A New Beginning

A New Beginning

Jean Chapman

PIATKUS

Copyright © 2001 by Jean Chapman

First published in Great Britain in 2001 by
Inner Circle, an imprint of Judy Piatkus (Publishers) Ltd of
5 Windmill Street, London W1T 2JA
email:info@piatkus.co.uk

The moral right of the author has been asserted

A catalogue record for this book is available from the British Library

ISBN 0 7499 3398 4

Set in Times by
Action Publishing Technology Ltd, Gloucester

Printed and bound in Great Britain by
Mackays of Chatham plc, Chatham, Kent

To my lighthouse ladies, Marjorie Selwyn,
Beryl Winchurch, Lorna Otway and Paddy Treece,
also their mother Doris Hewitt, and to all those who
were part of the traumatic double evacuation from
Gibraltar during 1940.

Acknowledgement

As an historical novelist I have shown readers glimpses of real people. In this book I had the permission of a family, whose wartime experiences form part of the story, to use their real names and real experiences. My thanks are due to Marjorie, Beryl, Lorna and Paddy who lived in the lighthouse keepers' cottages, Europa Point, Gibraltar.

Prologue

They had painted the lighthouse a long, long time ago, but Laura was always slightly shocked by the brilliant white and red; two white stripes, one red, like a giant jam sandwich. Not nearly so imposing, or dour, as the raw bare stone she had known as a young girl. Red and white against the brilliant blue Mediterranean sky. Patriotic, though. Perhaps just right for Europa Point, the tiny outpost of Gibraltar – an English irritation on the face of Spain.

She walked to the stone wall behind the lighthouse. The sea was calm at the base of the crags and, at the horizon at the edge of her sight, the Atlas mountains shouldered up the solid blue sky from the continent of Africa.

Behind her a tourist bus came swinging on to the point. She moved discreetly further away. They would not stay long, fifteen minutes or so, and she had nothing in common with their fleeting curiosity. She walked towards a grassy area where she could sit on a bank alongside an old roadway.

She wondered if it were only the sea that had not changed, the sea, the cliffs. Behind where she sat had been a military camp, way over to her left had been St George's, the Church of England where her mother had been christened, now an enormous golden mosque, one of the largest in the world, they said. Clever of the Muslims to have acquired that

1

impressive site for their opulent, domed building.

She wondered if the mosque was on the visitors' itinerary these days? She guessed they would have been to the harbour. Pleasure yachts there now, the dolphin patrol near the wall, then the long empty quays. It hardly seemed possible that all that activity, the navy, the convoys through the Med, were all no more, that Gibraltar was preparing itself for a new gentler invasion, a new industry of tourism.

She looked towards the coach; people were already climbing aboard. One or two looked her way as if they wondered if she was one of theirs. One woman waved. She could not bring herself to respond. She was a world away from a holiday-maker. Above, the gulls were screaming and swooping low; one of the bus passengers had foolishly fed them, probably the reason for the quick retreat to the coach.

She felt more at one with the birds, the sea, the dolphins, they too came in the spring to have their pups inside the calm fish-laden Mediterranean, swimming before the ships, racing, leaping.

Leaning back she watched the birds, felt they watched her. This place, this piece of rock fraught with so many emotions for her, sorrow, fear, love, security, heartache. She would never be free of this place – certainly not now. New roots were being pushed down and once roots took purchase in the rocky clefts it seemed they never gave way.

Chapter One

The Censorship Department, like all the rest of Gibraltar, was awash with gossip. Laura found the whispered rumours about civilian evacuation strange in this section set up specially to delete any careless gossip, or hint of information, from the mail.

She enjoyed her job for the glimpses she had into other people's lives. Reading for the most part letters sent between loving members of the same family, she learned to ferret out the unspoken messages of caring beneath the mundane words, learned not to censor such cryptics as B.O.L.T.O.P. and S.W.A.L.K. 'Better on lips than on paper' and 'Sealed with a loving kiss,' even H.O.L.L.A.N.D., which had at first seemed more seditious as the Netherlands were trodden under the Nazi jackboot. But after it kept appearing on letters from ardent young men to their girls back home, the department accepted that it did mean 'Hope our love lasts and never dies'.

She looked around at her fellow workers, women of all ages. She smiled as Doris Hewitt, wife of one of the assistant keepers at the lighthouse, caught her glance. Doris looked seriously worried: she had four children, four little girls, and her husband would certainly be judged to be helping the essential defence of Gibraltar and so have to stay behind.

3

Quite a few of the older women were incensed by the epithet 'useless mouths' which had been coined for all those not actively involved in the defence of The Rock, England's gateway to the Mediterranean. 'Want to see my husband try to cook for himself,' one wife had exclaimed, 'or do anything else in the house come to that, then they'd know what "useless" was!'

Beginning to censor her last batch of letters for the day, Laura wondered how she would feel if she had to be parted from Jamie. She hoped her and Jamie's love lasted and never died. She looked round guiltily as she realised she had without thinking scored a line under the initials on a letter she was reading – not part of her job at all. She stared at the underlining and wondered if by doing this she might have changed the course of someone's life? Would the girl it was addressed to believe this young man's hopes, his ardour, when otherwise she might not have paid much heed to 'H.O.L.L.A.N.D.'?

She finished the letter quickly, pushed it back into its envelope, trying to reassure herself that love could surely not be based on such a detail, such minutiae. Some letters she censored used the words 'my other half', 'my better half', not how Laura would have worded what she felt was her own more mystical emotion, but she knew exactly what they meant.

She had recognised Jamie's specialness the very first moment she had seen him on South Barrack Road. He had been with his father, walking towards her mother and herself. So the two women and two men had met, remet in the case of the older two, for Laura's mother, Queenie Maclaren, née Middleton, had been born and brought up on Gibraltar as had her mother and grandparents before her, and Laura had identified the son with awed and silent wonder. Afterwards she thought he must have believed her to be an idiot, inflicting her own tongue-tied silence on him, hardly finding gumption enough to smile, while their two parents chatted and beamed at each other. She had

4

never seen her mother so animated.

After that meeting Laura's life had never been the same. Immediately she had wanted to be different for him. She wanted to be extroverted and jolly, and shout, 'Wow! I really like you!' She didn't want to be shut back into the narrow world she and her mother inhabited, mentally scourged by her father's constant criticisms. She wanted to be as animated as, briefly, her mother had been with Freddie de Falla.

She had not had time to rehearse her wished-for careless rapture. Jamie had been outside the Censorship Department the next day. He wanted to tell her how much he enjoyed meeting her the day before, he said. She wanted to tell him the same, but perhaps her swift, shy glance was enough, for he was not put off. In fact as the days passed he declared himself 'only half alive until we're together'.

The idea that she had found some other half to herself had been with her from the first, but she could not find the immediate spoken word. On their tenth meeting, a kind of anniversary, she gave him a letter when they parted.

When they next met he was ablaze with love for her. 'I feel I could jump over The Rock, and back again. I'm invincible!' He had stood and beat his chest in the middle of the Main Street. She had laughed aloud, careless, released for a moment. Then she had hurried him along to a seat in the small burial garden giving shelter to the graves of Nelson's men from the battle of Trafalgar, where they sat very close, gripping hands, talking quietly beneath the tall eucalyptus trees, making promises that only God or the war could cause them to break.

'Dreaming again, Laura,' her supervisor accused.

'Sorry,' she said smiling, 'but I've nearly finished my last batch.'

'That young man has a lot to answer for.'

She looked up, a defensive denial leaping to her lips, but she was with her workmates, her friends, who could hardly have failed to see Jamie de Falla meeting her out of work,

5

cheerfully greeting everyone. She shrugged. 'There is a war on,' she said, though quite what she meant she was not sure, but the older women did.

'That's right! Don't you waste any time. If we all get evacuated it'll be too late. And he's a grand chap. All us girls fancied his dad like mad when we were young.'

'Even my own mother – I think?'

'She certainly did! I remember it all well. Then her father, your grandfather, got posted first to England then out to the Far East. And blow me, Queenie finally comes back married to a red-moustachioed army officer and with a dark-haired daughter . . .'

'Who's courting her old sweetheart's son.'

There was some laughter, but if she had wanted to ask more she was thwarted by home time and the general tidying of desks and scooping up of handbags. She wasn't sure whether her precautionary, 'As long as my father doesn't find out!' was either heard or taken seriously.

She walked out just behind Doris, who drew in her breath sharply and her step faltered as she saw her husband waiting. He looked serious, came forward immediately to meet his wife, took her arm, his eyes only on her. Everyone around heard the lighthouse keeper's words to Doris. 'You've got to go mate!'

They all knew what he meant, knew from his face, from the way Doris stood stock still for a moment staring unbelieving at him as he disguised his own emotion with the brief, stiff upper-lip English quip. Laura saw in Doris's face all happiness and hope disappear as her life of security and happiness was dashed to smithereens.

She watched Doris walk slowly away with her arm pushed through her husband's, leaning like someone suddenly old and tired as she listened and he talked quietly to her. The blow of compulsory evacuation was, it seemed, no longer rumour.

Other workmates called hurried goodbyes and some called, 'See you tomorrow, perhaps!' They joked, they hoped, but responses were uncertain. She looked around, but Jamie was not there. She needed to see him, needed not to go home, and decided to make her way along Europa Road towards Europa Point and the lighthouse, part of the same way Doris and her husband would have gone.

After a time she turned off. The general public was not allowed in the prohibited area around the lighthouse. She walked up through trees to a secluded spot that had become special to them, a mutually agreed trysting place. Laura waited by 'our tree', a sparse-branched tree growing on the sea side of the path, where often one of the bigger ginger apes sat as if contemplating the seascape. To the right, one wall of the great harbour was visible sweeping out a protective arm in a great curve; to the left, the blue of the inner Mediterranean, its horizon and nearer waters well dotted with traffic. Gibraltar was changing, she thought, changing from home to fortress, everywhere the preparations were for war and siege, for only combatants to remain.

She swallowed hard, willed him to come. Then turning to stare down the path, there he was. Slim to the point of slenderness, Jamie de Falla was said to have his English mother's tallness and his Gibraltarian father's darkness. Privately she added other ingredients, the elegant dignity one saw in the heel-tapping, hand-clapping flamenco dancers or caped bullfighters, a distant arrogance – which belied all he was, just as much as her own father's outward affableness hid the private man.

'Jamie.' She questioned the seriousness of his face which did not seem to lighten even to give her a greeting. She raised her face but he pulled her straight into his arms and held her as if they both had need of extra comforting. There was such a sad and yearning stillness in the moment, she knew to move or question was to precipitate the news, the disaster, hasten their mutual misfortune.

'I stopped to get a newspaper,' he said at last and releasing her he pulled a copy of the *Gibraltar Chronicle* from his pocket. 'It's the notice. The army chaps were saying it

7

was about to be made public.' He handed her the paper which he had folded to a neat square.

'Notice of evacuation.' She read quickly down, speaking aloud the categories 'aged men, children under fourteen, all women'. She glanced up at him but he was still staring at the paper in her hand.

'It's the order from the War Cabinet in London, so it is official.'

'But . . .' she tried to think of a way out, a category she did not fall into. There was her work for the Censorship Department, but it obviously wasn't exempting Doris.

'I know Spain won't take anyone,' he said. 'My father says they may come in on the side of Germany.'

'Why would they do that?' she asked, but it was a shock to realise he was actually wondering *where* she would be sent, not *if*.

'In return for Gibraltar, French Morocco and Oran when the Germans won.'

'Oh!' She was surprised by his pat answer and the sheer mercenariness of it. So did countries act just like people? *If I do this you must give me that?* She frowned and accused, 'That's just what your father thinks.'

'No, he hears things – and guesses others. He says Franco is dependent on the USA for food and oil, and they've not allowed him to build up stocks after Spain's Civil War, but old Franco hasn't decided on which side his bread is best buttered yet.' He smiled as he often did when he spoke of his parent, 'He doesn't miss much and he's usually right.' As a marine engineer currently helping with the problems ventilating the deep tunnels into The Rock which were to be used as air-raid shelters, Freddie de Falla came into contact with both the naval and army garrisons.

Laura frowned, turned away; one of the problems she had most trouble reconciling herself with was the adoration of Jamie for his father, when she found her own so difficult to live with.

'What are we going to do?' she heard herself ask and

8

when he did not answer she turned back to him. He had picked up a pebble and was throwing it from hand to hand, then suddenly he threw it as far out into the sea as he could, to the grumbling disquiet of the ape. Pulling itself up to its full four feet it shook the tree in retaliation.

'All right old boy . . . nothing personal,' he said and they stood quietly holding hands as the ape settled again.

'When you go I shall ask my father to release me from the engineering, so I can join the navy,' Jamie stated quietly but lifting his chin as if already taking pride and a proprietary interest in the Royal Navy frigate passing below them, 'like my grandfather and . . .' his voice trailed away.

She remembered him telling her that his great-great-grandfather had fought with Nelson at the battle of Trafalgar.

'He won't try to keep me when he knows I want to go,' he added.

Some vague bleak version of a song flitted through her mind, men marching, singing . . . *when he knows I want to go*. 'The war feels real for the first time,' she whispered as she tried to absorb the shock of this news. Would Jamie be in more danger in the navy, or staying on Gibraltar being bombed and shelled if Hitler tried to take The Rock, and what if Spain came in on the German side? She wondered if a ship on the high seas, a moving target, would be safer – but what about U-boats? So many ifs. She wondered how much time they might still have together. 'When do you think the evacuation will begin?' she asked.

'Soon. As soon as ships are ready.' He pulled her round so they faced each other. 'You know I love you,' he said. She raised a hand towards his shoulder, he caught it and interlaced his fingers with hers. 'I want to marry you. Will you marry me?' He rushed on as if to be sure she completely understood how he truly felt. 'If I don't marry you I shall never marry anyone.'

'Or me,' she answered bleakly.

'You won't be able to keep us a secret much longer.'

Though she knew he kept his voice light, almost whimsical, she dreaded what might be coming next.

'My father knows all about you,' he went on, 'why I rush off from work every day. I've met your mother, though briefly, she's *really* nice. Surely we must now tell your father?'

Her heart plummeted, heavy, cold, a leaden thing.

'He must give consent, at least to our being engaged,' Jamie was going on, 'before we have to part. I don't understand why you won't . . .'

'No,' she interrupted, pulling their interlaced fingers apart, 'you don't understand, Jamie.'

'I know you're never happy if I talk about your father, even mention him.'

'He would never allow me to be engaged,' she said flatly.

'But if we don't ask, how can we know?'

I know,' she said with certainty. 'I shall have to wait until I am twenty-one and legally able to do as I like, and even then . . .'

'Even then!' he exclaimed. 'What is this "even then"?'

She moved away to where pebbles became grown through with grass at the edge of the cliff, unable to look at him, or let him see the hurt in her eyes, to learn the real truth behind her seeming reluctance.

'Even then?' he repeated quietly. 'I don't know what you mean?'

'I . . .' She began, stopped, shook her head.

'Laura,' he pleaded, 'tell me.' He would have taken her back into his arms but she needed to be apart if she was to try to explain. She spread her hands and gestured for him to back off.

'Don't push me away. I want to help.' His voice was low, urgent. 'We haven't got time to play games.'

'Games!' she exclaimed, suddenly very, very angry. 'How I wish it was a game. How I wish I could talk to my father, like you apparently talk to yours.' She felt fury take

10

over her wit, her wisdom, her tongue as she went on. 'And you're lucky, do you know why you're lucky? Because your mother's dead. Because she died when you were three.'

She saw him take a step back, stagger under the enormity of what she was saying.

'You're not saying you wish your mother was dead?'

'No! Don't you see? My father, it's my father I wish was . . .' She gasped, stopped, appalled, unsure whether or not she expected the hand of God to strike her down immediately, or worse that Jamie should turn away from her revolted, for ever alienated by the murderous wish.

'For God's sake, what does he do?' He stepped urgently to her, took her hands and, almost unconsciously it seemed to Laura, examined her bare arms, distractedly turning her hands over and over as if searching for signs, bruises.

She shook her head at him. 'He's too clever for that,' she told him, 'and it's my mother more than me.' She could have added, he just pushes me out of the way.

'That's what I meant when I said, "even then",' she went on, 'I meant even then there's my mother to think of. We sort of guard each other,' she told him. 'You see, he doesn't like witnesses. The one good thing that will come from this evacuation is that my father won't have any say in the matter.'

'You said "more than me",' he persisted, 'so do you mean he does strike you?'

'He wasn't always like this,' she said as if he had not spoken. 'When I was little there was always laughter when he was at home, and love from my mother when he was not. The army is his career and he used to say he was a "galloping major", and run around with me on my shoulders. Mother used to have to beg him to stop, said he'd shake my head off careering around, but I used to laugh until my sides ached. Then as I grew older things changed; perhaps it was my fault for growing up.'

11

'How has it changed?' Jamie's stance suggested he would not move again until she answered.

She knew she could not put into words her father's devious ways, the derogatory remarks that had become their constant lot, or the way he could unexpectedly punish her mother with swift secret punches, even turning a corner into a deserted street, in corridors in public places, the threatening messages he could flash with his eyes across crowded function rooms.

'I always believed my mother,' she said, continuing her own scenario, 'until I was fifteen or so. When she told me she didn't feel well, or had had an accident, I believed her.' Her voice had fallen to little more than a whisper. 'But it has got worse since we came back to Gibraltar. My mother could have looked up old friends, he wouldn't allow that – and there's a man here, a major. He and dad were second lieutenants together. Now dad's a lieutenant, only one rank higher and the other man's a major.'

'A man doesn't take it out on his family because he doesn't get promotion.'

'Other things have mounted up since we've been here, like meeting your father again for instance, if ever he found out.'

He took her face between his hands and gently traced his thumbs over her cheeks as if wiping away tears. 'You can't stay with him.'

'With official evacuation that won't be the problem.' It was parting from Jamie that would be the trauma.

'In any case you're not going back to him. Never! Not today. Never! You can move in with me and my father, you both can, you and your mother.'

'Jamie!' she almost shouted at him in alarm, then tried to make a fresh start, more controlled. 'Jamie, don't you think I've gone over this time and time again, wanted my mother to leave, wanted us to run away together. She's always fearful that no matter where she went he would follow, that he'd find her, find a way to punish us, make things worse.'

12

She paused. 'I've come to realise two things. While we're with him we can see the dangers, try to avoid situations that enrage him.'

'And the other?'

'That when my mother finally decides that she no longer wants to play the part of happy army families, it will be her decision.'

'But now *I* know,' he began face stern, eyes blazing, 'it's different. I can't let you go on . . .'

'You mustn't interfere.' She shook her head at him with urgent emphasis. It'll only make matters worse. You'd be giving my father another reason for his spite. Until she is beyond his reach things must stay as they are. Once we're away, I could talk to my mother properly, freely.'

There was a silence, only a sudden breeze from the sea sighed about them, moving her skirt and hair.

'Please,' she asked.

'Once you're away,' he compromised adding, 'and that can't be long, not many days, you can take it that neither of you will ever go back to him. I'll see to that.'

'Jamie, you must promise to say nothing to anyone – not to your father, or anyone, not yet.'

'My father already knows all about you, that I intended to ask you to marry me.'

Disarmed by this revelation, she asked, 'What did he say?'

'He said not to make the same mistake he made with your mother, and let you get away.'

'Really! So they were . . .' She gazed at him in astonishment. 'I don't know how that makes me feel.'

'But you see how it makes me feel,' he stated, then added quickly, 'and I have a ring for you.'

'A ring?'

'I didn't buy it. It's more special than that. It's a ring my father bought for your mother before she left Gib all those years ago; he said his courage failed him at the last moment. They were both very young, and he thought he

13

would keep it and ask her to marry him when she came back.'

'Instead of which it was twenty-five years later . . . with a husband and a daughter.'

'And he wed my mother when he heard his first love had married an army officer.'

'What a disaster, well, it was a disaster for my mother.'

'But not for us, we're not going to repeat the disaster, not now we've found each other.' He took a small box from his pocket and opened it. On the satin lining was a diamond solitaire ring. Laura gasped at its magnificence. 'I think he bought it in Africa,' Jamie said pulling it from its box. He took her left hand and slipped in on to her third finger. He nodded his pleasure as the ring slipped easily but snugly on to her finger. 'My father said it would be just right.'

'And it is,' Laura said with a smile of apology for all the times she had been truculent about admitting his father was right about anything. She angled her finger in the sunlight and the diamond made wonderful prisms of every colour from yellow, to red, to purple to blue. 'It is magnificent. Oh!' she clasped her own hand over her heart, 'but I won't be able to wear it. Maybe you should keep it for me.'

'What, like my father!' he exclaimed. 'No chance. It's yours. I'll get you a chain so you can wear it around your neck until you leave, then . . .' He held her gently but with such intensity that the whole world seemed to hold its breath for his next words, 'once you've told your mother, wear it for me, always.'

'Always.' Her tears now made prisms around the diamond. 'With such pride. It is so very beautiful, and so valuable, but . . .'

'But?'

'That *you* want me to wear it,' she paused to display the ring on her engagement finger, 'is the most important thing.'

'I thought you might mind because I didn't buy it specially, if you had I'd have bought . . .'

'This is far more special,' she interrupted. 'But I wonder why your father never gave it to your mother when they met?'

'I asked him, he said it was always Queenie's ring. My mother had a very splendid sapphire ring he gave her.'

'So your father was truly in love with my mother. No wonder I felt as if I'd known you all my life, even when we first met. It was like recognising . . .' she stopped and laughed up at him. 'We might have been brother and sister!'

In the tree above the ape gave a loud derogatory grunt.

'I agree with that remark,' Jamie said. 'They'd lock me up if I felt like this about a sister.'

She was much later than usual when she finally arrived home.

The carefree loving moments, even the warmth of the May evening seemed to ebb swiftly away like a retreating tide as she entered the deeply shuttered house. Automatically she glanced at the hall table to see if her father's cap and officer's cane lay there. It was bare. She was drawing in a deep breath of relief when something, perhaps even just the stillness, the uneasy silence, warned her that something was wrong.

The sense of something wrong, something as yet undiscovered, she had begun to know this feeling too well since their return to Gibraltar.

She stood and listened for so long that she began to feel it might be difficult to move at all if she did not soon make the effort. She had seen the same inertia come over her mother at times as she strived, and failed, to find a way to please her father. She also remembered his devastating, raucous outburst when her mother had once lashed back with 'If I stood on my head and turned to gold it wouldn't be right for you!' For weeks afterwards she had hardly spoken at all – which had not been right for her father either.

'Mum!' she ventured towards the kitchen area, then hearing nothing she repeated the word more loudly up the stairs. 'Are you there?'

There was a noise, a small half cough, half cry before a voice, raised high to clear the throaty range of trouble, called, 'Laura, I'm in the bedroom.'

'Mum?' she queried at the door, then she caught sight of things strewn on the floor. She pushed her way in against a tide of hampering garments. Her mother sat on the bed surrounded by clothing, everything seemed to have been thrown from every closet drawer, the wardrobe, even the heavy wooden drawers lay thrown about. A stranger might have thought a powerful whirlwind had hit the place.

Queenie held up a dress she had recently finished sewing; it was torn almost in two. 'Why does he do it,' she said but without enough emphasis to make it a question.

Laura went to sit by her, took the pretty green and blue cotton into her hands and looked at the damage to the meticulous fine pleated bodice and panelled skirt. 'Best just forget it,' she advised, and put it to one side where her mother couldn't see it.

'I'm not sure I can stand much more,' her mother whispered. 'You asked me many times why I stay, now I have to admit I don't know why. I think it was after seeing Freddie again – and now you're grown up . . .'

'And we're to be evacuated,' Laura added. It was immediately clear that her mother did not know.

'Evacuated!'

'There was a notice in the newspaper, and Doris's husband came to meet her from work to tell her. They're really upset, with the four little girls.'

'Oh!' her mother exclaimed looking round the room. 'Your father didn't say anything, but that would be the reason for all this.' She laughed shakily. 'It never seems quite so bad if you can think of a reason.'

'Oh, Mum, stop making excuses for him. He's just a bully, a hateful, spiteful bully.' She stopped abruptly,

16

remembering her outburst to Jamie, then lowering her voice she added, 'But once we're away from him, where ever we get sent, we'll never come back to him, never.'

'How would we manage?'

'We'd manage,' she told her mother, the secret knowledge of Jamie's pledge like a coin in a child's pocket, burning to be spent.

'Yes,' her mother said quietly.

Laura turned slowly to look at her. 'You mean it?' she questioned and her mother nodded. This was the first time Queenie had given any hint that she would eventually make the break. The two of them hugged for a long moment as they sat side by side on the bed.

'It's taken me a while to be brave enough, hasn't it?' She glanced up and Laura followed her gaze to the dressing-table mirror which reflected them and the chaos all around them. 'I was sitting looking at myself before you came home. I thought I looked like an old, old woman, weighed down by every care in the world, surrounded by the scraps and rags of her life. At whatever price, there should be better than this, I thought. I'm forty-five, Laura. Middle-aged, not old.'

'Not old, no Mum, only worn out by . . . him!' She ached to tell her news, to show the ring, but she sensed it would be too much at this moment, just another secret, another deceit to be practised until they were clear of her father. Time enough when they could see Gibraltar disappearing over the horizon – and Jamie of course, going to war. She sighed deeply.

Queenie immediately caught her daughter's hand. 'We'll be very careful, stay together as much as we can when he's here,' she paused, then grimaced. 'He'll have to move into army quarters, the New Camp, I guess. He won't like that.' She looked at her daughter with the air of an old campaigner preparing for a brand new mission. 'So we must pack discreetly.'

*

The preparations for departure were soon everywhere to be seen in Gibraltar. Tea chests were in great demand as housewives tried to make some division of their household goods, leaving enough behind for their menfolk, but taking enough with them to make some kind of a beginning in a different country. 'Wherever that might be' was the phrase they used to each other, but French Morocco and Casablanca were the words coming from the harbour where freighters were being pressed into service for the purposes of a mass exodus. Those inclined to argue against what they called their 'deportation' were persuaded that it was a better alternative to either imprisonment or a thousand-pound fine.

From the moment Laura had helped her mother retrieve and fold the clothes Jock Maclaren had scattered, they too had been preparing to leave. The clothes were divided between cases secreted under the bed in Laura's room and those they decided to leave put back into drawers and closets.

Laura's discretion was further tested as for the first time she began to visit Jamie in his home, meeting his father properly and beginning to see why Jamie thought so much of him. He appeared to her a very still man, who did not make unnecessary movements or gestures (such a comfort after her own father) and who, when he met her in his own home as her father-in-law to be, beamed expansively and declared, 'Marvellous! Marvellous!' She was to learn it was one of his favourite words and it seemed to her no one could help opening out, blossoming under such enthusiastic approval.

'The ring,' she said, 'it is beautiful, and I still feel overwhelmed that you should . . .'

'It's right,' he interrupted. 'It's been in my safe all these years, a memento of a lost opportunity, and now it has a new beginning. Will you wear it for me while you are in this house?'

'But of course.' She immediately pulled the long thin

gold chain from under her dress, undid it and slipped the ring on her finger.

'Marvellous!' he said and with deliberation and took her hand and kissed it. 'Marvellous!'

'Has Jamie told you why I can't wear it all the time?'

'Your father wouldn't approve, you think,' he paused, then laughed. 'I don't blame him. I wouldn't approve of my son, or of me, if I were in his shoes. I'd still whisk his wife away from him if I could.'

Jamie had appeared in the doorway with tall glasses of fresh lemonade but stopped, watching Laura's face as his father spoke of Queenie. Laura felt her colour rise, not with embarrassment, but with the urge to say she wished he would whisk her away.

Freddie de Falla looked from one to the other. 'It seems to me you're making things more difficult for yourselves by not even telling Queenie. Surely she could...'

'Dad! It would make things more difficult for both of them – honestly!'

'There's always a right time for things to be told,' Freddie said mildly.

'I know, Mr de Falla...'

'Freddie,' he corrected.

'But you must believe me, it is not now.' Laura shook her head decisively. 'I shall tell my mother when we're on board ship and she has nothing more to worry about.'

'So, I guess she does not even know you are coming here, to our home?'

Laura saw for the first time how deep her deceit, or foolishness, or reluctance, must look to Jamie's father as she said, 'No, she does not.'

'But there is something you could perhaps help her with,' Jamie said.

'Name it,' his father stated without hesitation.

'She wants to take her sewing machine and...' he paused looking to Laura for help.

'And tailor's dummy, all her sewing aids. She can tailor,

19

and we could earn a living if need be . . .'she trailed away as she saw the expression on Freddie de Falla's face.

'A living? An officer's wife having to earn a living? And having to ask for help with the simple matter of a couple of chests to the docks, with all the army transport at his bidding? What is the real problem?' he asked. There was genuine bewilderment in his voice as he looked from his son to Laura. 'Just what kind of man is your father?'

There was a long pause. 'My mother will be glad to be evacuated,' she began but could manage no more of an explanation. The old habit of keeping a still tongue was hard to break, particularly to this man. She had told Jamie exactly what kind of man her father was, and he had been true to his word, he had not told anyone, not even his father. 'While I shall be heartbroken – to leave Jamie,' she added at last.

A sound like a low groan startled Laura.

'Another separation,' Freddie de Falla said, and she was again struck by his stillness at this emotional moment as he added, 'More heartbreak.'

Jamie moved quickly to his side and took his hand. The taller of the two by a good head, the gesture was still of a boy going to his father. Laura agonised over all the different kinds of loving. It was almost too much to bear and a small emotional 'Oh!' escaped her lips.

Jamie led his father a step or two nearer and the three of them embraced. It was Jamie again who took the lead, who suggested the practical to bridge over this emotional chasm. 'So what about these tea chests?' he asked. It was the same ploy Laura had used to keep her mother going forward, hiding the torn sewing and helping clear up the ravages of her father's tempers. The diversion was not lost on Freddie either.

'If we'd been in England I suppose you would have suggested a cup of tea,' he said with a wry smile.

Again she stayed longer than she should, so even her mother questioned her when she arrived back.

'I've found someone who'll help us with the sewing machine and all the other things,' she told her. 'He'll arrange for two or three chests to be delivered here and then they'll be taken down and stored at the docks until we know which boat we'll be going on.'

'He'll?'

Laura wished her habit of blushing would go away as the heat seared up into her cheeks. 'Freddie de Falla,' she said quietly.

'Freddie!'

Laura saw it was not just her own cheeks that were blazing.

'But when did you see Freddie?'

'I've been seeing his son, Jamie.'

Queenie stood quite still for long seconds as if reassessing her daughter in the light of this new knowledge. 'Seeing?' she queried.

Laura was smiling and nodding agreement with all the word implied, when they heard the sound of a vehicle screeching to a halt outside the house. Almost immediately the front door was opened and slammed to.

The looks they exchanged now were aware and understanding. Queenie clasped a hand to her mouth and before she could remove it Jock Maclaren stood in the doorway, cap still on, slapping his swagger-cane into an open palm. Six foot two, he was a colourful man, for though dark headed, his facial hair, moustache, eyebrows, were auburn. It gave a brightness to his face, a disguise to his nature, and he had a habit of half closing his eyes whenever he spoke.

'Day after tomorrow,' he announced.

Neither of them answered, though Queenie pulled her hand down from her mouth to her side.

'I've heard, day after tomorrow!' he repeated with an extra slap of his cane, and the edge to his voice warned them both he was beside himself with anger. His fury was lit by the fact that the evacuation of these so-called 'useless mouths' was beyond his control.

21

He came two huge, rapid strides nearer. Laura had to force herself to stand firm, not flinch, or move backwards. 'So will we be ready?' he asked, sarcasm twisting his lips.

'We'll have to be, I suppose,' Queenie answered the seemingly loaded question as best she could.

'We'll have to be,' he mimicked, but whatever he intended next was interrupted by the impatient hoot of a horn. Whoever was waiting for him outside must be a senior or fellow officer, no one else would dare hoot for his return.

They saw his jaw work as he ground his teeth. He had to go, but they could see there was something more. It cost him dear to tell them, 'You have to close the house down.'

He spun on his heel and they listened to his footsteps punishing the hall tiles, as if he wanted to leave his mark on them too. The door slammed, an engine restarted and the vehicle roared off back in the direction of the harbour and the camp.

'So he has to go and live in camp at once,' her mother surmised. 'I hope at once.'

'Two days,' Laura whispered, 'just two days left.'

Chapter Two

They both knew that all their preparations must be done while Jock Maclaren was out of the house. There was no way there would be peace or space enough to even think while he was around, and both knew he would stop Queenie taking her sewing machine and materials if he could. He would see it as unfitting for an officer's wife. He would rather see hat-boxes or vanity cases portered to the docks. His obsession with his public image was the one thing they could rely on.

It was decided Laura should go immediately back to the de Fallas' home, the chests Freddie had offered now an urgent necessity. Running in the heat would have drawn attention before this state of uncertainty and apprehension had fallen over the whole of Gibraltar, now anxiety quickened most people's steps. There could hardly be a single family that was not affected.

She had hoped her pull on the iron bell-ring would be answered by Jamie, but it was his father. He listened gravely to the news as he closed the door behind her.

'I've chests here in the house that can be used,' he said immediately, 'and if you help me empty them, I could arrange for a handcart and have them taken round at once.'

'Jamie's not here?' she asked.

'No,' he replied briefly as she followed him up the stairs to the first landing, where he pointed to a brass-bound chest that stood there, 'and there's a similar one on the next landing.'

'But these are too good!' she exclaimed, 'they must be heirlooms.'

'They're chests and Queenie needs chests.' He raised the lid; inside were piles of folded sheets. 'I'd really forgotten what was in here,' he paused, fingers stroking his chin, then he added 'but I know what we can do. There's an empty closet in my bedroom, these can all be put into there.' He led the way into the bedroom on the left, a large airy room.

'Another heirloom,' he said with a smile as he caught her astonished look at the enormous four-poster bed which stood in the exact centre of the room, its fine drapes catching the breezes from the windows front and back.

She walked to where he had opened the doors of one of the two built-in closets. It was empty. It struck her as so sad. This must have been Jamie's mother's clothes store, and the huge bed probably where Jamie had been born – and conceived. The thought sent colour flaming through her cheeks. She was glad his father was already on his way out of the room.

'You start on this one and I'll go and see what's in the one upstairs.'

'Where has Jamie gone?' she asked.

Freddie was halfway up the stairs to the next landing. He came slowly down again before he answered. 'He's gone to recruit for the navy. He wouldn't rest,' he paused then as if in justification of his son added, 'and once you've gone he'll need to be in the action. There's a strong naval tradition in our family. I'm the odd one out really.'

'He did say,' she told him, then shaking her head, 'why do we have to have wars?' It was more a remark than a question.

He made a noise in his throat, half snort, half moan. 'It isn't only wars that bring uncertainty,' he told her, 'there are other times when you can't see the way forward – or don't want to go on even if you *can* see it! Life's a journey and even when you can't see the point, it's best to just keep putting one foot in front of another – eventually the light and the way comes back to you.'

She felt he was talking of losing Jamie's mother, knew he was trying to help her face the coming separation. 'I'm sure you're right,' she said as brightly as she could.

'So in the meantime, plod on.'

'Plod on,' she repeated and stooped to take the first of the huge, heavy linen sheets from the chest. As she carried them, sachets of lavender fell from between the folds. On the way back she retrieved them and saw with what care, beauty even, each one was made; each was embroidered, cross-stitched with a motif or a name: a heart; Freddie; Jamie; a tree bearing minute pears; a bed – a replica of the huge bed these sheets must have been made for; a spout of water over a stone trough, surely she had seen that through the window. She had laid the tiny plump squares out on the remaining sheets and did not know Freddie had come downstairs again until he spoke.

'My wife was a marvellous embroideress; she made tapestries and pictures, everything she touched she beautified.' He stood with another pile of linen in his arms. 'Even me,' he said quietly. 'She knew I had loved Queenie, your mother, but Grace charmed me, made me worthy to love her. She gave me Jamie, then . . .' she heard him swallow noisily, 'she was gone.'

From where she knelt by the chest Laura looked up to the picture above it, a tapestry of a unicorn in a medieval setting with a young woman and a small boy. 'Yes,' he said 'Grace did that too.'

'How wonderful! These really are heirlooms, even these lavender sachets, the work, the tiny stitches . . .'

'You take them, put them in your clothes.'

'Oh! no, I couldn't . . .'

'You can't refuse the one with Jamie's name on – and the bed!' Balancing his load he picked up the two and put them in her hand, 'and any others you'd like.'

25

'I'd love to have them,' she said. 'Thank you.' She wanted to add that she seemed already to be in his debt for a lot of things, but she sensed it would not please him if she said so yet again, so just added quietly, as if to herself, 'You're a generous man.'

They were just closing the closet doors when they heard Jamie return. He called out for his father. 'I've done it!' he shouted up the stairs.

Freddie caught her hand. 'Be practical,' he whispered, 'concentrate on the things that have to be done. All right?' he asked and when she nodded he breathed, 'Good girl! Marvellous! I'll send him up to you, you can tell him the news while I organise the handcart.'

She heard their voices below, Jamie's at first enthusiastic, then quiet, solemn, then he came bounding up the stairs. She waited for him by the chest, still holding the sachets. He checked himself on the top step as if to curb the excitement of his successful expedition. He came slowly to her and how well she knew how he felt, joy to be going on the one hand, and sorrow and regret on the other.

He looked down at what she held.

'Your father gave them to me.'

'You don't need to have them if you don't want,' he said, 'he's a sentimental old . . .'

'He's . . . marvellous!'

For a second they both laughed then the tears she had managed to hold at bay so long overwhelmed her, and Jamie tried to help mop them from her cheeks.

'Two days,' she said between handkerchief wipes.

'Father told me.'

'And you've enlisted?'

'I'll have to go to England for training,' he told her, 'I wondered if you would be sent to England?'

'French Morocco's nearer and that's where we keep hearing,' she said, adding ruefully, 'my father kept us back when a lot of English women and children were being sent home.'

26

'We'll be apart for a time no matter what, but I'll have leave, and wherever you are, I'll find you.'

She thought he sounded invincible and some of the names of the navy's ships tumbled through her mind. *Dreadnought*, *Renown*, the *Victory*, towed into Gibraltar's Rosia Bay for repairs after the battle of Trafalgar. No wonder the excitement lingered in his eyes.

'And we'll all come through, you'll see, and we'll all come back to Gib, back to our homes, to our tree.' His voice fell to a tenderness and he lifted her chin and kissed her on the mouth. She wondered if Nelson made such promises to Lady Hamilton.

From downstairs his father called. 'I am going to Fatima's to see if I can find one of the men and arrange the handcart.'

'Who's Fatima?' she whispered, feeling brought back to a slightly ludicrous reality.

'Fatima? Her whole family works for us; she does father's office work, her mother housekeeps and cooks for us, her two brothers have qualified as plumbers and ventilation engineers, apprenticed to my father.' Downstairs the street door closed.

For a moment they stood in complete silence, then Jamie lifted her two hands which still held the sachets and smelt them. Then he took them from her and placed them on top of the chest. His action made her very aware they were alone in the house, for how long she did not know. She just hoped Fatima lived some distance away.

'Why are you . . .?' He turned her a little to the window. 'You are blushing aren't you?'

'I can't believe I think such things when world-shattering events are happening.'

'Such things?'

'I was hoping Fatima lived a long way off.'

'That thought *is* world shattering as far as I'm concerned. It makes me feel ten feet tall, or as if there's an extra fleet of ships on our side.'

27

'HMS *Invincible* then.'

'Well for the next half hour at least.'

'Gosh! All that much time!' Her feeble quip reminded her of Doris's husband and his 'You've got to go mate!'

'Enough to make count,' he said and kissed her with such sweet gentleness she strained upwards to make the kiss firmer, stronger. Her action brought a swift response. 'Laura, I love you.'

The statement held a question, but the shyness imposed by the years of her father's biting criticisms tied her tongue at this vital moment. She looked at him so hard; he had understood before, had not been put off – but this time she understood he was asking more. She knew she loved him, for wouldn't she lay down her life for him without a moment's hesitation? She might not be able to stop herself blushing at every moment, but surely she could overcome this hurdle for the man she loved – surely. 'It feels like the last half hour in the world,' she said at last.

'Don't let's waste it,' he said and drew her towards his father's room.

For a moment she paused, resisted; she hadn't thought of this particular place, *this* bed.

They stood on the threshold, and it was as if he were introducing her to a person as he said, 'This bed was my port in a storm during childhood, when I was ill or upset I slept here with my father.' He drew her a little nearer to the antique mahogany four-poster. 'My father used to tell me stories of Nelson's time, of the great battle of Trafalgar, of how the *Victory* and the *Royal Sovereign* sailed to take on the might of Spain and France, of how Nelson sent his famous signal, "England expects every man will do his duty" and how Collingwood on the *Sovereign* said he wished Nelson would stop signalling.'

'I didn't know that,' she said, sitting on the edge of the bed and feeling like a child beginning a new voyage of discovery. She turned to him intending to ask if he used to pretend the bed was a great sailing boat, but saw that the

28

wonder in his eyes was all for her. She slipped her arms around his shoulders and he picked her up and reached far over to place her near the middle of the bed. She laughed as then he had to climb up and crawl across the expanse to be by her side.

He kissed her lips, her throat, unbuttoned her dress to kiss the top of her breasts which rose above her bra. 'Take your dress off,' he asked. She sat up and he helped pull it up and off, throwing it with a flourish to land in a long straight line at the end of the bed.

'I always thought you were a bit like a bullfighter,' she whispered.

He pulled off his shorts as he denied any such ambitions.

He ran his finger from under her chin, down between her breasts, to her navel. He followed the fingers with his lips, then, still kissing her, he pushed his hands underneath her back to undo her bra. She arched her back to help, then slipped it off over her arms. He drew away a little and gave a low moan as he first looked and then lowered his lips to her nipples.

The effect was like an electric shock; she felt her nipples tighten as if a switch had been thrown. Her body arched upwards with desire, or instinct, she was not sure. Her hand fluttered upwards to his face; he caught it, held it for a moment then took it down between them until she felt his hardness. As she touched, his hand slid between her legs, then moved upwards. She felt herself open like a flower, aching for him – and he came to her, and she to meet him.

She had heard such stories of it not being good the first time, but she wanted to shout her completeness from the rooftops – she wanted to talk, of all times at this moment, released from all inhibitions. But she didn't. Instead she lay replete, revelling in the wonder, waiting for Jamie to move, or speak.

They had lain quiet it seemed only seconds when they heard someone walking about downstairs. Both sprang up like children caught in a grown-up game. Clothes were pulled on, then, as they stood either side of the bed, with a mutual gesture, they pulled the top cover straight.

Then, Laura biting her lip and Jamie frowning to keep a straight face, they tiptoed out to the landing. Here Jamie announced, 'So that's settled, as soon as father comes back I'll help him load the chests and you go straight back home and tell your mother to have everything ready to pack. We'll do it immediately and . . .'

'Take them down to one of the warehouses on the front,' his father finished for him as he came upstairs, swinging a large key from one finger. 'We may as well all go together. None of the men are free to help, they're all busy with their own families. We'll load the chests and go.'

The walk through the streets pushing the handcart seemed to make them all feel uninhibited, slightly crazy, a circus coming to town Laura thought as Freddie doffed his hat to people, acquaintances who, even though busy with their own affairs, turned to look after the trio. For Laura, who walked between the two men, every sense was heightened: colours were brighter; scents of sweet jasmine and pungent geranium seemed to lace the breeze; sounds were sharper but more than anything else her body remembered Jamie's every touch, and moistening her lips she could imagine she could still taste his.

Coming to the door of her mother's house Freddie stopped and just stood for a moment, looking all around. 'It's a long, long time since I stood on this step,' he said.

She was surprised, she had not realised he had *ever* been there before, but as she opened the door and the men carried the first chest in, her mother came through from the kitchen. 'Freddie!' she exclaimed and half lifted her arms as if she might take him into an embrace, then shaking her head she added, 'It's a a long time since you last came to this house.'

'And you were going away that time too,' he said quietly.

'And last time you brought roses, not . . .' she gestured towards the chests, 'not furniture!'

30

'What I didn't bring was enough courage,' he said.

Laura wondered if the ring she now wore on a chain around her neck had been in his pocket. She also wondered briefly if this was the moment to show it to her mother, but as the arrangements for the immediate packing and portering of the chests to the docks were told, she knew it was not. Such a revelation might dangerously delay them. There was always the possibility her father could return yet again; it was one of the tricks he enjoyed, coming back when they least expected him.

In spite of all the uncertainties ahead, or perhaps because of them, they all fell into a kind of madcap mood as they worked. Jamie came downstairs draped in one of the many lengths of material Queenie had bought over the years from the brilliant range the Indian shopkeepers kept. It was a secret indulgence she had been able to hide from her husband. Then Freddie surpassed all by dancing with the tailor's dummy on its way to be dismantled and laid between the folds of the materials. The precious Singer sewing machine was even more carefully packed into the other chest – but the time passed quickly and soon the chests were packed, locked, roped up and labelled.

The four of them stood quite silent around the boxes when it was all done.

'I don't know how to thank you for this,' Queenie said.

'Take care of yourself,' Freddie told her, 'and take care of this daughter of yours for my son's sake.'

'Second time around,' Queenie said wistfully.

'Better than never at all.' Freddie went to her and taking her shoulders kissed her lingeringly on each cheek. 'God speed if I do not see you, or at least not this close again. Don't worry about the chests, I'll see they're on your boat.'

'I'll see you again later?' Jamie asked Laura.

'By the tree,' she confirmed, as her mother nodded approval.

When the men had gone the two women stood for a moment in the silent hall. 'He could have been your father,'

31

Queenie said quietly, 'I loved him . . .'

'I know . . .' She knew that this *was* the moment to show her mother the ring – the ring that should have been Queenie's.

The story was quickly told. Her mother stood as if spellbound, until her daughter had finished, then she took the ring between her fingers. 'It is magnificent,' she breathed, 'and he had bought it for me.'

'Let me take if off the chain, so you can . . .'

'No. Oh! No.' Queenie shook her head. She didn't want that, it was too late. 'We were so young – much too young. It is enough to know.' She angled the stone to see the rainbows of colour from the facets. 'But isn't it marvellous!' Then realising she had used Freddie's word she gave a quiet but most loving chuckle of laughter which gripped Laura's heart like a ring of pain for her mother as she added, 'I bet you're glad he *didn't* give it to me.'

The two stood, arms about each other, and in the gentle embrace Laura felt more best friend, sister, elder sister even, than daughter. She was so grateful her mother had not said 'if only' or yearned for the *might have been*.

Into the moment of joyful absorption came the sound of a vehicle stopping outside. Not merely stopping, *screeching*, to a halt.

The embrace became a convulsive grasp.

'Your father – driving himself,' Queenie said, and their open expressions became the anxiety of the beleaguered. The ring was pushed quickly out of sight and Queenie gestured Laura to go upstairs. 'Tidy things up,' she breathed, both aware of the pulled-out drawers and cupboards, the denuded sewing room. How would they explain where everything had gone?

But they were too late, the front door opened and Jock Maclaren stood there, like the wicked genie from some evil lamp. He closed the street door. 'I've come to help you pack,' he announced, then looking from one to the other, he asked, 'What's been happening?'

32

Neither answered.

He came closer and Queenie instinctively stepped back. 'What have you been doing? You both look flushed.'

'We've been looking for sheets for the furniture, as well as trying to pack,' Laura told him. 'It's hard work, makes you hot!'

'Getting a bit chirpy, aren't you girl!' he exclaimed.

She expected the usual 'speak when you're spoken to'.

'So where are the cases?' he asked looking round.

'They're upstairs,' she answered, remembering the cases that were half packed but hidden under her bed.

'I'll be up to inspect them then.'

She did not move or answer.

'There is,' he said, advancing on her, 'such a thing as dumb insolence. Go on, up you go. I'll come and see what you're planning to take with you tomorrow – see if I approve.'

'Tomorrow?' she queried. 'I thought we had two days.'

'Ah! so you may have done, but you know what thought did!'

She hated him for his stupid, glib, hackneyed 'jokes' and the way he laughed at them. 'They can't keep altering it like this!' she exclaimed.

'This time tomorrow, my girl, you'll be packed, house shut up and aboard.' He turned to put his cap and cane on the table, 'And I'm off duty now until you're embarked.'

He couldn't be. There was her promise to see Jamie.

'Laura,' her mother was prompting, not, she realised, for the first time. 'There are more sheets in the spare room cupboard. Even some in the attics. You could *go* and look.'

Laura glanced at her mother who neither nodded nor moved but whose eyes held a new purpose, a new defiance. 'I'll go, yes,' she acknowledged and hurried to the stairs.

'That's more like it! And don't forget the mattresses,' Jock shouted as if she was almost out of earshot, instead of one foot on the bottom stair.

'Mattresses?' Queenie queried.

'Yes, mattresses! My wife and daughter will be travelling in the comfort of an Egyptian freighter, where no doubt you will find some spot to unroll your own bedding and lie down. Very fitting for an officer's wife and daughter!'

'Perhaps we should have gone earlier.' Queenie ventured a jerk of her head at Laura.

'You mean you *wish* you had gone earlier,' Jock said, then adding with sarcasm, 'You both wish you were not here. That's it, isn't it, little Laura?'

Laura looked at him. The contrast between him and the two kind men who had so recently been there made the truth loosen her tongue. 'No, it's not true as it happens,' she heard herself say, 'and it was your fault we didn't sail to England with the other English wives and families on the *Dorsetshire* weeks ago.'

'Oh! Oh! My goodness,' he pretended to be staggered by her outburst. ' "As it happens" indeedy. Well "as it happens" we'll have you upstairs packing and looking for sheets. *And* when I want you to come down I'll call.'

'Just *go*, Laura,' her mother said, a new assertiveness in her voice.

Her father looked from wife to daughter and laughed. Laura's heart thumped with apprehension, knowing that matters in the Maclaren family were racing towards some traumatic conclusion and that once her mother had left Gibraltar she would never again live with her husband. But there was some time to go until then, and she was reading all the bad signs. The sequence was so familiar – the irritation, the sarcasm, then would come the physical domination, standing too close, towering over, then the first contact, maybe no more than a slight push with his body, but once made some bullying would follow.

34

'Can't I help you downstairs?' she asked still lingering.

'No, of course not, there's no time to waste. *Go on*!' Queenie turned and for once in her married life preceded her husband out of the hall, towards the kitchen.

Laura stood listening a moment, torn between being a presence to protect her mother and saying what might be a final goodbye to Jamie, if not final then for a long, long time. Then she ran up to her room and dragged out the half packed cases, placing them in the middle of her parents' bed for her father's inspection. After closing cupboards, drawers, rearranging the ironing board and draping a discarded length of cloth over the table in the sewing room, she shut the door. Breathless, listening first at the top of the stairs, she descended step by step.

She felt her stomach tightening, constricting into a silent ache of anxiety. While other teenagers had fretted over disloyal friends, or uncaring youths, this had been her secret pain. She had learned very early that any outward show of distress served only to make her mother feel so much worse.

Near the bottom of the stairs she could hear talking. Her mother. Speaking out? Speaking up for herself? She tiptoed and stood open-mouthed, her ear against the kitchen door. 'There'll be no chance of letting the house while we're away,' she was saying, 'no one will want to come and stay on Gib – and if you've to go into quarters . . .'

He must suspect something, she thought, it hardly even sounds like my mother, but her father seemed to be remaining silent – and Jamie would be waiting. They would be gone tomorrow. Holding her breath she tiptoed to the front door, let herself out and closed it with infinite care – then ran. With luck she could be back before she was even missed, she told herself – with luck.

She was out of breath long before she reached their

tree but forced herself on, gasping in the heat and on the uphill path. When she arrived she thought he was not there, but then a movement brought her eye to the shade of a rock further up on the land side. She had the impression that he lay languid but attentive as she came into his view. He would have risen but she hurried to throw herself down by his side.

He reached over and pushed her hair back from her damp forehead, then held her hand waiting for her to recover her breath before asking, 'So what is it? What's happened?' When she did not immediately answer he added, 'I heard you coming, running as if Beelzebub himself was on your tail.'

'Nearly true,' she said, then leaning across his arm to put her head on his chest she told him the news of the earlier departure.

'Hell!' he exclaimed quietly. From the corner of her eye she saw he jaw working as he clenched and unclenched his teeth. 'I did hear that the Moroccan authorities want you all to arrive in the morning so you can be processed in daylight,' he said, 'but I didn't know they were bringing the sailings forward.' He paused and she sensed him gathering his thoughts together more resolutely. He sat up away from the rock so he could look at her more directly, and when she would not meet his gaze, he added, 'But there's something else.'

'The trouble is, my father's home until we embark . . . and . . .'

'And?'

She stared hard at the ground. 'I must go straight back.'

'You're afraid for your mother?'

She could still hear in his voice the reluctant belief of someone who had no real experience of domestic attacks. 'He may indulge in some parting punches. Yes,' she told him.

'I'll come back with you,' he said positively and was

36

on his feet holding out a hand to help her up.

'I'll have to slip back in,' she said half informing, half musing. 'I could go round the back, through the court-yard. I can listen near the kitchen, try to find out what he's doing.'

They were by their tree now and both automatically stopped, looking up. 'Where's our ape?' she asked.

'Didn't expect us today.' Holding hands they looked out over the stretch of sea she thought of as theirs, at least as much theirs as the tree and the ape. Neither spoke, there was everything and nothing to be said. They just looked, watching the mesmeric shoals of glittering silver shapes the sinking sun created over the rippling waters. Then their hands tightened and both drew in their breaths as in the middle of the seascape appeared a hole, a huge circling of descending waters. Charybdis and Scylla, a myth come to life. The hole in the waters swirled, deepened, filled. They waited. Watched, not just where the hole had been, but all around. She had a vivid picture in her mind of ancient maps where seas were shown inhabited by great monsters and whirlpools, which of course they were. Then they both exclaimed as not too far from the sudden sinking came the water spout, thirty, forty feet into the air, blown by the evening breeze, caught and transformed by the sun into a glorious falling rainbow wide across the sea.

'A sperm whale,' he said then as if the fact was too blunt for such a spectacle he added, 'we have to believe in such things.'

Such things as myths and legends did he mean? She glanced up at him as he watched the last rainbow shower falling back into the sea.

He lowered his gaze to her. 'We have to believe that everything will come out right in the end,' he said. 'We have to keep faith.'

No, she thought looking up at him, he means mira-cles, and . . .' Her reasoning stopped as she thought how

37

handsome, no, how beautiful he was, the sun lighting the flat plane of his cheek as he bent towards her. She felt such a rush of love and affection for him and her hand went instinctively up to cover the ring where it lay below the neckline of her dress.

'Put it on now, wear it for all to see,' he asked.

'But my father, I . . . it will only cause trouble.'

'I shall be with you all the time until you leave,' he said.

'But you can't!' she exclaimed. 'I have to go home.'

'I've told you, I'm coming with you.'

'But not – not to the house. He doesn't even know I'm out. I have to creep back in.'

'Wouldn't it be better just to confront him? I'm not much for this hole-in-the-corner way of going on. I think now's the time for some introductions – confrontations if he prefers them.' He took her hand and began to lead her at a brisk pace down the hill.

She literally dug her heels in, pulling him to a halt. 'You still make it sound like a game, a stupid child's game – and it's not.'

'What is it then?' he demanded. 'You tell me, exactly.'

'It's a power game, a secret, violent game of strength he knows he always wins,' she said, then felt he had tricked her into the admission.

'Time, then, that he realised his game is over.'

'But he's so strong . . .'

'I'm not afraid of him.' He started to walk again. 'Bullies are usually cowards when faced, particularly by someone their own size.'

'We can't just walk in on him.' She could not begin to imagine the result of such a confrontation and while Jamie might be as tall, he did not have the muscled strength that regular keep fit and army life had given the older man.

'What do you suggest? We haven't got time for a great

deal of manoeuvring.'

It was his purposeful pace that made her realise that if she did not come up with some reasonable suggestion he was going to just walk straight into the house. 'We could go to the back, listen without being seen in the courtyard, then...'

'Decide what to do.'

What she had not expected was that her father's jeep was no longer outside the house, but she still led the way through the high arched gate into the courtyard. Here figs, peaches and pomegranate trees had an abundance of small immature fruits, and many red and while oleanders and geraniums were in full flower. The place was her mother's creation and pleasure. Cautiously she skirted the garden until they came near to the kitchen window. She paused and listened. Jamie came to her side, then cautiously leaned over to peep through the window. She heard him draw in his breath and immediately stride for the door. Heart in mouth she ran too, overtaking him, and entered the kitchen first.

Her mother lay slumped over, her forehead on the table, while her hands and arms were wrapped around her middle.

'What's he done?' Laura demanded.

'Nothing.' Queenie's denial came even as they startled her, even as she straightened and was forced to use one arm to help herself upright from the table, while the other she kept tight across her stomach as if to contain the hurt. Then she saw it was useless to try to fool either of these young people. 'Nothing worse than usual,' she said, with an attempt at a wan smile.

When neither of them answered, Jamie too appalled and Laura too sick at heart, she turned to her daughter. 'He's gone looking for you. I couldn't stop him. I've no idea where he's gone, or how long he'll be. You'd best make your goodbyes and let Jamie go back to his father before he comes back. He's furious, beside himself.' She

39

made an appeal to Jamie, 'Don't tell your father about any of this, it won't help, and . . . we can cope.'

'You're coming with me,' Jamie told her firmly. 'There's no way I'm leaving either of you here now.'

Both women regarded him, the idea of a possible escape, an immediate way out very difficult to accept.

'When he comes back, he'll just find you gone. He'll have no idea where.'

'Why not, Mum, this is the perfect opportunity.' Laura was the first to see that it was just possible. 'We could take a case each, hide at Mr de Falla's house until it is time to embark.'

Queenie shook her head, but it was obvious she was giving it some thought.

'I'll go and get our cases, we could take those,' Laura said hurrying to the stairs.

'I'll get them, which room?' Jamie said. 'You make sure you have your handbags, all the papers, bank books whatever else you will need.' He nodded urgently. 'Go on Laura, hurry!'

Bags and coats were collected and soon they were following Jamie as he portered the two large heavy suitcases towards his home. Queenie was totally devoid of colour, a ghost in the early evening light, one arm still pressed to her side, as they hurried. But she had not said a word against the idea and never glanced back. Didn't dare, Laura thought, as she herself glanced fearfully around whenever vehicles approached.

At the house Freddie greeted them with surprised enthusiasm, then looked at Queenie's pallor with concern. 'What's happened?' she heard him ask his son who drew him away but he was quickly back. 'Should I get the doctor to look at you,' he asked Queenie, 'or a nurse?'

'No, no,' she said, 'it'll just be bruising.'

The remark which tried to make light of the trouble succeeded only in making it obvious that it was part of

40

the normal treatment meted out by Jock Maclaren.

'For God's sake, why did you stay with him?' Freddie demanded, then shook his head.

'He wasn't always like this, not at the beginning,' Queenie murmured into the slightly embarrassed silence. 'It's easy to ask such questions now.'

Freddie left the room but was quickly back with coffee and brandy. 'Sorry,' he said, 'I shouldn't make judgements, I know nothing about such situations – thank God. But there are beds here to spare and I'll go to the docks right away and find out exactly what is happening. Jamie will stay with you both, you will not be left alone.'

'I just can't believe we're doing this,' Queenie told him. 'I feel it's all wrong involving you two. If we all fall foul of Jock . . .' she looked from Freddie to his son. 'To get away like this, is . . . too easy.'

'Too easy!' Laura shook her head vigorously at her mother, 'It's what we should have done years ago.'

'And I'd just like the chance to fall foul of Jock Maclaren,' Jamie said.

Their attention was diverted by the sound of a door slamming, then of someone singing.

'It's Fatima,' Freddie told them, 'she comes in to make our evening meal now. Her mother's had to go to La Linea as their grandmother is ill. I'll tell her we have two guests for supper and for the night.'

'But not who we are,' Queenie added anxiously.

'Don't worry,' he reassured her. 'You're completely safe here.'

Freddie came back nearly two hours later with the news that Lieutenant Jock Maclaren had been seen at the checkpoint on Europa Point demanding to be let through to the lighthouse cottage, because he believed his daughter was there. 'He was in a rare state of excitement I understand,' Freddie said mildly.

'He must have thought I'd gone to see Doris,' Laura

41

said, adding for Freddie's sake, 'I worked with her.'

'He'll scour the whole of Gib,' Queenie said fearfully.

'But he won't find you,' Freddie assured her, 'and I have commandeered a friend of mine in the Green Howards, Sergeant Bill Milloy, to be your personal escort. The Green Howards have been detailed to help with the embarkation and to sail with the evacuees and help everyone disembark the other end. Bill knows the score. He will be here at eleven o'clock and we'll *all* escort you aboard the *Dar es Salaam*. And I've arranged for the chests to be loaded.'

In the light of such specific information she saw her mother begin to relax.

'So,' Freddie went on. 'Fatima has laid a meal for us, let's go and eat it, drink a bottle of wine and let the rest of tonight and tomorrow take care of themselves. Yes?'

'I'll drink to that,' Jamie said.

Laura felt his gaze pointedly directed at her and she blushed furiously.

'Marvellous!' Freddie ushered them to his table.

Chapter Three

Jock swept the jeep to a screeching halt precisely on the spot he had left some two hours before. Frustrated in his attempts to find his daughter, he intended to learn more from his wife. She must have some idea where their daughter could have gone – must know. She had talked enough when he had first returned with the news of the earlier sailing. Thinking about it, there had been something quite different about her. Had she even then been covering up for Laura, chattering away like she never did, not for all their married years. He clenched his teeth hard; neither of them was going to escape the consequences of tonight's escapade.

He closed the front door behind him, then stood and repeated the slapping of his cane very hard into the palm of his hand. It both hurt and helped to pull his resolve together, for he remembered his mother making the same threatening promise with whatever she had in use – hand brush, clothes tongs, wooden spoon. Not threatening him of course – not always.

He strode through to the kitchen where he had left Queenie. She usually stayed where he left her – but this time not. She was wise to hide, he thought, after the way he'd been made to look a fool in front of his own kind. The wrangle at the checkpoint leading to the lighthouse complex had not been pleasant – or successful. The men on guard had, he supposed, done their job in a proper manner – no unauthorised personnel to pass – and he certainly wasn't authorised. But he had been careful after that. Careful to the extent that he had asked no one else, only driven round and round looking. But now he judged the girl must be back home – would be upstairs packing and finding dust sheets as she should have been doing instead of sneaking out of the house. To where? Whom to see? These questions were going to be answered.

She had defied him silently often enough, hung around when he wanted her out of the way. He'd tried to protect her from the consequences of her mother's stupidities. He had tried for God's sake! But now she had gone too far. She had defied him and made him look a fool, made him look as if he was a man, an officer, *not* in charge of his own private affairs. She was no better than her mother.

He returned to the hall. 'So you're back!' he shouted. 'Come down here!' He turned and strode into their sitting room and slapped the tall white flower of the peace lily on the side table with his cane. The flower toppled sideways, then recovered, leaving a great sprinkling of pollen on its wide dark leaves. He moved to the far side of the room, turned and waited facing the door.

'God in heaven!' he shouted his patience wearing thin. His mother had been a religious woman, church three times every Sunday, prayers mid-week. 'I pray for your father's enhancement,' she had once told him. At the time he had thought his father's job as a clerk at the Council offices was special. 'You must get on in life.' His father's advice had been, 'Get away, boy.'

What were they doing? 'Can you hear me?' he bellowed, rushing to the hall as if trying to outstrip his unease. 'Get down here!'

Only silence, falling as palpable as an all-enveloping blanket of fog might – only silence. But hadn't Queenie said something about there being sheets in the attic? That's where they would be. Out of earshot.

He hurled his cap and cane savagely on to the hall table, then ran up the stairs, noting as he passed that the cases that had lain open and half packed on their bed had gone. He was faced by three closed doors at the top of the third-floor stairs, even so he opened each one, then went with slow thoughtfulness down to search the bedrooms, which he did with thorough fury, wrenching open closet doors, even peering beneath beds, for he knew what fear could do. He had often seen his father cower. It was the reason he had determined he would never show funk, never be shamed, always be in control, particularly in his own household.

Where was his household? One racing after the other – looking out for each other as usual? It seemed the most likely explanation. Queenie had known all the time where Laura was – and while he was out she had gone to fetch her – that was it.

They would hope to sneak in. He nodded to himself as he thought of a way to foil that idea. He ran down to the hall, strode across to the front door and shot the bolts home, smiling as he secured the heavy wrought-iron bars top and bottom. Now there was only one way in. He felt secure now, secure because he had the situation under control and it could not be very long before his family were where he could put his hand on them again, for a little longer at least. The evacuation was bad enough, he did not deserve this 'rebellion' as well.

As time crawled by the feeling of being that impotent child again began inexorably to take over. If he did nothing the old anger surged to bursting point inside his skull. So all the time listening for their return he roamed around looking for clues. He realised first that Queenie's handbag was not in its usual place in her shopping basket. He ran back upstairs. So where were the cases? Had they taken them to the dock, carried them down there themselves, part of another stupidity to bring shame on him? But as the evening wore on he knew this was not the answer.

Now the search took on new implications. Cases and

45

bags gone. He looked now for money. There was always money in a pot on the dresser, money to pay the few casual people who sold things door to door, or delivered heavy items from shops. Nothing – and evening was fast becoming night.

Beginning with the drawers in the kitchen he pulled out everything looking for a Post Office Savings Book he knew existed. He ran back to the bedroom, rifled more thoroughly through the contents he had already tipped out. He realised this was more than a temporary absence, this was desertion – but they could not leave Gibraltar until their boat sailed tomorrow. He knew exactly where they would be at eleven-thirty. He closed his eyes as he planned. His breathing became heavier, deeper as his fury rose. 'How dare they,' he muttered, 'how dare they treat me like this.'

He cast about in his mind what he could do. If he went knocking on doors asking for them he'd make a fool of himself – but he needed action. No, what he needed was revenge. He ranged the possibilities. Then he laughed and went out into the garden, where the flowers loomed like pale ghosts floating in the darkness. He opened his arms wide as if in thanks for the inspiration.

He used his feet to begin with, savagely knocking over all her massed geraniums, spinning them against walls and troughs until the terracotta pots lost their ring, cracked apart; then he trampled the flowers thoroughly. He'd seen Queenie's capacity for retrieving broken plants. She would not be saving these. No, she would not. These would be beyond anyone's rescue.

The oleanders broke easily as he used his strength to pull off the flower-laden branches. Soon the slender trunks gleamed white like peeled corpses among their own floral tributes. Everything he destroyed, on and on, stumbling over the debris he created, upending great stone troughs with strength increased by his fury.

At last, exhausted, he went back to the kitchen, poured himself a tumbler of whisky and planned for the next day.

He would find a way to make it one they would always remember. He'd waylay them, somewhere in the crowded passageways to the quays, he'd make opportunity to wreak his revenge properly. Something to remember him by, he raised his glass. 'Until we meet again,' he promised himself.

'The quays are crowded now,' Sergeant Milloy, a ruddy-faced, stiff-necked Scot, reported once he had been introduced to his personal charges for the voyage. Arriving at the de Fallas' home he proposed they should leave immediately. He spoke in short sharp sentences which, volume increased, could be imagined as parade-ground orders, or derogatory comments. 'I think it would be wise. First on we will secure the best positions. There'll not be much mattress room come night.'

'Mattresses!' Queenie exclaimed. 'I'd forgotten we had to take our own mattresses.'

'Will it matter?' Laura, with the agony of being parted from Jamie so imminent, felt little mattered.

'I think so,' the sergeant said.

'Yes,' Freddie agreed, 'you never know how long you might need your own bedding for. Hundreds of people arriving at the same place at the same time. There must be some here you can take.' He looked at Jamie and the two of them ran upstairs and in minutes returned with two single mattresses dragged willy-nilly from beds and down the stairs.

'They need rolling up,' Jamie said beginning to try to do just that with the rather rigid flock bedding, while Freddie went in search of trunk straps. He found one and took over from Jamie, aware that the sergeant was uneasy and already off-limits as regards his day's duty. 'Look,' Freddie said as this strap proved barely long enough, 'you all go ahead with Bill and I'll follow with the mattresses once I have them rolled.' He refused offers of help. 'No problem, I'll carry them with the straps, one on my shoulder, one under

47

my arm. Just look out for me. Go on,' he urged his son with a nod towards the women, '*two* of you should go – just in case.'

They were still the stragglers, for though there were people moving ahead of them the roads were not busy, but as they neared the area of the docks they could hear the hubbub of people. Through the alleyways running from the wider streets they glimpsed an incredible picture. It looked as if the whole of the population of Gibraltar and much of the naval and army garrisons were assembling on the edge of the land, and the quays were lined with a multifarious collection of ships already loading their passengers.

'Freddie'll never find us,' Queenie said as they approached this mass of people. Many seemed to be looking for people themselves, crying out for someone's attention at the tops of their voices, waving, gesticulating. If for one second they did spot someone they knew, the next they were lost again in the swaying arms, in the general unease and shifting of the crowd.

'We have to report to the man at the gangway,' Bill Milloy said.

'One of us should wait here,' Queenie suggested. 'Freddie will come this way. If you take my bags, then I can carry one of the mattresses when he comes.'

'I'll wait,' Jamie said, then Laura grasped his arm, caught up in the trauma of this last-minute parting and he added, 'if you like.'

A loudspeaker called from the freighter the sergeant was leading them towards. 'That's us,' he said. 'Best we get aboard.'

'Oh! I can see him coming,' Queenie announced and stepped back a little out of the crowd. 'Go on, we'll catch you up.'

As she turned back Laura felt a lurch of alarm. She should not be letting her mother out of her sight. But Jamie was pulling her arm to move after the sergeant and she was diverted by the sight of her workmate Doris Hewitt and her

48

four young daughters being helped through the crowd. The smallest girl was crying and the others looked totally bemused as they struggled to hold on to bags and bundles as they were buffeted by the throng. The next moment they too were out of sight and, looking back, so was her mother.

The Green Howards' corporal on the gangway checked their names and allowed them to wait against him until the other members of their party arrived. It seemed like ages and, when finally the two of them did appear, the press of people was so great Freddie had difficulty passing the two mattresses over to the sergeant. He then turned to urge Queenie to go aboard. 'Go on, my dear, he can't hurt you now.'

She gripped his arm, her lips parted but no words seemed to fit the intensity of the moment.

'I know, I know,' he reassured her as if she had spoken, 'don't worry, I can take care of myself.'

It was then Laura noticed Freddie's bruised and cut lip and that her mother's blouse and slacks were covered in dust as if she had fallen or been rolled along one of the town's crumbling white-washed walls. 'He found you,' she gasped, but neither of them answered.

'We're holding people up,' Bill said, drawing attention to a small group looking for them to move on. 'We must go aboard.'

Queenie pushed out a hand and gripped Freddie's arm, then turned and began to climb the gangplank.

Laura spun round into Jamie's arms for a last desperate embrace, which ended only when Freddie put his hand on his son's shoulder. The ship's hooter blasted out at the same moment startling them all and, as Jamie released her, she was carried a few steps backwards by the sudden press of people who too had been saying their last goodbyes.

Even with the feel of his arms still about her she felt bereft, knew the wild misery of separation. Had she been able she would have fought her way back to him. As soon as she was on the deck she turned aside and clung to the rail

49

so she could not be carried further away and she might see him for as long as possible. 'Where will we meet again?' she wanted to shout, and, 'When?' Then, as if she had shouted aloud, he cupped his hands to his mouth and called to her, 'I shall find you, wherever you are, look for me!'

All around bewildered and heartbroken people were clinging to the rails in tears, waving, or staring with disbelief as their enforced exile began, as the gangway was hoisted aboard and the mooring lines were dropped from the quay into the sea. The ship's hooter sounded once, twice, and they were cast off. Cast off. She gripped her mother's hand as they stood staring down at the two de Fallas. Freddie raised both hands and made a gesture reminiscent of an Eastern act of worship. Jamie gave her a naval-type salute, then blew her a kiss. Afterwards she could not remember whether she returned it, or whether she just stood rigid with despair.

A little boy nearby suddenly screamed as if he had only just realised his father was being left behind. He turned on his mother and as she tried to hold him, fought her and cried out, 'Daddy, my daddy!' Then he pushed at his mother with all his strength and catapulted himself away, and would certainly have dived from her arms and overboard had Sergeant Milloy not grabbed him before he went over the rails. Gasps of alarm and relief were intermingled; it all happened so quickly.

'Come on, old lad. You give your dad a fine salute.' He showed the boy how and, surprised by the intervention, the child did just that and allowed himself to be hoisted up onto the sergeant's shoulders. 'Right, now Captain!' Bill Milloy asked him, 'see any smoke?' The immediate cry and pointing to the column of thick black smoke issuing from the freighter's funnel was enough to divert the boy's attention and Sergeant Milloy, with an aside that he would be back, carried the boy away, another soldier coming to help with the young mother's mattress and bags.

The incident distracted her for a few moments and when

Laura looked back the gulf of water had widened. The faces of those left behind began to take on the anonymity of distance, floating like a pale haze in the midday heat and, as the ship turned away, the two of them threaded their way between people and baggage towards the stern, a final viewing platform others too were seeking.

At the stern rail people moved up, made room for them, and they joined the line of unhappy people wrenched away from their homes and loved ones. They watched with silent concentration as the coastline receded behind them and Gibraltar hung in the sky like a dark cloud low in a sun-bleached sky. Soon all they could perceive was the flash of the lighthouse against the bulk of rock. She thought of Doris and the children; to them that light pinpointed their home.

Soon most turned away to begin trying to select and settle themselves in a space that suited them, and the two women were a little apart from the others remaining at the rail. 'What happened?' Laura asked and the question made her realise that her mother had not spoken since before they boarded. She reached out a tentative hand and brushed some of the dust from her mother's slacks. 'Mum?' she prompted gently.

Queenie shook her head, closed her eyes.

'I need to know,' she said and struggled to find words to express their growing dependence just on each other, 'I do need to know . . .'

'His parting present,' her mother said bitterly. 'It's what he said he had for me.'

'But where was he?'

'I didn't see him. I was watching Freddie. There was a family, and all I could see for a moment or two was the top of the mattress Freddie was carrying on his shoulder. Then someone grabbed my arm,' she paused to clasp a hand over her own forearm, 'and I was jerked violently sidewards.' She shook her head at the memory. 'I saw an archway over my head, heard a door slam behind me and . . .' she spread

51

her hands in bewilderment, 'there I was facing him in a kind of yard, full of boxes and crates and sacks, and . . . he looked so evil.'

Another passenger came and stood near them for a few moments, murmured, 'Not much left to see now' and moved away again.

It had given Queenie time to try to recover and she went on in a strange light voice aping normality, 'My goodness, he must have planned well, been planning all night I shouldn't wonder.'

'He can't reach you now. Not ever again.'

'He told me he'd hunt me to the ends of the earth, that I'd never escape.' She pressed a clenched fist over her lips for a moment, then continued, 'I tried to turn, get away. He clamped his hand over my mouth and nose. I couldn't breathe. He dragged me across the yard. I thought he was going to . . .' she glanced at her daughter then away out over the sea, 'rape me, or kill me – or both.'

'And Freddie?' Laura murmured wanting to move her on from that recollection.

'I didn't think Freddie could possibly have seen what happened to me. I thought he'd just walk by. I was beginning to pass out. I couldn't breathe. I couldn't breathe. I couldn't breathe,' she repeated, drawing in a huge panic-stricken breath as if she still needed to gulp in the air. 'He was pushing me towards a pile of sacks. Then suddenly I fell. He'd let me go. For a moment or two I couldn't see properly – then I realised Freddie was there. I was terrified for him. Your father looked like the devil, his black hair all fallen over his face. Freddie was so pale. He towered above Freddie, but he stood his ground, shouted at me to get out of the yard. Then I came to my senses and knew if I could get someone . . .'

'He would stop.'

'That's what happened,' Queenie confirmed. 'I fell out of the gate over the mattresses which lay just outside. A couple of Royal Air Force boys were walking by, they laughed for a moment. I suppose I looked comical, then one helped me up. I told them someone was attacking my friend. The other ran into the yard. I heard him shout then Freddie came, picked up the mattresses, and . . . we came to the boat.'

'I hope they thumped him good and hard before they let him go,' Laura said. 'Was he in uniform?'

'Isn't he always.'

'They might not, then.'

'Ready for you now, ladies.' Sergeant Bill Milloy stood behind them waiting to help carry their cases and mattresses. 'Let's find you a sheltered spot. Likely be cool tonight.'

They followed him and saw that those with elderly relatives or young children were beginning to unstrap their mattresses. A heavily pregnant woman and a soldier were helping an ancient man down to the deck. It seemed there were to be no cabins or bunks for anyone. Bags and coats were being piled to make back rests and pillows. Among the many were familiar faces: she recognised their greengrocer's wife, the lady from the sewing shop, and she saw Doris being helped by another Green Howards sergeant to remove a well-knotted rope from a mattress for her children.

'Thank heavens the sea's calm,' Queenie said as they passed the day on the crowded decks, shading themselves as best they could from the sun. Neither Queenie or Laura had thought of food until those nearby began to pull out packed meals and flasks of cold drinks. Exchanging looks they wondered, then explored the bags Freddie and Jamie had given to them along with their cases. They found a wealth of goodies: meat and cheese sandwiches, biscuits, fruit and fruit drinks.

The evening came, Laura made her way over to Doris and found her much concerned for her children and, like her mother, so thankful that the sea was calm, and hoping the voyage would be short. 'Casablanca, I keep hearing,' she told Laura.

53

Eventually the packed deck became quiet except for the occasional murmur of a child, a snore, a cry, or someone having to thread their way between the sleeping hoping to find the crew's overworked toilet facilities available.

Laura lay listening to the mesmeric sound of the engines and the stir their passage made through the water. Above them the sky became like soft black velvet sewn with brilliants. She disciplined herself to lie quite still, for she was sure her mother was at last sleeping. She herself was wide awake, though she had slept very little the night before. Last night. Her night with Jamie.

She pushed away the awful thought that it might be the only night she *ever* spent with him. They had all gone to their allocated beds: her mother into Freddie's huge bed, Jamie to his own, and Laura to a room near the top of the stairs. Freddie had elected to sleep on a sofa in the hall 'just in case' he said, 'I'll be watchdog.'

He had not, she thought, been a very alert watchdog or he might have investigated the comings and goings in the night. Jamie had arrived in her room almost before she was in bed. 'Your father will hear,' had been her first reaction, but he had slipped in beside her, only to decide his own bed was much less noisy and further away from the stairs. Holding hands they had tiptoed from room to room. He had hurried her along the corridor like a naughty boy escaping with the contents of the pantry.

As they slipped between his sheets he had whispered, 'You'll soon have been in every bed in the house.' She had smothered her laughter with a mouthful of sheet.

'Sssh! we'll have my father up here,' he said.

'Or my mother.'

'Or both,' he had said and it had taken them both many minutes to come to some sort of sanity, which kept bursting out all through the magical loving and dozing night.

She wondered now why Freddie had not put her into that huge four-poster with her mother – unless . . . Her face burned as she wondered if he had either been giving his son

54

a last opportunity to go to his fiancée – or himself a chance to go to his former love. 'Or both,' she whispered up to the stars. 'Or both.'

Last night she and Jamie had looked up at these same stars. Jamie had pointed out the bright Pole star. 'The mariner's star, that's in the tail of The Little Bear, see how it lines up with the stars on the back of The Great Bear.'

'We call that The Plough,' she had told him.

She wondered if he was looking at the stars tonight, at that star, the brightest. She concentrated on the bright evening star and imagined her own personal constellation, a triangle. The points at the base were the two points where she and Jamie were, the star was at the peak of the triangle, the point where their thoughts and their love met. The trouble was the two earthly points were every minute becoming further and further away from each other.

Carefully now she undertook what she had promised Jamie she would do as soon as she was safely away from Gibraltar. She lifted her head to pull the chain from around her neck. Then running it through her fingers she found the clasp, carefully undid it and slipped the ring on to the third finger of her left hand. A shaded deck lantern still provided enough light to sparkle the diamond to life as she lifted her hand to admire it.

They could write. She would write as soon as they had an address. 'H.O.L.L.A.N.D.' she would write on her envelope – and underline it.

Chapter Four

Her first waking sensation was of tremendous hunger. The lack of a proper meal the day before and being on deck all night was making most of the deck passengers search their bags. By her side her mother was doing the same.

'Hungry?' she greeted, adding the offer, 'biscuits and cheese?'

'Starving.'

'We'll have to make do until we get to . . .'

'Our secret destination.'

'That won't be long.' Bill Milloy arrived as if on cue.

'How do you know?' Laura asked.

'Go and look,' he told her. 'I'll roll your mattresses.'

Munching biscuits they went to the rail and leaned there, marvelling at the long rollers of the Atlantic breaking along a seemingly endless beach. After the small sands and tideless Mediterranean this was grand scale. Above Africa rose a sun cloaked in the mantle of land colours, brown, dull bronze, then leaving the horizon it shrugged off the earth, rose and brightened to the brilliance of highly polished brass. The warmth of it reached them like a benison. The beaches became golden, the long waves blue and white.

'Will there be camels to ride?' a young voice asked.

They turned to see it was the young boy who had so nearly taken a tumble over the railing.

56

'There might be,' his mother humoured as the boy tried to free his hand from hers.

'You hold on tight to your mummy,' Queenie told him, 'you don't want to lose her.'

'Oh, dear.' His mother smiled woefully as she allowed herself to be pulled away. 'He does need his FATHER,' she spelled out. 'Or I do.'

'Making a rod for your own back,' an elderly man, face the deep-lined brown of one who had spent a lifetime around the Med, called after her. He looked to them for agreement as the young mother did her best to steer between passengers and baggage apologising as she went, but the spelled word had driven the brief smiles from their faces. They were all missing their men.

They stayed leaning on the rail as the low outline of the white city of Casablanca came on to their horizon. Soon they could see the long curving arm of the mole thrown out around the straight lines of the shorter quays. The port and the fishing harbour area were already busy and soon to be more so as their flotilla of merchantmen with human cargo arrived.

'Thank goodness it's morning,' Queenie commented as they were ordered to prepare to disembark, and she struggled to keep their mattresses and bags in some kind of tidy pile. 'We'll swelter when this sun gets to its peak.'

Standing in lines around the decks, clothes and hair tidied as far as possible, but unwashed, they were stoical, leaning or sitting where they could. The young children looked anxiously at their elders and matched the sombre mood with their own frowning concern, staying close, holding tight to those they knew. Laura felt she had some idea of what it might be like to be a real refugee: powerless, at the mercy of politicians, policemen and soldiers. She looked around at the men lining the rails – helping, many really kind, but in charge – very much in charge. Watchful for any rebel, anyone stepping out of line.

By ten o'clock they were on land, but all restricted inside

57

the walled port area. There was some delay as a service was being set up for the evacuees to change English money into francs. Through the gates they could glimpse high, blank, white walls where the ancient houses of the casbah gazed inwards and only low shaded archways gave access to the narrow winding streets beyond.

Her gaze was drawn to the many swallows which continually swept across the docks, the walls, the city, with proprietary assurance, at home if they liked to be, or free to cross continents. They made her feel even more trapped where she had no wish to be, surrounded by people, baggage, walls and gates. The money-changing had seemed to take for ever, and everyone was now so hungry and their throats so dry. She looked impatiently at the officials with their sheafs of papers who appeared to be just standing about. Nothing was seen to be happening, children became fretful, mothers and the elderly short-tempered.

Then there was a shift in the crowd, a palpable uplift of spirits. Laura could suddenly smell strong aromatic coffee, and soon French Boy Scouts came carrying great trays of coffee in enamel mugs. Girl Guides followed bringing trays loaded with crispy French bread and freshly barbecued sardines. Never had fish, bread and coffee been so welcome. The supplies were seemingly unlimited and those serving and supervising were friendly and sympathetic. 'It's a bit like the miracle of the loaves and fishes.' It was the elderly man from the boat but this time everyone turned to smile their agreement.

In the early afternoon the crowds began to be organised, names were called, and families directed to different areas. While they still waited they refound Doris and her four daughters who were, to Doris's weary despair, being sent on a further journey by train. This would take them back along the coast towards Rabat and Oran, the way they had just steamed.

Laura tried to make contact with one of the officials now busy ticking off the names for the train. She asked in her

58

politest schoolgirl French if they could go with Doris Hewitt so they could help look after the four young girls. 'She needs help,' she appealed but the official shook his head without looking up, though he asked, 'Names?'

They were moving away when he called after them. 'Queenie and Laura Maclaren.' He wrote an address on a piece of paper, and finally looked up as he passed it to them. His utter weariness made his brown face sallow, and drew attention to the grey in his moustache and hair. Something in the sudden sympathy he saw in their eyes made him give a slight bow and he added, 'If you wish to get a taxi...'

'We can go? Queenie asked.

He nodded and indicated the main way out into the street. 'You must not move without informing the authorities,' he said.

'We have chests in the hold,' Queenie suddenly remembered.

'They will be delivered to you. It is all organised.' He smiled as if to add it may not look so but it is. They thanked him as he moved on to the next group.

They portered their cases, bags and mattresses through the crowds to the gates, where they produced their piece of paper with the scrawled address. The Moroccan policemen stepped back smiling, gesturing as if offering them the freedom of Casablanca. Outside taxis and horse gharry drivers were eager for their business.

Queenie lingered just outside the compound, taking time to buy a round flat loaf and a bottle of mineral water from the proprietor of a tiny stall. 'I mean to keep our supplies up after that experience.'

Laura smiled agreement as she also indicated a gaily red, yellow and blue tasselled horse gharry tended by a broadly smiling boy. Laura's heart and spirits lifted as her mother took the initiative. She would become a different woman, Laura thought, a swallow released from a cage, into the blue, away from the tyranny of her father.

Before they could reach the gharry, someone called their names again. A man's voice but not, she thought, the official, this was younger, more English. For a moment she could not see who spoke, only knew it came from the direction of the gate they had just passed through.

Then she saw an officer, an officer in the Green Howards, coming quickly their way.

'Mrs Maclaren?' he inquired smiling.

Queenie nodded cautiously.

'Nearly missed you. I have a message for you.'

'A message?'

'Who from?' Laura asked.

'I presume if you are this lady's daughter, from your father.'

Her father! She wanted to scream at the man, can't he leave us alone.

Her mother's hand had flown to cover her mouth. The officer saw her alarm and hastened to tell her that there was nothing wrong. 'It was just that he felt circumstances might make him miss you at the docks when you left Gib. He wanted you to know that he'll be keeping up with news of you wherever you are, and I promised to let him have your address. I'm going back on one of the freighters shortly.' When neither of them answered or moved the lieutenant added, 'It's absolutely no trouble.'

'We saw my father at the docks,' Laura said, adding a stiff and belated, 'thank you.'

'But you wouldn't have known your address then,' he said smiling and nodding down to the paper in her hand. 'It'll be quicker than writing if I let him know.'

'No,' Laura said bluntly, moving so her arm touched her mother's as they stood side by side. 'When we're settled we'll let people know who we . . .'

Her mother leaned into her and she stopped, the gentle pressure enough to remind her of their long-standing conspiracy of silence.

'He may worry, don't you think?' The man's smile had

60

disappeared now and, as they both stood absolutely silent, he shrugged and asked, 'Any message then?'

Queenie shook her head.

'No!' Laura exclaimed, the word coming louder than she meant. 'No message.' She raised her hand to the boy who was watching intently, hands already curled around case handles. In seconds all their baggage was loaded.

'Thank you for your trouble,' Queenie said climbing in beneath the fringed canopy as the lieutenant still lingered, uneasy with his unfulfilled mission.

Laura glanced back as they moved off and saw him talking to the men on the gate, including the old man with the list, which he was leafing through once more. Even as she hoped her mother would not turn, she did so. 'He'll never give up,' she breathed. 'Never.'

'What can he do if we're in different countries?'

'He'll always keep tabs on us.'

'If he can.' She was grimly determined that he would not be given the chance. 'We've made up our minds, Mother, he'll never come back into our lives.'

Queenie did not answer, she just looked old and utterly weary.

The youth, after clicking his tongue to speed up his horse, called to them, 'You want mint tea? I know nice tea shop.'

'No thank you,' Laura said, beginning to be thankful her teacher had insisted on French conversation, 'just to the address as quickly as you can, please.'

From the port he took them along wide boulevards lined with palm trees. Here, in contrast to the uneven plastered walls of the old town, elegant French colonial buildings lined the way. There were pots of hibiscus on the ornate balconies and purple and red bougainvillaea climbed between the ornate balustrades.

Their address was of an older three-storey apartment block in a side street. Less elegant, Laura thought, but perhaps more practical, for there were many small shops

61

and street cafés nearby. They were greeted by a tall, almost skeletal-looking, old man in an all-enveloping brown djibbah who smiled, bowed and introduced himself as Ibn Mustapha. His daughter, he told them, was out but they were welcome to Morocco. He gestured up the stairs and handed over a key. 'To the top,' he instructed.

The boy carried up their cases and was back down for the mattresses before they had reached the second flight. They paid him off, giving a discreet tip which he was delighted with and insisted on carrying all their belongings right inside.

Once he was gone Laura closed the door and leaned back on it. They exchanged looks, heaved huge sighs of relief, both so thankful to have some privacy after the crowded hours on ship and quays.

Then they inspected their new home. 'Not over furnished,' Laura commented ironically. There was a small kitchen with a minimum of equipment, a second room with a table and two upright chairs and a tiny bedroom with two bare iron bedsteads which looked like cast-offs from a derelict hospital. This room faced the street and had shutters which Laura pushed open to reveal a minuscule balcony just large enough for the shutters to be swung open.

'This would be the only way out,' Queenie said peering down over the larger windows and large balconies below them.

'What do you mean?'

'There's only one door.'

'One door?'

'If that official gave the lieutenant this address.'

Laura gasped as she, too, glanced down to the street far below and realised her mother was thinking of being trapped there by her father. She refused to believe it could happen. 'Dad's in the army,' she stated. 'He may be an officer, but he still has to obey orders.'

'He'll have leave, even in wartime they all have leave sooner or later.'

Laura slipped her arm around her mother's waist as she stood at the open window, the lowering sun colouring the white city in shades of orange and pink, while still the swallows scythed the air close by. 'So we'll move,' she said. 'we'll look around, starting tomorrow. We'll find our own quarters – as long as we inform the authorities . . .' she paused remembering their instructions, 'and we could ask them not to pass on our *new* address.'

'Not even to a husband.' Queenie shook her head. 'It's not how these things work – not in the army.'

She was afraid her mother might be right, but she said, 'We'll just have to be cleverer than they are.'

After the first week Laura realised that being clever would have little to do with whether they moved or not. The problem was that every suitable free room in and around the city had already been commandeered for the many displaced by the war. There were places at either end of the residential scale. Casablanca had many sophisticated addresses, but these were way beyond their financial reach. At the other end of the scale they saw places where just the presence of two English women alone aroused such interest and begging, so many hands reaching out to them, touching them, they were glad to scuttle back to their flat.

Queenie was always watchful, in no way reconciled to being there, though everyone they encountered in the shops and markets was helpful, welcoming and friendly. 'The first time you have been to Morocco? You are welcome.' Many times this was said to them. The only sour note came in the shape of M Mustapha's daughter, who had only shown an interest when their chests were delivered from the docks. Her eyes had devoured the ornate carving and inlaid brass and she had muttered, 'There must be many valuable things in such magnificent chests.' Queenie refused to allow them even to be unroped.

Laura came to feel if she would only agree to unpack the sewing machine it would be good for her. Over the years the more difficult and abusive her father, the more intricate and perfectly made had been the garments coming from Queenie's sewing room. She could lose herself completely in the making of clothes. There were some wonderfully attractive materials to be bought cheap from the small shops in the medina and she knew her mother was tempted. Every time they passed the bright materials she stopped to finger them. Laura urged that they could well afford some small luxuries. Each evacuee was given an allowance of fifty francs a week, with the exchange rate of 875 to the pound, they could eat well and improve the apartment.

She did eventually persuade her mother to buy spreads and cushions for the beds, and colourful hand-woven mats for the floors. When clothes or curtains were mentioned, things that needed sewing, Queenie was still adamant. 'If we find somewhere to move to we might not get the allowance, then we'd have no money to fritter away.' Then, looking at the chests still strapped as Freddie had prepared them for the journey, she added, 'It just doesn't feel right to unpack them.'

Certainly the war situation gave no reason to feel secure or settled anywhere. Italy officially entered the war on Hitler's side on 10 June. News filtered through that in the Bay of Gibraltar six Italian merchant ships had tried to scuttle themselves, but the Italian Navy was a powerful force and England would need to hold on to Gibraltar if they were to protect Malta and Egypt.

Worse was to come. Ten days later, on 24 June, France sued for peace with Germany.

The English held their breath, feeling betrayed and alone. Laura and Queenie wondered what their position would be in French Morocco, or was it German Morocco now? There were solemn faces everywhere, almost in some cases they sensed people were ashamed that England had been abandoned. Rather shamefaced Queenie put into words what her daughter had only thought – there would now be no chance of British troops being allowed to come on leave into Morocco. It seemed a selfish and insensitive thought as the Fascist war machine rolled ever wider and more murderously across the map of Europe and the Mediterranean.

It was on the morning of 4 July 1940 that, as they descended the stairs to do their food shopping, they were startled by the swift and violent closing of the door below. M Mustapha usually sat in the doorway to wave them cheerily in and out. His more eagle-eyed daughter gave more attention to their returns and their purchases.

Today streets approaching the old walled medina felt different, quieter than usual. Once they passed in through the main archway people who were standing about in tight groups halted their conversations while they passed. Something's happened, Laura thought, and wondered if an order had been made for all English evacuees to be rounded up and put into camps. There had been speculation on the wireless. This might make these French colonials even more ashamed of deserting their former ally. They approached the open-fronted grocery shop where the proprietor had obliged them by weighing up small quantities of his stock to suit their meagre storage facilities. He had proudly boasted of having a Parisian great-grandmother.

The shopkeeper looked up as if to give his usual amiable greeting, but his manner changed, his face became malevolent. 'Out of my shop!' he ordered, 'I never serve you again! Murderers! Mothers and sisters of murderers!'

Laura turned to look behind to see who he addressed, felt foolish when there was no one. Her mother instinctively stepped back, hampering other shoppers in the narrow street, but Laura demanded to know what he meant. 'We've never murdered or harmed anyone,' she said and felt she might just remind him it was France who had capitulated, but as he began to come round from behind his counter another customer, an Arab woman, white robes concealing all but her eyes, stepped forward and murmured, 'They do not know.'

'What don't we know?'

The shopkeeper bristled and began shouting in one of the Berber dialects. The veiled woman walked away from his shop but waited for them a few paces away.

'The British Navy shelled the French fleet in Oran yesterday afternoon, many many French sailors have been killed, hundreds and hundreds,' she told them in a cultured voice which told of education, or a longish stay in England. 'It seems your Mr Churchill did not trust us, was afraid we would let them fall into enemy hands and be used against you.'

She dipped her head in farewell and before they had recovered from the shock of this information she had moved away to complete her morning shopping elsewhere. Laura wondered if they would be treated in the same way wherever they tried to buy. She moved to go further into the medina but her mother caught her arm. 'We'll manage with what we have today,' she said.

'The authorities will surely contact us,' Laura speculated as, without thinking of any other consequences, they began to make their way back by the shortest route out of the medina, across a main street and through a large market where vegetables, fruit, fish and meat were sold. Hardly had they entered the market complex before they were being remarked about, and Laura caught the words, 'Killers!' 'Killing your allies.' 'Shelling ships at anchor.' Her mother seized her wrist and they began to walk faster. Laura happened to catch the eye of a man who was behind a double stall, with huge jars of honey on one side and hand-woven baskets on the other. His lips twisted with hatred. They gasped as he suddenly leapt up on to the stall scattering baskets, pointing, drawing everyone's attention to them. '*Assassinat criminel des matelots français à Oran!*' he accused.

The shoppers suddenly coalesced into a united crowd and Queenie and Laura were jostled, cursed, furious faces pushed close to theirs, anger more frightening, more focused as this charge of criminal assassination of French sailors was repeated. Mouths were pursed with new venom and Laura felt spittle land and run down her cheek.

Queenie gave a sobbing cry of alarm. Laura, whose first reaction had been to cover her face and curl up against the nearest wall, now pushed her mother before her as she glimpsed a possible escape, a narrow cobbled alley. She took the lead now, pulling her mother, fearful of pursuit, fearful of finding the way barred by a high locked gate. But in moments they were in the greater anonymity of the business streets and then back to their apartment building. Here they made as little noise as possible, thankful that M Mustapha's door was still closed as they scuttled on tiptoe up the stairs.

Inside Queenie's hands trembled as she turned urgently to try to wipe the spittle from her daughter's cheek and neck. Laura caught her hands. 'It's all right, Mother. I'm all right.' Then her hand touched slime on her dress, and she saw the skirt of her mother's dress was also stained.

'Take them off,' Laura said and shakily she pulled it over her head and used the inside to wipe her face, arms, legs, though she could see no other evidence of the crowd's censure. She remembered what Jamie's father had advised, be practical, do what has to be done. 'Right,' she said, her voice high, tremulous. 'We'll have a thorough wash, our hair and everything, then a cup of tea, and wait quietly for news.'

'And stay in,' Queenie added.

'Yes,' she agreed, though both knew they could not exist long without venturing out to buy supplies.

They spent a wretched time wondering what was going to happen next. They lay talking and speculating long into that night and the next few days were a nightmare. When they did have to venture out for food very few wanted to serve them; all courtesy had gone. They were the enemy. It began to look certain they would all be rounded up and put into concentration camps.

Early one morning they were woken by a tremendous pounding on the flat door. 'My God!' Queenie exclaimed. 'they've come to arrest us.'

If there had been any other way out Laura was sure they would have taken it, so frightening was the persistent hammering, then shouting at the door. In French and in English they were ordered to open the door.

'We'd better open it before they knock it down,' Laura muttered as she went to the door, her mother just behind her.

At the door was one Moroccan policeman. 'You have twenty-four hours to leave French soil. You are to take just what you can carry to the port tomorrow morning, otherwise you will be interned.'

'But where will we go?' Queenie asked.

'Perhaps to the same place you sent 1,300 French sailors – to die in the sea.' He turned abruptly and left, repeating, 'Be at the dock early tomorrow morning.'

'They'll never forgive us,' Queenie whispered.

'And history would never forgive Winston Churchill if he'd let those ships be used by the enemy.' Laura had spent much of the time thinking about the situation, worrying about Jamie. Was he already at sea, already on active service? 'Those seven battleships could have turned the war at sea against us,' she went on. 'Then where would our island nation be?'

'It's all like a mad game of chess,' Queenie despaired, 'and we're the poor pawns.'

'Yes,' she had to agree, but the thought came that at least Jamie was an active pawn. She resolved that if ever she had the chance she'd 'do her bit', be practical, be active, do something.

She assumed a stout, Churchillian resolve. She made lists of 'fors' and 'againsts' what they might do, what was possible. First what they would take with them. They decided it would be wise to take their mattresses if they could possibly manage it, though after their experiences in the last few days they doubted whether any taxi or gharry would take them to the docks.

Laura experimented tying up each mattress inside one of the rugs so that if necessary they could drag the mattresses and carry their cases. 'It'll take us a long time,' Queenie said. 'We'll need lots of rests, I should think.'

'So we start out early, very early,' she refused to allow herself to sound daunted by any difficulty.

'And the chests?'

There was no choice. Laura had no suggestion beyond writing a note to Ibn Mustapha asking for their chests to be sent on after them, and enclosing a little more than the rent they owed. When they left the next morning they both bade an unspoken farewell to the brass-bound boxes and could well imagine the daughter of the house confiscating them and their contents.

The first horse gharry they saw they almost automatically raised a hand to, but they were ignored, so did not persist when the taxis began to appear on the streets. They soon saw other groups of evacuees trying to find help with their burdens but they were being harangued, pushed aside and spat on. An elderly Moroccan with a cart drawn by an old and decrepit donkey lingered on a corner as they approached, but hardly had Laura taken a step towards him when other Moroccans ran forward threatening him and shaking his cart so it looked in danger of collapse and the donkey near to being pulled off its feet.

Most of the robed residents just watched from their doorways as the evacuees dragged their belongings along, but the hostility hung in the air as palpable as the growing heat of the day. All Laura's hopes were directed towards a ship, any ship, that they could all board immediately, and be away from this alienated French colony.

Their numbers increased rapidly as they drew nearer to the port area. Ones, twos, threes, family groups, the hundreds moved ever forward like human detritus into a wide funnel with a blocked end. And still they came. When the first reached the barred dock gates and high wall the rest piled in behind them. It became impossible to see the extent of the thousands herded there. Around them, to see they did not stray back, or anywhere else, French Moroccan soldiers stood guard, rifles at the ready.

The expectant minutes of waiting grew to despairing hours. The afternoon came but there was no issue of water or food. Old people began to pass out, mothers did their best to shield their babies and children from the blistering African sun. The dark shiny faces of the troops were impassive. If anyone asked questions they were ignored or shouted at and more than one rifle butt threatened – but those closest to the gates were gleaning some information.

The story was gradually passed back that there were ships. Fifteen cargo vessels under an English admiral had entered the harbour, carrying 15,000 French soldiers and sailors, survivors from Dunkirk. These men wished to join the Vichy government set up by Marshal Pétain in the empty hotels of that southern spa town. To Laura it seemed strange to let trained fighting men have the option to join the marshal after his capitulation to the Germans – illogical after the extreme action taken to prevent the French battleships at Oran falling into enemy use.

The gossip filtering back from the gates was that the British admiral had been ordered to load all the Gibraltarian evacuees immediately or his ships would be impounded. Standing in the heat, perspiration ever running and drying on their bodies, they wondered what the delay was. 'For God's sake just load us, take us somewhere,' an old man murmured at Laura's side. She felt a pang of concern for him, but at her side her mother suddenly wavered and fell forward. She grabbed her arm, caught her before she could topple those around her. 'Bear up, Mum, we're not going to let them win.'

Quite who she meant at that moment she was not sure, perhaps she just meant the sun, but she was astonished to find that her mother was shivering, her skin felt clammily

70

cold. She supported her weight, tried to find some remark to make every few minutes, forcing her to answer, thinking she needed to keep her mother conscious. Queenie was quite strange, remote, like one concerned with other problems, bigger problems than those they already had. 'Sunstroke,' the old man muttered.

When it began to look even to the optimistic that the French authorities and the English admiral were willing for them all to perish there on the dockside, the gates were opened and the flood of desperate old men, women and children surged through. They did not need directing to the gangways and soon these steep narrow slopes were filled with people fighting to get aboard. They had stood and waited peaceably enough, but all were now sufficiently desperate, tired, hungry and beside themselves to push others aside if it meant leaving on one of these ships. Children were crying and screaming as their adults became like wild beasts to secure places for them.

Laura had been part of an army family long enough to know the stories that those involved in the worst fighting never talked about it, and as she pulled her mother after her, past older and younger to board a small cargo ship, she knew why. They would be ashamed of some of the things they had to do to survive.

Some of the reasons the English Admiral Creighton had hesitated to load the evacuees quickly became evident. The troops, who had just vacated the holds, had been in them for fourteen days without a break; the stench, between farmyard and dungeon, was appalling in the heat, many people were already retching as the smell overwhelmed them. Nor, they learned, had the ships been reprovisioned. There was nothing for them on board, just standing or sitting room on the deck, a thousand to each of the fifteen ships.

Too stupefied to talk or speculate the majority of them just collapsed to the deck and waited. It was night-time when they finally cast off and nearby somebody murmured, 'Destination unknown.'

71

'There's only one place they can take us,' another voice answered. 'The nearest place – back to Gibraltar.'

Beside her Laura felt her mother sag forward and begin to weep. It was the most desolate sound, and with a shock she knew it had been the realisation of where they would be taken back to, not sunstroke, that had made her mother shiver so uncontrollably.

Chapter Five

The freighter rocked its human deck cargo gently as it steamed over a calm sea beneath brilliant stars.

Laura gazed fixedly at the Pole star, but did no Galileon calculation of distances, imagined no triangle with Jamie, herself and the star at its extremities. She was not sure where Jamie would be now, there had been no news in the three weeks they had been in Morocco, but her instincts and commonsense told her he would be far from Gibraltar, already training in England.

She had tried to console her mother a little by reminding her that Freddie would certainly still be there. 'So will your father,' Queenie had answered, turning away, shielding her face from view with her hands. She lay still, making no effort to find any degree of comfort wedged on and between their baggage, and a thousand other bodies and all their belongings.

Though they were packed tight, the chill of the night became increasingly penetrating. The crew, many of them with the thick but cheery accent of Tyneside, brought every spare blanket and pullover they had, and distributed them as far as they would go. An ancient, but huge fisherman's guernsey was their allocation and Laura gratefully pulled it up over her shoulders and Queenie's back. The seamen also mustered up a hot drink in huge jugs which had to be passed from hand to hand. Each in turn gratefully cupped the hot containers and drank. No one was sure what it was, but even the guessing brought relief. Bitter chocolate made with water and a hint of rum was Laura's guess – it warmed the stomach as well as the hands. No one worried much about the taste.

'As good as the old laudanum,' an elderly grandma commented as fretful children became quiet and soon slept.

For some hours there was relative quiet. In the coldest hour, just before dawn, when she guessed hardly anyone slept, someone, a boy she thought, began to sing, very quietly. No more than a haunting shade above the gentle noise of their swishing chugging passage through the sea, the soprano voice was sweet, pure. The prayer in the words of the old hymn voiced the fears that had plagued many through the long hours – fears of reprisal attacks – of submarines – of bombers. 'Eternal father strong to save ...' The young chorister knew every verse, there was not a movement among the passengers until the voice rose to the final chorus of the final verse:

> O hear us when we cry to thee,
> For those in peril on the sea.

As the last notes lingered, drifting out over the waters, there was a concerted easing of breath, a sigh that appreciated the beauty of song and voice. Laura sat up and looked over towards the east. The sky was noticeably less grey and before long the rising sun began to colour first an area which looked no larger than a man's fist, then to seep ever wider and with even more brilliant colours from palest aquamarine, to pinks and reds, to the dull gold in the middle, like a sunken furnace moment by moment rising more gloriously to the surface. Finally, the rim of the sun lifted spectacularly above the ocean, and Laura understood all about Hephaestus, the god thrown down from Olympus and said to work his forge beneath the sea.

It was another hand, like a dark raised fist, she was

reminded of later as the familiar outline of The Rock loomed, and the singing began again. Not a single sweet voice and the sombre beauty of a hymn this time.

'Roll out the barrel.' A thousand sore, dry throats hoarsely roared out the celebration. Laura glanced round but no one seemed to be aware that the two of them were not sharing in the rapture. Many were crying tears of sheer joy, there were emotional shouts of 'Home! Home!' and then someone began singing croakily, 'There's no place like home', but another song was beyond them. A boy with his hair bleached white by the sun and his face blistered and near burned black looked around to tell them that it was his birthday. 'I'm eleven. I'll be home with my dad for my birthday now.'

Before they entered the harbour proper many had already assembled their belongings, some even standing holding cases and bundles, all their hardships temporarily behind them as they saw their homes coming ever nearer.

Their anxiety to be ashore turned to bewilderment and disbelief as they realised that no preparations were being made to land anyone. Men, husbands, fathers, were assembling on the quayside, while women and children crowding at the rails could see their loved ones and were waving and calling.

'What is happening?'

'What are they doing?'

'Why can't we go ashore?'

'I don't believe this!' Exasperation and frustration caused more tears while on shore the crowd grew and began to look angry.

On board word spread that they were not being allowed to land, but were to be evacuated straight on to England.

'Not in these ships, hen,' a hefty Tyneside deckhand put in as he overheard the story. 'Us had field kitchens aboard to feed froggies us brought back from Dunkirk. They was took ashore in Casablanca. Tell us 'ow us can feed yous all? Might as well throw yous all overboard

75

now, as try to take yous anywhur else in these ships.'

That somebody might actually jump overboard began to be a possibility, people were becoming really desperate. The same Geordie came back to tell them that their menfolk had brought the whole city of Gibraltar to a standstill, on strike until their families were allowed to land. 'They say a deputation's going to the governor.'

Shortly afterwards they saw a small party of civilians and a smartly uniformed ship's captain leave the dockside on the way, they presumed, to the governor's residence. The problem was that the governor, Sir Clive Liddell, was convinced that if he allowed the evacuees ashore he would never be able to persuade them to leave a second time. Laura felt Sir Clive was probably right. She also knew the Geordie deckhand was right too. There was no way any of them could be taken further without provisions and sanitation. People would certainly die.

The deputation returned and waved. They had pledged their word that if the evacuees were allowed to go to their homes, even for a short time, they would willingly and immediately report back to the docks for re-embarkation as soon as requested. This would be as soon as the freighters had been cleaned, adapted for the needs of the women and children and reprovisioned. There was no question of anyone disagreeing and hardly had the governor's proviso been made known to everyone than army lorries began to arrive at the docks.

'One thing is sure, no one on Gib can be unaware that we've arrived,' Queenie said. There was no irony in the observation as she watched the frenzy of activity, listened to the hubbub. Weighted docking lines were thrown to the shore, which dockers used to haul ashore the thick wire hawsers, and heave these over the bollards; the deck winches took up the slack and the freighters were finally neatly docked and gangways put into place.

Laura and Queenie allowed others to make their way eagerly forward. The boy with the birthday gave Laura the thumbs-up sign as he reached the top of the gangway. She rejoiced for him and returned the gesture with both thumbs. She watched him down into the crowd on the quay then lost sight of him as she repeatedly scanned the crowd. She could see neither her father, nor Freddie, and though common-sense told her Jamie could not be there, she searched for him too.

When to delay longer would have been ludicrous, when already lorry after lorry had left the quayside and some had already returned for second loads, Laura reluctantly led the way down to the quay. It felt like a walk to the gallows, a walk down into the pit of despair. She drew her mother into the shade of one of the warehouses, away from the remaining small crowd and the army personnel arranging the final lifts.

'What shall we do,' she asked, 'go to Freddie's?'

'Or to a small boarding house,' Queenie suggested. 'I don't want Freddie getting hurt.'

'No,' she agreed. 'So it'll be best to walk towards Irish town and Tuckey's Lane to find lodgings without any of these men taking notice.'

Queenie nodded briefly, both aware that Gibraltar was a small community to try to disappear into. 'Pity we can't leave the mattresses somewhere,' she was saying as a jeep came screeching on to the dock. Both drew in their breaths and Queenie stepped back against the warehouse wall. 'Remember he can't force us to go with him,' Laura said. 'He can't!'

Queenie gave her a look which was full of anguished doubt and glanced back towards the ship with its stinking holds, as if even that might provide escape.

The jeep made a wide sweep around the rapidly emptying area before the driver seemed to locate and head straight for them and for the first time they could see the driver prop-erly. Both gave gasps of relief. The man who brought the vehicle to a stop alongside them was not Jock Maclaren, but Sergeant Bill Milloy. Laura felt her knees weaken with

77

relief. She wanted to throw her arms around him, to greet him far more heartily than the handshake he offered. 'We're pleased to see *you* again. We thought it was my father.'

'We should hurry,' he said already loading all their baggage and inviting them to climb in with a swift hand gesture. 'We're not sure where your husband is,' he added putting the jeep back into gear and swinging them sharply right towards the Rosia Bay area of the town, then added, 'the duties were all suddenly changed.'

'To do with us all coming back,' Laura supposed.

He shook his head. 'Not sure.'

'We thought of going to a boarding house,' Queenie began as they moved off.

'I've to take you to Fatima's house. It's the safest place Freddie could think of.'

'There's been more trouble,' Queenie stated.

There was no answer.

'At Freddie's home?'

'Aye.'

Bill's monosyllabic answer had the effect of sending both their minds skimming over the nastiness Jock Maclaren was capable of.

The home of the de Fallas' widowed housekeeper, her daughter and two sons was, as Laura remembered, within walking distance of the de Fallas' home, 'half an hour' Jamie had said it would take his father to walk there and back.

Close, but, she hoped, not too close. They would have to be very careful. Then her lips relaxed almost to a smile. 'All that time,' she remembered saying to Jamie and had blushed – then there had been the huge bed. 'This was my port in a storm as a child,' he had told her.

She sighed as they jolted and swung around the many turns, vaguely aware that her mother and Bill were talking, but she could not wholly leave the recollection of her first love-making. It was only as the jeep stopped in an estate of

78

houses and flats built on a steep incline and at right angles to Rosia Bay, that she heard Bill say, 'Fatima's brothers have been living with Freddie.'

There was no time to do more than draw the conclusion that her father had been seriously threatening Freddie de Falla for as the jeep stopped Fatima Valerio flung open the door. She had been at Freddie's home and set supper and made beds for them the night before they embarked for Casablanca, but they had not met her. She was they found as flamboyant and exotic as her name; and her black skirt and beautifully crisp flowered blouse made Laura aware of the hours she and her mother had spent lying on the deck of a coal-burning freighter. Laura was wondering just how sympathetic Fatima might be towards these English women, who had already caused her employer so much angst and now apparently had her brothers sleeping out as body-guards.

It was the state of the black smutted clothes and their sunburned and blistered arms and faces that changed what-ever reservations Fatima might have had into cries of instant concern.

'Oh! you poor things! Come in, come in. What to do with you first is the problem,' Fatima exclaimed, then immediately went on making the decision. 'Tea! Hot sweet tea, washes and lots of sunburn lotion, then a meal.'

'Sounds wonderful,' Queenie said gratefully.

Laura nodded agreement, wondering quite which she was most – hungry, she thought. 'We've only had a sip of cocoa since yesterday,' she said.

'Ah!' Fatima exclaimed and her plans were immediately rearranged. 'Eat first then, other things can wait.'

Fatima led them through to a kitchen where a huge table was laid ready for a formal meal, but in no time a huge, round, crisp loaf, tomatoes, and some cold meat was put before them. 'Begin, please,' Fatima urged, 'while I make some fresh orange juice.'

'Your mother?' Queenie inquired trying to bring back

some kind of social normality as their first ravenous pangs were eased. 'We heard she had gone to nurse her mother, your grandmother.'

'That's right,' Fatima said, 'and with Mr de Falla's help we have persuaded her to stay there, otherwise she would have been evacuated like you. My grandmother's very frail so it made sense for Mother to stay with her until the war is over. My grandparents are Spanish,' she said with a shrug, the enigma as to which side Spain would eventually join left unspoken, though Fatima went on with a stream of information as she brought a freshly sliced melon to the table. 'Because my two brothers and myself are all employed in Mr de Falla's business we are exempt. I am doubling as secretary and housekeeper while my mother is away. He is a marvellous employer.'

'And friend,' Queenie said. 'I'm afraid my husband has caused him a lot of trouble?'

'Yes,' Fatima answered, then gave a hoot of laughter and threw up her arms, 'but not nearly as much as he has caused your husband.'

'Really!' Laura's exclamation was so delighted that all three women laughed.

'Really,' Fatima confirmed motioning to both to continue eating. 'I tell you what Mr de Falla has done if you promise not to tell the police.'

'The police!' they both exclaimed.

'What has he done?' Queenie asked, then added confidently, 'nothing I would ever fetch the police for, I know that.'

'Well,' Fatima was relishing the telling. 'He broke into your house, then he let in a locksmith and has had all the locks changed, all the windows provided with bolts, so that your husband could not get in and destroy anything else.'

'Anything else?' Laura queried.

Queenie pulled herself upright in her chair, drew in a deep breath, then let it out in a controlled and protracted sigh. 'What has he done?'

It seemed to Laura that Fatima knew some details but did not volunteer them, instead she said, 'Mr de Fella was determined to stop him going in and out of your family's old property for no good reason. But he'll be here later, if it's safe, that is if he finds out for sure where your husband is.'

'How will he do that?' Laura wanted to know.

'Ah!' Fatima tapped the side of her nose. 'Not many people like the lieutenant. We have good sources. We usually know his duties before he does.' She hooted with laughter again, then was just as suddenly serious. 'But today something happened. We thought it was to do with the boats coming from Casablanca, but no . . .'

'I don't want Freddie to run any more risks,' Queenie began.

'I think for you he does not mind,' Fatima interrupted quite matter-of-factly.

Laura glanced at her mother who was looking as if she needed time to assimilate that remark.

When they had eaten all they wanted, both found it difficult after three days of real deprivation to leave food on the table. 'I want to wrap it up and take it with me,' Queenie admitted.

Fatima reassured them there would be a proper meal later when the men came. She showed them to a room with a double bed. 'My mother's room,' she told them, 'and the bathroom is next door.'

Left on their own they looked at the pristine whiteness of the bedspread and pastel shades of upholstery on chairs and both began to pull off their soot-smutted clothes.

'Being unwashed and splattered with filth goes with being a refugee,' Laura said, reminded of being spat on as she pulled her dress inside out.

'Evacuee,' her mother corrected.

'Feels the same,' she answered, looking round their latest superior resting place. There was an elegance here, an inherited taste perhaps, certainly old quality furniture,

81

which hardly told of a woman who had to make her living housekeeping and cleaning for someone else. Laura wondered what Fatima's father had done for a living and how long her mother had been a widow.

Once washed and in clean underslips they both lay on the bed to rest. They had learned to make the most of whatever comforts came their way, and this was luxury.

Laura woke with the uneasy feeling of being unable to recollect where she was. She looked up at a strange ceiling, a window where the light told of late evening, then realising she turned her head to see her mother deeply and peacefully asleep. She rose slowly and quietly and went to the half-shuttered window to look at her wristwatch: half past nine. She decided not to disturb her mother, but she would finish dressing and go down. She left the room carefully, nursing the handle so it made as little noise as possible, then began to go downstairs.

Immediately she was aware of a sombre rumble of men's voices in discussion. Just before she reached the kitchen door she heard Freddie de Falla say, 'None of this must be told to his wife and daughter.' The remark made her an unwitting eavesdropper, stopped her in her tracks. Then she raised her chin and stepped forward into the doorway. The three men who sat at the table all rose. Jamie's father, and two stocky young men who showed their half-Spanish blood as did their sister Fatima, but she was taller than both her brothers.

Freddie de Falla came immediately to embrace her, inquired about Queenie and quickly introduced her to the two brothers, Joshua and Carlos. She reassured him that she and her mother were unharmed, told how they were thrown out of Casablanca. Her mind went briefly to Doris and her four daughters, who had been sent by rail further along the coast, towards Oran. She had not seen them at the docks. What had been their fate? 'They treated us as if each one of us was personally responsible for the decisions of our government.'

82

'That's how it is everywhere,' Carlos said solemnly. 'Spain, France, England, Germany – your leaders speak for you.'

'And the world judges you by your leaders,' Joshua added.

'I suppose so,' she said a little surprised by this joint show of wisdom.

Freddie stood between his two sturdy young engineers but looked, Laura thought, as if *he* had been through a hard time. His face, his cheeks were planed down, a new sharpness about the angles of his cheekbones, a more rigid set to his mouth.

'What mustn't we be told?' she heard herself ask. 'I'm sorry, but I overheard as I came downstairs.'

When he did not answer immediately she went on, 'It's my father, isn't it? What's he done, and where is he?'

'Oh, we know where he is,' Freddie answered. 'He's been detailed to set up patrols to keep an eye on the situation over the border. The Germans are at the Pyrenees and, with Spanish consent, are attempting to make a survey of Gibraltar from the lighthouse in Punta Carnero and from La Linea.'

Laura wanted to ask if he thought an invasion was imminent, but glancing at Fatima and her brothers remembered this was where their mother and grandmother lived. 'But this is not what you didn't want us to know surely?' Laura was looking at Freddie when she spoke and saw his face change, his attention leave her entirely. She turned to see her mother standing in the doorway.

They walked towards each other as if compulsorily drawn and embraced for long moments without speaking. Such was their total absorption in each other that Laura felt she intruded by just looking. Carlos cleared his throat gently and Joshua stood obviously amazed, but beaming his full approval.

Queenie at last stepped back and studied Freddie. 'There've been more battles,' she said quietly.

After a moment's thought, he nodded, then grinned. 'Not physical,' he said, 'more a battle of wits.'

'Which you are winning,' Fatima put in from the stove where she was rearranging large steaming pans.

'W . . . e . . . l . . . l,' Freddie drew out the word, 'I was, or thought I was.'

'And now?' Queenie asked.

It was Freddie's turn to sigh, and he looked at Laura as much as to say this is what I did not want for either of you to know. 'Maclaren is managing to sabotage my work for the army. How he's doing it, and when, I've yet to find out. My guess is he's paying someone a lot of money, but I shall lose the MoD contract if things go on as they have today. We had a serious rock collapse in one of the tunnels, and it's been made to look as if the ventilation work we've done caused it.'

The brothers shook their heads and growled their disagreement. 'We'll have to guard our work until it's finished,' Carlos said. 'We could work out a rota with the men.'

'Looks like it,' Freddie sounded momentarily incensed, then he made a throw-away gesture with his hands and drew Queenie and Laura back to the table. When everyone was again seated, he looked round and exclaimed, 'Marvellous! Marvellous!'

Laura saw the look on her mother's face as he smiled and that smile spread to them all. She was reminded of a song she used to sing in the Girl Guides, how did it go? Something about a smile being a funny thing and lightening up your face, then the memory of sitting in a ring with other girls in blue dresses and leather belts came with the words:

> But far more wonderful than this,
> Is what a smile can do,
> One smiles at one, one smiles at you
> And so one smile makes two.

Her heart warmed to Freddie all over again. He was one of those who cheered you up by just being there. Part of this she knew was because he never *dwelt* on his own troubles, he showed genuine concern for everyone else before himself.

'And I want to know about Jamie,' she put in quietly.

'Of course you do,' he tutted at himself. 'I have a letter for you.'

Laura felt her heart begin to hammer in her chest as he reached round to his back pocket and brought out a letter with an English stamp on it. The envelope was open but Freddie drew from it a second sealed envelope and held it towards her. 'It came three days ago.' He shook his head as if quite exasperated with himself. 'Matters just drove it out of my mind.'

'I wrote to him care of you,' Laura said.

He shook his head. 'Nothing arrived.'

She took the envelope with the thought that this was the first thing that had passed between them, the very first thing they had both touched, since the day of the first evacuation. She experienced it between her fingers with an awareness that was so sensuous it made her feel an exquisite pang of sexual appetite. Then the adult feeling gave way to a blush, and she felt her face blazing as she grasped the envelope to herself with both hands.

'Do you mind if I go and read it upstairs?' she asked.

'And I may take your mother to your home for a time,' Freddie said, 'while we know your father is well out of the way.'

If there was any query in her mind about this it was completely submerged by the need to be alone with Jamie's letter. She sat on one of the pale pink chairs and, eyes closed, held the precious letter gently to her heart, so as to savour every possible sensation. Now before opening it, it was anticipation, love, happiness that these small pieces of paper had come from his hands to hers. She remembered letters she had censored where one lover had kissed the page leaving an imprint of lips for the other to kiss. She had been scornful then, until she had met Jamie, until she had received this letter.

Carefully she pushed her fingers under the envelope's flap and tore it carefully open so as not to risk tearing across one word of address he had written: 'Laura Maclaren, c/o Señor F de Falla.'

My darling Laura,
Every day at post call I hold my breath waiting for a letter – or even small bundle (as happened to one happy chap yesterday). I am sure you are writing and I wonder if you are getting mine. Then I worry about you and your mother. Are you still in French Morocco, I wonder?

She glanced up at the date of this letter, 2 July, the day before the French fleet had been attacked.

So far this war has done two things, one terrible – separated me from the girl I love and ache for. The other thing is, it's given me the chance to go to sea – not quite made it yet, but think it won't be long now. Our courses are pretty concentrated, navigation and gunnery seem the most interesting to me – but we'll see, and I mustn't say too much or this'll be censored. But you know all about that . . .

Gunnery? Gun turrets would be targets surely, so would the bridge, of course. Did they do navigation on the bridge or tucked away in a safe cabin? 'Why can't you be a cook or something safe,' she breathed then tutted at herself, nothing and nowhere was safe on a ship if it was bombed, torpedoed, shelled, the French losses at Oran proved that. 'Oh! dear God,' she exclaimed quietly and as tears welled she could not read on for a time.

One thing I can tell you all about. I've learned to play

Solo Whist, going either 'abundance' or 'misere' – the first means getting as many tricks as you can (I think), the second means you don't have to take one single trick – seems impossible to me. If you think the war's serious you should be in on one of these card games, talk about a breathless hush, then a barrage of bad language.

I love you, Laura, although I write about all these other things there is not a moment in any day when you are not in my mind. Do you remember the little lavender sachets we found in the linen chests. You are embroidered on to my heart just like that – part of me for ever.

'Part of you for ever,' she pledged and glancing then at the address on the top, the letters and numbers of a stone frigate, as the navy called shore bases, somewhere in England but, at least, she realised with a great surge of joy, she could write to him now with some certainty that he would receive the letters.

She must do it now, she thought, at least begin a reply. She was bursting with words of love. She found paper and envelopes from her case and began rapturously to tell him how she felt, how she had slipped his ring on to her finger as the boat sailed from Gibraltar. Then more carefully she began to tell what had happened to them, trying to condense the experience into words and phrases which would not invite the censor's blue pencil.

By the time she went back downstairs her mother had been gone some time with Freddie.

Chapter Six

Freddie opened the door from a small ring of brand new keys, then stepped back to allow Queenie to walk into her hall first. She advanced only far enough for him to follow her and close the door. She stood listening, glancing up the stairs and all around as if assessing the mood of the house, feeling what it held for her. She shuddered in the cool dark entrance.

'He's definitely away,' Freddie reassured her. 'I wouldn't have brought you here otherwise, or so soon, but there are things I need to know rather urgently, things I think are missing.'

She frowned at him. 'I don't understand,' she said, 'and I don't think I care about anything in this house any more.'

'This house is yours,' Freddie said firmly. 'It belonged to your mother, your grandparents, many of the contents are heirlooms. No one but you has the right to . . .'

'To?'

'To plunder it – or at least I think that's what your husband's been doing.'

'Plunder?' she was interested now. 'But why?'

'If I'm right,' Freddie said darkly, 'he's using your valuable things to pay to have my business sabotaged.'

Queenie stood quite still, the lines of her face becoming set and hard as she thought about this. 'Yes,' she agreed at last, 'if it's a way of hurting both of us he'd enjoy doing that.'

'It was one of the reasons I broke your kitchen windows

and had your locks changed. He's not been in since. He's tried of course – but someone saw him and he was reported to the police as a burglar.' He grinned as he held out the keys to her.

She did not take them. 'It would be like taking back part of my life I never want again,' she said. 'You keep them.'

'This was all part of your life before you met your husband,' he said quietly, 'as I was,' he paused. 'All the time you've been away, these weeks since I've really known how it was between you and ...' he could not bring himself to name the man. 'I've been letting myself retie all kinds of links with the past. I've imagined taking up that past, our past.' He offered the keys again, but she made no move to take them. He thought she looked lost, unsure, he remembered seeing that expression on Grace's face when he had led his wife over stepping stones in a flooded creek – unsure where to step for the best, confused, not quite able to reach his outstretched hand – but certainly committed to step one way or other, for better or for worse. His heart quickened as Queenie at last put out a hand, not to take the keys, but to cover his own.

'Don't you think *I've* remembered and yearned for it all to have been different. Half of me wants to be here with you in Gib more than anywhere else in the world – the other half would sooner be anywhere, Timbuktu, anywhere other than in the same place as Jock.'

'I never stopped loving you, Queenie, never will.'

'And you're dearer to me than ever before.'

He stepped forward and took her gently, carefully, into his arms and while she could have wept for this gentleness, this contrast to Jock Maclaren, an inadvertent shudder ran through her whole being.

'What is it?' he asked.

'Just excitement, I think,' she answered, but it had felt like a premonition. She leaned her brow on his shoulder. 'What fools we were,' she whispered, 'what innocent, inexperienced young fools.'

'Perhaps life's giving us a second chance,' he said, 'a strange beginning to it,' he admitted with a laugh, 'but don't let's miss it, Queenie.'

'No, don't let's,' she smiled up at him and she caught his hand and held it tightly and with a certainty people usually only acquire after being together many trusting years and having friendship as well as love to cushion them against all life can throw at them.

He led her by the hand to show her what he suspected. In the sitting room a cabinet that had been full of colourful pottery, Italian majolica and blue and white Delft, was looking sparse, and a smaller cabinet, which had held a collection of intricately and beautifully carved ivory scrimshaws, was empty.

'Oh!' Queenie cried, 'the ivories! They were my grand-father's pride and joy, my father added to them. Surely ... Perhaps they've been put away for safe-keeping, or ...' She knew it was not so.

Freddie shook his head. 'I don't think your husband is into preserving things, only selling them, or giving them as payment for the underhand damage he's been doing. One of my workmen saw a small narwhal tusk changing hands.'

She nodded sadly, running her hand along the top of the empty cabinet. 'There were two in the collection. It would be like him. He would choose his accomplices very care-fully, men as ruthless and avaricious as himself. He can if necessary put quite a lot of thought into his acts of malice.' Looking back at Freddie she asked, 'What else has he done? What else is missing?'

'He's ransacked pretty well everywhere,' he began, 'particularly in the kitchen.'

They walked through. Queenie raised her eyes, shrugged as if it didn't matter.

'I intended to try to tidy up when I had time and opportu-nity,' he said, 'but it's been a bit cat and mouse – like now really.'

She moved to a drawer near the window. It still rested

half open. 'He won't have found anything here.' She stirred some fallen papers with her foot. 'We took our savings book and papers with us.'

'I'll pick them up then,' Freddie stooped down. 'Show me which drawer to put them in.'

'It doesn't much matter,' she said but bent to help, then as she put a pile of recipe books and sundry guarantees and receipts on the table to straighten them she looked out through the window to her walled garden.

'My garden!' she exclaimed, 'my plants.' Any inertia, any blunted feelings she had shown about the rest of the house, about the contents of the kitchen drawers instantly disappeared. She went to the door asking, 'Open it for me.'

He fumbled the keys, not sure which one. She stood very still, very straight holding her hurt in, her jaw working as she clenched and unclenched her teeth. He had seen the extent of the wilful destruction, wished he could spare her. In his anxiety he dropped the keys. 'I need to go outside,' she said as if suspecting him of delaying deliberately.

Once outside she walked out into the middle of the walled garden, for a moment making him think of a schoolmistress on playground duty, as turning slowly all around she saw the extent of the devastation. Then the detail impinged on her, the broken pots, the overturned troughs. Her hand went to cover her mouth and she shook her head in disbelief at the amount of damage done, at the strength and violence some of it would have needed to accomplish. Then she saw the containers where her oleanders had flourished. She almost stumbled forward to look more closely at the stripped stems spearing upwards from each pot.

'Oh! how could he?' She sank to her knees among the broken slender branches, their leaves gone from glossy green to sharp spiky brown and withered papery flower sprays faded from red and pink to beige. She scooped up a mass of the broken shrubs and held them to herself, grieving for what had been alive and beautiful and now

91

lay wilfully broken down and ruined.

'He destroys everything I care about,' she said so low it was as if she spoke only to herself, 'everything I try to make, or grow. He would kill me if he could.'

'No,' Freddie said sharply and knelt down beside her, trying to ease the dead branches from her arms. 'No, he won't destroy you, or me, or us, or your daughter and my son. He can't touch any of the important things. He can't force anyone to love him.'

'Not now,' she said surrendering the dead sprays to him. 'Laura told me when we had to sail back here that he couldn't force us to go back to him. I didn't believe her. Now I know he can't, he never will. I *would* sooner die.'

'No! No,' he softened his voice to a gentle chiding. 'We'll do better than that. We'll live, we'll take this second chance, as soon as this war lets us we'll be together, that'll be our victory.'

'He'll kill you if he can get away with it.'

'He won't get at me.' He edged closer on his knees trying to reassure her. 'Fatima's brothers have kept too close a watch. I've felt like royalty I've been so well guarded and now we'll all guard you and Laura.' He silently agonised about the magnitude of the task, and wondered how safe any of them were with Germany planning an attack on The Rock. He couldn't lie, couldn't brush away the reality of an enemy thought to be poised to attack. He put his mouth close to her ear and whispered, 'I took the lead in the school pantomime once, *Babes in the Wood*. I had to kneel down in dead leaves, just like this.'

She glanced down and gave a short half laugh, half sob, then turned to push her head down against him. 'I would sooner die than be with anyone but you.'

The hope for such a thing, and the fear of all that could prevent it, stifled the word that usually sprang so easily to his lips.

Chapter Seven

The tune broke into her sleep, roused her gently, the whistle rising with quiet melodic insistence. Laura lay quite still by her mother's side listening. Someone in the street? In the next house or garden?

It must be early hours of the morning, but she felt too languid, and reluctant to risk disturbing her mother to try to see the luminous hands of the clock on the bedside table.

She felt rather than saw her mother raise her head from the pillow, listen, then very cautiously slide out of bed, pull on a thin kimono and go to the window. Outlined by the predawn lightening of the sky Laura saw her lean forward and lift a hand. The whistling stopped. A prearranged signal. She listened to the rustle of the robe as her mother slipped from the room.

Laura too rose after a few moments and from the cover of the inner curtains and the outer shutters looked down at the figure who stood so still in the shadow of the old bougainvillaea which climbed the opposite wall. She had no doubt it was Freddie, he had in the ten days they had been hiding at Fatima's come at many strange times, very early morning, very late at night. This time, she glanced at the clock, three in the morning. She knew he only came when there was no risk of her father, or any of his paid spies, following him. She wondered if 'this unearthly hour' as her

93

mother might well call it on another occasion, held some special significance.

She moved back a fraction as her mother appeared, looking almost as if she floated across the yard in the white flowing robe which seemed to take on a luminescence in the greyness. Freddie moved forward to meet her, hands outstretched. Marvellous! Laura silently supplied his word as their hands were clasped and they stood facing each other, his head bent close over hers.

She caught the gentle sibilants of their whisperings, before they walked slowly into the shadows out of her sight. They were like young clandestine lovers, latterday Romeo and Juliet. She reflected that those Veronese lovers had also been beleaguered. She smiled at the thought of her mother's dead-of-night assignation, the romance of her being called there by a prearranged signal; she deserved some happiness, she deserved all she could snatch.

Then going back to the bed she sighed theatrically thinking of her own absent lover, of Jamie somewhere in England. There had been another letter, Freddie had sent it with Fatima as soon as it arrived. This letter had received different, more drastic, treatment at the hands of the censors. There must, Laura assumed, have been an issue of special scissors with right-angled blades which could cut square-cornered pieces from the mail. So many words and sentences had become no more than rectangular holes in the writing paper, this letter resembled a handcut doily. She felt as an ex-censorship employee she must warn him never to write on both sides of the same sheet of notepaper again. All she knew for certain was that he *was* on a stone frigate and that he sent all his love.

In the hours that hung so heavily during this imprisonment in the Valerio home, she had made exact copies of both sides of his letter and tried to match words to the gaps. She had found many alternatives, some startling, so on one page, as the letter began:

My darling Laura,
Still I wait for your letters – but I live in greater hope as
I have just received a letter from my father date   Life
goes on here at   much as I have described in my
other letters. The difference is we have some chaps

    – they come in here to the NAAFI to frighten us all to
death with their stories – or they try to! But stone frigates
are pretty unsinkable.   Dad tells me how busy he
is   – I should think he could be employed anywhere.
I'm sure   would love his services.

His writing was flowing and bold, the paper small, so the
second side was more or less nonsense from the cuttings-
out on the first page, the lines of which did not exactly
coincide with the writing on the back, so all there was in
some places was either the loops at the top or the bottom of
the letters.

    There is not a lot to do here in the evenings, some of the
chaps have been into town but as they borrowed   they
might have   they hadn't been caught. Because I am
oli   they all feel I should be

She had supplied 'olive-skinned' and 'some kind of Romeo'
when she first read it and had been making up her own
variations ever since, but the remnants of the next sentence
had given her the most pleasure.

    taken up serious stargazing – as well as card games, it
makes me feel closer to you, remembering how we
looked at the stars and   I'll tell you what I'll   not
if the stars were out. In any case if you were with me
I   nyway. Yours until the stars (our star) stops . . .

She wondered all about those words and sentences cut from
letters, all those tiny bits of paper. Did they have baskets on

their desks to collect the banned phrases? Was someone in charge of 'collection and destruction'? She could imagine having to recapture fallen slips then sprinkle them like confetti into an all-consuming furnace. All those private words written by one person or another, the full meaning only known by the writer and the recipient, or the would-be recipient. 'Like our star' she murmured. She had learned to be careful that her longing for Jamie did not become an all-enveloping impossible craving, did not take on the anger they said came with real bereavement. She tried to find a distraction, something to do, comforted herself with the thought that when the evacuees were re-embarked Freddie was quite sure they would be taken to England.

She woke late the next morning and was again alone in the bedroom. She found her mother, dressed, breakfasted and working in Fatima's garden. She watched her as she dead-headed the geraniums, busied herself picking up fallen hibiscus blossoms, generally tidying this other garden – occupied, happy. The word came into her mind unbidden but it made her look at her mother more carefully. Happy? Had last night's liaison made her happy?

A second blossoming, she thought, that was exactly what she was watching. Happiness had renewed her looks.

'You look quite pale,' her mother said. She had been unaware her mother had stopped gardening and was watching her closely.

'While you ...' She turned away, walking over to a stone bench, giving herself time to accept that her own state of mind also showed in her face.

'While I?' Her mother asked coming to sit by her.

'While you look blooming.'

Queenie pushed her hands under her thighs, rocked forward as if to study the stone slabs. 'Freddie came last night, in the night,' she said as if in explanation, before going on. 'He came to warn us that your father is narrowing his search – closing in. He realised that his men were being questioned by two particular soldiers while they were

96

working on army projects. Now some of the men have reported being aware that their houses are being watched, and with Fatima, Joshua and Carlos all working for Freddie, that must include this house. We have to be extra careful, not put a nose out into the streets.'

They looked up as Fatima came out from the kitchen; the tall girl with her sleek coiffure looked as exotic as any hibiscus flower. Laura thought to put a flower behind one ear would enhance her black skirt and floral blouse and look entirely appropriate.

'I've told Fatima,' Queenie added.

Laura smiled at the young woman, who with her brothers seemed genuinely delighted their employer had refound the love of his life, and all so devoted to caring for their guests. She wondered if they would ever be able to repay them.

'Mr de Falla has been getting more worried every day,' Fatima said. They both moved up so she might sit between them a few moments before leaving for work. 'He . . .' she stopped and bit her bottom lip, 'he's really worried.'

Laura felt she knew more. 'So what else is happening?' she prompted.

'Your ships are being cleaned and refitted as you know, and Josh says they're recruiting more carpenters to speed up the work.'

'Our ships.' Queenie tutted. 'Will they really try to take us out in those old freighters? Will they ever get rid of the stench!'

'I didn't mean the ships,' Laura said with quiet insistence.

'There was talk of more shipping being attacked. The Italians again. The raids are getting awful.'

Neither of the other two women answered. The air raids had been more spectacular than frightening so far. The wailing of the sirens and, at night time, the searchlights shining up from behind the heights of The Rock, great waving wands of light wiping across the sky trying to catch the Italian aircraft sent in to bomb the fleet in the harbour or out in the Mediterranean.

'I didn't mean the air raids either,' Laura persisted.

'No,' Fatima admitted giving her a faint sideways smile as they all sat so close together on the short stone bench.

'It's my husband we're more afraid of,' Queenie said. 'I don't want any of you to be hurt.'

Fatima shook her head. 'Mr de Falla has tied his works and systems up well, so well he believes this is why your husband has changed tactics ...' she paused, looked at Laura who she could see was still not satisfied. She clicked her tongue resignedly and added, 'He believes your father has become unbalanced. He thinks trying to find you both, knowing you're both here on The Rock, so near, and yet he cannot find you, has affected his mind.'

'I could believe that,' Queenie mused.

'Seriously?' Laura questioned both statements.

Her mother nodded. 'You know he's obsessive about things.'

'Mr de Falla is taking it all very seriously and so must we.' Fatima got up to go. 'This house has never been so well fortified, and our neighbours are loyal to us and very vigilant. I'm sure you'll be fine.' She looked at Laura. 'You will be fine. I know it's boring. I'll try to get you some English novels.'

'I'll cook the evening meal and tidy up,' Queenie said. 'I like to be busy.'

'No, I'll do that, you can do the mending and turn those shirt collars for Carlos and Josh,' Laura said.

'Never had anyone arguing about the housework before,' Fatima said waving goodbye. 'What is it you say "it's an ill wind that blows no one any good?" But keep the front door and the back gate locked at all times, until we give our special knock.'

Laura watched her go thinking their lives had become like those of underground agents, or prisoners: special whistles; secret knocks; locked doors, and events reported to them second hand. She would like to be out there seeing for herself.

She found herself thinking about Doris Hewitt and the four little girls at the lighthouse and felt envious of their spectacular view over the wide open sea. She remembered how Doris had told her a little about their lives, how the girls took their father's supper tray up the winding stairs to the lighthouse's service room when he was on duty. How no way did they dare put one finger on the shiny brass rail which circled the stone staircase. How the little girls – Marjorie, Lorna, Beryl and Paddy – ran around the unprotected base of the lighthouse dodging the waves when it was rough.

Chores done she went upstairs to write Jamie a long letter, about the sea and the sperm whale and the view the Hewitts must have from Europa Point. In fact she told Jamie all she knew about the lighthouse girls. She told him how she and her mother were being protected and keeping a low profile 'no – an invisible profile if there is such a thing' but how she longed to walk freely on the cliffs, stand beneath their tree, talk to their ape. 'I wonder if he misses us? I miss him!'

She began a new sheet. 'Our respective parents have refound each other in a big way,' she wrote, 'but I can't wait to be on my travels again.' She had to put the memo about not writing on both sides of the notepaper as a postscript to this six-page letter. She went to bed satisfied with her efforts and would ask Fatima to post it the next day.

In the early hours of the following morning they were awoken by the wailing of the air-raid siren, and even though the raids had not so far been severe the urgent rising and falling wail still sent a chill of apprehension down their spines. Mother and daughter sat up in bed listening, wondering if they should get up. They were not in doubt for long. They heard planes, very close, and without thought went to the window, each pane criss-crossed by sticky tape – like every other window on Gib – to help protect against flying glass.

Searchlights already scanned the sky in wide arching

lines and they saw briefly but with startling clarity a plane caught in a beam, another beam joined it so the aircraft appeared transfixed like a silver moth in the middle of this cross of light, guns opened fire, puffs of smoke appeared around the plane, then it dived. For a moment Laura thought it sounded like an express train hurtling down towards them as it manoeuvred to slip the lights, but the engine note changed again as it climbed away. Then another plane appeared higher at the edge of the highest searchlights. The beams swung dizzily, catching, holding then losing this target.

For a moment there was only the sound of engines, going away it seemed, almost they were breathing properly again, when there was a strange whistling sound, like the whistle some fireworks make as they hurtle skywards – only this was coming down, getting louder. The next moment the whole house felt as if it had been shaken in the jaws of some gigantic furious dog. Both of them fell to the floor and the bedroom was full of swirling dust.

'That was close,' Laura heard herself say some seconds later in a strange shaky voice, but before she could say more a second bomb fell and another – stupidly she began to count aloud. There was no good reason apart from the fact that if she was counting they were still alive. Her mother threw an arm over her shoulders and they flattened themselves to the floor as the bombs still fell.

'Five, six, seven, eight.' She wondered if it was right that sticks of bombs came in eights.

'Nine.' She heard her mother swallow hard as she took up the counting.

'Ten, eleven, twelve, thirteen, fourteen, fifteen ...'
Together they counted, together they waited, grasped close, covering their heads with their free arms. When her mother made as if to lift her head Laura pushed it down again sure there would be one more explosion.

Moments passed and they heard voices in the house, and running. Their bedroom door burst open as they struggled to their feet. Fatima and her two brothers rushed in.

'Are you all right?' The question was asked and re-asked as all five reassured themselves.

'But I think it was near,' Josh said. 'It *felt* near.'

'It sounded all around to me,' Carlos said grimly, 'near us in front and behind near the water catchment. I'm going to see.'

They followed him to the front door and looked out. Not far away was a tangled heap of something, as they walked nearer they could see it was two cars, one thrown on top of the other, then from not too far away came the sound of crying and pleas for help.

It was very obvious that this raid was the most serious Gibraltar had suffered. This time it seemed there must undoubtedly be casualties.

They were soon stumbling over rubble and were among people pulling aside bricks and splintered wood. There were children in night clothes, tousled, distressed and while the men went to help with the search for survivors, Queenie took over the children. She pushed a child at each of Laura and Fatima. A man came carrying a medical bag. 'Thank God! Over here!' someone called. The man raised a hand but paused briefly to look at the children then went to where the men were calling to him to hurry. The women moved a little further away with the distressed children as an ambulance sped up and soon they saw stretchers being loaded into it, stretchers with blankets completely covering the people being taken away.

A nurse came and took over the care of the children and they were taken away to the hospital in a private car. Quite soon they were mere onlookers as more people arrived, relations, anxiously looking for those they knew to be in the area.

'Nothing more we can do here,' Carlos said. 'I'm going over to the catchment, and I'll check on the boss at the same time.'

'I'll see these home, then come,' Josh told him and

turning to Queenie and Laura said, 'The boss would *not* be pleased to see you two roaming about like this.'

'This was different. I hope those children will be all right,' Queenie said her voice falling as she added, 'and none of them belong to the people who've been killed.'

'No,' Fatima breathed and they all fell silent each thinking of the distress and injuries they had seen. Laura thought of the handkerchief in her pocket smeared with the blood she had wiped from a little girl's cheek and neck so it did not stain her nightdress, as if it mattered, she thought, but she had seemed such a sweet dainty little thing. She had reminded her of Doris's youngest, about five years old. It had been all she could do for her. It would perhaps be a good thing that the children were to be evacuated to somewhere safer.

'I didn't see anyone outside when we left,' Fatima said as they returned to her home. 'No one keeping watch or anything.'

Laura felt a cold shiver run all over her body, gooseflesh stood up on her arms, the hackles rose on the back of her neck. She had not even thought of her father in the immediate panic of checking everyone was all right and then rushing out into the early morning to help. Now she peered under the arches of bougainvillaea framing neighbouring front doors, but could see no one outside watching their movements. Even so she felt more and more apprehensive as Josh pushed open the front door and went inside, Fatima following behind.

It was pure instinct that made Laura catch her mother's arm. She held her back, then saw Fatima miss her step, her hand flying to her mouth. She looked back, then stooping picked up something from the table and silently turned to display what she held.

It was an officer's cap and cane. It was her father's cap and cane.

Chapter Eight

The bombs had finished dropping and the raid was over but a tremendous drum-beat had taken over Jock's head. It had begun like 'taps', the drummer's call that focuses attention, the moment Blondie Fulmer, his batman, had come with the news that one of his watchers had found Queenie and his daughter.

Fulmer he knew had hired extra men and he had left this part of the new strategy to his batman. He had no wish to deal with anyone as low down the military scale as his batman – he despised Fulmer enough. His batman was, he considered, a blond covetous Cockney beneath contempt. His only use was that he could be bought. If the price was right he reckoned Blondie Fulmer would do anything if he could get away with it – and having his officer as collaborator obviously made him feel safe.

The raid had been fortuitous. He had been unable to rest or think of anything else since Fulmer had brought him the news that the house where *three* of de Falla's employees lived – and which he would have dismissed as being too overcrowded to take in anyone else – had proved to be the place his wife and daughter were said to be hiding.

His mind ran ever more sinister scenarios as he planned confrontation and capture. He watched the camp's cat stalk a song thrush and admired the slowly lifted paw, revelled in the bird pecking so unaware beneath a tree, turning dead leaves, so busy. The cat sank slowly to a crouch – then sprang. He chuckled delightedly. Queenie, or rather the bird, had no chance as the cat crippled it then played with it for a long time before it died, its screeching cries for help like stabs of sheer pleasure to his heart. He had watched, then suddenly realised he was not the only watcher, other birds seemed to have gathered on nearby fences and trees, like voyeurs at a hanging. When the bird had given a particularly raucous despairing appeal they had all flown away as if knowing all hope was gone, the agony was over. For a moment he wondered if the birds had expected him to intervene, he could remember his father knocking the window to stop sparrows fighting – and his mother's contempt. Jock had glared at the cat, it could have been more subtle, he thought, made it all last longer.

But to last longer the thing had to begin, nothing would stop the pounding in his head until it began, until he took action. The raid had provided the excuse he needed to leave the camp. He had found and bullied Fulmer into driving the jeep so he could show him the house, telling the guard at the camp gate that they were going to see what damage had been done 'to installations'. The barrier had been lifted, no questions asked, but Fulmer was fidgety, obviously nervous about his officer's intentions.

'Want to stop and 'ave a look?' Fulmer had asked then as they passed the end of a street where smoke and dust rose in a long lazy plume into the morning haze and a small crowd of people were collected around a busy core working over debris.

'Sir,' Jock reminded him.

'Sir?'

'D'yu wanna stop and 'ave a look, sir?' Jock mimicked the man's tone and accent coarsely and crudely.

Fulmer had driven on, gritting his teeth. It was going to be hard graft polishing this man's shoes when every day he hated his guts more, even now he contrived to do the chore without putting his hand inside each shoe. It was only when they reached the house that surprise lifted his mood and the sullenness from his voice as he noted, 'The door's open.'

'Stop around the corner,' Jock ordered as they swerved to avoid a heap of cars, piled and contorted by bomb blast. A piece dropped from the top wreck as they walked back.

'What d'you think's 'appened?' Fulmer asked as they stood in the doorway of the silent house.

Still no 'sir'. The lack of it thudded with extra pressure inside his skull. He would soon have to rid himself of this batman, he was becoming too sure of himself, knew too much. They reached the open door and he thought for a second Fulmer was going to call out. He raised a swift silencing hand. 'Stay here and keep watch,' he hissed, 'give me a whistle if anyone comes.'

He had to constrain this man – permanently – but he would have to do it carefully. He knew only too well each was at the other's mercy, revelation of the damage done to defence works and air-raid shelters to discredit de Falla, and the army time and manpower used to try to ferret out his family, had only to be leaked to bring the authorities down on his head. A court martial would be the final humiliation. He would go to any lengths – any lengths – to avoid that.

'What'y going to do?' Fulmer called after him, adding a derogatory, 'sir.'

His officer was already several paces into the hallway, but came back and confronted him, eyes blazing with such fury and contempt that Fulmer swallowed hard and instinctively took a step away. What was worse Maclaren did not speak again, he didn't have to, the promise had been in his eyes. 'Christ!' Fulmer breathed as he was again left at the door. What he wanted more than anything was to get the hell out of this situation. To leave was more than he dared do, but he began to feel a real sympathy for Maclaren's wife and daughter.

In the house Jock paused to listen, then reassuring himself that he could justify his presence by saying he was investigating the open door, he walked on through the rooms, downstairs first.

He found early confirmation that he had been brought to the right place in the kitchen. Piled on a chair was sewing. Queenie was never anywhere long before she was sewing – or gardening. Here were men's shirts, the collars being carefully turned, the neatness of the work was hers without doubt. Working on other men's clothes. 'Not for much longer,' he promised.

By the second bedroom he was sure no one was in the house. He calculated that if these people were willing to overcrowd their home with people they hardly knew, they would also be the sort that would rush out to help other folk in an air raid. Queenie and Laura would have gone too – of course they would.

In the third room, a double bedroom, he found their clothes. He recognised his daughter's skirts and blouses lying around, sewn by her mother of course. He stood for many seconds with a flimsy smocked blouse tight drawn between his fists, but he did not tear it, he placed it aside, his hands trembling, his face sweating with the effort of this restraint. He would store his anger. Slowly he went back downstairs. There was such opportunity in this situation, he needed to think it through very carefully.

He paused in the shadows of the hall, his hand rested on a small table holding a vase of oleander sprays. Their fragrance rose to him as the table tilted under his hand. It was like the sweet talcum-powder scent which lingered after a woman's bath. It reminded him of Queenie and her garden.

From the doorway Fulmer turned to look as Jock took off his cap to wipe his forehead as he pondered his problem. What he needed was cheese for a trap – a bait – and suddenly he realised he held it in his hand. He let out a great guffaw of laughter – and startled his batman, who swore blasphemously at him. Jock lodged it in the pigeon-hole marked 'getting rid of Fulmer', but for now he was too busy making other calculations.

He placed his cap and cane on the small table, where they could hardly be missed. His wife and daughter would certainly *not* overlook them. The bait was laid.

The direction of the de Falla house from Cumberland Place seemed of vital importance. He consulted Fulmer on the geography of the area. 'Right! For a start we'll wait either side of that bush over there. We should see all and hear all,' he sneered and fell into a mimicry of his man again, 'but say nowt, as you might so charmingly say.'

They pushed close in by a huge bougainvillaea which arched over a doorway, one each side, so that even anyone coming in and out of that door would have to be vigilant to see them. It was not long before they saw three women and a man walking uphill towards the house. They had been careful to leave the door slightly ajar, exactly as they had found it.

The thudding beat in Jock's head increased as he recognised Queenie in a dressing gown – out in the streets in her night clothes – an officer's wife. She had an awful lot of lessons to learn. Laura had on slacks over her pyjamas, and the other, taller woman, had on an outdoor coat.

His anger turned almost to pleasure as he saw the man say something, go inside, then the tall woman went in after him, only to come back into the doorway carrying his hat and cane. He felt his stomach twist with pleasure as he saw the consternation the objects caused. He heard Fulmer give a little gasp and wanted to laugh aloud for, as he anticipated, they assumed he was inside. He saw the girl motion his family to run, get away.

He felt triumphant as he saw the first part of his plan succeed, as he watched his wife turn immediately and do just that, run – just as he wanted her to. Laura hesitated for a moment. Pushing your luck again, he silently told her. Defy me once too often you will, but after a moment's hesitation Laura followed her mother.

He let them get away from the house, out of sight, then

signalled Fulmer to fetch the jeep. *This part of the hunt was where the cat lifted its paw.* It was a matter of anticipation and timing. He must balance how far to let his women go against how long it would take those in the house to find it was empty and *perhaps* decide to go after the two runners.

Once in the jeep he had to swear at Fulmer several times before he understood what he wanted. 'Slowly! Go bloody slowly! I want them further away from the house before we catch up.'

In his mind's eye he saw the beginning of the cat's slow crouch. He tried to put himself in the minds of those he wished to outwit. His wife and daughter were intent on flight – *the crouch took a deeper shape in his mind*. Those left behind in the house, the man and woman, they were the imponderables. *The crouch froze before it sank to the full power needed for the pounce.* There was another element to gauge – distance – but as sure as night followed day while he was nearing his prey, he was also leaving the imponderables further behind every second.

Yes, the spring of the big cat would be possible as soon as he sighted the prey. He laughed with delight at the prospect. He had waited many weeks for this, had been humiliated as he tried to find his family, had seen the puzzled and amused looks on the faces of those he had inquired of, and had promised himself this sweet revenge.

Fulmer muttered something and Jock laughed again at the look on his face. 'You can go a little faster,' he told him as if indulging a child.

His amusement died when even going faster they did not come upon their quarry. This would surely be the way they would take. There were no short cuts, Fulmer assured him.

Then he saw them. They were leaning over a low wall. 'Taking their breath,' he whispered, then louder, 'they won't need it!'

'What 'yer mean?' Fulmer looked at him, repeated the question and bumped the kerb.

'Keep your eye on the road – and them.' He stabbed a

108

finger towards the women who were moving away again, walking and jogging to keep up a good pace.

Jock suddenly realised just how near the de Falla house they were, four or five hundred yards, no more. 'We must stop them,' he said urgently, 'swerve in front of them.' The man grumbled discontentedly under his breath and though he increased the speed a little did not do so sufficiently for Jock's ends. 'Put your bloody foot down!'

'I'm not going by those women now!' He hurled a hand towards the windscreen, to the road which narrowed and now had only a very narrow pavement at one side. 'I could kill them.'

'Not straight away,' Jock shouted. 'Go on, man, go by, swing in front of them.'

'Not on your . . .'

'Double your money,' Jock promised grimly, 'just swerve in front of them and leave the rest to me.'

Fulmer pressed the accelerator more firmly; in the confines of the narrow street the jeep leapt forward. The women turned at the sound of the engine, then the older woman in the white robe stumbled and fell to her knees. At his side the officer laughed. 'Down you go, dear! Down you go! Once a bundler always a bundler.'

Fulmer eased up as the younger woman stooped to help.

'You get nothing if you slow up.'

Anger made Fulmer slam his foot down hard – for a few seconds – then seeing how the distance shrank between the vehicle and the women; how little chance they had of escape from injury, and seeing the panic-stricken backwards glance of the younger one as she struggled to drag her mother clear, he braked as hard as he could. The jeep skidded alarmingly. Jock Maclaren swore and tried to seize the steering wheel. Fulmer fought back, trying to prevent Maclaren pulling the vehicle hard to the left and on to the women. He felt a breath-stopping punch deep into his ribs and he was pushed hard at the door which he felt give. Again he was struck but he hung on to the steering wheel as

109

hard as he could pulling it to the right. He saw Maclaren swivel slightly and, while still trying to force the wheel down to the left, the officer brought up both feet. The thrust sent Fulmer tumbling out. His head hit the pavement with a noise resembling the cracking of a gigantic egg.

As she stooped over her mother Laura saw her father again, from under her arm in an upside-down frame made by the jeep windscreen. His face was a portrait of evil, his upper body looming up as if he was launching himself out of the vehicle towards her. She saw him lurch violently towards the driver as in desperate panic she hauled her mother up, off the ground with strength heightened by fear. She threw them both sprawling against a house wall, then froze as she felt the outside leg of her slacks suddenly become very tight, and she realised the jeep wheels had gone over the fragment of loose material. She had come as near as that to being crippled if not killed.

They raised their heads and could see the jeep speeding on. 'He'll be back,' Queenie stated and though she struggled painfully to her feet holding her shoulder her voice was chillingly matter-of-fact.

'He's got to find somewhere to turn,' Laura said, 'if we run back.' She stopped as she saw the prostrate figure stretched out on the road.

'There's someone on the road,' her mother said in the same moment.

They ran back. The man was lying very still, his head raised as if on a pillow by the edge of the pavement. Even as they knelt by the man Queenie pointed to where the jeep was again in view. 'He's coming back!'

Laura bent over the man and immediately recognised her father's batman. She also saw the stream of blood coming from the back of his head. 'We need help quickly!'

'He's going to run us all down,' Queenie said, distracted from the man lying at their feet by the sight of the jeep speeding back towards them.

Laura knew they could not move the man even if they had time. She stood up and holding out her arms as if this would in some magic way stop the progress of the vehicle she advanced up the road to meet it. Behind her she heard her mother scream out her name in a long appeal. 'L . . . a . . . u . . . r . . . a!'

The vehicle came on and she went forward. She had stood her ground with her father before but this, she thought with a grim twist of humour, could be the ultimate challenge. Jamie, she thought as she watched the jeep loom larger, I love you.

He saw the figure, and it enraged him. He was also aware of Queenie in the white robe first stooping down then straightening. Fulmer was still lying where he had fallen he supposed. Then two things happened at once, in his mind's eye the bird escaped, his bird flew away, and his foot went from accelerator to brake. Even so it could be too late and his stupid defiant daughter still stood in the middle of the road.

The jeep veered, hit a house wall, jumped back into the road and stopped within an arm's length of Laura. After it had stopped she stepped to one side and shouted at him: 'You'd better go and get help quickly, your batman is bleeding to death.'

It was only in retrospect that Laura could make sense of all that happened next. She remembered her father's face leaning from the driver's seat of the jeep, hard, inscrutable, shock at seeing so much blood pouring from the back of Fulmer's skull, deterred from whatever he intended. Then so many people seemed to arrive within minutes of each other, Josh and Fatima, Freddie and Carlos, and later at Freddie's house both the police and two officers from the New Camp.

Fulmer was dead on arrival at the hospital. The inquiry began almost immediately, first with the army and then the civil authorities.

There were a lot of questions to be answered, statements

to be made, and only later did Laura begin to piece together what she thought must be the truth. The hat and stick left at Fatima's house were the clue she thought, but Lieutenant Jock Maclaren had no one to either corroborate or deny his story of hearing someone in distress in the house, going in and then being summoned by his driver to the scene of what they thought was another bomb.

Fulmer was not there to contest his officer's story of his 'faithful batman of long standing inexplicably losing control of the vehicle.' His story was never believed by those who knew him, nor could it be disproved.

Chapter Nine

The day the inquiry into the death of George Albert Fulmer was concluded in the coroner's court, the six of them all walked silently back towards Freddie's house, brooding.

Freddie walked by Queenie, his arm around her waist, steadying her as she in turn supported the arm she had in a sling. The three Valerios and Laura walked behind, not trusting themselves to speak, such a flood of anger might be loosed – yet each one knew they would not be so restrained once they reached the privacy of the de Falla house. There would be another inquest all of their own.

The verdict of death by misadventure had left them feeling dissatisfied and distressed, and they were all silently pursuing their own particular line of grievance.

Once Freddie's front door closed after them he helped Queenie to a comfortable chair and said bitterly, 'He said he was going to inspect the installations for bomb damage.' Freddie's voice shook with rage.

'He's done more damage than any bombs,' Carlos growled.

Laura could see her father being driven away in the staff car with his senior officer, sitting ramrod straight, the picture of a wronged husband. He had managed to give the impression that in spite of his heavy private burdens he was doing a good job for his country in time of war and was a disciplined and trustworthy officer. Did the army really not see through him? She sighed heavily. 'I think he's managed to get away without a stain on his character.'

'He had a glib answer for everything,' Fatima said as she brewed tea and sliced lemons, 'and he gave his evidence as if *he* really believed it. If I hadn't known anything about the affair *I* would have believed how his driver "seemed to go to pieces, lost control of the vehicle, fell out as he tried to take the wheel ..."'

'How he raced back to the aid of his driver ...' Laura added shaking her head at the lies that had been told under oath.

'I watched some of the soldiers, officers and men, while he was giving evidence,' Josh said with gentle certainty, 'they know the truth about him.'

'But no one spoke out!' Carlos complained.

'When *we* tried we were reminded it was "a sudden death, not evidence for a divorce case",' Josh recalled.

'Someone laughed at that,' Fatima mused.

'You know what chilled me the most ...' Queenie began and both Freddie and Laura made faint murmurs of assent and when her mother did not go on Laura finished for her.

'When he said though he had marital troubles *at the moment* he regarded his marriage vows as life-long ...'

'... and would do all in his power to make sure they remained like that,' Freddie finished.

There were a few seconds of still reflection.

'And you felt people in the court *were* on his side when he said it,' Josh added.

'There was a shift of opinion at that moment,' Freddie agreed.

'He didn't even look as if he had much on his conscience,' Carlos said, punching a fist fiercely into the palm of his other hand. 'Even when we told all we knew ... *all* of us,' he paused to sweep an arm around the five of them, 'he *still* talked his way out.'

'The devil looks after his own,' Queenie said.

'The army seems to,' Carlos concluded.

114

'Circumstantial,' Josh said. 'What *does* that mean?'

'Inconclusive, or hearsay, I think, not first hand, not seen,' Freddie said.

'Did Private Fulmer have a wife?' Queenie wondered.

'Just a widowed mother,' Josh answered. 'I asked one of the army drivers.'

'Poor woman,' Queenie said very quietly. 'Poor woman. In other circumstances we might write to her ...'

'Yes.' Laura knew they would not, there would have to be too much suppression of what they suspected to make for a genuine message at such a time.

'His officer will write,' Queenie said, then realised, 'your father ...'

'That's awful!' Freddie proclaimed, making Laura think it was a long time since she had heard him pronounce his favourite word. Nothing had been at all 'marvellous' in these long, long days following Fulmer's death and the trauma of her mother's arm for which, whatever was said, she felt personally responsible.

Queenie let her head fall to her chest, chin resting over her sling, appalled by the thought of Jock writing a letter of condolence to Fulmer's mother. Freddie was immediately by her side. 'Come on,' he said, 'you're going for a lie down.'

Since the night of the air raid they had more or less all lived at the de Falla house. Freddie had arranged it so that the two women were never alone. Fatima did the office work at the house, and her brothers divided their time between their own home and his. They all worked different shifts so that there was at least one man with the women all the time.

Freddie supported Queenie up the stairs into one of the smaller bedrooms. They had decided she would rest better alone so that her left arm, plastered from shoulder to wrist, could be supported by as many pillows as she needed. Freddie carefully rebuilt the pillows around her. She looked up at him as he stood so obviously calculating whether moving a pillow a fraction this way or that might make her more comfortable. 'You make me feel like one of your MoD construction jobs,' she told him. 'Not going to cement me in, are you?'

'I wish I could,' he said solemnly.

'Oh, Freddie, you're like The Rock anyway,' she told him, 'my dependable rock. I wish you were coming with us, I wouldn't worry about anything then.'

He sighed. 'They say the boats are all nearly ready.'

She patted the side of the bed and he sat down.

'You'll soon be going,' he added, 'only days I think.'

'If the inquiry had been delayed we might have missed the boat!' She smiled at her own pun.

'You can laugh and joke. Marvellous!'

'Why shouldn't I? While I'm still with you everything is marvellous.'

He raised his eyebrows at her, shook his head at her attempts to sit upright in spite of the weight of her plaster. He put his hand behind her back to support her.

'I can't bear to think of leaving you behind,' she said earnestly.

'Whereas Laura,' he reminded her, 'can't wait to go.'

'She's hoping to see Jamie as soon as she sets foot on land – that's if we are sent to England. Carlos said today he'd heard Canada.'

'I pray she's not to be disappointed.'

'I hope this war won't go on and on, so those two miss out on all *their* young lives – all those years, Freddie, like our years, lost.'

'I think the world has become too good at killing people from a distance for that to happen.' He bent to her and kissed her lips with the lightest of touches. 'It makes the politicians at home think harder about their own safety.'

Coming up the stairs Laura smiled to herself. When Jamie's father made such a long statement she felt she could rely on it being good commonsense.

'So you don't think the war will go on that long?' she heard her mother ask.

116

'A year or two, because so many countries are becoming involved, but not many, many years.'

'Promise?' her mother asked just as Laura reached the bedroom door.

She was about to speak but while Freddie supported her mother's back Queenie's hand went gently to Freddie's cheek and prolonged the kiss he began. It was a moment of sweet intimacy not to be interrupted. She turned to go but not before she saw Freddie's hand slide gently down her back and perhaps without intention beneath the waist band of her skirt. She saw the movement of the skirt as he gently caressed the bottom of her spine, his arm still supporting her back and his lips still on hers.

Laura moved on along the corridor, startled, aroused. She had felt as if the hand had moved over her own back, as if it might have been Jamie massaging her. 'Damn it!' she whispered as she sat on the edge of her own single bed and pressed her knees tight together, aching for her own lover.

First thing the next morning the order came for all evacuees to reassemble at the docks the following day. The freighters that had brought them from Casablanca were ready, or as ready as under three weeks' furious activity and the limited resources of the authorities could make them. 'They're clean and provisioned,' Fatima said, 'but I hear the facilities are a bit primitive.'

'Meaning?' Laura asked.

'Cooking,' she answered. 'The soldiers they unloaded at Casablanca had field kitchens aboard each ship, now ...'

'Now?' Laura questioned the doubtful look that came on to Fatima's face.

'Now I'm told they have iron cooking stoves lashed to the rails.'

Laura blinked, trying to envisage this – then she laughed. 'You can't cook like that. What if the sea's rough?'

'Black coal ranges tied to the ships' rails,' Fatima

insisted, 'I'm telling you. Carlos saw them being loaded, *and* . . .'

'And? Come on Fatima!' Laura exclaimed.

'Well, the toilet arrangements are a bit primitive too.'

Freddie came into the room where Fatima was supposed to be typing his letters. She beckoned Laura to come near so she could whisper.

Laura listened, then shook her head and laughed again.

'So what's all this about?' Freddie asked.

'She's pulling my leg!' Laura told him. 'Pull the other one Fatima Valerio, it's got bells on.'

'All right, you'll see.' Fatima went back to the type-writer.

'Well, it made me laugh,' Laura said then asked Freddie. 'How did you get on at the hospital?'

'You'd best go try to make your mother laugh. The hospital won't take her plaster off before she sails.'

'I thought they might put a lighter one on,' Laura echoed. 'Oh dear.'

'They're going to try to make sure you sail on a ship that has a nurse on board,' Freddie told her.

Laura looked sceptical, nurses were not regarded as 'useless mouths' on Gibraltar and she knew of none that were being shipped out. But when she spoke to her mother she soon realised it was not her arm that was making her unhappy, it was the thought of leaving Freddie.

'We seem to be doomed to be always living on different parts of the globe,' Queenie said, adding ruefully as Fatima came into the kitchen, 'we're being sent to safety, while those left here will face heaven knows what – invasion, bombardment – no one knows.'

'Gibraltar may suffer,' Fatima said, her voice falling for a moment, 'but we have guns and the navy, and all those air force boys; we shall fight back.'

No one answered. Laura thought fearfully of the navy fighting back, then of The Rock being pounded by high explosives, and of her and Jamie's special places. The tree, their ape, all the Barbary apes, they had to be kept safe, or the saying was that Gibraltar would head for disaster. Then as the other two were talking she found she was planning a last expedition to their trysting place. Then when – and not *if* she told herself, pushing back all her fears for Jamie on active service – *when* she met Jamie again she could tell him how it was looking before she was evacuated this second time.

There would be only once chance, that evening. She glanced up as Josh came in, Josh the gentle one, should she ask him to go with her? Really it would make more sense to ask Carlos, he would make a fight of trouble. But she knew she was not going to ask anyone, she wanted to be alone.

News of the next day's embarkation meant there was a lot to do quickly. It was a tiresome, troublesome thing to have again to roll mattresses, again pack what provisions and items of household goods they felt would be essential when on board, or when they reached their destination. Queenie regretted her sewing machine and chest full of materials. 'I wonder what's happened to them? All the clothes I could have made!' Laura just stopped herself saying that not at the moment she couldn't, then felt a new guilt about the hurtling fall which had broken her mother's arm *and* about the chests which, though Freddie made nothing of, she was sure were heirlooms from generations back.

It was after their evening meal that she realised Freddie was watching her curiously. 'What are you thinking?' he asked. 'Or should I ask *who* are you thinking about?'

'Who, I suppose,' she said. 'Before I go tomorrow I want to walk up to the cliffs where Jamie and I used to meet . . .' She had not planned to tell anyone and now felt rather stupid, with so much to do, so many practical things, she felt he must think her a fool, wasting precious time.

'There is always the risk . . .' he began but stopped as he saw the shuttered look of intention on Laura's face.

'It's stupid I know . . .' she admitted.

119

'If Carlos went with you to the beginning of the cliff path, he could wait there.'

'And I could have my few moments alone with our tree, and we have a particular ape who sits in the tree, I'd like to say goodbye to him.' Her voice was full of sudden enthusiasm, her face vibrant and young and she blushed as she added, 'I really do know why my mother loves you.'

'I'll find Carlos,' he said.

But they had barely left the front door when Laura saw an army officer standing in a doorway opposite. She walked confidently by Carlos's side, quite sure her father would not prevail on a fellow officer to stand watch for him, the man's presence was just coincidence. Her father's power was over those of lower rank, those he could order without fear of being talked about in the mess. She mused how much her father would hate that. She wondered if it had happened after Fulmer's inquest. She could imagine conversations stopping as he entered the mess. He could well become even more paranoid if he thought people were talking and laughing about him behind his back.

'Walk past me, would you!'

She spun round as a man called sarcastically after them. She recognised the voice immediately, but had not recognised the figure in the doorway.

She stopped, staggered, with the shock of it being her father. Carlos bristled like a dog on guard, or one sensing something odd and dangerous about the man who approached. There was certainly something strangely distraught about him, his face was unnaturally pallid, filmed with perspiration, and he was jerking his neck with a strange and seemingly uncontrollable twitch.

'Why are you here?' she asked, gratefully letting Carlos take his stand between the two of them.

'Come to say goodbye. Give you both a goodbye kiss.' He pushed his face towards her, pursing his lips, at the same time his head jerking with the violent nervous tic.

'Keep your distance,' Carlos growled.

'Who the hell do you think you're talking to!' he exclaimed, but his voice had for the moment lost the hard edge of authority and Carlos did not even bother to answer. He tried to shoulder by the Gibraltarian and ordered Laura, 'Go and fetch your mother.'

'She doesn't want to see you now or ever,' she told him, her heart thumping but emboldened by the unflinching Carlos.

'What she, or you, wants is not in the equation.' His voice slurred over the words like one the worse for drink, but she was sure he was not. '*I* want! Me! I want her here!' He jerked his forefinger down to a spot in front of his feet. 'Now!'

Carlos hit him in the mouth, without preamble or warning. The punch toppled him over, left him sprawled on the road holding his mouth. 'We're not in your bloody army,' Carlos told him and taking Laura by the arm he steered her back towards the front door.

'You'll regret that for the rest of your days,' Jock spluttered as he checked his teeth were still whole inside his cut and bleeding lips.

They were at the door and looking back briefly when they saw an army jeep stop against the officer now struggling to his feet. It seemed to both of them that he was hustled aboard in no gentle or respectful manner. As they stood on the front doorstep the jeep went by and she heard her father shout, 'Tell your dear mother I'll catch up with her ...' The rest was lost as the vehicle sped away.

After it had gone Carlos wanted them to set off again, but she felt too shaky – the jeep, the same street, her father – she felt the mood was lost. The whole household was upset once more by the incident. Freddie wanted to go at once to the camp and complain to the commanding officer. Queenie begged him not waste their last evening in such a way and that it could make trouble for Carlos.

Carlos shrugged, blew out his lips in noisy derision.

121

'There would be no witnesses, he could not prove anything,' he said.

'No, that's right,' Laura said adamantly. 'Just like the inquest, no witnesses.'

Later when all the packing was done and Freddie was sitting in the garden with her mother, he said, 'You may regret not going on your walk in the days to come.'

'Go,' Queenie nodded, 'he won't be back, he'll be hiding his swollen lips, and Carlos is very willing to take you.'

'You don't need to worry about Señor de Falla,' Carlos told her as they restarted their walk. 'We shall look after him, you believe me. Tell your mother.'

'I do believe you,' she told him, 'and I will – and I shall always remember your ...' she turned to look at him and smiled, 'your courage.'

He laughed, punched one hand into the palm of the other. 'Wham!' he said, 'it felt good.' He took her to the beginning of the walk along the cliff edge and without being asked stopped and perched on a wall there. 'Be as long as you like,' he said.

She went slowly, climbing up the steep rocky path on the edge of the cliff, living in retrospect the times she had waited there. Sometimes Jamie had already been there, sitting with his back against – she looked over to locate it – yes, that huge rock, looking out over the Med with that solitary tree and that solitary ape. Only this evening the ape wasn't there, nor the whale – 'nor you Jamie,' she breathed, 'but I'm coming, I'm coming to you, I know I am.'

She started violently as behind her something moved and scuttled, and as she turned an ape swung himself up into the tree, on to its favourite perch, grunting as it settled itself. Like someone coming in late for a performance at the theatre, she thought, as it regarded her with its coal-black eyes, its head nodding slightly up and down.

'I nearly didn't come,' she told it, 'and you were nearly late. I shall tell Jamie.' She moved forward a little to the

122

edge of the cliff looking down and to the right towards the harbour. 'And I shall tell him about how many ships were in the harbour,' she stopped realising that many of them, some twenty-four they said, would make up the convoy of ships she would sail in the next day. The wind stirred her skirt, moving it against her legs, bringing her back to the moment. She looked further out to sea. 'And I shall tell him how the sea looked – how brilliant and blue – and how the Atlas mountains are still there, another continent, another country, and tomorrow, ape,' she turned to look at the beast, 'I'm going to another country, I'm going to Jamie. You'll have to look after things here for us.'

Chapter Ten

This time their luggage was better managed. In a whirl of last-minute organisation Fatima supervised everything.

Carlos said the freighters would have quarters for their thirty or so crew. The living space for 500 evacuees would be in the holds.

'We travelled on the decks before,' Laura reminded him.

'They couldn't keep you all on deck for more than a day or so,' Carlos said, 'not practical. If there was an attack, or ...' He tailed off and they did not dwell on the prospects, as the cases were strapped up and labelled. Josh came with a small can of white enamel paint and added their names prominently on each side of the cases, adding the number they had been allocated.

'That'll be dry in no time and won't come off! Make them easier to find if they do have to go into luggage hold.' He added a final flourish to Queenie's name, then shyly a small flower by the side of Laura's.

This time the collection points were at several places throughout the town, theirs at the far end of Freddie's street. Husbands, relations – anyone not travelling was told to keep away from the marshalling points. 'They don't want a last-minute rebellion on their hands,' Freddie said. No one answered but everyone tacitly agreed it was always a possibility. The disastrous trip to Casablanca and back, plus the thought of another voyage 'destination unknown' for the women, children and old men was hardly to be borne.

It was decided to make their goodbyes at the house rather than be kept at bay by troops trying to load lorries. So it was a sad coming and going as Carlos and Josh carried the cases and the mattresses to the accumulating pile at the end of the street. It was worse standing on the steps of the house watching, knowing the moment of parting was very near.

These were the long moments when they did not look at each other for fear of becoming upset too soon and making everything much more difficult for everyone. It was a time of stiff upper lips, remarks about time and glances up into the sky, as if it could be anything but blue. Then urgent, silly, panicky, last-minute thoughts about passports and papers – and writing letters, promises and quick covert glances at those soon to be lost for a long time.

Then it was time. Queenie turned and Freddie took her into his arms, encompassing her, the plastered arm, all in a silent embrace, his face in her hair. Their stillness was a private place, set them apart from the others who busied themselves making their goodbyes.

'We'll all meet again,' Laura said. 'We'll be back.'

'Take care of yourself, write as soon as you can,' Fatima said as the two girls hugged and Laura realised how deep their friendship had grown in so short a time. There was a mutual respect – even admiration – between them.

Carlos and Josh both kissed her and she found tears on her cheeks for all the Valerio family, for these two brothers so alike in build, so unalike in natures.

Queenie coming back to them from Freddie's embrace begged them all to go inside. 'I can't bear to think of turning round and seeing you all. I'd want to run back.' She smiled at Freddie through a haze of tears, then embraced them all in turn, Freddie again but swiftly, not looking at his face.

'No matter how many times we do this,' Freddie said with an attempted laugh, 'it never gets any easier.'

'Let's hope this is the last time we ever have to do it,' Queenie murmured. 'Now go inside, Freddie.'

It was only as they reached the lorries and the crowd of equally heart-sick evacuees that Laura remembered she had not really said a final goodbye to Freddie. She glanced at her mother and thought he probably would not have noticed anyway. The way those two had clung to each other had been painful to see. They had parted as if each tiny loss of contact brought instant pain. She wondered if this was what tearing people apart really meant. She looked back. The steps of the house were empty, the door closed.

The docks were much quieter for this evacuation. This second time had no novelty. There was no waving, no calling, hardly any talking at all, just orders being called by more men with lists, mothers rallying children, daughters elderly parents. Everyone might have become a lot more frustrated and resentful but for the arrival of an ambulance bringing several people, and children some looking severely injured – air-raid casualties – to join the evacuation. There were to be no exceptions.

They found they were allocated to a freighter called the *Dromore Castle* belonging to the Union Castle Line. They learned it was a coaler as they filed aboard, and were shown their living and sleeping quarters – in newly white-washed holds. Five holds were each to take ninety to a hundred women, children and old men.

The descent into their accommodation was traumatic, many young children clung to their mothers and screamed as they were firmly clutched and carried down through the hatches on wooden steps (marginally wider than a ladder), built to allow people access in and out of the huge whitened coal bunkers. Any luggage they could carry they were allowed to take with them. Trunks and tea chests were consigned to a baggage store.

The shoes of old men and children reinforced with metal segs scraped and echoed on the metal floor as each group reached the bottom and stayed there, unwilling to move further into the already suffocatingly hot hold, but as the numbers grew some yielded and moved further inside.

126

'Some of those old people won't get back up those steps unless they're carried,' commented a robust woman, mid-brown hair crisp waved over her head with tiny tight rolls at the ends, her face and arms the same shade of heated pink. She was hung and strung around with bundles and bags so she resembled a pack mule, and had two boys clinging to her skirts. She moved past them, adding, 'If we get to the far end at least everyone won't be walking over and around you,' she said.

Queenie did not answer, but she and Laura slowly followed her, Laura thinking that at least they would be further away from what looked like a table with bowls and buckets, but it hung from the ceiling on wire hawsers and on closer inspection proved to be part of an old hatch cover. It hung steadily enough, but what if they went right out into the Atlantic to avoid submarines? And was it to be where all these women, children and old men washed? For the first time Laura began to think the lavatory arrangement Fatima had described to her might also be true.

'Find yourself a spot to unroll your mattress and make the space around it your territory,' a uniformed sailor called, overlooking them from a standpoint halfway up the steps.

The hold full of people shushed each other and listened attentively, expecting details of routines, or who they might go to for advice or help, but the only other thing he told them was to: 'Listen for announcements.'

'And the only things they'll tell us'll be things we don't want to know,' their new companion quipped glancing at Queenie.

Laura felt embarrassed by her mother's silence as they carefully pulled out the long stitches on their bedding rolls, saving the sacking and string under the mattresses, then folded up their blankets and put them under their pillows.

The woman with the boys had two mattresses for the three of them. She put her mattresses close together. 'Give my boys a bit more comfort of a night,' she said.

'Then you're entitled to a bit more space round your

127

two,' Laura decided, heaving their mattresses a few inches further away. One of the boys tried to help and tripped. Queenie caught his hand saving him from falling.

'Steady as you go, young man.' The contact broke her silence, eased words from the heartbreak. 'Twins?' she asked the mother.

'Four years old, and ten minutes between the two,' she replied proudly. 'I hope you like children, because it looks like we're all going to get to know each other pretty well. I'm Mabel Macintyre,' she introduced herself, then pointing at her boys added, 'Ian and Alec. Everyone calls me Mabs.' She nodded at Queenie's arm, 'Not a good time to be in plaster.'

'I fell,' she said briefly, then introduced herself and Laura.

'Your husband?' Mabs asked and for a delicate moment Laura wondered if this stranger could have heard about Fulmer, the inquest . . .?

'In the army, and yours?' Queenie said, long practised in putting on a brave face – and running answers into questions.

'Merchant navy. He hasn't seen our boys for seven months, and he adores them. We never expected to have any, see, we'd both left it late. He planned to leave the sea and stop at home, watch them grow up – but the war came and . . .' All the time she talked she unstrung bundles, tidied and stacked.

'I'd like to go back on deck,' Queenie said.

'Say goodbye to the old Rock *again*. Come on m'lads.' Mabs caught hold of her boys, one each hand and swung and jumped them along so they did not fall or step on other people's bedding. Many were of the same idea, there was a steady stream climbing back out of the hold.

'You won't want to do that many times wi' that arm.' A deckhand standing at the hatch top reached down, put a huge strong hand under Queenie's good armpit and helped her out on to the deck. 'Let's 'ope we don't hit any heavy weather.'

'You're right,' she said. 'Thanks.'

Laura's heart gave a jolt as they looked out over the Bay.

The ships she had seen from the cliff the night before, all seeming so casual at their various angles and anchorages, now had purpose, all faced out to sea, their funnels belching smoke. There was pattern, order and intention. Jamie had told her that in a convoy each ship had a place and had strictly to keep to that position. They didn't, he had said (though she had hardly believed it), even have to move out of their spot to pick up survivors, their own men or the enemy. He had also told her that the speed of any convoy was always the speed of the slowest vessel. Her gaze went doubtfully around the disparate collection of ships. She did not think they would be travelling very fast.

She had never imagined any of the things Jamie had said would ever greatly concern her. Now, part of a convoy about to leave the shelter of the Bay of Gibraltar with U-boats prowling, Vichy, German and Italian air forces waiting to strike, it seemed to be of most vital importance. She wondered if Mabs knew much from her husband about ships sailing in convoy.

She glanced at her mother supporting her arm on the ship's rail. She prayed for fine weather so they could spend their time on deck. She looked at the two boys, standing on the bottom rail, gazing with rapt attention at the sight of so many ships all moving together. How were they going to fare? She felt a terrible moment of pessimism, which she immediately tried to shake off, this was not her normal self at all. Make the best of everything, whenever it was possible, was the way her mother had taught her to be. For a long time she had thought all they were doing was following the old adage 'when the cat (in the shape of her father) is away, the mice will play' – mostly at pretending he did not exist and wasn't coming back. Now he wasn't going to reach them again – never would – she promised herself.

'We'll soon be outside the bay.' Even as Queenie made the remark the ship began to be lifted and dropped by larger waves. The boys were immediately aware of the change, looked up to see the adults' reaction, then grinned delightedly.

129

'We're second. Look!' Laura pointed to the boat in front of them. 'That's the first and we must be very important because we're number two ... in line,' she added, almost as if she could sense what Alec had in mind as he looked up at her.

'My dad's a sailor,' he said.

'Yes, and he's taking 'portant things like oil to ...' Ian looked up to his mother for guidance.

'To mummy,' Alec said triumphantly.

'To the motherland,' Mabs corrected. 'To England. Nearly right though.'

'I wonder how fast we shall be able to go?' Laura mused aloud.

'Ten to twelve knots,' the deckhand who had helped them up from the hold said as he stood behind them, 'that's after working on the engines, we limped into Gib at six knots.'

Laura had no idea how slow ten knots was but several nearby who seemed better informed drew in their breaths sharply and muttered between themselves.

One piece of information was followed by another as a long piercing whistle focused their attention on an announcement being made over a megaphone. 'Hatch covers will be fastened through the hours of darkness for your own safety.' There was a pause then the voice added, 'In the event of disaster you will be battened down.'

The shock of the last stark proclamation made Laura shiver as if the temperature dropped a dozen degrees and a silence full of imagined horrors fell over all those standing at the rails. Those still climbing out of the hatches seemed to scramble out with more alacrity, then stood around looking incredulously from one to another. The new fear was finally put into words by an outraged woman who declared, 'We won't have as much chance as the rats.'

There was an angry murmur of agreement, then Mabs brought a bit of sense back as she said, 'Neither will we be trampled to death trying to get up to the hatch if we know it's bolted.'

The deckhand who had already spoken to them gave her

a pat on the shoulder. 'We need a few more of your sort with a bit up here.' He tapped the side of his head.

Then Queenie, as if she had heard neither announcement nor the remarks murmured, 'My chap's still there.' She was gazing fixedly back at The Rock.

Laura thought, I suppose if we were sinking they'd let us out, and also that it was unlikely that Mabs would ever know that her mother's chap and her husband were different people.

'Mine's on Atlantic convoys,' Mabs said gazing out to the wide bright ocean, the way they were heading. 'On the high seas as they say.'

'Mine can't wait to be at sea.' She shyly extended her hand with the engagement ring. 'I'm hoping we're going to England and he'll still be there training at his shore base.'

'My what a ring!' Mabs exclaimed. 'I didn't think chaps bought rings like that nowadays.'

Queenie and Laura exchanged quick glances, another secret. 'This one does,' Queenie said sniffing away the threat of more tears.

'Are you better now?' a young voice asked from her feet.

'Oh! yes thank you, Alec.'

'Mummy, I want to ...' Ian was dancing about holding his crotch.

Inquiries were made and they were pointed towards a length of sacking hung over what looked like a separate compartment up a step. Laura led the way. 'I heard ...' she began lifting the sacking for Mabs to lead her boys through, then she turned back, hand over her mouth, suppressing the laughter, 'and it's true,' she said.

The seemingly unflappable Mabs followed her up the step and then stopped aghast at the sight of a long wooden plank slung out over the side with a row of circular holes cut in it – with nothing below, far, far, below but the blue sea. 'We can't surely ...' she began turning to Laura her face a comical study of consternation and disbelief.

Before she could recover the sacking was pulled aside

and a elderly man in a Sunday-best black suit was about to enter, but seeing the women there bowed himself back out. 'I beg your pardon,' he called, 'I will wait.'

The boys both pee-ed with great interest and concentration out down through the holes into the sea. Mabs looked at Laura, 'We'll all be hearing more from him later.' She jabbed a finger towards the top of Ian's head. 'He thinks about things for a time, then his tongue will wag.'

They left the breezy 'lavatories' and found several men waiting outside.

'All right for men,' Mabs said, 'they're used to going all together. I couldn't even go if someone came into the school lavs with me!'

They laughed but it was going to be a different matter when they had to use these facilities before night-time – then it was the communal buckets.

It was the buckets long before then because, as Mabs had predicted, some of the older men and women, many arthritic, could not be hauled up and down the steps every time they needed the lavatory. The heat of the hold began to take on its own particular aroma.

Their first meal aboard was sandwiches of bully beef served with plenty of strong sweet tea. Those wishing to heat food were shown the black iron ranges lashed to the deck rails and given the fuel. Initiations into the hardships of life aboard were immediate.

When night came and the women had settled themselves on their mattresses, and the boys were finally asleep, they were to watch Mabs perform her nightly hair routine. She carefully combed out her hair then, with large metal 'crocodile clips', trapped each wave on the top of her head, and with a mass of small metal rollers she rerolled all her ends.

'Do you manage to sleep in those?' Laura asked.

'The only time I don't put them in is when the old man's home – then I have them in during the daytime and take them out at night.' She made a cheeky click-clicking noise with her tongue.

Chapter Eleven

If Mabs's personal bag contained a large quantity of curlers and clips, Laura's held notepaper and notepad. To write to Jamie was part of her life, and not to be abandoned just because there was no chance of posting anything for the duration of this new sea trip. She made up her mind to keep a kind of diary of this latest journey – a log perhaps she should call it.

Laura's Log:
28–29 July 1940. Boarding and settling in on *5033 Ship M* as it is officially called, though once aboard it is quite clear to see the name *Dromore Castle* beneath the painting out. Love you.

Tuesday 30 July. The story of our chances should the worst happen has become an ongoing saga. It hasn't taken long for everyone to realise that there are in any event not enough lifeboats or life jackets for everyone. Even so Albert Young, the giant Tynesider with hands like hams, who helped Mother out of the hatch the first day, has become a regular acquaintance and he is quite sure we shall all arrive at our destination safely. When questioned about where this might be, or how long it will take, he just shakes his head. Mabs has been told by another seaman that there is a 'mixed crowd' on board, probably even a 'Fifth-columnist'. There are certainly some Czech soldiers. I presume these are going to join us in the fight against Hitler, Mussolini & Co. Keep safe my dearest.

31 July. Another beautiful blue day, quite out of sight of land now. We have decided to stop questioning Albert, it's not fair – and today he made me feel very ashamed. I stood looking at some of the other ships, many seem to have just one gun tacked on the front – sure that's not the proper terms – we have two or three along the sides, and I said sort of flippantly, 'A few guns and optimism, is that all we've got?' 'No,' he answered very quietly, 'there's faith in the good Lord.' I felt very humble, particularly when as we talked he told me he was reading the Bible – and he meant from beginning to end. He has nearly reached the end of the Old Testament.

Mabs's two boys came running up to him at that moment, hurling themselves at him, gripping a leg each. He's almost adopted them – entertains them whenever he has time. He took them off to help dole out our meagre ration of washing water. We get a kind of double scoopful each in the morning for washing ourselves – it about a quarter fills a bowl. Not a lot! Nor any privacy to use it. Tonight I think I should say 'God Bless You.'

1 August. Albert is not the only optimist on board, everyone who talks to the sailors comes back with the same message. They seem sure to a man we will reach our destination safely. I wonder if having faith is the only way you can stand life aboard such ships in such times – or at any time. Faith and the rum ration the crew get – spirits incorporeal and spirits bottled, they certainly need and deserve both.

These first few days out from Gibraltar have had an unreal quality for those of us who can climb the ladders and spend them on deck. The sun shines, the sea reflects the brilliant cloudless blue sky and it is a beautiful sight

134

to watch the ships all moving in concert. If it was not for the stern waves it would be possible to believe we were all standing perfectly still, so precisely are the convoy positions kept. Albert did confide that we are making big zig-zag movements out into the Atlantic to avoid U-boats. It doesn't look true and the war hardly seems real.

In the holds is a different matter, as Mabs predicted there are many elderly and sick who can't climb the ladders. Their relations and many other kind people take turns tending their needs, feeding, washing, emptying their slop buckets over the side.

Mabs and I have made friends with a Scotsman 'Jock' (what else) and he has begun rolling us a few cigarettes from the ship's supply of tobacco. When the smell below gets too bad we light up and blow the smoke around our little corner when we're confined to the holds. It makes the twins cough – well, all of us really – but it does help mask the smell of urine, sweat and sickness (and the latter has got worse since we've begun to experience a few real Atlantic rollers) that grows daily, or more particularly, nightly, below decks.

Jamie, not only is the stench awful, but we're all infested with fleas! We have rolled up stockings and padded the top of Mother's plaster. The thought of one getting down there . . . it also helps keep the edge of the plaster dry and from chafing. Now I know how those apes feel when they are scratching away, their mutual grooming procedures I could be envious of right now. Wish you were 'ere! Our fleas are big robust beasts which we're told breed in coal and in spite of the white-washing must still be living in all the crevices – or on us. The first I knew about them was big itchy spots all over my body. 'Orrible!

The ship is also overrun by cockroaches, bigger than any of us had seen on land, even in the Med. Many women screamed hysterically at first and the children picked up the habit – for a time but, as Albert says, 'You

135

can get used to anything in time.' I hope your Royal Navy run their ships in better order. I dread to think what other creatures lurk in the bottom of this ship – there's us of course! And none of this would matter if you were here.

2 August. I mentioned the sea was getting much rougher and now many more people are being seasick (we'll all three be expert smokers by the time we've reached wherever we are going). But worse happened this morning – very early, just before the hatch was opened to allow people to empty slop pails, the ship gave a tremendous lurch and our table slung on its wire cable slid to one side, toppled, then fell with a tremendous crash, spilling the contents of bowls on its top and pails underneath, as well as knocking over many standing nearby. The stench was indescribable. We got the twins topside as soon as the hatches were opened, where Albert thank goodness was on hand to take charge of them while we tried to clear up. Young Alec shouted down the hatch 'We're on water duty.' Someone shouted back 'What about an extra ration then?' 'Not on your Nellie!' pipes Alec.

Mabs went all prim and on her dignity wanting to know where a son of hers had picked up such an expression. Then not to be outdone Ian pulled Albert back to the opening and shouted down 'Nellie-belly!' Well his brother had got a laugh so you could hardly blame him. Then he spotted his mother making for the ladder and was off!

I thought that was going to be the only bright spot of the morning but then, in the midst of all the terrible cleaning up, I spotted a familiar back, then she turned round and it *was* Doris, my workmate, you remember, the lighthouse man's wife, from the Censorship Department. She asked about Mother and when I pointed to the far corner of the hold, she pointed to the opposite end. Obviously the reason we haven't seen each other before.

When I asked about her four little girls she pulled her mouth down at the corners. She says she worries about them all the time, particularly about the little one, Paddy, five, who tries to help her mother make porridge. But now their stove is useless. It's on the weather side and the spray just keeps putting it out. She's going to see if the cook will let her use his galley. No one else has tackled him but that won't put Doris off. I told her he's Portuguese but she says her sign language is good! It must be, because later I heard that Doris has become the 'self-inflicted' cook for their group, allowed to use the galley which, like the holds – but worse – is overrun with cockroaches. Her main problem is preventing them falling into her porridge and broth. Think I prefer our bully-beef sandwiches – monotonous but at least not boiled with beetles.

I realise I am never going to be able to post this to you – the censors would have a field day, so I am writing a 'postable' letter as well, and shall keep this log to give you when – and please soon SOON – I see you. I don't like to think about seeing you too much or the yearning becomes an unbearable pain. So, like your dear, dear, father advises, I find something to busy myself with. Not difficult with the twins around. Mother is having a field day; not having time to do her mending and darning before she sailed, Mabs brought all the sewing aids with her. Mother fell on it all as it if was manna from heaven and has developed a technique of holding the work in her plastered hand and working on it with the other – at arm's length. She says she can see it better anyway!

3 August. Saw our escorting destroyer really close up today for the first time. I thought destroyers were much bigger – or perhaps I just feel this one should be with all us lot to look after. One shepherd and too many straggling sheep. Albert says it takes twelve hours for it to make a circle all around this zig-zagging convoy, then he grinned and said 'So we have guns, optimism, faith *and* a destroyer.' Do you see a future for all four of us after the war – our parents and us? What a double loving we will have.

4 August. I was almost sharing Albert's optimism until we had some sort of an alert today. Lights were flashing signals from all over the convoy and obviously enemy action was expected any moment. Our guns were found to be jammed and the Czech soldiers were called out to put them right, which they did, and then manned them for the whole of the alert. We were all holding our breaths but just nothing happened except that we zig-zagged at much more regular intervals. I overheard one of the Czechs say, in perfect English, that it would have been a relief to have had something to shoot at – and I knew how he felt. Goodnight. God Bless. I shall pray 'For Those in Peril on the Sea' for the rest of my life.

5 August. Doris was busy on her girls' behalf again today. She was off to try to find someone to rootle out the children's warmer clothing from her tea chests in the baggage hold. Later I saw Beryl and Lorna in their Fair Isle jumpers skipping on the deck, the heaving motion of the deck just adds to their enjoyment, and with metal segs in their shoes they make a fine old clatter as they slide as well as skip. Another victory for Doris! Mother says you have to be a mother to know how to fight for your offspring, then she looked at me and said or a daughter who fights for her mother. We had a hug and stood with our arms around each other at the rails watching the children – most of whom in spite of everything are having a great time. They all have so many play-mates. Though I saw Doris's eldest, Marjorie, leaning over the rail all by herself just watching the sea. I remember Doris saying her eldest loved going up the lighthouse to her father and would spend hours on the outside gallery watching the ships go by. She seems a

138

more solitary child, like me. I feel very solitary without you.

6 August. It is colder, much colder. I keep wondering where we are. We seem to have crossed an awful lot of water. I would have expected to be at least in the Bay of Biscay (it's rough enough) or even in the English Channel by now. I may get used to being a sailor's wife – I will I promise – but I'll never make a sailor – dis ocean is jus *too* big.

Our little Alec is not enjoying himself at the moment, he has since midday lain in Mab's arms. I fetched one of our light blankets to wrap him in. Mother is putting spare socks over her hand, so stockings at the top, socks at the bottom. We're reserving our Pond's face cream for the sore spots around her plaster now.

7 August. Alec did not want to get up today at all, he's really feverish. Mabs won't leave him so we took Ian up on deck – but the weather is awful. Later Doris caused a sensation. It was just getting dusk and she was drinking a mug of cold tea, which an off-duty Welshman had just laced with a drop of rum, when we all saw a light flashing in the distance. 'That's Nantucket!' Doris declared confidently. The Welshman looked as if he had been shot. 'How the bloody hell do you know that?' he asked as soon as he recovered from the shock. She told him she had not been a lighthouse keeper's wife for so many years for nothing! But the thing was we all knew she must be right.

Later we were talking and some old boy who had been a geography teacher said Nantucket was an island between New York and Boston. So we have come right across the Atlantic. Is our destination Canada? Very mixed feelings about that – if you were there it would be a different matter. I must have looked devastated because Albert came and stood by my elbow and told me confidentially that sometimes convoys make a huge circle across the Atlantic to avoid the U-boats.

139

Alec is not so well. Albert came down into the hold this evening and put two fingers gently on the boy's forehead. He did not need to tell Mabs he was burning up. Then he pulled two oranges from his pocket. 'Squeeze the juice out for him, dilute it with water and add some of this.' He pulled a small packet of white powder from his other pocket. 'Glucose,' he said.

We managed to get Alec to swallow some of the sweet fruit drink, then turned the orange peel inside out for Ian to eat the pulp – too precious to waste. There are many children who have colds and chills, the change from heat to cold and so many of us sleeping together can't help. Albert says there is one little boy they are really worried about in another hold. Look after *yourself* dearest Jamie.

8 August. The weather gets rougher and it really is not safe to be on deck. The waves hit the ship with tremendous force. When we are in the holds it sounds like great steamhammers hitting the sides, deafening, makes the whole ship ring, then it shudders as the propeller lifts out of the water.

Alec is very unwell. Mabs went in search of help and found the invaluable Albert, who says there is a doctor in the convoy and they are thinking of trying to get him across to the *Dromore Castle* by breeches buoy, apparently the other little boy is giving serious cause for concern. I shall ask the doctor to look at Mother's arm when he arrives.

Albert came down to see Alec again and sat for a time between the two boys holding their hands. Ian sat looking very solemnly from one to the other and this time when Albert brought out another orange – his last – Ian would not eat the squeezed fruit. 'No,' he said, 'it's for Alec.' Self-sacrifice at four years of age. Children should be exempt from war.

9 August. The ship with the doctor aboard has been manoeuvred as close alongside as they dare and the breeches-buoy line shot across by rocket. We are all waiting anxiously for the doctor to come over. Watching the line which one moment is high above the sea, then dipping into it, I don't envy him.

We waited and waited, many struggling up to the deck to cling to the rails watching and waiting for the crossing to be attempted. It soon became clear that the doctor was not going to come. There was anger and many tears among those close to and so anxious for the little boy. Eventually the breeches-buoy line was cast off and hope of the doctor coming abandoned, at least for the time being.

10 August. The little boy in the other hold has died of pneumonia. Mabs is now in a dreadful state about Alec. Mother is helping care for him, keeping his lips moist with her fingertip and spooning water into his mouth whenever she can. Mabs replaces the blanket every time he throws it off. There is nothing more we can do – except pray. I hope Albert is praying because I feel his prayers would be more valid than mine, carry more weight with God. I feel God, like shopkeepers, should look after his regular customers. I seem to be a prayer-in-emergencies person. Mabs did not put a single curler in.

11 August. Today Colin Douglas Machen was buried at sea. It seemed terrible to me that I had not known his name until this moment. The captain made a dignified job of the service and the ship's carpenter had made up a small coffin. None of us will ever forget the moment when that box slid out from under the Union Jack and plummeted down, down into the tossing waves that seemed so eager to take it – and the flag that lay so flat, so soaked through by the spray on the empty board. Colin Douglas Machen, aged seven years, consigned to the deep.

12 August. Alec is much better, sitting up and taking notice. He even had a mouthful of bully beef and a drink of sweet tea. Mabs said 'Thank God!' Mother voiced what I thought, 'And God for Albert, his oranges and his glucose.'

And we have sighted *land*! Wales we're told.

An incorrigible Irishman offered to dry last-minute 'smalls' in the engine room, Doris (who else) availed herself of his generosity. Later on, holding up a pair of her bloomers, he shouted 'Here's your bloody knickers, ma'am.' Three weeks ago we might all have been shocked, but we have nearly forgotten what modesty is. Goodnight. I at last feel I am coming closer to you, my love.

13 August. Land! Land ho! We are constantly in sight of the green land of Wales. According to Albert we are steaming up the Swansea Roads and will dock in Cardiff probably tomorrow! None of us can really believe it. This evening we are anchored because there is an air raid going on, we think it is Cardiff that is being attacked. Even though this is so I know we shall all sleep soundly in our little corner tonight, after the anxiety about Alec, and the voyage, an air raid in the distance is small beer.

Oh! how I wish now that I could contact you, let you know where we are! Have you meet the *Dromore Castle*, be standing there resplendent in your naval uniform. I know, I know, that's all ridiculous – but we're all so excited to be actually arriving somewhere.

Chapter Twelve

Early the next morning everyone was roused and issued with a disc identifying them by the ship they had travelled on.

'Like cattle market labels,' Mabs said as she fastened one on each boy, then straightened quickly, ignoring the tugs on her skirt and the questions ready to burst from their lips. Queenie patted her own label as if proud of it and nodded to the pair, who immediately looked down at their own with new interest, comparing the message *5033 Ship M* and were satisfied that whatever this new activity might be they were included.

A good ploy, but Laura could imagine the faceless bureaucrats sitting in their offices devising schemes for dealing with these 'useless mouths' from Gibraltar. Such men dealt with problems not people, with logistics and statistics, not little boys with over-large labels on their chests. She found her mother looking at her and responded to her 'All right?' with a rueful smile and a nod.

Everything packed ready to go, once more they looked like an anonymous crowd of evacuees, or were they now refugees? Mabs had again strung herself around with her parcels, this time Laura knew the contents of each: boys' outer clothing; boys' underwear; boys' jackets; boys' story books with their board game, 'Snakes and Ladders' – and her bag of curlers. These had become a kind of yardstick of how things were going; ranging from none used, equalled total disaster; to all put into her light blonde hair with perfect symmetry, things were as well as they could be.

Leaving their infested mattresses behind, they began to move. Laura wasn't sure afterwards whether she heard the commands, or just followed the others, climbing out of the hold. Her mother, swinging her way up the ladder with one hand, bags slung around her neck, was an expert now.

Once on deck they looked around for Albert, anxious to say a proper goodbye. The decks were a packed throng of humanity, everyone slowly shuffling forward towards the gangways carrying, pushing, dragging their belongings. Below them on the dockside the first ones were already being directed out across the quay towards a huge shed into which they vanished. From above they looked like ants carrying great cumbersome loads to their nest. Laura remembered Casablanca, queuing all day waiting for something to happen, for someone to make a decision. At least the sun was not going to be a problem, she thought shivering slightly in the chill Welsh morning.

Then she saw Albert at the head of the gangway helping lift awkward baggage up and over rails. She dropped all her baggage as she reached him. 'I shall never forget you,' she told him holding out her hands. He took them both. 'Or me any of you,' he said as she stood on tiptoe to kiss his cheek, knowing his kindness and his mammoth task of Bible reading would always stay in her memory. 'Take care,' she heard her mother say as those behind began to shuffle more resolutely, as if to say 'get on, get on'. 'Thanks for all your help.' Mabs embraced him heartily. 'Sorry we were so much trouble. You'll probably be glad to have the coal back after us lot.'

He grinned. 'It doesn't have so much to say,' he said, as he picked up both the twins in his arms. 'Feel in my shirt pocket,' he told them. They dived and brought out two small hand-made yachts, complete with a sail on a mast that let down. 'A little parting present, so what about a kiss?'

The two boys now dived at his cheeks and clung to his neck. 'Right off you go, you're on shore duty now.' He put the boys down and turned hastily away to help haul the next baggage up and over on to the gangway. When they got to the quay they all turned back and waved. He returned the wave and nodded to them. Then his work and their journey went on, and all were aware that it was unlikely they would ever see each other again.

Once inside the huge shed they realised they were to be given some kind of medical. There were a number of tables set in an orderly row at the far side, with a white-coated doctor sitting on the one chair, a nurse standing by his side, all looking equally orderly.

Laura felt unreasonably resentful as they were all kept crushed to one side, herded together en masse, with a vast space between them and the line of pristine white beings.

'Looks like we've got to cross over to the other side, to the angels,' Mabs quipped.

Laura's resentment eased with a sudden snort of laughter, the comparison was so apt and how she warmed once more to Mabs and her sense of humour.

'That's if we pass the exam,' Queenie commented, supporting her plaster.

'Anything we've caught was on their blooming ships,' Mabs muttered as the waiting began to be irksome. She let the boys stoop down so they could 'sail' their boats on the floor, until they were eventually divided into groups in line with the distant tables. They were summoned over the divide one at a time by a perfunctory wave of the nurse's hand. They watched the procedure, a listen to the chest, a look in the ears and at the tongue, this appeared to be the cursory examination most received, but there were screens and some were directed to these and seen by yet another doctor. They could see that after their examination each person got yet another badge to stick on themselves.

When they reached the head of the queue Mabs took the two boys forward, then it was Queenie's turn – and Laura followed determined to draw attention to her mother's badly chafed wrist and shoulder.

'One at a time,' the brusque woman, who must have been a retired nurse by her appearance, for in spite of her white overall which she rounded out to capacity, the slash of scarlet red lipstick on her mouth – and teeth Laura noted as she bore down on her – no matron would have tolerated.

'I just want to make sure the doctor looks at my mother's arm,' she began.

'That is not our job,' the woman retorted and arms outstretched as if she were keeping a flock of geese at bay she advanced on Laura again. Beneath the nurse's flapping arms she noticed that the doctor never raised his eyes.

'Your mother will be referred if necessary when you reach your final destination.'

'Which will be when?' Laura demanded. 'I'm worried about the state of my mother's arm under the plaster.' She was worried about the unhealthy smell that was beginning to come from it and knew her mother was also aware of this.

'*I'll* ask the doctor,' Queenie reassured her, going forward to the doctor who was now drumming his finger-nails on the table.

Laura watched intently, as far as she could see her mother received exactly the same examination as the others.

'So what about my mother's arm? Do you think the plaster should come off?' she demanded as she reached the table.

The doctor's white moustache contracted as he pursed his lips. 'Aggression,' he said, 'will get you nowhere.'

'Oh, you're wrong!' she exclaimed. 'It was Hitler's aggression that's got me here!' Someone clapped, probably Mabs she thought.

'Would you like to go and queue at another table?' he asked still not deigning to look at her.

'I don't want to be here any more than . . .'

'My daughter,' Queenie's voice broke unexpectedly into

the exchange, 'has fought for me all her life, has saved my life, she is now concerned for my well-being. If you are a parent I'm sure you understand that.'

For a second he looked up, then his eyes hardened and he gestured curtly to his helper. 'Move on!' she tried her herding method with Queenie, who stood her ground.

'I'll just wait for my daughter,' she said.

Laura opened her mouth to continue the exchange but Queenie shook her head. 'Another few hours won't make a lot of difference.'

'We will know who to blame if it does.' Laura's examination was more cursory than most and at a nod from the doctor she was presented with a second label.

'So what's it say on your label?' Mabs asked satirically as they joined her. 'NAD – Naughty and Dangerous.'

Laura looked down at her label; it had got the letters 'NAD' on it. 'Nice Adorable Daughter,' Queenie suggested. 'Not All Delightful,' Laura said looking sourly back towards their nurse. Then they realised that not everyone received the same, some discs they noted bore the initials 'VD', 'TB' or just 'V'. The guessing game stopped as one woman went by in tears, these people were all kept to one side as the examinations went on. 'They must feel like lepers,' Queenie whispered.

'Don't feel too welcome myself,' Mabs said keeping the twins at arms' length from each other as they now attempted to stamp on each other's toes.

'Let me have Ian,' Laura said spotting Doris and her girls. 'I'll go and see if she has found out what NAD means.'

They watched her go, saw her nodding and smiling with Doris. 'You've got a daughter to be proud of.'

'No one knows how much,' Queenie said. 'While I have Laura I've got a friend and an ally. I just hope her fella is still here and they can get together before he has to go on active service.'

Mabs laughed. 'Some mothers would be hoping their

daughters kept out of the way of young men just off to war. Dangerous time with all those emotional separations.'

'I have no fears on that score,' Queenie said, but what she meant was that if Laura did get herself pregnant there would be no problem. Jamie's child, Freddie's grandchild, should it happen, would be welcome in or out of wedlock, though it would never do to say such an outrageous thing. Then watching Laura as she came back towards them smiling, obviously with the answer to the question, she felt her heart turn over at the thought of the pain and the heartache motherhood always brought in one form or another.

'NAD – no apparent disease,' Laura said.

'Well, thank the Lord for small mercies,' Mabs exclaimed, 'and it looks as if some of us are on the move again.'

'Anything you do not have immediate use for,' they were now told, 'will be taken straight to the railway station for you to pick up later.' Their journey would shortly continue to the familiar 'destination unknown'.

Laura wondered if you could be moved on all around the world 'destination unknown' and finish up where you started from.

Their baggage gone, they were led on foot to a nearby chapel. Here there were refreshments laid out, a really splendid tea, supplied by the ladies of the chapel. The long expressive 'Oooh!' from Ian had the ladies of the chapel laughing. 'Come you in then and tuck in my fine boyos. Twins?'

The ice broken it was a jolly meal, with such lovely fresh bread, cheese, cakes and tarts, arranged on snowy-white tablecloths with broad edges of hand crochet work. She exchanged glances with her mother who in turn nodded to the beautiful crockery the tables were embellished with, as if they were honoured guests, not very scruffy-feeling evacuees. They were hospitably pressed to eat as much as they could and the cups of hot strong tea flowed as fast as they could drink it.

After the meal she saw Doris light up a cigarette and be politely asked if she would mind going to smoke outside. Poor Doris looked mortified, Laura guessed she had forgotten they were in a chapel. She told Mabs and her mother she would take the boys outside to be with Doris. There was a square of grass to one side of the building.

Outside Doris was enjoying her cigarette and watching a boy of about ten kick a football around. 'Giv'us a game?' he asked the twins.

'He means would you like to play football with him,' Laura stooped to whisper.

They both immediately stripped off their jackets which pleased the young Welsh boy no end. 'M'name's Selwyn,' he said, then to Laura, 'if you play we can have sides. You take a little'un and I'll take another.'

'Right! You choose.'

'Not much in it is there,' the boy grinned. 'You'll do.' He tapped Alec on the shoulder. 'We all 'ave to play the same way and count the goals.'

Laura felt she definitely owed Selwyn. Kicking the ball between the goalposts he'd chalked on an outbuilding wall was very satisfying. She was almost guilty of hogging the ball, had to remember to give the twins a more than even chance. 'You're good,' Selwyn said. 'Wish you were on my side.' Then as she scored another goal there was applause, and she looked round to see that Mabs, Queenie and quite a few others had come out to enjoy the fresh air.

Laura declared herself exhausted but had hardly begun to get her breath back when they were all startled by the sound of a siren very close. Another air-raid warning, its loud and long, up and down wail going on and on, making hearts thump and the rush of adrenaline urge them either to flight or fight, but where to and who with?

'I'll have to go home now,' Selwyn said when the screaming whirr of the siren slowed, the pitch dropped and finally whined itself to silence. He stooped to retrieve his ball.

'Thanks for the game,' Alec said. 'Yeah! thanks,' Ian echoed.

'How many air raids do you have?' Queenie asked him.

'Oh, all the time,' he said, 'find some smashing bits of shrapnel.' He plunged his hand into his pocket and brought out a jagged and twisted piece of metal. 'Off a Heinkel bomber,' he said proudly. 'I pinch mam's Brasso and polish it.' Ian reached over and touched it then looked up into the boy's eyes as if he were seeing a God displaying the wonders of the world. Selwyn was so flattered he pushed his hand into his other pocket and brought out two smaller pieces of shrapnel and gave Ian and Alec one each. 'What do you say?' Mabs automatically prompted.

'Thank you very much,' Alec said, while Ian's breath was quite taken away by this latest gift.

'That'll take the linings out of their pockets,' Mabs added more realistically.

'They'll mend,' Queenie said as this latest friend left them strutting away, ball under arm.

The raid was distant, the far side of the city, but prolonged, making the raids they had suffered on The Rock seem like passing events. How much damage and how many casualties did raids of this proportion cause? The images of cars and houses reduced to meaningless piles, of children dusty and bleeding in their night clothes came flooding back, as did the return to the Valerio home; the cap and cane on the hall table; their flight, just as Jock Maclaren had planned – and the jeep.

It was late in the evening when the all clear finally sounded and ten o'clock before they were all aboard a train with a prepacked meal to sustain them – but for how long, and to where?

The train was crowded, in each compartment there was much moving up to accommodate everyone, older children were squashed in between adults, smaller children taken on to knees.

In the early part of the journey while Ian and Alec slept,

the women quietly discussed where they might be going. There was little else anyone could do as all the bulbs had been removed from the carriages; all that was seen as the night deepened was the passing shapes of houses, vast expanses of countryside and once searchlights in the distance.

'It has to be away from anywhere that might be bombed. They wouldn't send children into danger areas.' Queenie made Alec's head more comfortable as he lay across her lap. 'It wouldn't make sense ... not bringing us all the way from Gib.'

They agreed on this, ate the remains of their meals, dozed, and arrived at Paddington Station at two-thirty in the morning. London! So they would be moving on *again*. This could not be the end of their journey.

Laura lifted the leather strap and allowed the window to slide open shivering as the predawn chill swept into the compartment. Except for a solitary porter at one end and at the other, near the exit, a close huddle of two men and two women – obviously officials though not, it seemed, concerned with their arrival – the platform was empty.

The porter began to open the train doors, and the understanding that they all had to get off filtered along. Many children had to be woken, old people roused, stiff limbs eased into action again. She felt they emerged from the train looking a sorry lot. Their clothes had not been very special before, but after another thirty-two hours in them any sort of order had long since disappeared. At the far end of the train unseen hands were throwing their baggage out on to the platform where the original porter was struggling to load it on to a series of the station's handbarrows.

Most of the travellers looked and felt completely bewildered, and paid no more than fleeting attention to Ian as he pointed out a line of London buses, red double-deckers standing in the station forecourt. 'Like in my picture book!' he insisted. 'Are we going on the buses?'

There was more attention when the buses which they had

151

thought empty suddenly erupted with women and children, smartly uniformed schoolgirls, who all headed their way. They were so smart, so spick and span even at that hour of the morning, that many of the Gibraltarians moved aside, almost shrank back, to allow them uninterrupted passage to wherever they were going. The group of officials now came forward to usher this orderly crocodile of young ladies, from about eight to fifteen years of age all in grey skirts, blazers and hats, red blouses, badges and hat bands, on to the train they had just disembarked from. When this manoeuvre was complete, the Gibraltarians were ushered, in a rather more perfunctory manner, on to the buses the girls' school had just vacated.

'All change,' Mabs muttered, but they were so half stupefied by lack of sleep, lack of most things that made for civilised life, no one was able to put their doubts about this very odd situation into words. They followed instructions – and climbed bone-weary on to this next transport – ship, train, bus ...

Laura and her mother sat close behind Doris and another woman, whose tiredness seemed to disappear as they began to recognise places they both knew. 'Hyde Park,' 'Westminster! See!' They pointed to outlines familiar even to those who had never been to London before, and it was obvious they knew the capital well for they were soon intoning names of places that meant little to the others. Some of the districts they had heard of: Camberwell; Brixton; Dulwich; but not the one they finally announced 'Anerley', as their bus followed the others through huge wrought-iron gates set between high walls into parking spaces before a large building.

Prison was Laura's first thought, but as she saw the front of the extensive building she altered that to hospital, or convalescent home – or a school, a boarding school. Could it be the self-same school the orderly girls had come from to board their train? English children being taken out of London and ...

152

'They've brought us here just for a rest, a staging post,' her mother said as she helped Alec and Ian off the bus, encumbered as they were with small suitcases, boats and shrapnel.

Members of the Women's Voluntary Service in their dark green uniforms emerged from the main entrance and ushered them inside. In the elegant entrance hall, where a noble staircase swept elegantly up to the first floor, and where the polished wooden floor had been covered with matting, they were divided into groups of about twenty and given their own personal WVS lady they were told to follow. Their lady, Mrs Moss, was a homely body, apple-cheeked, and would have looked more at home wrist-deep in a bowl of flour in a Devon farm kitchen. She led them along corridors, past classrooms, a dining hall where tables were set and from which filtered the unfortunate but unmistakable smell of burnt porridge. Then upstairs, and they came to the dormitories, long rows of rather short beds from which they were invited to choose for their own.

'Oh! why didn't they leave us on The Rock,' wailed an elderly woman sitting on the edge of a bed, 'we could at least have been bombed in the comfort of our own homes.'

The more cheerful decided that proper beds, even short ones, were an improvement after mattresses on the floor of freight holds, and the view between the anti-blast tape on the windows was of extensive grounds. These optimists were silenced when they learned from Mrs Moss, as she helped them sort their beds and bedding, that their stay in the school might be 'lengthy'. They also learned that of other groups of Gibraltarians, 750 had been taken to a skating rink which had been converted into an evacuee centre.

'Not the Empress Hall?' one astonished Cockney woman asked.

'That's right, in Earls Court. They're having to manage on camp beds wedged in between the rows of tiered seating.'

'But that's got a bleeding glass roof!'

153

Mrs Moss's neck reddened to match her cheeks but she did not answer this point; neither did it help, as it never does for more than a moment or two, to know that some had fared worse than they were doing. They also learned that the residential school they had been brought to had been evacuated 'long since'. The straight and immediate swap they had suspected was apparently not the case.

The mood was now such that Laura felt they would have preferred it the other way, would have welcomed the last straw, the final insult to them as British evacuees from a British base put into a London school considered too dangerous for its regular residents. Instead, once more, they faced coming to terms with this latest communal billet, they had thought might be only very temporary. Many had even hoped they might at last find some privacy, even their own door to close on the world whenever they wished. Vain hope, and all their frustrations were suddenly played out by the normally placid Mabs.

'Open your hand, for goodness sake!' she said very loudly, for once really losing her patience with Ian as she struggled to remove his jacket, and he refused to unclench his fist so she could pull his arm through the sleeve. She repeated the order then, as he shook his head, she seized his fist and forced open his hand. He immediately began to cry, and Mabs to repent, as the piece of shrapnel he clutched cut into his palm. He changed it to his other hand and held out the injured one dramatically at full stretch, the blood dripping on to the bed cover. Mabs grabbed his hand and held it over the floor. 'You did it,' he accused.

A tall WVS officer of late middle age, with elegantly waved grey hair, had just walked into their dormitory and hurried over. 'Oh, dear, a wounded soldier.' She stooped over the hand. 'Never mind, old chap, we'll get a bandage and make you look like a hero.'

'She did it.' Ian made sure everyone knew the facts.

The officer looked up at Mabs and winked. 'Not enemy action then. I'll just get the first aid kit.'

Laura was to remember the roll of lint and a tin of Germolene in that first aid box later as her mother undressed and she saw how the top of her arm was rubbed raw. 'I'll go and see if I can find that WVS officer again and cadge some lint and cream.'

'Ask her when our luggage'll be here.' She acknowledged the call from further along the dormitory with a lift of her hand.

Laura found her working by herself in an office, she knocked and was beckoned in. 'Not more wounds?' she asked.

'I'm after a favour.'

Their WVS lady listened as she told her her worries about her mother's arm.

'Unfortunately, we've no doctor attending, just a district nurse tomorrow ...' she paused not needing to say that her concern would be head lice which had infested certainly all the children and many adults since confinement in the boat holds. 'But I can get what you need now.'

She went back to the dormitory with Laura and helped smear the pink tacky ointment around the top of the arm then tuck in a broad strip of lint. 'I'll be at another centre, but ask whoever comes tomorrow about taking your mother to a doctor or a hospital.' In answer to the inquiry about their luggage she said it should arrive anytime, she was surprised it had not already done so.

The next day Laura was to feel fobbed off, labelled as a nuisance if not a trouble-maker. The nurse who came was so elderly and so hot and bothered by the duties she had already to perform, it was impossible to distract her mind from the problem of the head lice. Laura then tried to intercept the new WVS officer, but her arrival coincided with the delivery of their baggage. The news spread and everyone converged around the entrance hall anxious to claim their long-awaited possessions. The situation was made more frantic because it was soon obvious that not all the luggage was there.

Laura abandoned her immediate quest to waylay the officer. She found and reclaimed their cases, then heaved them upstairs to their dormitory. Queenie's face lit up as she saw her coming. The cases were flung on to their beds and unstrapped and unlocked at once.

'Thank goodness!' Queenie exclaimed, 'now I'll be able to walk out and feel decent.' She picked out a dress and cardigan and clasped them to herself with one hand. 'Only needs pressing and ...' her voice dropped as she added, 'I must do something about this arm.' She wrinkled her nose in distaste as she turned her head towards the plaster.

'Tomorrow,' Laura decided at that instant, 'I shall take you to a doctor, a proper doctor. There must be one not too far away.'

She went immediately to approach the new WVS person in charge, but was told no one could leave the premises without permission, and that a system of passes was being organised and they must be patient.

'Your mother was seen by a doctor when she entered this country.' It was a parting shot as she left the office making Laura miss her stride. She considered going back, launching into a factual harangue, but decided it would not be a fruitful exchange, perhaps very much the opposite.

Queenie looked anxiously at her as she returned.

'We can go early tomorrow morning,' she reassured her. There was no way her mother was going to wait until some office somewhere sorted out rules and bits of paper to be handed to policemen on gates. They were not prisoners, they were British citizens evacuated for the convenience of the British war effort.

She did not sleep much that night as she hatched plans to leave the school the next morning. She even thought of rising and making them a kind of pass, she had enough experience of officialdom. She could creep to the school secretary's office being used by the WVS officers, write herself a pass, find a rubber stamp of some kind, smudge it sideways as she applied it so no one could read what it said.

156

It was planning such deceptions she finally fell asleep, waking to the certainty that bluff would be her best weapon.

Armed with their medical cards Laura led her mother to the front gates early the next morning while everyone else was busy having breakfast. She pulled open the huge gate and was confronted by a policeman but before he could speak she said, 'This is an emergency, I have to get to the nearest doctor's surgery, but I forget where they said it was, could you direct me?'

He looked down at Queenie's plastered arm.

'It's been encased too long they think, and what with the salt water and the fleas and cockroaches in the holds of the ships, well . . .'

The man straightened, swallowed. 'You should have passes.'

'They are not operational yet,' Laura said with a shrug, 'that's what I was told.'

The official-sounding jargon seemed to convince him and he took some trouble to direct them the shortest way.

The morning was fresh, sweet, a smell of grass probably cut the day before hung in the air, and traffic was background to bird song. Not the first impressions they expected from wartime London, and the roads they passed on the way to the surgery had names like jasmine, hawthorn, woodbine and laurel.

The surgery was in the converted front room of a large Georgian house and was full. People moved up to make room for them on the long upholstered benches lining the walls. They took note of all those who would be before them. In the two and half hours they had to wait Laura wondered whether they had yet been missed – escapees – though from what she was not sure, not the law surely. Queenie whispered the wish they had found time for something before they left, even if it had only been a cup of tea.

The doctor was a woman, her speech, like her short cropped grey hair, severe. She asked a lot of short sharp

157

questions, examined the top of the plaster, felt Queenie's hand, had her moving all her fingers and thumb separately, then agreed that yes it was time the plaster was removed. She wrote a note and directed them to the nearest hospital outpatients. 'Take the train, it'll be quicker.' She looked up, then seeing their expressions of doubt she tore a piece of paper from a notepad and drew them a map of how to get to the station, where to get off and a map from there to the hospital.

'Thanks so much, that is really kind,' Laura said, 'we'll find it now no problem.'

The doctor surveyed them once more, then with her pencil homed in on the map once more, making a dot that went through the paper. 'And when you get off the train, there is a small café where you can get a cup of tea and something to eat before you go and wait at the hospital. I use it myself sometimes when I'm on emergency standby at the hospital.' The smile she gave them transformed her face. 'Good luck!'

Neither of them had anticipated quite such a journey across London. When they reached the station it was crowded and when the train came in they found themselves almost bodily carried aboard by the crush. Workers, mostly boys and older men, but women of all ages, greeted friends and acquaintances, these were the regular travellers. Laura marvelled at their seeming cheerfulness. Then there were many men in uniforms of all ranks and nations, with bags, cases and kitbags helping to fill the corridors, even the spaces between the seats in the carriages, a swaying kaleidoscope of khakis, blues and mufti. An American army officer stood up to let Queenie sit down. Laura stood close, her eye immediately caught by the dark blue uniform of a naval officer standing in the corridor with his back to her, his brown hand gripping the window rail as he swayed to the gait of the noisy rattling train. She tried to remember what two gold rings around his sleeve meant.

Her heart began to thump stupidly as she stared at the

back of the man's neck. Of course it couldn't be, it really would be too great a coincidence, and wasn't his hair the wrong colour under his cap, and wasn't he too broad. Jamie was tall but ...

'Excuse me, miss,' an American voice said gently near her ear, so close his lips touched her hair, 'what's he got that I haven't?'

She swung round on her own leather thong to find her face inches from the American army officer. He gave her a captivating smile. 'I'm nearer for a start.'

'Perhaps,' she said with a grin, for like many a reasonably good-looking man the uniform added almost film-star glamour, and his transatlantic drawl was a real-life novelty, 'it's the naval uniform.' She raised her free hand to display her ring.

'He's a lucky guy,' the American said pulling a rueful face. Then as the train came to a jolting halt he, and the naval officer, who was not one bit like Jamie as he turned to alight, both joined the surge of people getting off. The American gave her an exaggerated salute from the platform as once more the doors were closed and the train jerked and rattled away.

They were more than grateful to find the small café the doctor had pinpointed on the map. It was crowded with a good many weary-looking people. 'They look as if they've all worked nights,' Queenie whispered as they sat down with tea, good hefty golden brown slices of toast and margarine and, as if in confirmation, the plump, brassy blonde Cockney buttering the toast asked, 'Wot's up, bleeding hospital canteen defunct agen?'

'S'right Mavis,' a young woman with what looked like a nurse's uniform under her coat agreed.

'Reckon they'll have to conscript somebody to look after that place,' Mavis added.

'And chain them to the counter,' someone else called, to which there were several humphs of ironic agreement.

Listening as they ate they began to have the feel of

159

Londoners in wartime – cheerful, ironic, soldiering on –
and then to see it, as they walked on to the hospital, past
sandbagged doorways, and statues, hoardings with posters
urging them: 'In the Blackout pause as you leave the
station's light' and women variously to: 'Join the Women's
Land Army'; 'Come into the Factories', or that 'London
Needs More Women Bus and Tram Conductors'.

'We should be able to find jobs,' Queenie said, 'we
shouldn't be "useless mouths" here for long.'

They walked in silence after that and Laura was beginning to wonder just what the posters had put into her
mother's mind. Then as they only had a road to cross to
reach the hospital, she had to grab her, snatch her back
from the path of a passing taxi.

'You're heading for the right place, missus!' the startled
driver jerked his thumb at the casualty department.

'Sorry,' she apologised both to the driver and to Laura.
'Sorry.' They gripped hands and crossed very circumspectly.
Laura did not speak, her heart was still thumping. The taxi
had reminded her of the jeep in the moment of alarm.

The casualty department was not in fact as crowded as
the doctor's waiting room had been, though busy enough.
They stood by the reception desk watching the coming and
going of nurses, doctors, porters wheeling trolley loads of
files or patients in wheelchairs or beds; there was no
mistaking that they were in a huge hospital.

Their details were handed to an attractive dark-haired
young nurse who told them, 'You're lucky, we have an
extra doctor in clinic today.'

This time the doctor was a young man. They both fleet-
ingly wondered why he was not in the forces – until before
he attempted to stand when he fished around under the desk
and brought out a crutch. It was soon clear that he was
struggling to acquire the skill of balancing himself so he
could use both hands to examine a patient in spite, Laura
thought, of echoes of great pain still marking his gaunt
face, his black-ringed eyes. He caught her glance of sympa-

thy and dismissed it with a half grin, half grimace. 'Always in the front row for things, me,' he said, 'others waited until Dunkirk!'

He asked Queenie to give his hand a good squeeze, 'as hard as you can,' then nodded as he made his decision. 'I'm sending you to the plaster department for this to come off, then I'll see you again when they've cleaned your arm up a bit.'

A combination of saw, huge shears and a lot of effort by a young nurse directed by an older one finally opened and removed the plaster. The older nurse supported Queenie's arm as the younger gently manoeuvred the spread-eagled plaster mould away.

'Good riddance to that,' Queenie breathed.

'We'll clean you up a bit,' the older woman said, 'then the doctor can see what he thinks, but I'll tell you now it'll hurt you more out of the plaster than it has in, for a time anyway. All the muscles that have done nothing will have to start working again. Can you lift your arm for me?'

'Ooh!' The cry was reaction to a maximum of effort with no more than a minimum of movement. 'I can hardly move it at all and look at my skin!'

The flesh was white and flaccid as if it had been deep under water for a long time. The smell too was of something very long neglected and unwashed. Queenie compared her two arms, one so much thinner and whiter, quite unlike the other browned by sea and sun, strengthened by doing so much extra work.

'Will it be all right?' Laura asked.

'You'll be amazed how quickly it will rejuvenate now the air can get to it.' The younger nurse brought cotton wool and a bowl of warm antiseptic water. She began to work very carefully but they both gasped as the skin began to scale off in large pieces, but soon they saw that underneath the skin was palest baby pink. The nurses smiled at the expressions of relief they both made at the sight of healthy new skin.

When they returned to the doctor, he was more concerned to find out if the healing of the bone was satisfactory and decided he would have an X-ray taken. It all took a long time: following the signs to another department, waiting there, waiting for the result of the X-ray, returning to the doctor. He took some time considering the plate then decided that the healing process was going well and was sufficiently far advanced to allow the arm to be left unplastered. 'But we'll get nurse to put your arm in a support and you should use the sling for another two to three weeks. Don't let your arm hang down unsupported if you can help it.'

As they left the hospital Queenie decided they should go back to the café and celebrate. 'They had egg and chips on the menu, with a bit of luck we won't be too late.'

All thoughts of their reception back at the centre were forgotten as first they anticipated then ate the delicious mound of crisp fat golden chips and two eggs each, with Queenie managing everything just with a fork. 'I feel like a new woman,' she announced as the last forkful disappeared. 'We'll have one more cup of tea, then we'll get back. They'll be wondering where we are.'

Laura reflected that her mother had no idea how true that might be, but she did not care. The arm had been attended to, whatever they said back at the school she could deal with.

Let in through the gates by the same policeman he asked Queenie, 'Get on all right did you, ma'am?'

'Better than I expected, thank the good Lord,' she replied.

'People been looking for you, miss,' he nodded to her, 'quite a few people from in 'ere,' he nodded towards the school building, then with a smile that broadened to a grin he added, 'and one from outside. Handsome chap in navy uniform.'

162

Chapter Thirteen

For a moment neither of them could see anything or anyone as they walked into the school foyer and passed from bright sunlight to shadow, then figures emerged, closed in on them, from two sides. From the office Mrs Moss came, her step irresolute, her face set into neutral mode, and behind her a tall elderly man, 'like a judge with the toothache' – a phrase she had heard Mabs use sprang to Laura's mind.

From the passage leading to the classrooms and stairs came Mabs herself, her walk very animated, lifting her arms in greeting, lips opening to pour out her greeting to them – until she too came in sight of Mrs Moss and the stern-looking man. Their attention was diverted back to the man as he asked abruptly, 'These are the persons?' and as Mrs Moss nodded he added, 'Would you both please come into the office, I need to talk to you.'

'And you are?' Queenie asked.

'My name is Mr Marsden. I'm from the Colonial Office.'

Laura glanced at Mabs who now stood so still, arms stiff and thrust out by her sides, as to look wooden, quite unnatural.

Something, Laura thought, has happened to Jamie, someone from the navy has come with news – but how would they know where we were? 'Mabs?' she appealed.

'No,' Mabs said shaking her head with hasty vehemence,

163

turning away, 'it's nothing. I'll see you in the dormitory later.'

'Will you come into the office,' Mr Marsden repeated in a manner which suggested he was not used to having to repeat an order.

Laura had to stop herself running after Mabs, very clearly there was *something* – but equally clearly it was not anything she wanted to tell in front of these officials. Reluctantly she followed her mother and hoped this interview would not take long.

While they were both invited to sit down and Mrs Moss ventured to ask after Queenie's arm, Mr Marsden stood with his hands behind his back, lifting his chin as if waiting for a prolonged chat rather than a single inquiry, to end.

Queenie nodded confirmation that the arm was all right.

'*This*,' he dropped the word with such weight they could have no doubt that what he had to say was official and would undoubtedly be acrimonious, 'unauthorised expedition has been viewed with extreme seriousness.'

'But ...' Laura began gesturing towards her mother's sling, 'this was a serious matter.'

'Your mother's condition was being monitored.'

'We had permission,' Queenie began, 'I was really worried about the state of my arm under the plaster, the hospital confirmed it was time the cast was taken off.'

'You did not have permission. There is to date no system of passes in operation at this centre.'

'We knew that, we told the policeman on the gate ...' she stopped, looked at her daughter and fell quiet.

'I have to tell you now,' he began, taking a few officious strides away from his point of oratory and back again, 'that if you take any further unsanctioned actions the Colonial Office will not be responsible for repatriating you to Gibraltar when the time comes.'

Queenie was silent as she wondered what this might mean to them in the future. Laura was silent because her mind was full of other questions, though she wondered

164

whether the man had consciously or unconsciously echoed Mr Chamberlain's word when he told the country that they were at war with Germany.

When neither women made any reply to what he obviously thought was a very damning sentence for misbehaviour, he waved a dismissive hand. 'That is all,' he said. 'I have other matters – of import – to deal with.'

'You have no other news for us?' Laura asked. 'There's nothing else?'

'You will be kept informed in the same way as everyone else as to your future here in England.'

Mrs Moss opened the door for them and nodded, lowering her brow at them as if to signal where her sympathies lay.

'Pompous oaf!' Laura muttered as they began the walk along the corridors.

'So we didn't have permission,' her mother said quietly, 'glad I didn't know.'

Laura thought that while her mother had learned to suffer and not strike back, she had learned more devious ways in order to protect her mother and herself – and the way the authorities were treating the Gibraltarians it might not be long before others broke 'the rules'.

'So glad it's done though.' Queenie held her arm with her free hand. 'But Mr Marsden, he obviously knows nothing about a naval officer calling.'

'No, but perhaps Mabs does,' Laura said.

'She does,' a voice said from the bottom of the stairs.

'Mabs! What is it? Is it Jamie?'

'Yes!' Mabs gave her a quick excited hug.

'He's not hurt, or . . .'

'No! No! He's fine,' she leaned forward and whispered, 'and he's not gone either. They told him to come back tomorrow – a man on leave before going on active service – but I've got him hidden in one of the groundsman's huts.'

Laura's mouth opened wide in astonished joyful disbelief. 'He's here! Mabs!' she exclaimed. 'Where?'

'I'll show you,' she breathed looking along the corridor

conspiratorially, 'but it's perhaps best if just the two of us go.'

'I'll go up. Go on,' Queenie urged, 'give him my love – ask for news of his father.'

Laura followed through a passage leading past the kitchens, out of a side door, along a narrow path under the outer wall. 'Good job the boys and I have been exploring,' Mabs whispered, 'or I would never have known about these sheds – or the overgrown side gate. I fetched him back in through that.'

At the next corner of the path she paused and indicated a line of three wooden store sheds. 'The last one in the far corner. Will you be able to find your way back?'

Laura nodded as Mabs gave her arm a final squeeze and whispered, 'So I'll make myself scarce.'

She was reminded of the moment Freddie had put his son's letter into her hand when they were shipped back to Gibraltar. It was both wanting to run, and wanting to savour every second. The first two sheds had heavy padlocks on them, but the third, much older, slightly ramshackle had only a hasp on a catch, no lock.

Her heart was beating so violently now it seemed to shake her whole body. She stumbled slightly as she reached the door, her hand going out to steady herself fell heavily on the wood – like a knock or a summons. She listened but there was nothing to be heard, she pulled the door open a slight creaking crack and whispered, 'Jamie! It's ...' before she could finish her sentence there was a slip, a slide, a resounding clatter from inside the shed, as things fell, then she heard a muffled voice.

'Laura! Oh, damn it!'

It sounded as if a great many more things were falling, but it *was* Jamie, without doubt it was Jamie, even the sounds of his impetuous battle with the continuing cascade could be no one else. She looked quickly around, but no one else was about, no one could be within earshot. She felt a nervous giggle threaten to become hysterical at the

166

thought of him being in this stupid hut, fighting gardening tools like Sancho Panza tilting at windmills. She pulled the sagging door wide, letting out a thick haze of dust, and across a fallen tangle of wooden-tined rakes, decrepit wheelbarrows, hay forks, broken plant pots, she saw him.

She stepped over into a gap in the jumble, stretched out her hands, reached wordlessly for him. He jumped recklessly over the debris his side and they had to cling to each other to balance in their tiny clearing. They held on for long silent minutes as if each was afraid the other might swirl away, be as insubstantial as the dust they had raised.

'I thought I'd never find you,' he gasped, kissing his way from brow, to cheek, to lips as if he still sought her, still must hurry. 'This is the third day of my leave,' he agonised. 'I've been everywhere – all over London. I was off to try to track down the surgery or the hospital you'd taken Queenie to, when your friend Mabs waylaid me.'

'Your leave . . . how long?' she asked, remembering with a pang that it was said to be the one question you should never ask when your man first came home on leave. She pressed her cheek up to his as if in apology. How warm his flesh was, how prickly his stubble. She swallowed hard, however long would be too short a time.

'Seven days,' he said, 'then I'm posted to my first real ship.'

'To sea,' she whispered remembering what Mabs had said, a man on leave before going into active service – seven days, three gone.

He didn't answer immediately, then he whispered back. 'Yes, so let's not waste any more time. I don't understand what's happening here, police on the gate, as if you're prisoners. Let's get out of here.'

'Let's,' she confirmed.

But before they could attempt to jump out of the debris that surrounded them so closely he suddenly gave a great gasp of joy. 'Laura,' he breathed and clasping her around the waist lifted her and turned in a slow wondering circle.

167

'It's really you,' he said and looked as if he might well break out into cheering.

'Really me.' She laughed remembering him beating his chest in the Main Street of Gibraltar. 'And you've got a tiny yellow and black spider on top of your cap.'

'What do I care, I've got my woman in my arms.'

He looked so directly and gallantly into her eyes, a wave of love engulfed her, swamped her senses, leaving her feeling much as she had had done the very first time she had met him, tongue-tied, awestruck – and as then willing him to understand how she was. Instead of words she self-consciously reached to the top of his cap and picked up the thread to which the tiny spider was still attached and holding out her arm watched as the thread lengthened until the spider touched down on the side of an upturned wheel-barrow. Then she began to brush the dust off his shoulders with gentle sensuous strokes and as she did so she looked down at him.

'You're a brazen hussy,' he accused gently as the brushing continued. 'All those days – and nights – wasted. Can you leave now?'

'I will leave now,' she promised herself and him, 'but I must go and tell Mother and Mabs that we're going.'

He lowered her to the floor, then leaping out of the shed door, he reached back and gave her such a lift as she jumped she fairly flew out. 'Shall I come with you to get your things?' he asked as he reached round and picked up a small case from the shed side.

'I think that would be a very bad idea, we're already in trouble with the Colonial Office.' She laughed at his surprised expression. 'I'll tell you all about it – and we've been to America, well to Nantucket Light.'

'*I'm* supposed to be the one in the navy,' he protested, then kissing her once more added, 'don't be long.'

She could hardly bear to go at all, looking back several times before she turned the corner, then she ran. Once inside she slipped off her shoes and ran in her stockinged feet, thankfully seeing no one but fellow evacuees who looked startled at her haste, but she waved cheerily to dispel any thoughts of trouble. In their dormitory both her mother and Mabs were waiting.

She quickly told them what she intended.

'No problem,' Mabs said, 'take one of the boy's little cases. It'll hold all you need – and just go. I'll make sure that side gate is open for you in four days' time. Though if these passes are not around by then I reckon they'll have a riot on their hands.'

She looked at her mother. 'Go on Laura, you made me take my chance, now you take yours. We'll deal with any trouble that crops up here.'

She stooped to kiss her mother, give Mabs a hug, then there was a flurry of finding clothes and packing the small case. 'I'll give you a tip,' Mabs said, 'turn that ring of yours round so it looks like a wedding ring, save a lot of questions.'

Laura blushed and glanced quickly at Queenie. 'Good idea,' her mother endorsed, 'did you remember to ask about Freddie?' then she laughed, 'of course you didn't.'

'I will though,' she said giving them both another kiss, 'I'll bring back all the news.'

When she got back to the shed the door was closed and Jamie stood waiting case in hand. He had brushed himself down and straightened his cap. She noted the thin gold band and circle decorating his sleeve, the same insignia on his epaulette. He was, she decided, far more handsome than *any* other man in uniform. She tossed back her head with pride, walked taller. His face was so tanned, he looked super fit – fighting fit was the epithet she regretted as it sprang to her mind. But it was, she reminded herself, what the country wanted, fighting fit men *and* women. There were the posters she and her mother had seen screaming appeals for women to release men for active service, 'wanted 200,000 women' one had proclaimed. Invasion here in England was, she had learned, as much a threat as it

169

had been to Gibraltar. The capitulation of France left the enemy on both doorsteps, the Mediterranean and the English Channel. If Jamie could fight so could she, for a moment she imagined them both posterlike striding together towards the bright light of Victory.

Then as she reached him and they clasped hands the war image faded, all she wanted was for them just to be together – no more separations – no lives spent apart, there had been too much of that already in their two families.

He led her to the spot where a great mass of ivy hung nearly to the ground. Bending double they came to the gate the twins had first found and later Mabs had prised open to let Jamie squeeze in. They emerged into a quiet avenue, both covered this time with bits of dead ivy and more dust.

'No one told me I should bring a clothes brush to elope with.'

'Elope?' she questioned as he took her arm and they began to walk towards the main thoroughfare. 'OK but where to?'

'Look,' he said, 'I have a bit of a confession to make. I had to take my sea chest north after I finished my training courses, so presumably I'll sail from up there, but ...' he paused and frowned a little then rushed on, 'a friend I've made used to work in London, but his wife's taken their children and gone back to her mother in Scotland for the duration. He's gone there for his leave.'

'So ...' she began speculating.

'He told me I could have his place ... if we want it. He told me where to find a key.'

'You mean a house ...'

'Well no, a cottage, he said, it's well south of London near the Downs. I'm not even sure we could get there tonight anyway.'

'A cottage. Oh! let's try shall we.' She was enraptured by the very idea of a cottage, and grasping his hand she ran a few steps ahead. 'Do let's try.'

170

'OK.' He grabbed her hand and ran her to the end of the avenue, hailing a passing taxi. 'Paddington as fast as you can.'

They climbed into the back, sat hand in hand and grinned at the ridiculousness of the driver cutting corners and weaving through traffic to catch a train of uncertain existence at an unknown time.

'Half fare for the forces,' the driver told them as he swung expertly into the station forecourt and flatly refused to take the offered shilling tip. 'No way, mate, least I can do for you chaps.'

'Thanks very much then, and good luck.'

'And good luck to you two. Don't do anything I wouldn't.'

'Wide scope then!' Jamie quipped and the driver went off roaring with laughter. 'Right,' he said turning to Laura, 'keep up the momentum, let's run see if there is a train.'

There was. 'In one hour and twenty minutes' time,' Jamie worked out.

'Just time for a cup of tea,' she responded pointing out the buffet.

'So tell me some of what's happened to you,' he said as he put down the tea in thick white cups and saucers and went back for fish-paste sandwiches. 'Well, at least the bread feels fresh,' he said.

'They'll taste wonderful, whatever,' she said, then they gripped hands under the table, drinking and eating with their free hands. 'I feel more liberated every second,' she said, 'free, just you and me, not hundreds of other people all crammed together whether we liked it or not. I'm here with you, just you, because I want to be. It's ...'

'Marvellous!'

The esoteric burst of laughter was noted at other tables, some turned to look, some smiled, others kept their eyes strictly averted from such public display.

Jamie told her of his training. 'Having been on the sea all my life helped. I've learnt the gunner's trade but naviga-

171

tion's my first love,' he said, then grinned at her and added, 'well, second.'

'In view of your great-great-grandfather I don't mind being second to the sea.'

'There's a lot of things I can't do with the sea.'

For a moment the remark and the way he looked at her, blatantly desiring her, confused her back into silence, freezing her every natural reaction, until he reached under the table and squeezed her knee. A blush swept up her neck and face, then she laughed at herself, began to tell him more details of the traumas of their return. Their sparse meal over, they sat on as she told more quietly of her father's action with the jeep, the death of his personal servant, the inquest – then of *his* father's protection and kindness, of Fatima and her brothers. 'I pray that family will all come through safely,' she ended.

Furious as he listened to the story of the attack in the street, and stricken as she told of her mother's hardships aboard the coaler with her heavily plastered arm, he asked, 'So this was the reason you said you were in trouble with the Colonial Office?'

'I took my mother to the hospital without permission. I honestly thought she might be in danger of losing her arm if it was neglected any longer.'

'Then you did right,' he affirmed. 'Surely they can't keep you all enclosed for the duration.'

'They'll have a riot on their hands if they do. Doris – you remember Doris from the lighthouse and her four daughters – Doris is up in arms because they say the children have to be taught by Gibraltarians inside the grounds, and of course all the teachers that came with us are Catholic. I don't think Doris will accept that for long.'

'Knowing Doris, no, there'll be a mass breakout,' he said, 'and you've led the way!'

She glanced at the huge station clock. 'We should go out on to the platform,' she said, 'stupid to miss the train after sitting here all this time.'

172

They travelled first class as was expected of a naval officer however new and junior. Their entry into the only compartment where they could see space hardly seemed welcome. They slid back the door to find there would be just room for the two of them facing each other if the senior officers already seated moved up a fraction.

Jamie saluted and led the way in. 'Room for you here I think, m'dear.' He settled her facing the engine, put their suitcases on the rack then looked quizzically at the space opposite. 'Will I get in there I wonder,' he asked of the *Daily Telegraph* which completely screened the occupant of the neighbouring section of seating. The paper was shaken irritably and a senior air force officer, with stiff grey tooth-brush moustache and crisp grizzled hair, regarded him without enthusiasm but moved up a fraction.

'Thank you, sir,' Jamie said saluting the newspaper which again concealed the face, and sat down opposite Laura, winking and stretching out his long legs so one brushed hers. Almost as if his neighbour saw he cleared his throat authoritatively. Jamie lengthened his face at her and she had to clench her teeth not to laugh. She caught the eye of an American officer sitting near the window; he shrugged his shoulders, grinned broadly then turned, still smiling, to look out of the window.

Before long Jamie cleared his throat. 'It's a bit stuffy in here,' he said. 'Shall we retreat to the corridor?'

The American gave a low impetuous guffaw, but as the *Daily Telegraph* was lowered as if to deal with children misbehaving at breakfast, he grimaced and returned to the view.

'They weren't all stuffy,' she said as they moved out of sight of the officers in their compartment.

At the end of the carriage there were people standing who had obviously come through from the third class which, glimpsed through the narrow swaying tunnel connecting the carriages, looked a packed mass of uniforms, kitbags and cases.

173

They leaned near a window, thrown against each other as the train swayed and rattled along, and when they could comfortably make themselves heard above the tiddle-dum, tiddle-dee racket of metal wheels over rails, they chatted – silly things to an outsider, important things to them, reliving precious moments, re-exploring and retying the knots of simple events they had shared. They recalled their tree, how it looked, how it clung to the edge of the cliff, about their ape and his favourite branch. '*He* could be a grandmother for all we know,' he said. She remembered the wonder of the whale, its huge water spout, sending rainbows over the sea, and the view of the harbour. She told him that she and her mother would both try to do some kind of war work, but as they touched on their future they fell silent.

The long summer evening was beginning to fade as they drew in to the station some halfway between Paddington and Plymouth on the northern edge of the South Downs. 'Are you sure this is right?' she asked as he collected their cases and the train drew in to a station, like so many others, awash with golden nasturtiums, pink geraniums and blue and red asters, but no name board so enemy spies or parachutists – or strangers in the area – had no chance of really knowing where they were.

'I tried to count the stops,' he said, 'but here's the porter, he'll tell us.'

He handed the two halves of their tickets to an elderly man with sharp, damson-dark eyes, and a stained railway waistcoat with a heavy silver metal watchchain looped across it. He took the tickets, glanced at them as Jamie asked 'We're right, aren't we?' He nodded and looked around the two as he closed the carriage door behind them and waved a green flag to the driver.

'Right!' he said. 'Who do you want?'

'Not so much who, it's my friend's cottage, his name's Duncan, Alistair Duncan. He said . . .'

'Honeysuckle Cottage,' the porter cut in and walked

174

ahead through the booking office to the street the other side. It was deserted, hazy with the last moments of the dying sun, warm, peaceful. Behind a row of cottages the Downs rose, capped with woods which were full-headed, dense, in full summer leaf. 'About a 150 yards up on your left, woods just at the back.'

'Thanks!' Jamie said.

'Pleasure,' he replied and threw him one up, a salute from old civilian to young naval officer, then bent to begin rolling two churns of milk through towards the platform. They began to walk away aware that however busy he appeared he was watching them go.

'I suppose he'd know Alistair well, he used the railway to go up to London.'

'I can't wait until we've shut the world out,' she said, 'the whole world. No one but you and me, no hold full or dormitory full of people, no sharing the toilets with hundreds of others, no washing in public, no bugs, no fleas, no ...'

'Well, we hope not.'

'... headlice.'

He pushed his hand under his cap and scratched vigorously. Then as the road went to the right and a lane veered off to the left he stopped and pointed, 'That must be it!'

The cottage standing back from the lane was thatched, the front garden was full of pink phlox, white branching daisies, sweet-smelling old moss roses and all around the front door on a wooden trellis was a mass of red-throated and yellow-blossomed honeysuckle.

'Honeysuckle Cottage, and,' she breathed in deeply, 'I can smell the honeysuckle from here.' She followed him quite enraptured as he pushed open the gate and led the way.

'Now,' he said 'third plant pot on the right, and ...' he stooped to slightly heel over a hefty plant pot a bit and feel underneath, 'here it is.' He produced a largish iron key. 'Bit like a church key,' he said.

The front door opened smoothly, but before she could follow him he stepped back out. 'Let's have a little cere-mony about this,' he said and sweeping her up into his arms he carried her across the threshold. Then kissed her before putting her down.

'Close it,' she said, 'close the door. No, let me ...' she wriggled out of his arms and with some theatrical show closed the door. Turning, she leaned back on it and experi-enced the sheer joy of privacy. She smiled blissfully at Jamie. 'You don't know what it means. Just to have a front door of our very own to close, even if it is only for a few days.'

He swore very gently under his breath. 'Don't look at me like that or I'll find hammer and nails and board it up.'

She reached for his hand and pulled him after her. 'Oh look!' she exclaimed pulling him into the kitchen. 'An Aga, a wood store, a huge dresser with,' she turned back to him, laughing, delighted, 'of course – blue and white willow pattern plates. What is the rhyme? "Two little blue birds flying up high ..." My mother would love this.' She rushed over to the brown stone sink and, hands on the edge, swung herself forward to peer out of the window. 'The garden's got all overgrown,' she turned back to him, 'my mother would like to get her hands on that too.' The sentence slowed to a stop as he just stood looking at her almost as if waiting his turn in this catalogue of discovery.

'It wouldn't mean anything if you were not here,' she said going slowly to him and lifting her arms to slip around his neck. 'I always want to talk at the wrong time.'

'Let's explore upstairs shall we?' he asked.

They made love in a room where the ceiling sloped low over their head and when they pushed the windows open the smell of the honeysuckle flooded the room, becoming more concentrated as the night air cooled trapping the hot scent of the vine near its source.

They slept and woke in the chill of early dawn, crept further under eiderdown and blankets and made love again,

176

enchanted by the act now not so fevered, Jamie more caring so at one moment she thought it was like being comforted and nursed, before being thrown to the lions of love. Only after this time they did not sleep. Jamie got up to go to the bathroom and she shivered in the bed, shivered lacking his warmth, shivered thinking of four days and three nights, of how quickly he would be gone. After such loving how would she bear another separation? She remembered stories of women who in olden times dressed like men and followed their husbands or lovers to the front. Then she found herself fretting because she could not remember the willow pattern story. 'A bridge ... and lovers,' she mouthed.

'You know I'm ravenous,' Jamie said when he came back, but she opened the bed for him and he climbed in, took her into her arms and warmed her with his body and his kisses.

'Are you hungry?' he asked.

'I don't think so,' she said and thought her voice would give her sudden melancholia away, that she might spoil this night when there were so few others. She nuzzled into his bare shoulder and repeated a muffled, 'I don't think so.'

'Do you think there's anything to eat anywhere?' he asked in a little while.

'Come on,' she said springing naked from the bed.

'Like Aphrodite from the waves,' he said as she reached down the woolly brown and mauve check dressing gowns that hung on the bedroom door and threw one to him.

Would have to do with the sea, of course, she thought, as pulling on a dressing gown she led the way downstairs. They reached the hall before she risked a light, then thinking there were no windows from hall to street, she found and flicked down a switch. Almost immediately they were startled by a thunderous knocking on the door. 'Put that light out!'

He dived at the switch and put it out.

'Sorry,' she said her heart still thumping as he drew the

door curtain over the small bull's eye glass she had forgotten. 'He must have been right outside. Never expected a warden round here.' She remembered the pounding on the door in Casablanca.

'We should though,' he answered from the kitchen where she could hear him drawing curtains, 'there's plenty of air activity all over the south and the Channel.' He put on the light, adding, 'It was irresponsible of us. They say the newspapers are calling it the Battle of Britain, the battle to stop Germany invading.'

'It was pretty irresponsible not to think of anything to eat,' she said peering into a container marked 'Bread' and another marked 'Biscuits'. Then she opened a cupboard, which again held only empty containers, biscuit tins preserved for storage. Then she hit gold. 'Tins!' she exclaimed. 'Some without labels – and a soup!' she exclaimed holding the tin aloft.

'Smashing!' he exclaimed, 'and I've found the tin opener.'

'Oxtail,' she told him, 'that'll be warming, and tomorrow we'll have to go shopping.'

'Shall I open any of these without labels?'

She shrugged. 'It might be wasteful.'

'Wait a minute, this one's got something scratched on the top. P it looks like. What do you think?'

'Peaches! Peas. Yes, it'll be peas.'

'No, it'll be peaches, on *such* a night as this, it will be peaches.'

'Or plums, they tin plums – or jam, the Americans bring jam into their PXs in tins so Mabs was saying.'

'I'm opening it,' Jamie said, using the tin opener, exclaiming with exaggerated joy as she stood stirring the soup over the small electric ring she had also found in a cupboard.

'What is it?' she asked. 'If it's peas they could go in the soup. We made all sorts of concoctions on the boat. Everything thrown in.'

178

'Well, you're not throwing these in.'

'What are they?'

He peered into the tin. 'They begin with P.'

'Pig's trotters or something equally revolting. I know, pilchards!'

He shook his head and when she came over and tried to see he held the tin high above his head. She stretched up to reach it, then saw liquid lapping over the edge down his fingers.

'Don't waste food,' she said sternly, 'we ...' she stopped short of telling him of their long day and night with only a sip of cocoa to warm their stomach. More juice trickled from the tin.

She tried to guess again. 'Is it fish, or vegetables, meat, or fruit?' she asked. Then decided, 'fruit,' as he licked his fingers very sensuously, very suggestively, 'definitely fruit,' then she burst into tears.

'I'm sorry, I'm sorry,' she grieved as he quietly put the tin down and came to her. 'Only it's all waste and pretend, isn't it. Lives wasted and us pretending ...'

He held her tight, almost to the point of stopping her breath. 'The important things are not pretend,' he told her. 'We love each other, that's real. We have a short time together this time – that's real – but we're hoping for a lot more. I found you again against all the odds ... that's real.'

She pressed her forehead hard into his shoulder, tongue-tied. 'I'm stupid – but it doesn't feel real – none of this. There must be something wrong with me. I can believe all the bad things, but the good things ...'

'Perhaps you just need more practice with the good things.'

'I couldn't even remember the story of the willow pattern plates, that's a love story.'

She was shaking in his arms like one overcome with shock or fever.

'Perhaps you will when we use the soup plates,' he said and took her over towards the dresser, reaching down two deep blue and white dishes. 'And while you do the soup, I'm going to light the Aga.'

'Do you know how?'

'Alistair's a very practical man, he gave me detailed instructions.'

She took the plates from him.

'All right now?' he asked. She nodded thinking about Freddie – do something practical, he said. She turned down the soup and balanced the plates on top of the saucepan to warm while Jamie opened the firebox of the stove, put in some crumpled newspaper, small sticks, then a couple of larger logs, lit it and when the flames began to take firm hold he gently pulled out the damper. The fire immediately began to roar up the chimney. He closed the door and the damper a little. 'See how it goes.' It was soon obvious it was going very well. He stoked up again and they began to revel in the warming kitchen.

She was bringing the steaming hot soup to the table when she remembered the other tin. 'What *is* in there?' she asked.

'Pears,' he said reaching down two smaller bowls.

Chapter Fourteen

They had walked to the highest point of the Downs they could see from the cottage, and sat down breathless and triumphant looking over rolling green, golden and brown countryside; pasture land near the tops, and lower, fields of tall golden wheat still bent to the breezes, this way and that, colours deepening in swathes then lifting and lightening.

Like fur stroked the wrong way, then smoothed, she thought.

Like the sea under a capricious wind, he thought.

On the wind too came the sound of machinery. Jamie stood up to try to locate it. He pointed it out to Laura who sat with her knees drawn up to her chin, arms clasped around her legs. 'There, look, a tractor with a cutter and binder.' He watched as the sails of the binder turned the wheat on to the blade of the cutter and behind the bound sheaves of corn emerged. 'They've begun harvesting,' he said needlessly, though he supposed he was trying to convince Laura and himself there was a continuity of sorts.

'And there's the flock of sheep we walked through,' she said pointing more directly in front of where they sat, 'and the shepherd who spoke to us.'

He could see the man standing with his jacket held over one shoulder, crook in his other hand. He raised his hand but the man was not looking.

'"Where sheep may safely graze". It's a hymn, or an

anthem, I think,' she said bouncing her chin on her knees. 'It all looks so timeless, so peaceful. So tiny and manageable.'

Like the squadron of fighter planes he remembered seeing, but not mentioning as they had walked to the village shop that morning, very high, climbing up into the sun. He had wondered if they were off to intercept the enemy, defending the coast. He thought of the quotation he had so proudly learned from the *Manual of Seamanship* early in his career. 'Remember that your life's vocation, deliberately chosen, is War: War as a means of Peace, but still War; and in singleness of purpose prepare for the time when the Defence of this Realm may come to be in your keeping.'

He knew the time had come, this time, these precious days and nights were his preparation.

She wondered if there were censorship departments in London, surely she would get war work there. They could get a reference from Gibraltar. She must do it straight away, leave herself no time to mope, to think and fear.

He also knew the posting he had been given would probably take his destroyer on convoy escort duty. Four, no five, days ago he had reported to the dockyard and had been directed to a destroyer in the throes of a refit. He had found his captain seething, and largely inaudible above the din, in what looked like the only untouched bit of his ship, his cabin. With signs and notes and bellowed greetings and goodbyes, he learned that neither he nor anyone else was wanted aboard for another seven days, when the chaos should be less and they could begin preparing her for sea.

'When we went to the shop this morning,' she said, taking egg and cress sandwiches out of the basket and the Thermos of tea, 'the woman behind the counter told me her sister lives in Dover and that there are planes shooting at each other, dog-fights, every day now. One Spitfire came down near her sister's house, she said it sounded like an express train rushing at her. She says it soon won't be safe to be picnicking out of doors any more,' she paused. 'She sounded quite alarmed. But even though we saw that squadron of fighters in the distance this morning, it just doesn't feel real to me.'

He wished he could say the same. Leaving the ship he had met the surgeon-lieutenant coming aboard. He already knew their new captain and 'liked the cut of his jib', mostly, it seemed, because he had already seen action, been blown from his bridge by a German mine and his ship lost. Of more importance to Jamie had been the information that he had survived several hours in the North Sea before being picked up by a trawler.

'But it does to you,' she added quietly still looking fixedly out over the Downs unsure whether he had heard her, he was so still. 'At some moments, like now, it feels as if you've already gone, that it is already happening to you.'

'I'm sorry,' he said pulling his mind back from the surgeon-lieutenant, who looked so worryingly young, to catch her last words. 'What were you saying? What's happening to me?'

'This is not working, is it?' she said gently and when he looked down at her with swift alarm she went on, 'I don't mean ... I mean it's not working our not talking to each other about what's really on our minds.'

'You were so upset the first night, I thought it was best not.'

'It had all happened so quickly – I couldn't come to terms with everything then.'

'And now we are trying to come to terms?' He wondered if it was possible.

'Yes, I think we're trying – but separately. We trying to save each other some kind of anguish by not talking, and it's ... terrible,' she said passionately. 'I don't even know what kind of ship you'll be sailing in, we haven't even talked about that. It could be an aircraft carrier, a submarine ...'

'A destroyer, been in cold storage since the end of the last war.'

'An old ship,' she said in horror.

He laughed. 'I've no fears on that score. She's better built than anything being made today. She'll stay afloat when others won't.'

'You sound very sure.' Laura looked at him askance.

'She's a grand old boat – a displacement of 1,500 tons, should be able to reach a speed of thirty-three knots and more.' He stopped himself adding that she had six torpedo tubes, four 4.7 inch guns and a complement of 150 officers and men.

'Right,' she said, 'so I needn't worry about you.'

'You better had, or I'll want to know the reason why.' There was no resonance in his voice as he evaded the real question.

She was silent, then sensed that if she let this moment go they might never approach the subject again, and the time would go by without the honesty between them, however harrowing, she knew they needed. 'So what are you afraid of?' She posed the question lightly, adding, 'You said you had no fears about your destroyer.'

He did not answer but sat down some arm's span away from her. Then, looking out into the far distance he said, 'Do you know what I'm really afraid of,' he paused because he felt to say it sounded ridiculous and he made excuses first. 'I think it's being born and having lived on the Med, but I'm afraid of really cold seas, the waters of the North Atlantic and above the Arctic Circle. Isn't that ridiculous?'

She watched him carefully, but he was very still.

'And you think sailing from the north means you'll be in those waters.'

'I do,' he said, 'from time to time we're bound to zig-zag north, I'm not afraid to go, it's just this stupid thought of being sunk in such waters. I think in a way it's just the thought of that first immersion, the breathtaking clamp of icy waters, so cold you can't draw a single breath – which, when you think of all the other things that can happen aboard ship, is pretty ridiculous.'

184

'I don't think so. Fears are personal things. The worst come from our pasts. I know mine always do.'

He was silent thinking about this. 'I do remember diving into a newly filled swimming pool and thinking it would be like the waters off shore at Gib, then really believing I was going to die, that I'd never get my breath again. Perhaps that's what's in my subconscious.'

He reached a hand out but she did not take it. 'It must be pretty easy to guess what my fear always is,' she began. 'When I couldn't remember the story of the willow pattern plates it worried me, then when I remembered it worried me more.' It was her turn to give a short humourless laugh.

'You didn't say you'd remembered.'

'No, there's a lot we haven't been saying to each other.'

'And the story of the plate?'

'It was about a beautiful Chinese girl who fell in love with one of her father's servants. She would not give him up so her father made her live on an island in the middle of one of his lakes. The servant went across the bridge to rescue the girl and run away with her, but the father saw them.' She stopped for a moment then added wistfully, 'so the three figures on the bridge are the two lovers running away together, and her father chasing them with a whip.'

'So your fear is . . .'

'Always that my father will catch up with us one day. Which,' she said turning her head on her knees to look at him and echo his words, 'is pretty illogical seeing all the other things that could happen to us in this war.'

They smiled at each other, then clasped hands over the dividing yard of grass. 'Like a sandwich?' she asked.

It was at suppertime when she was frying the last two of the few eggs the shop had let her have that the subject of fathers came up again.

'I had a letter from Pa just before I set out to try to find you,' he said, 'with instructions to let him know immediately I heard anything of you both.'

'And I was supposed to ask after him. Is he all right? I

mean, no more trouble from my father.'

'He's fine, but he says it's strange Maclaren seems to have quite disappeared from duty rosters, and he can't find out why.'

'Oh!' The thought of her father as a loose cannon anywhere was appalling. She lifted the frying pan as the eggs began to spit viciously. 'You don't think he's been sent back to this country?'

'Wouldn't have thought so. Most likely he's still on the Spanish border. It's all getting very fraught in the Med.'

'I suppose ...' she began then obliterated the people on the willow pattern plates with the fried eggs. 'Oh, don't let's talk about him. It's Freddie – tell me all you know so I can put Mother's mind at ease.'

'I should think Pa's about as safe as anyone else. If Spain keeps out of the war, Germany won't be able to invade Gibraltar, and the navy's always going to have a big presence at Gib.'

'And his work?' she queried, 'no more disruptions?'

'No problems. In fact his words were that it was "going well" and he'd soon be finished that particular MoD contract. I was wondering,' he added tentatively, 'if we should go back a day early so I could perhaps help you and your mother find somewhere to live, get you out of that school place before you think of work.'

'That would mean leaving tomorrow morning,' she said very quietly, 'that I really could not bear.'

They did not discuss leaving again and their last full day, a day of mellow heat reminding them that autumn was coming, they wandered around the garden. They picked late raspberries and loganberries from Alistair's neglected fruit cage, then blackberries from the field briars in the back hedge. Then found themselves tidying overgrown rambler roses, rooting out canes from the garden shed and tying up the heavy-headed hollyhocks. They even tidied the honey-suckle around the front door, weaving in the long shoots rather than cutting them off.

Jamie decided the one thing he still wanted to do was sample the beer at the local pub. 'Perhaps they might find us something for lunch,' he suggested.

They found the landlady, a plump overheated body, pulling a steady stream of beer into a variety of tankards, pewter, glass, pottery until, as she was filling one decorated with a pheasant's head, the tap hissed, fizzed foam and nothing else. 'That's it,' she said as she found space for the tankard on the tray, then topped it up from a jug which caught the drips from the tap.

'Are we unlucky?' Jamie asked.

'Got a dozen or more thirsty harvesters ordered these when they went up to the farm with the full wagons,' she told him, 'be back any minute. Regulars. Sorry 'bout that!'

'We were looking for something to eat and drink,' he said.

'Could do you cider and sandwiches,' she told them, 'if you don't mind waiting a few minutes while I get this lot sorted.' She nodded back to the road where, as if on cue, two wagons drew up, each pulled by a huge handsome black shire horse. 'There be a table out front if you want to enjoy the sun while you be waiting.'

'We'll be killed in the rush,' Jamie joked, for as soon as the wagons stopped a crowd of older men jumped agilely down and came flooding into the bar bringing with them the dry stalk smell of the harvest field mingled with the odour of hard honest work, and calling, 'Ready for us, Doris?'

The beer was quickly drunk while outside youths were busy taking buckets of water from the horse trough to the horses, unhooking one side of their bits so the animals could drink unimpeded. The boys in turn were brought out shandies and Vimtoes.

In no time it seemed the beer and pop was gone and the men back on the carts. 'That was quick,' Jamie said to one old man whose back was well bent but whose smile was broad, 'don't you eat?'

'Not much midday, can't stook with a full belly. We'll

do justice to a good meal when the sun's gone down.'

'Got to take advantage while this weather holds,' Jamie said.

'That's right.' He began to walk away then turned back and tipped his cap with his forefinger. 'Enjoy the rest of your leave, Lieutenant.'

'Come on, George!' came voices from the wagon, 'always gossiping.'

'So how did George know I was a lieutenant?' he asked as they watched the carts roll away and the landlady came back with loaded plates and mugs of cider.

'Oh, George, his son's porter at the station, he sees all the comings and goings.'

'His son ...' Jamie began and Laura saw a possible indiscretion coming.

She picked up a sandwich. 'This is wonderful.'

'Ham,' she was told, 'home cured – them's said as you were the sailor staying at the Duncans' place.'

'Final treat for us,' Laura told the older woman, 'we're away tomorrow.'

'Good luck to you both then,' she said giving them a passing rueful kind of smile.

When she had gone inside Jamie exclaimed, 'His son! That must make him ninety I should think.'

'At least!'

They ate, drank and giggled like hysterical children, reminding each other in whispers of the porter's looks, his watchchain, his waistcoat – 'he had the same sharp dark eyes though' – and didn't know when to stop.

'Know what I'd like to do now?' she said replete as much with suppressed laughter as food. 'I'd like to walk back to the cottage over that hill and through that wood.' She pointed to where the road ahead curved around the far side of their hill, which was three-quarters capped by woodland. 'Look, there is a path.'

'Hmm,' he contemplated the walk, 'it's a deal, as long as I can have a sleep under the trees at the top.'

They called their goodbyes and thanks, then unexpectedly Jamie turned back into the pub. 'Won't be a mo.' He came out smiling. 'I've left a drink behind the bar for George and son the next time the beer comes in.'

They walked hand in hand along the road, around the bottom curve of their hill, then turned through a gateway where a well-defined path was clearly to be seen running up into the wood.

They didn't talk now, there was no need, and there was no awkwardness, just each aware of the other's hand. From time to time one or the other gave a gentle squeeze and they would glance at each other and smile.

It was further to the wood than they had thought; the slowly rolling countryside made distances deceptive. By the time they reached the first shade of the trees Jamie wanted to sit down at once, but Laura was enraptured by the green shadiness.

'I've never been in a wood as big as this before. How quiet it is, even the birds.'

'I should think it's too hot for them to sing, they're having a siesta if they've any sense.'

'Come on,' she said, 'I'm not sitting down until we're right at the top of the hill.'

'How will you know?' he asked.

'Because I'll start going down again,' she called back.

Her voice already sounded distant, weaving between the tightly growing trees, all stretched up towards the light, but with many small saplings edging the path. With a sudden sense of panic he started after her. 'Wait!' he called.

He caught up with her as she stood quite still on the edge of what looked like a central growth of older trees. Huge, tall conifers, their branches unbrellaed so densely that the light filtered through only darkly and underneath mosses and ferns grew in great abundance. 'Isn't it strange,' she breathed, 'it's so cool, so still, so green, it's like being underwater.'

He suppressed a shudder. 'It's certainly ... well, cold.'

189

She wandered slowly on through the middle and he watched her go for a moment, wishing there was a way round he could take and that the words of the old psalm had not come into his mind. 'Yeah, though I walk through the valley of the shadow of death ...' He hurried after her but found the ground damp and slippery.

'Ugh!' he exclaimed in disgust, wiping the soles and sides of his shoes. 'I feel as if I walked through the Slough of Despond and the Forest of Despair,' he said.

'Well, we've come out the other side.'

He caught her hand and led her to the far side of the wood and they sat down at last overlooking the cottage. A sudden whining drone made them look up and search the sky. In the far distance what looked like a small swarm of bees drove around and into each other with some ferocity.

'A dog-fight,' Jamie said, then as two planes detached themselves from the main mêlée and came screaming towards them they sprang to their feet to see better as the two planes hurled themselves around the sky.

'It's one of ours – a Spitfire, and he's got Jerry on the run. Wow! Look at them go!'

The two planes climbed, then the Messerschmitt, trying to out-manoeuvre his pursuer, dived then turned and seemed about to get behind the Spitfire. But the Spitfire was too quick and followed him round on the same angle, as if stuck to his tail. They held their breaths as the Messerschmitt dived again, following the very contours of the Downs.

'He's gaining on him, you know.' Jamie clenched his fist as the Spitfire closed the gap between the two planes. 'Go on, now, let him have it.'

As if in answer they could hear the machine guns of the Spitfire; they waited for something to happen to the Messerschmitt, but it flew on, then disappeared over the rise of the next hill and, as the Spitfire followed so close on its tail, there seemed barely any sky between them. They stood motionless, waiting, searching the sky, then there was a tremendous impact and a sheet of flame followed by a pall of smoke from behind the hill. They held their breaths until, swirling up and up above their heads, came the Spitfire, circling for a moment then heading back towards the other planes still engaged in the distance.

The two of them stood and cheered and clapped.

'One to us,' Jamie said, and by tacit consent they began to walk back to the cottage, too excited now to sit and rest.

When the excitement died they moved, it seemed to Laura, with extra quietness through the evening towards the night, their last night. They ate sausages and jacket potatoes in the garden and drank a bottle of Alistair's wine, then sat on watching it grow dark. She wondered if they were moving slowly to make the time last longer; she smiled at Jamie in the dusk at the thought. She rose, took the crockery and the glasses inside, then came out and took his hand leading him towards the stairs.

'You,' he said, 'are a brazen hussy.'

She had laughed at the expression. 'You make it sound like a compliment.' Her laughter turned to tender sorrow as watching him undress she saw him fold his civilian trousers and place them in his case. He is already preparing to leave, his mind already turning to tomorrow, to what is ahead, she thought.

'I met our ship's doctor – briefly,' he said. 'He only looked a kid but he was off to find lodgings for his wife. She was going to stay nearby so they could be together as long as possible.'

'That sounds like a wonderful idea, but ...'

'No, I know, but I just thought if, in the future ...'

'Yes, of course,' she assured him, 'like a shot.'

The next morning, their last day, Laura was up early. She spent some time dusting and setting the place in order. She carefully polished a large studio portrait of Alistair and Fiona Duncan with their two little boys. 'Thanks for having us,' she whispered.

'What are you doing?'

She started, not having heard him coming. 'Saying thank you for the time we've been their guests.'

'Come here,' he said and they stood in each other's arms, very still, very aware that these could be their last private moments. 'At least for these days I have been truly thankful.'

'Amen,' she said quietly.

'Yes,' he said acknowledging it had sounded like a prayer, and even though she could see his case standing at the top of the stairs with his naval cap on top, his jacket hanging on the banisters, she smiled at him and hugged herself close to his crisp white shirt and the warmth of his body through it. 'We've become friends too, as well as lovers. Do you feel that?'

'Mates.' She nodded against his chest, then made herself let him go, or she felt she might never be able to.

They put the key back under the plant pot. 'Alistair said anytime . . .' he said as he straightened up.

'So we may be back.'

Collecting their cases they began the journey back to London. He had little time and she crossed London with him to Euston for his train north. Their last embrace on the platform was swift; time was short and that was merciful. He looked at her quickly for reassurance, a last glance of intense questioning. She held her breath, lips tight, and nodded. He turned and boarded his train. Only as it pulled away did she let out her breath in a great gasp of pain.

Chapter Fifteen

She felt quite unreal, like a kite cut loose, staggering about the sky, free to float or sink with every breeze that might touch it – undirected, a crazy thing without a guiding hand.

She saw people going into the buffet and, following them automatically to the counter, bought herself a cup of tea, then sat staring hard into her cup, feeling screened by the rising steam, remembering sitting in Paddington station's buffet as they waited for the train to take them to the cottage, and Jamie's audacious squeeze of her knee. Audacious, he was; ardent, he was, but he was also so much dearer to her now she knew his quieter side, the one with fears – the one that must have taken him tumbling into his father's huge bed as a boy. She would be able to find the right words to tell him all this in her letters. She would say that absolute perfection in all things would be difficult to live with permanently. Permanently? Would life with him go as quickly as their time at the cottage, that had passed in the twinkling of an eye? If they were lucky enough, if both survived ...

The tea nearly gone and the steam clearing she became aware of a small family party looking at the three empty chairs at her table: a middle-aged woman, a soldier, her son undoubtedly for he resembled her, and a younger boy who was carrying an army kitbag.

'I'm just going,' she told them.

193

'You don't mind then?' the woman asked touching the top of one of the chairs.

'Of course not.'

'My brother's kitbag,' the boy said toppling it carefully from his shoulder, manoeuvring it to stand by the seat he took.

She exchanged a rueful smile with the mother. 'I've just seen my fiancé off, he's in the navy.'

'Not easy, is it?'

'I shall go when I'm old enough,' the boy told his mother.

'Sit down, and be quiet,' she told him, then looking back at Laura added, 'all the luck in the world, love.'

'And to you and yours,' she replied as she left them. She certainly wasn't going to be alone in her sorrows, no one would be in this war.

Once she was on the move again and having to take note of where she was going, she thought her return journey was into a very different London. Then she realised that the change was in herself. As the girls in the Gibraltar Censorship Department had often told her 'when your chap's about you've eyes for nothing and nobody else'.

Travelling alone she was aware of seeing, for the first time in England, the aftermath of the bombs. There was debris as there had been on Gib, but the people she found amazing. At a bus stop she saw a city-dressed gentleman display the headlines of his newspaper to his elderly neighbour in the queue.

'It's like the football league, we've reached the final now,' he said. 'We're out on our own.'

'Bloody right,' the Cockney replied, 'an' I'll tell you something for nothing. We're playing at home, on our own ground!'

The two enjoyed the aptness of their joke as did those around. The Cockney caught sight of her solemn face. 'Don't worry, love, it may never happen,' he told her.

She felt awed by the ease with which these Londoners

thought of the escalating seriousness of the war in terms of the games they played, particularly when she also saw a news placard: 'Seventy-eight to twenty-six. England still batting.' She had no idea what the figures meant, unless it was our planes lost and German planes shot down. It seemed so many, yet it must be that; she wished she knew which figure was for their side. She remembered the aerial battle they had seen only yesterday. She and Jamie had leapt to their feet and cheered – just as if it had been a game.

By the time she had travelled by tube, bus and a fair amount of walking to reach their billet she was determined that it was a game she was going to get into as soon as possible and help win. The nearer she came to the school the more her first resolve became focused on walking up to the main gates. There was no way she was going to sneak back in by the side gate like some wrongdoer. Neither did she intend to take any kind of a lecture from Mr Marsden of the Colonial Office. She could imagine how he would enjoy strutting up and down, hands clasped behind his back, 'dealing' with her 'totally unauthorised absence'. Her *second* unauthorised outing. She would have news for him, because unless they locked her up she did not intend to stay confined behind walls when there was a war to be won. She wondered whether it was possible for both her and her mother to go north, find work there? Though Jamie had said it didn't always follow that where a ship was refitted it would be based there once the sea trials had been done. Some on his course had been sent to Portsmouth.

Back like a ramrod, case firmly in hand, she approached the main school gates at something like a march. The policeman straightened up as he saw her coming, and as she got nearer he seemed to look her up and down and appraise her in some detail. Then he saluted and said, 'Afternoon, miss,' and opened the gate for her.

It was the attaché case, she thought. He must think I'm official. She inclined her head a fraction, unable to believe quite this much luck, and went inside feeling as if she had shoulder-charged a door that had been already open.

Inside the school was very quiet, there was no one in the foyer. Then she realised the classes for the children must have started, for in the distance she could hear the unmistakable raised voice of someone teaching, emphasising a series of points to a class.

She glimpsed one or two women at the far end of the dining room talking quietly as they finished clearing away after the midday meal. Upstairs there was no one in the dormitory. She surveyed the long lines of beds with dismay, and tried not to think of the double bed with its puffy aquamarine silk eiderdown and counterpane, the pretty floral curtains – the privacy – Jamie.

All the windows in the dormitory stood open and she could see little groups of evacuees standing and sitting around talking, enjoying the sunshine. She put her case on her bed and noted that her mother's, Mabs's and the boys' things were all still in the same places.

She walked out along the passage Mabs had taken to the groundsmen's sheds, but pulling open the door came abruptly upon Mrs Moss, the WVS lady attempting to push her way in. She was carrying a sleeping baby. In spite of her resolve not to be overawed by anyone in authority, Laura's heart gave a little skip of alarm at this unexpected encounter.

'Hello,' Mrs Moss greeted her, laughing as they had to manoeuvre round each other in the doorway, 'I'm pleased your mother's looking so much better. We've got another casualty now. This one's mum has gone and scalded her hand.'

'Oh, I'm sorry, is there anything I can do?' she heard herself ask.

'You couldn't just hold him for a few minutes, could you? I've got some grocery returns to finish – take me about half an hour.'

'Can I take him back outside?' she asked as the baby was

transferred to her arms. Was it possible she wondered, that this particular WVS lady had not heard of her absence? Or was she providing her with some kind of cover to return to the fold? She glanced at the round face glowing as if from some energetic baking session and could not believe her capable of such conspiracies. She might be friendly but she would never fly in the face of such as Mr Marsden.

She walked away with Mrs Moss's thanks and assurances she would be as quick as possible. She left the path towards the sheds on her right and continued towards the playing fields and tennis courts. The baby was robust, heavy and stirring to wakefulness. She was not sure who was the most surprised as she came upon her mother encouraging Mabs who was playing tennis with great gusto and little skill.

'Laura? How did you get back in?' Her mother looked at once delighted, then aghast at the baby, 'but what's this?'

'I just squared my shoulders and walked up to the gate. The policeman wished me good afternoon and opened the gate for me, and,' she looked down at the baby now blinking his eyes and stretching in her arms, 'Mrs Moss asked me to hold him for a bit ... I ... she didn't seem to know I've been away. Is everything all right?'

'Hey!' Mabs shouted from the court and came running up to the netting, curling her fingers through the mesh. 'That was quick work!'

Laura began to explain again, but Mabs laughed. 'I know whose baby it is.'

'What I don't understand is why Mrs Moss didn't march me straight off to the office?'

'Because ...' Mabs began, then said, 'no, wait a minute.' She hailed a young woman to come and take over the racket and the game.

'He's gone back then?' Queenie asked quietly.

She looked soulfully into her mother's eyes and compressed her lips, nodded quickly several times.

Queenie squeezed her arm.

'I'll be all right,' she reassured her, 'and you do look better.'

'Knowing my arm's OK has made the difference, that and getting outside in the sun . . .'

'And all the excitement we've been having.' Mabs came rushing at her, kissing both her and the startled baby on his forehead. 'Come here, let me have him.' She took the baby and led them to a grassy bank in the shade. 'Let's sit down.'

'What excitement?' Laura asked.

'No, you first,' Mabs exclaimed. 'How's it been?'

Laura leaned back on her arms and lifted her face to look up into the leaves of the trees.

'That good?' Mabs said quietly.

'That good, wonderful, marvellous – and I never wanted it to end,' then prompted by the word she sat up and told her mother, 'and Freddie's fine, his work's going really well now. Jamie had a letter just before he found us.'

She saw the pleasure in her mother's eyes replaced with caution as Freddie's work was mentioned, but she would tell what little more she knew when they were alone.

'Where did you stay?' Mabs wanted to know.

The description of the cottage held both spellbound. 'A whole house to yourselves,' Mabs said wistfully. 'It sounds more like the kind of place we should all be in, there's more air raids here every day.'

'We saw a dog-fight,' Laura said, 'but there's so much I need to know. First of all, why haven't I been run in by the Colonial Office?'

'Because . . .' it was her mother who took up this story and enjoyed the telling of it, taking her time, adding to the suspense. 'Because . . . no one knows you've been gone, well, no one outside the dormitory, and I don't think all of them guessed.'

'But?'

'We've taken turns sleeping in your bed, and sitting at your seat in the dining room, so the same seat and bed were

198

not always empty. There are always people wandering about and it was never questioned. Our only worry was how you were going to get back in.'

'And whether you would get back before we all broke out,' Mabs added.

'What do you mean?'

There was a general settling down, Mabs putting the baby on the grass, dangling and slowly twirling a leafy twig above him so he kicked out and tried to reach up to it. 'People are getting really restless, many have got relations or friends they could go to if they were allowed. Doris in particular is determined to go to her family's home in Northfields. I think she'll slip away as soon as she has the chance.'

'I understand she's written to the Colonial Secretary for Gibraltar whom she knows personally,' Queenie added, 'asking about this threat not to repatriate us if we don't do as we're told.'

'And?'

'I know no more, presumably if Doris goes then we'll know she's been reassured about it.'

'If Doris goes I think there'll be a mass exodus,' Mabs said, then nodded at Laura again, 'particularly you, now you've had a taste of privacy.'

'Many a true word . . .' Laura said.

'There is some talk of passes,' Queenie said.

'There's *some talk* of us being sent to the West Indies,' Mabs said. 'I've heard it several times and I tackled our Mrs Moss, she'd obviously heard something but was under instructions not to talk about it.'

The thought of another sea voyage after the one they had just suffered was appalling. 'We must all refuse to go,' Queenie said quietly.

The rumours occupied their minds until, with the baby restored to Mrs Moss and Mabs off to supervise the boys' tea after classes, Laura and her mother walked away from the general movement towards the buildings to make time just for themselves.

'So you didn't have to turn your ring around,' Queenie said, 'pretend it was a wedding ring.'

'I'm not sure mothers and daughters are supposed to have this kind of conversation,' Laura said with a grin.

'No,' she agreed, 'but then we've shared a lot no mother or daughter ought to have ...' she paused as if reluctant to say the word, 'suffered.'

Laura caught her hand and held it. 'Not any more, Mum,' she vowed, 'no more bad times with my father. He's out of our lives. Finished. Kaput!'

'But I worry about Freddie. What did he say about his work? Has there been any more trouble, any more sabotage?'

She told her mother all Jamie's news, her mother stopped walking, let her breath out in a great sigh. 'So no one knows just where he is. I'm not sure which is worse, knowing or not knowing.'

'He's a long way away, that's all we need to know for now.'

'He'll turn up again,' Queenie said with quiet certainty. 'I don't believe I'll ever really be free of him in this life.'

'You're free of him now,' she insisted, but remembered how her own heart had plummeted when she had merely recalled the story of the father with the whip on the willow pattern plate. She had to draw in a deep steadying breath to continue. 'If Doris does go then we'll take it that the authorities won't penalise any of us, and we'll go too.' She did not specify where. 'Do our bit. We won't be "useless mouths".'

'That would be good,' Queenie reflected, 'to be doing, rather than being done to.'

The next morning Laura was passing one of the classrooms and saw a school atlas on one of the desks. She was looking to see exactly where Portsmouth, the Firth of Clyde and Liverpool were, and other places Jamie had mentioned, like Scapa Flow, when someone called her from the doorway.

'Mrs Moss,' she exclaimed, 'I was just . . .'

'I've come to tell you the passes have arrived,' she bustled into the classroom full of enthusiasm. 'From Monday you'll be able to go out. There'll be a man on the gate, you'll have to fill a form in, he'll give you a pass. When you come back you hand the pass back in to him.'

'Oh!' She gave the woman a swift hug. 'That's wonderful.'

'Let everyone know for me will you,' she said. 'There's going to be a notice put up, but . . .' she pulled a face at that formality.

The procedure was exactly as Mrs Moss had described it and with their first passes in their hands Queenie wondered if Laura would insist on them staying together. She had an idea she badly wanted to explore on her own.

When she tentatively suggested that Laura should go off to find the Censorship Department and leave her to have a general look around, then they could meet up at the café near the hospital for a snack, Laura had, she thought, looked almost relieved. She reminded herself that even devoted daughters didn't always want their mothers around, and she would have found it difficult to have explained her own intentions.

Her plan was vague to say the least and had been triggered only by listening to other people's conversation when they were last in that same café. It was just something she felt called to do.

But first she had to make her way back to the hospital. She went to general reception, and was greeted with some enthusiasm when she told them what she had in mind. 'Can you wait *now*?' the woman with the knife-edged waves of a recent perm in her blonde hair asked with some eagerness. 'I'm sure one of the administrators would be only too pleased to see you.'

'Of course,' she said and sat contemplating the fact that this was the first real job she had ever applied for. She was almost put off by the enthusiasm of the receptionist. She watched the constant bustle of people, white-coated doctors, stiffly uniformed nurses, the general public coming in looking worried: a fireman in dusty uniform with a bloody bandage pressed to his temple; several children looking distressed and terribly pale; harassed mothers and grandmothers. What on earth was she doing there? What made her think she could do anything to help in such a place? She rose slowly to her feet.

'Mrs Maclaren?' the receptionist called startling her, 'our Miss Chandler will see you now.' She beckoned Queenie to the counter, then lifted a flap to usher her through, indicating an office door at the back. 'Go straight in,' she was told with a beaming smile.

Miss Chandler, a small neat little woman, with greying hair but the figure of an athletic schoolgirl and enthusiastic eyes, rose to meet her.

'My dear Mrs Maclaren,' she said, 'do sit down. I can't believe what our receptionist has just told me. You're applying to run our staff canteen – though canteen is an embellishment.'

'I've no qualifications for anything ... at all ... really. In fact ...' Queenie stopped, overwhelmed by all the reasons she could think of for not being in this woman's office applying for a job in England. 'I suppose,' she said lamely clutching her handbag tighter in preparation for leaving, 'I've done this all wrong?'

'Carry on from "in fact",' Miss Chandler prompted gently.

She listened carefully and patiently, then rose from her desk. 'I think before we go any further you should see exactly what it is you are offering to do.'

Queenie followed her through the reception area to the far side, put off rather than encouraged as the blonde receptionist gave her a wave. They went through a swing door and down two flights of stone stairs. This she quickly realised was not an area where the general public were permitted. The corridors were lined with store rooms and the only people they met were porters pushing trolleys with oxygen cylinders, clerks with bundles of files, doctors, nurses.

'Our canteen had to be moved after we suffered bomb damage and we needed extra space for surgical cases,' Miss Chandler turned to tell her, 'there just was nowhere else. This way.' She held open another door for Queenie who had begun to feel wherever she was going was in the bowels of the earth as she passed doors marked 'Boiler Rooms. Danger No Unauthorised Admittance'.

The corridor got narrower but there was a man white-washing the walls which were of rough brick. Miss Chandler suddenly stood aside, having to squash herself against the wall for Queenie to pass. 'Welcome to the staff canteen,' she said.

The room was divided by a series of upright steel girders, and encumbered by a large number of bentwood chairs scattered all around, some few of these containing resigned-looking staff drinking cups of tea. The counter was a trestle table placed in front of a galley-like space, behind which was a broad shelf holding an urn, a teapot, cups and saucers and a toaster – but there was no assistant behind the counter.

Queenie was aware Miss Chandler was watching her closely, while she in turn was peering into the far corner. 'Does that work?' she asked nodding to a small Baby Belling electric cooker resting crookedly on its stand.

'No one's tried for some time,' she was told.

She thought of the *Dromore Castle* where cooking had been done for hundreds in much worse conditions. At least as far as she could see there would be no cockroaches to fall into the food.

'Our last lady walked out two days ago. Since then the doctors, nurses and staff have just made their own drinks when they have time and there's been nothing to eat.'

'I wouldn't be able to keep it open all the time,' Queenie said.

'You mean you'll come and do it?'

'I'd love to.'

There was an immediate cheer from everyone scattered around and between the girders in this strange room.

'Good old ...?'

'Queenie,' she supplied.

'Good old Queenie! When are you starting?'

'Tomorrow?' she queried of Miss Chandler.

Beaming, Miss Chandler patted her on the back. 'Welcome aboard, Queenie.'

When Laura arrived at the café she had expected her mother to be waiting, but she had not expected her to be in animated conversation with two young women, nurses with civilian coats over their uniforms, and for them to bid her a cheery, ''Bye Queenie, see you tomorrow.'

'What's this?' she asked taking a seat by her mother who was agog with her news.

'I thought you'd probably find some kind of sewing or tailoring, I never dreamt you ...'

'It was in here,' Queenie gestured around the café.

'I remember,' Laura said reflectively, not wanting now to tell of lingering outside the recruiting office for the WRENS, carried away by the posters of smart young Wrens working alongside handsome naval officers, wanting to rush in and join, to be one of the same branch of the forces as Jamie.

But she had gone to the Censorship Department, and been totally surprised to find they had all her details from Gibraltar and were only waiting for her to contact them. A position was waiting, she too could start immediately.

Chapter Sixteen

'It's the chairs,' Queenie pondered as they sat in the evening sunlight, 'they're the problem.'

'It *all* sounds awful to me,' Laura said, 'I still don't understand what really made you do it.' If she was honest she felt ungracious, peevish. This unexpected initiative by her mother might be a problem if the chance ever came to move nearer to Jamie's home port. There was the dawning of another idea too, which as yet she had hardly admitted to herself, was perhaps not even possible.

The end of the first day at their new jobs had resulted in a lengthy retelling of their experiences to each other and the fascinated Mabs.

'It was almost like a calling,' Queenie laughed deprecatingly at her own words. 'When I heard those people talking in that café, then went to see,' she paused and shook her head, 'all those weary doctors and nurses having to make their own cups of tea and no food, not even a bit of toast to offer them. I can at least do that – and I'll do something about the stove and the place and those chairs everywhere so you can hardly walk. I don't know what yet, but ...'

'You two make me quite envious. Off out to work,' Mabs was thoughtful, 'and me stuck here with the boys. But then ...' She leaned back dropping the sock she was darning on to her lap; Queenie immediately reached over and took up the work, shaking her head when Mabs tried to take it back. 'But then,' Mabs repeated, 'I wouldn't dare go and leave them. If anything happened while I wasn't here, or to me while I was out ... No, however, much I'd like to I couldn't, my John would never forgive me.'

The length of time since Mabs had heard from her husband was becoming something they no longer talked about easily. With the help of the WVS she had contacted his shipping line so he would be told as soon as he docked where his wife and children were. Mabs confidently expected news every day, outwardly at least; only those closest to her saw the compressed jaw line at the end of each post call.

Letters were coming in greater numbers as relatives and friends learned of their evacuees' whereabouts: thousands were in the Kensington area, Palace Mansions, the Royal Palace Hotel; 1,000 in Marlborough Court; 300 at the British Empire Hotel, plus 750 at their centre in Anerley.

Queenie watched hopefully for a reply to the two letters she had already written to Freddie. A letter came from Jamie telling Laura the sea trials were 'coming along *very* nicely'. This had her agonising about the '*very*'. Was there a secret message here, was his destroyer off to active service almost at once?'

'So your day had one big surprise,' Mabs was saying to Laura.

'Oh! yes, Doris, already working there. I should have realised she might be. She's got the children into school, she's living with her family – and things are working out for her.'

'She's *making* it work,' Queenie agreed. 'Could do with her to help organise my chairs.'

There was a concerted outcry from the other two.

'Not those chairs again!' Laura exclaimed.

'Never mind about the air raids and the casualties, it's just these chairs we have a problem with,' Mabs added.

As the days and nights passed the air raids were more and more a constant anxiety. People's faces grew pale from lack of sleep and many had an almost permanent frown as they listened for that first rising note, which quickly plummeted along with their stomachs, to rise again, wailing up and down, warning of yet another raid.

When they had first arrived in England Hitler was still ordering his bombing campaign against shipping, ports and particularly the coastal area facing the Pas de Calais where, after the capitulation of France, his invasion fleet was known to be massing.

Then later in the summer the air attacks moved to the airfields, menacing and crippling the Royal Air Force on the ground as well as in the air. Hitler's clear intention was to wipe out the air force as any kind of a threat to the success of his seaborne army. He had marched over many borders but never attacked an island. If he could finally lure the depleted and exhausted RAF into the air and finish them off his invasion could be a more speedy success.

On 7 September 1940 he switched to civilian targets. Hitler decided to try to bomb the heart out of London, and for the first time 300 German bombers accompanied by 600 fighters took part in a daylight raid. The sky was dark with planes, enemy planes.

The day went on and every time there was a pause everyone waited for the All Clear to sound, the long continuous note that said it was over for the time being. Many reasoned that the raid was to be in daylight *instead* of at night-time. But where they had been able to see the explosions as bright orange flashes surrounded by palls of black smoke, once evening came, then night, the fires had new spectacular fury.

The sky became all shades of orange and furnace reds, like a sunrise and sunset, as at east and west – all points of the compass – fires started by earlier attacks blazed. To this was added the demonic fireworks of the bombs and incendiaries still being dropped, and all night the noise went on: the pulse of the German bombers like an intermittent malevolent heartbeat; the earth-shattering thudding explo-

207

sions; the woof of gunfire, and the wail of sirens as emergency services rushed hither and thither.

Crouching in the long dug-out shelters in the school grounds, Mabs muttered that to become used to something was not to like it any better – and the scale of this raid was beyond anything they had known before. Then there came a new noise, like a sheet being torn, of the heavens being wrenched from the earth. The three women looked at each other for a few seconds, then they realised it was the whine of bombs falling through the air. All three of them instinctively threw themselves over the twins, spreading themselves over the boys like mother hens defending their clutch of eggs. They crouched tighter as the whine became a screech, then came the massive explosion, the quake of the ground. Great clods of earth and stone rained down on the arched shelter, and all of them held their breaths, too terrified for coherent thought, or prayer, as they waited to see if their shelter held.

They had not moved and had only just begun to draw breath again when a voice from well beneath them asked, 'Can we go and look for shrapnel in the morning?'

Someone made a noise, a half whimper, a half sob of laughter, then Mabs, still in the middle of the huddle, said, 'Your Auntie Queenie will bring you some back.' The sob became something like a snicker of tremulous laughter, then it teetered towards hysteria as they still lay over the top of the boys, until Alex protested, 'You're crying, our mam, and it's all wetting me.'

The raid stopped shortly afterwards, about three o'clock the All Clear sounded, but no one moved from the shelters until daylight. Queenie decided she would leave early for the hospital. 'I wonder if the trains will be running,' she said, 'but if I can't get . . .' She left the rest unsaid. Though he didn't dare repeat his request she felt Ian's eyes on her. She gave him a secret wink. There wasn't much joy in the world for these boys at the moment; if a bit of shrapnel helped she'd see what she could do.

The morning was full of the smell of smoke and dust and its haze hung in the sun as far as she could see, but as she made her way to the train the birds were singing. It looked as if properties had been damaged on the far side of the school's extensive grounds. On the underground platforms some of the people who had slept there still lingered, folding blankets, being given tea by more WVS ladies.

It was not until she emerged from the tube to walk, or to try to walk, to the hospital that she began not just to see but physically come up against the scale of the disaster. Streets she had begun to recognise as familiar on her way to the hospital were gone; façades had fallen outwards or inwards, some blocking most of the roadway, some piled in on themselves leaving half a block of apartments as if sliced through with a knife.

Impeded by the rubble, the hosepipes, the firemen dragging themselves wearily on still dousing smouldering ruins, Queenie was brought to a halt by the sight of people scavenging about in the ruins of their homes, pausing as they found a pan, or the remains of some other possession and picking it up as if retrieving a treasure, only to have it crumble to a black nothingness in their hands. These people were black like the remains of their worlds they foraged in, while above them towered the broken buildings, rooms torn apart, exposed to anyone who had time for an upwards glance.

It was like glancing from black and white to Technicolor Queenie thought, for some of the standing sections of flats looked by comparison so colourful and clean; there was even a clock on a mantel shelf with envelopes still tucked behind it. On a high floor something appeared to roll and teeter on the edge of the broken floor then, swift as light, it shot to the far end of the room making her hand fly to her throat in alarm. A cat! She looked around as if she must tell someone, must help the poor creature. Then she became aware that besides the firemen, the wardens, the police, other people were coming along carrying what must be all they had left in the world in bags, sacks, battered cases.

209

She caught the eye of a woman who had dust covering her hair, and blood which had run down and caked one torn stocking, though she carried nothing. The woman stopped. 'Been bombed out twice I 'ave. What d'you reckon to that! House went, I was under the stairs with me case of valuables, they dig me out send me along to the church hall where all us bombed-outs are, and that cops it. Don't reckon many got out, not the woman next to me anyhow and she had two kids.'

Queenie was appalled by the thought of the 'two kids' they had giggled over so hysterically. It made her feel so much worse about this woman's state. 'You'd better come with me, I work in a hospital canteen, going there now. Get your knee looked it.'

'Nah! It's nothing. I've got some folks in Bethnal Green, find my way there I will. My old man's sister lives there and he was at work on the docks last night, so we'll meet up there I suppose.'

'I hope so,' Queenie heard herself say, 'I do hope so.' But the woman was on her way again shuffling through brick ends and splintered wood, stepping over hoses. She turned round and looking back shouted, 'Just what I stand up in.' Then raised her arms to heaven in a gigantic shrug.

By the time she reached the hospital Queenie was expecting the worst, and there it was, packed tight, spilling out of the swing doors. It seemed as if the greater part of the population of the district were needing attention. The blonde receptionist, Wendy, was staunching a child's head wound, Miss Chandler was wheeling a trolley through to the corridor leading to the wards. Queenie hurried towards her canteen.

She was in the newly whitewashed corridor when she was suddenly overwhelmed by a sense of dread. She stepped back against the wall, leaning there, paralysed by terrible apprehension, or some kind of premonition. She looked up and down the long arched corridor, all whitened now but with curious alcoves and recesses into doorways.

The safest place in the hospital one of the boilermen had told her, 'Arched roof like a bridge, the whole hospital could come down on you there and you'd be safe.' She knew what he meant and felt he was probably right, but this sense of dread was greater than commonsense and it sprang from what? She drew in a deep breath and in that moment knew exactly where it came from.

She had smelt this tangy metallic, smoky odour before. *Now* it was filtering in from the devastated city, *before* it had lingered on Jock's clothes when he came from the firing range. Cordite, smoke, hot gun barrels – fear and dread as her husband entered the house.

'My dear?' a voice queried, 'are you all right?'

She looked up to see Miss Chandler hurrying towards her. 'Not hurt?' she queried. 'Not caught in the raid?'

Queenie shook her head to both queries, aware the administrator looked both anxious and weary.

'Not claustrophobic?' she asked. 'I mean working down here? It happened to our last lady.'

Again she shook her head. 'No, nothing like that. I'm anxious to get on with my work.'

'Thank goodness for that,' Miss Chandler said with relief. 'Come on then, m'dear, that's where I'm heading for. A cup of very strong, very sweet tea. I do hope there's some sugar?'

'There's condensed milk,' Queenie told her.

Miss Chandler had her tea, then fetched bread, margarine and some cheese from the patients' kitchens and soon the smell of cheese on toast was the most prevalent smell in the long underground corridor.

It was many hours after her normal home time that Queenie finally realised she had to stop, for she reeled and nearly fell as she turned for the many hundredth time from shelf to counter. She clung on for a few moments until her head cleared. The momentum of doctors with blood-stained coats and nurses with dishevelled hair under their caps was easing. Now was the time to leave, to put Laura's mind at

211

ease, and her own about her daughter's safety. Bone weary she rearranged a few of the chairs with their backs to the upright girders, so those who wished to get to the counter to help themselves could do so unhindered.

She made her way to the exit, but reaching the swing doors she knew she would not make it. She had to sit down before she could travel anywhere. There was a free space at the end of a bench, wearily she turned back, as she did so someone caught her elbow.

'What's this?' Miss Chandler stood there with handbag and gas mask slung over her shoulder. Then hearing the journey she had to make she said, 'You're coming home with me. Five minutes' walk and we're there. Manage that.'

She tried to protest but Miss Chandler shook her head. 'I've seen enough exhausted people to know that's about all you can manage for the time being.'

'My daughter . . .' Queenie began.

'Tell me when we get to my house.'

The house was literally just around two corners from the hospital. As they walked the nearest air-raid siren screamed out once more, to be repeated from district to district, the echo of one falling into the rising alarm of another. 'Let's hurry along. I've got a cellar built like London Bridge *and* I've made it comfortable.' The small brisk woman led the way without waiting for a reply as the familiar intermittent drone of enemy bombers could be heard.

The cellar *was* comfortable. Reached from the back kitchen of an impressive early Georgian terraced house, the stone steps ran down under huge arches, newly white-washed like the corridor, and down there were two camp beds, two easy chairs, a radio and a telephone.

'I'm organised, you see,' Miss Chandler said with a smile. 'I usually crash out on the far bed, so if you'd like the other, I'll fetch us both a mug of cocoa.'

Too exhausted to argue Queenie pulled off her shoes, took off her skirt and lay down, and before the hostess

212

came back with her drink she was asleep. They were both woken by explosions at about four o'clock in the morning, and then the telephone rang, its proximity startling Queenie with its shrill clamour.

'Billie Chandler.' Her voice was crisp, lifted above the slur of sleep. Queenie noted she looked elegant in white satin pyjamas with a black monogrammed W on the jacket pocket. She put down the receiver and said, 'That was the hospital. We've had a hit, oxygen store's gone up and my records.'

Queenie was out of bed and slipping back into her skirt.

'Not part of your duty y'know ...' Billie began but when Queenie ignored her she added, 'Good show!'

The sky was lightening as they hurried back; it seemed to Queenie only minutes since they had left, so deeply had she slept.

This time the chaos was inside the hospital, firemen and hoses were everywhere. Attempting to go through to her canteen Queenie was stopped by a fire officer. 'Your corridor's full of fumes. It'll be tomorrow at the earliest before we could let you go down there.'

'There's your daughter,' Miss Chandler reminded her. 'Come back when you've made sure everything's all right. I dare say there'll be plenty of clearing up to do when these chaps are finished with us.'

'Well, us and old Adolf,' the fireman agreed, 'don't forget he helped.'

To her surprise Miss Chandler walked with her out of the hospital. 'I just wanted to say that I've been in that great big house by myself since my married sister took her children into the country a few weeks ago. If you and your daughter wanted to come and live nearer to where you work there's a self-contained flat on the second floor, and you know the cellar's good. We could soon get another camp bed.'

Queenie was so astonished she had not begun to answer when Wendy appeared in the doorway loaded with a huge

213

carton of files dripping water. 'Miss Chandler,' she appealed.

'I'll see you tomorrow.' Miss Chandler nodded her on her way as Wendy looked about to give way to tears over the sagging carton of paperwork.

She saw another woman weeping, weeping with rage, as she made her way back past the devastated flats where she had seen the cat – where still the letters stood propped behind the clock, and a man now scavenged in the fallen ruins. 'Stop him,' the woman was appealing 'this is my home, he has no business here.'

The grey-haired man was shouting back that he too lived there, but the woman screamed back that she had never seen him.

'Even so,' the man replied with great dignity standing in the midst of the black wreckage, 'my belongings are here too.' He lifted the remains of a bird cage and displayed it to her.

Instinctively Queenie's eyes went up to the floors above. Was the cat still there? Then she realised the woman was shouting at her.

'What do you want? You didn't live here! You got big pockets like some of the demolition men?' She started across the rubble towards Queenie. 'Shouldn't have pockets those men.'

Queenie walked quickly away from the two who now stood shoulder to shoulder, as if at last recognising each other as neighbours they were uniting to repel this intruder from their pile of rubble.

The incident was disturbing. After the unstinting work she had seen being done in the hospital this seemed tainted with – what? Not selfishness or greed, not when they had lost everything they owned, homes that probably meant more to them than any place she had ever shared with Jock. Yet she still hated the thought of Jock purloining her grandfather's treasures, particularly to pay for the sabotage of Freddie's work.

214

She had reached the tube station and an irascible old newspaper woman who had taken up a new stand inside the station was complaining. 'Where were the RAF that's what I want to know? Should be shooting the buggers down. No reports of any enemy losses. Where are they?' She slammed a pile of newspapers to the ground. 'Never make a living at this rate.'

Human nature, Queenie decided, perhaps that was the problem; you couldn't be a saint all the time.

She had hardly arrived back at the school when she heard Laura calling her. She turned to see her running down the front steps looking distraught. 'Oh! are you all right? I've been so worried all night.'

'Are *you* all right?'

Laura nodded urgently asking, 'What happened to you?'

She explained about the hospital, the raid, the exhaustion, Miss Chandler's cellar, then in the pause to find the right words to tell about the offer of the flat, Laura cut in with astonishing news of her own.

'Things have happened here. Mabs has gone, with the boys; her husband came, John, a great giant of a man. He's taken them off to live with his mother, she lives near Carlisle in the Lake District. He's sure they'll be safe there.'

'Oh, so I've missed them,' Queenie lamented. 'I wouldn't have done that for all the world. Those boys . . .'

'She's going to write. She made John wait until late last night, hoping to see you, then they just had to go. He'd arranged a lift with a lorryload of goods going north from the docks.' She paused and linking arms with her mother she said, 'Ian left a message for you. If you found any shrapnel can you please send it on.'

Queenie laughed, then remembered the woman walking to Bethnal Green, the two children that woman had seen killed.

'He was lovely, her husband,' Laura went on, 'huge, a bit like our Albert on the *Dromore Castle* – perhaps that's

215

why the twins took to Albert so quickly. They spotted him first, we were near the tennis courts and Alec went running across shouting "Daddy! Daddy!" and Ian followed shouting "Are you a captain? Are you a captain?" By this time Mabs is in his arms and has a boy hanging on each leg.'

'Like Albert,' Queenie recalled.

'Yes. Then Ian began to get upset shouting and tugging at his trousers. "No, are you a captain?"

'"Oh!"' the big man exclaims as he realises what the boy means. Then sort of making himself a space he sings and does a kind of tap dance.'

> A captain? A captain?
> Yes, of course, I am.
> I'm Captain Sam
> Of the *frying pan*.

'"Yes!" Ian yells and hurls himself back at his daddy and we all stand around crying our eyes out.'

Chapter Seventeen

Not letting Hitler disrupt the daily routines had become both a matter of stubborn pride, and a framework in which to try to deal with the random onslaught on civilian targets. They all, Londoners, Gibraltarian evacuees, everyone, shouldered the burden of the terror together; never was a city or a country so grimly united.

Long after Laura had dutifully gone to make her way across the devastated city, the silly rhyme stayed with Queenie. She even felt she could imagine the dance, half clog, half tap as John Macintyre had sung to his son. She was so grieved to have missed saying goodbye. They had shared so much with Mabs. She had mended their clothes and Mabs and her boys had lightened their hearts.

She doubted they would meet again for a long time – if ever. Years of fatalistic realism told her other things came into life, people moved on, and however good the intentions, time flew by and then it was suddenly too late. But they had their address in Carlisle, they would write, keep in touch that way, and she would certainly send Ian and Alec shrapnel.

Perhaps if she went for a walk along the far side of the school grounds later, or even investigated the debris thrown up around the shelters she might find suitable pieces. Was shrapnel bomb casing, or pieces of shot-down planes, did bullet cases count? She needed the footballing boy from

217

Cardiff, or perhaps someone at the hospital had children, grandchildren . . .

She sat on her bed nursing her arm, suddenly registering how intolerably it ached. She had worked it for too long and consoled herself that properly rested she would be far more use the next day. She pondered the question of why she had not immediately told Laura about the flat she had been offered? It might be more in the city but there was the cellar *and* the telephone – *and* privacy. Laura's lack of enthusiasm, even dismay, for her job at the hospital was no doubt the reason, but now her delay only made matters more complex.

She fell unwittingly to wondering why she should have been overtaken by such a sense of dread in that subterranean hospital passage, when there was so much real drama, real need, real cause for fear in the city? For sure some animal instinct had recognised the smell of the cordite as a past evil and paralysed her muscles so she could not continue into possible danger. The horse that will not cross a broken bridge. The dog that cowers at the sound of a cruel master's step.

She felt her skin grow cold; she had suppressed so much for so many years, though things were changing – she was making them change, would go on making them change. In the midst of all this suffering, all the agonies of people bombed out, with air raids becoming ever more part of their lives, Queenie Maclaren was slowly becoming her own woman again. Perhaps she could become more like Queenie Middleton once more. What had she been like, that young girl born on Gibraltar, raised in the sun?

She dug back into her mind. What had it been like? Happy. All her young life was happy, her parents were loving – in love. She had friends at school, out of school.

The permitted Friday evening outings, walking down the narrow Main Street in groups and gangs, boys with boys swaggering; girls with girls giggling. Later couples. Freddie. No, not later Freddie, always Freddie. Even at school, even amongst the gangs of youths her eyes had sought him out, and he too had been aware. Freddie had hovered and both had been totally mesmerised as they finally singled each other out. It had been traumatic, so sensually disturbing that neither of them had known how to deal with it.

She remembered the first time Freddie had put his arm around her waist as they walked into the more secluded alleyways off the main shopping street. She had been so aware of the warmth and pressure of his hand and arm, her mouth and throat had contracted so she could hardly talk. She might have uttered a word or so, but they had certainly not *talked*. It was as if they had both been pole-axed by the experience, for she remembered he had never moved his hand or arm one inch once it was in place – not that first time.

When she had undressed that night she had looked to see if the contact had made a mark. She would not have been surprised to see a great broad band of burning red running around her waist. The surprise had been that there was nothing to show.

The intensity of her own feelings had frightened her. She had known nothing like this awakening, had no benchmark. She had been too young. She shook her head sadly. Too young to really be in love, proper adult, life-long, love? She knew better now. Then she had nothing to compare her feeling with, no gauge to know that she had been the most fortunate of girls to have found *the* man, her fella. Found him and let him go – as he had her.

But they had refound each other, and the passions had rekindled. The nights he had come late to Fatima's home had been a rediscovery, a new courtship and marriage in one. She almost dropped her head at the memory of bathing so carefully, of smoothing her night clothes and borrowing the silky wrap before slipping quietly from the bedroom.

She walked to the open window and lifted her face up to the sun. There should be nothing but rejoicing about such a love. She smiled at the thought of all the young people who foolishly thought they had such a monopoly of love and passion. She thought of Laura and Jamie, separated but at least engaged, and with the ring Freddie had bought for her. 'Marvellous,' she breathed, 'just marvellous.' Then she remembered the day she had been told of her father's posting to Singapore.

It had been as if a sudden black fog had blanketed her world. She had tried to resist, find ways not to go, seemed to remember encountering Freddie from time to time in this miasma of misery. He hadn't known what to do either. In their dilemma they had quarrelled. It seemed to her now that they had quarrelled so they could bear to part, only at the last had Freddie come with flowers – and the ring in his pocket.

But if Freddie had been guilty of youth and shyness, her own mistake had been sheer foolishness, blind stupidity.

Her mother had made a new home for them in Singapore, and a new garden, where her beloved plants grew at a tremendous rate, and orchids took the place of oleanders as favourites – and where, as she moped for Freddie, her mother said there was all the time in the world, and that one day they would go back. But it had not been true.

Shortly afterwards in the tree-lined Orchard Road in Singapore her parents were both killed in a bizarre traffic accident involving a rickshaw, a man carrying an impossible load on his bicycle and their car.

She had gone through the joint funeral in a daze of grief and unwelcome and unwise sedation. She knew it had been wrong at the time, knew she should have been allowed to show her grief to the whole world. For an army orphan it had apparently not been fitting. They meant kindly, every-one meant kindly. Jock Maclaren most kindly of all. She remembered now that the army had offered to escort her back to her mother's home in Gibraltar, but Jock was already in the role of protector – and she had been grateful. In trying to bury, or at least to continue to live with the loss of her parents, she had inadvertently buried Freddie.

Her features became hard as she gritted her teeth, her face suddenly feeling stale and old, bleak, as she recalled how totally she had been deceived. How once he had been sure of her, married her, Jock had changed, or reverted to type, to someone either his mother or father must have been, or at least had made their son.

The caring, almost the reverence, with which he had seemed to regard her had lapsed into sulky monosyllabic insults in private, and scathing and hurtful gibes in public. Other young women who tried to befriend her had been discouraged by being ignored when in his company. One bright young Cockney had faced the seemingly impassive Jock at a Christmas party for other ranks and their wives, and told him loudly, 'She'll never please you, will she? Stood on 'er bleeding 'ead and turned to gold!' Then she had turned to Queenie, 'Leave 'im love, while you still can.' That night had been the first time he had struck her.

Desolate she had not known who she could appeal to for help or advice. Shortly afterwards she had realised she was pregnant. When Laura was born it seemed better – for a short time, and Jock's army prospects had seemed brighter for a while. But she had quickly learned that a child does not improve matters in a disastrous marriage, it only gives more to disagree about, fight about, more to take opposite sides about. Then his hopes of a good promotion were dashed. Then *she* had really begun to suffer. He could only see what he had wanted, not what he had.

She sighed. Poor Laura, she had not known a happy childhood, not a childhood at all once she had begun to try to take her mother's side. She had noticed how Laura now referred to her father as Maclaren. 'Nothing had been heard of Maclaren,' she said as if the man was a stranger, with a name that had nothing to do with them.

If only it were true. If only she could totally convince herself they would never see him again. She wondered if the army were keeping a more watchful eye on him after his batman's death? Could this be the reason Freddie's work was going better? Was it still going well, or had there been more sabotage? But what would Jock pay his helpers with now her house was locked and barred against him? There was at least some satisfaction in that. She ached to hear from Freddie. Just to have his words on paper would be to recreate his quiet voice, his sincerity. 'Marvellous.'

She smiled, sniffed herself back to the business of the day, there was this shrapnel to find, and she would write again to Freddie. She intended to keep sending messages into the blue in the hope that one would land sooner or later and be answered. She sighed deeply then pulled herself upright as she saw Mrs Moss coming into the dormitory.

'You look tired m'dear,' she said approaching quickly. 'You should put that arm back in its sling for a bit.'

'Good idea, I think I will,' she replied but her eyes were on the envelope Mrs Moss carried.

'You missed the post call this morning,' she said, 'and I think Laura was outside looking for you. I've just remembered.' She handed the envelope to her. It had a Gibraltar stamp.

Queenie took it, at once totally involved with it to the exclusion of all else as she saw it was Freddie's writing.

'I'll leave you to it,' Mrs Moss said unheard.

She sat on the side of her bed, then with shaking, hasty fingers opened the envelope. There were several pages. She meant to read them slowly, to savour, to soak in every word, but instead her eyes flew across the lines in his bold open hand, the opening without any formal preamble rushing her straight in.

Queenie, my darling, I have made a resolution. I made it the moment you asked me to go indoors so I could not watch you go. The resolution is that it shall never happen again. The next time we come together it is until the end, until death do us part. Not war, not fate, nothing shall come between us ever again. And now, my first love, I have this off my mind I can write more calmly.

222

Gibraltar is a real fortress now the children have gone from the streets, the schools. Everyone misses their laughter, just the sound of them going about is so different to the boots, endless military boots, that echoed everywhere. All that can be heard in Main Street in the evenings is the sound of tramping, drowning every noise – even the traffic at times – as all the forces come off duty and head for a few hours' relaxation.

Fatima took it into her head to try to obtain permission to go over the Spanish border to see her mother and grandmother (not so well), but the Spanish will not allow it. She created a scene at the crossing point. I can understand how she feels with so many bus loads of Spanish women (thousands I think) still allowed in each day to do domestic work, washing for the forces etc. (as usual one law for the Gibraltarians and one for the Spanish). I intervened to take her home otherwise I thought she might be arrested! She was not only questioning the Spanish border guards but she was supplying the answers as well – in her usual manner. They went from astonishment to disapproval, to downright aggression before I could persuade her away. She sends her love to you both.

Every day the *Chronicle* comes out with new lists of restrictions, either new places out of bounds, new curfew rules or the city's gates being closed, but we all survive. The cinema queues are long because there is little else to do when the day's work is done. There is plenty to watch in the harbour and in the air as always. I went to the cinema to see *Destry Rides Again*! Very noisy!

Now I have more meaty news. Maclaren is having some kind of treatment – but for what I do not know – all I can find out is that he is hospitalised. But it is at least keeping him from under our feet while we finish our contract. There are more things in the air, but I would not be able to guess just how fortunate these might be for us. We have to be like Mr Micawber and be ready in case anything turns up.

Queenie, I was remembering our time together when we were young. We knew then we were born for each other. We were so happy then without knowing. Soon we will be happy again, but this time every moment we will know how happy and lucky we are to be together again. I love you. Take very good care of yourself – for my sake – you see I am completely selfish. Your love until the apes leave Gibraltar. Look for me. Yours Freddie.

'Look for me,' she breathed, 'I have been looking for you all my life.' She read and reread the letter, wondering what he meant by 'more things in the air' and not being able to guess 'how fortunate these might be for *us*.' She decided she must write to Freddie at once, then she would find shrapnel and write to Mabs and the boys. It would be a good chance today.

The writing took her over; once begun she could not stop, filling both sides of each large sheet of thin airmail notepaper with memories of the streets, gardens and beaches of Gibraltar, of expeditions up The Rock itself, the views. Then, without change of pace, she told him of the offered flat, and her determination to take it. She told him the address, described Miss Chandler and the circumstances that had left the flat empty – then paused to wonder why she was so certain she would do this when it seemed obvious that Laura did not approve of her venture into the world of hospital work.

When Laura came home that evening she found her mother neatly tying up a small parcel for the Macintyres in Carlisle.

'That can only be one thing.'

She nodded asking, 'How's the city?'

'Battered,' Laura shook her head, the scenes and smells of devastation fresh in her memory, 'but smiling, still making jokes.'

'Hitler'll never win, Germans haven't got the right sense of humour.'

224

'So you've been collecting shrapnel.'

'Well, no, I paid twopence for some from one of the boys here. He'd been to his grandparents' home in Bethnal Green. He said if I scratched a swastika on it, it would make it worth a lot more.'

'So did you?'

She laughed and shook her head as she watched her daughter kick off her shoes.

'I hope we can sleep in our beds tonight,' she said, 'short as they are, they're better than the shelter.'

Her mother made no answer.

After a moment or two she looked at her mother who was gazing at her, with a certain look in her eye. It was, she thought, the kind of look people had when they were going to tell you something they didn't think you would like.

'I heard from Freddie today,' she said 'and I have something to tell you before I post my reply.'

Laura listened with a growing sense of disbelief as her mother told her about Miss Chandler and the flat, then produced the letter to Freddie, already sealed, she noticed, as her mother added that she had told Freddie the address.

'The address of this flat?'

'Yes, of course. You must want to leave here as much as everyone else does. It'll be easier for both of us to get to work, just walking distance for both of us. There's such a good cellar, built like a fortress and arched like a bridge. Anyway,' she went on in a casual, light-hearted manner, 'they say if a bomb's got your number on it you've no chance wherever you are.'

'Do *they*,' Laura said, hearing the denigration in her own voice. 'I wonder how many people are moving further *into* towns.'

'Quite a few from here,' Queenie reminded her. 'There's Doris and her girls for a start, then the family with relations in Bethnal Green, they're moving out of the evacuees' scheme with five young children.'

'More fools them,' she said shortly.

'Laura, what is it? You weren't very happy when I took the job at the hospital ...'

'I was just so surprised. I thought you'd do something like sewing or tailoring,' her voice fell a little, 'something safe, something you could do here, or anywhere.'

'Here! No thanks,' Queenie said very definitely, 'particularly not now Mabs has gone. And I wanted to do something that was more directly for the war effort.'

'Me too,' Laura answered her voice low and intense.

'You *are* in a government department doing war work ...'

'I want something a bit more active, a bit more involved, not just the same as I was doing on Gib, in an office – but ...'

'But?' her mother queried. 'But?'

'But I can't ...'

'Can't?'

'I couldn't leave you isolated in the middle of London, if ...'

'Isolated? I thought you'd be so pleased for us to have somewhere of our own again. You so loved the cottage Jamie took you to, having your own front door again and all that ...' she paused and reassessed what Laura had said. 'Leave me? So where would you be?'

'I want to join the WRENS.'

'The WRENS?'

'The women's branch of the Royal Navy.'

Queenie was staggered, aghast. She had never believed her daughter would ever want to enter the forces after experiencing regular service life from the family's point of view. But at least she was practised in hiding her real feelings and held back all her misgivings to ask a practical question, 'Would you be allowed to go? I mean, be allowed to leave the Censorship Department?'

'One of the senior people there has a daughter high up in the WRENS, he talks about her all the time. I mentioned how I felt. He said it's an elite service, but he could work it for me

226

and would recommend me for special training because I'd worked in censorship. But the sooner I applied the better he said. So I didn't get too established in his department.'

All this came out quickly once started and, as she talked, from the uptight recalcitrant woman emerged the bright-eyed, eager youngster Queenie loved to see.

'Jamie does know where you are now,' she felt she must remind her daughter. 'It could mean you'd be further apart, if your postings took you to opposite ends of the country.'

'I can always let him know where I am. And it might be the opposite, that we're closer. I should feel closer, in the same service. But obviously I can't go now.'

Queenie watched her as she sat down on the edge of her bed and began to carefully take off her precious stockings to be washed ready for the next day. She recognised the self-sacrifice she had seen so many times in the past; the outings forgone because she thought her father would come home while she was out, and vigils kept when as a child she should have been long in bed. 'You must go or I'll feel it's my fault,' she said, adding a silent 'again'.

'That's not how I meant you to feel at all.'

'But I do. Why can't you go? Explain to me, please.'

'I just thought that wherever I had to go you could come, find lodgings nearby, but now you're at the hospital, helping everyone, you won't want to leave, and . . . now there's this flat.'

'Oh! I see,' Queenie relaxed, shoulders slumping as all the tension of not understanding left her. 'My dear, dear, girl this *is* just what *I* want. You've mothered *me* for far too long, it's time we both had a life of our own. I want this flat, I want this job, and I want you to go off and join your WRENS.'

'Truly?'

'Truly.'

Laura began to roll her stockings back up her leg.

'Now where are you going?'

'I'm going to post your letter to Freddie at the corner box.'

227

Chapter Eighteen

'Listen to the midnight news?' Miss Chandler asked, check-ing the clock as she and Queenie began to undress next to their cellar camp beds. 'Three minutes to go.'

'Just time to show you this. It came today,' Queenie finger-tipped through the contents of her bag and found an envelope, from which she drew a studio photograph of Laura in WRENS uniform. She held it for a moment feeling a new thrill of pride in the solemn but happy face of her daughter, newly completed 'basic training' and posted 'north'.

Miss Chandler came and sat on the camp bed next to her. 'She's a handsome girl. She'll set the navy's hearts throb-bing.'

'She's already engaged to a naval officer.'

'I did notice that splendid ring when we were introduced. Y'know there's a frame in the flat upstairs with a rotten photograph of me, you could put Laura in that.'

'Oh! but . . .'

'Go on. I can always emerge again later.'

'Miss Chandler,' Queenie felt suddenly quite over-whelmed by this woman's kindness. 'I want to say thank you properly for letting me come here into your home . . .'

'Please call me Billie, my family always do. I've never been given my full moniker since I left school, anything's better than Wilhelmina.'

228

'No,' she rejected the interruption, needing to make a very solemn statement of thanks. 'We're so grateful.'

'Oh! tosh! It's far better for me not to be on my own.'

'You hardly know us . . .'

'Anyone who volunteers to work *where* you do, and *how* you do, and whose daughter volunteers for active service when there's no compulsion for her to do so, they're both first class in my eyes. And . . .' she rose quickly from the bed and turned the knob of the radio, 'we're nearly missing the news.'

Here is the midnight news and this is Alvar Liddell reading it. Up to ten o'clock this evening 175 aircraft have been destroyed in today's raids over the country.

'Oh! ripping! That caught the buggers a treat!' Miss Chandler exclaimed and whirled her satin pyjama bottoms around her head.

'Listen!' Queenie urged, anxious not to miss one detail.

. . . in daylight raids 350 to 400 enemy aircraft launched two attacks against London and south-eastern England, about half of which were shot down.

'At last we're hitting back,' Queenie relished.

'Thank God! Perhaps we can all relax a notch or two . . .'

The rest of the news passed them by as they both ducked to the sound and quake of a huge explosion. They looked up again to see flakes of whitewash and plaster falling from the arched ceiling, then listened intently. 'Relax, did I say?'

'I've faith in this cellar,' Queenie said as no more imminent danger sounded and the last of the flakes flittered down on to her camp bed. She thought to herself that she had just as much faith in the presence of Wilhelmina Chandler, who's so well known at the hospital they'd soon be dug out.

229

'What're you grinning about?' Billie asked. 'You're extraordinary!'

'Not me, you, you're the extraordinary one.' She pushed her weary limbs down into the bed, made a long mound of the eiderdown down by her side to support her arm, then went on, 'Lots of things really.'

'Tell!' The order came from the adjoining camp bed.

'The photo, and I'm glad my daughter's ... well, I'm just glad about my daughter ...' a pang for the absent Laura took the words from her mind. Until she had gone with Jamie to the cottage on the Downs the two had never been separated for more than hours. She did miss catching up with her news every day. 'Time she was away about her own business,' she paused to watch as Billie manoeuvred the string she had tied around the tiny knob on the distant brass light switch and yanked it from her bed, putting them in the dark before she added, 'and being glad she's been posted north as she wanted.'

'Though Liverpool is probably only halfway to where her chap will be docking,' Billie speculated. 'There's a globe up in the flat.'

'I found the Firth of Forth when we first carried my things up,' Queenie admitted, her eyes closing, feeling herself on the brink of sleep, 'it is about as far again as Liverpool is from here.'

'I know and if he gets based at Scapa Flow, that's in the Orkneys, four times as far.'

'I think I should be knitting balaclavas and scarves in my spare time,' Queenie said, feeling her arm give a reminder of its present maltreatment at the thought.

Billie hooted with laughter. 'What spare time?'

As the autumn passed the daytime raids ceased, and the great flocks of birds seen wheeling over the city during these raids could, like the city, get on with their daily business. Night-time was another matter. Each night she pondered the foolhardiness that had ordered and kept thousands of Gibraltarians in the capital to endure this Blitz, the continuing nightly onslaughts.

Queenie had quickly learned it was not foolhardiness or stubbornness that kept many Londoners in the city. Stories told in her canteen were often of relatives who could not bring themselves to leave the elderly or the mortally sick behind. The agony of one mother who had stayed to be with her grandfather and whose child had been seriously injured by flying glass, and died on the children's ward, left doctors and nurses alike sitting sipping their mugs of tea in dejected silence.

The only way the hospital could deal with the daily influx of casualties was by moving every patient well enough to stand the journey out to what was jokingly called their 'place in the country'. This was a converted mansion, surrounded by the wards in Nissen huts – out of the bombing, but also out of the reach of relations, so that there were long intervals between visits. Many patients resisted leaving the city hospital, and one or two 'favourites' whose relatives were known not to have the wherewithal to bus it out to the country were allowed to remain.

Queenie saw these Cockney reunions as she helped with tea on the wards when staff were hard pressed. Such an outflowing of good humour and banter, such huggings, as a neighbouring patient commented, 'It does your 'eart good just to watch.' She saw too how the patients' eyes were always on the door as the bell rang and the visitors came trooping in, hoping against hope there was someone for them.

There was a venerable old man, who they nicknamed Mr Moses, in the first bed inside the men's surgical ward. No one knew who he was, no one had inquired after him, and though he did not speak his eyes followed those who passed him by as if he searched for a familiar face, a clue to who he was.

The nurses and the auxiliaries tried to spend a few extra minutes with those like Mr Moses, but Queenie knew how they must yearn for their own folk, those who could give titbits of news about friends and acquaintances, those who laughed at the same things, understood without explanation.

She found much of these things in Laura's enthusiastic weekly letters. There was no doubt her daughter was feeling fulfilled in her new life, which increasingly seemed to be hush-hush; 'plotting and planning' she called it.

Queenie slid the handsome photograph of her daughter over the youthful Billie, and was almost shocked by how much the silver art nouveau frame enhanced the portrait. She had it in the flat during the hours she spent there, sometimes a whole day when she was forced to rest her arm. At night-time the photograph went with her to the cellar.

The flat had one large, elegant sitting room with a splendid view, or it had been a splendid view before the war, over a tree-lined square. Now the ornamental railings had been sliced off for the war effort; the trees on the far side, stripped of leaves and branches, looked like those of a First World War battlefield and several houses had lost cascades of tiles.

The flat kitchen was not large and had a gas geyser which frightened the life out of her by booming into life some long seconds after being turned on. The bedroom was restfully elegant in aquamarine, pale green beryl, placid sea colours, with a three-quarter-sized bed used so far only to rest on during the day.

They were just settling in the cellar one evening some three weeks before Christmas when the telephone pealed out. Billie was immediately on the alert.

'Chandler.'

She admired the authority this diminutive woman managed to summon up whatever the hour of day or night, but this time she took the receiver from her ear and held it towards Queenie, whose heart leapt with apprehension as she was told, 'It's for you.'

'Hello.'

232

'Mum! It's me, Laura . . .'

There was the sound of a scuffle and a husky male voice said, 'So that's your name, gorgeous.'

'Will you get out of here,' Laura said as if off stage, laughing.

'What's happening?'

'Nothing, Mother, just high spirits. I'm at a dance and there's this phone box so thought I'd give you a call. Can you hear the racket?'

She could – music and laughter. 'Sounds like a crowd.'

'They're a great lot up here, these scousers. Are you all right? You in the cellar?'

'Yes to both,' she said, 'don't worry. Everything OK your end?'

'Fine! There might be leave at Christmas. Keep hoping.'

'Fine!' She was aware of the repetition, tried to make an effort to sound normal in the excitement at both ends of the telephone. 'Sounds like a good do.'

'It is. Heard from Gib?'

Queenie felt herself shake her head, heard the sound of money rattling into the box the other end. 'Only what I told you in my last letter . . . nothing more . . . they seem to be having less trouble than we are here.'

'I'll have to go Mum, no more change and there's a queue for the phone. Love you, 'bye!'

Queenie opened her mouth to say goodbye but the line went dead. She tutted, 'There was so much I wanted to say.'

Billie reached over, took the receiver and replaced it on its cradle. 'Just to hear the voice is enough.'

'Yes,' she said, though she felt the voice she had heard had sounded more like Billie's, as if the uniform had given Laura a new status, a lift up in the world. It made her feel rueful, left behind – then thoroughly impatient with herself for thinking such things. She pondered the brightness and energy in her daughter's voice, having fun at a dance, with other men. She hoped she'd be careful, sensible.

233

'Lights out?' Billie queried.

She nodded, watching as the string was manipulated with that expert upwards twitch. She wondered why Billie had never married, had children, grandchildren, by now. She must have been an attractive woman in her youth, very attractive, with a good background, wealthy, aristocratic too, for she had seen letters begun to 'Dear Aunt Lottie', and addressed to 'The Honourable Lady Phipps'.

'There may be chance of leave for Christmas,' she said into the darkness.

'Oh! that *will* be ripping. Hitler may give us a rest at Christmas. And if her chap gets leave you must all stay here. There's bedrooms to spare.'

'Thank you, I really do appreciate ...'

'Don't go formal on me again,' Billie protested.

'No, I won't, but ...'

'Get your eyes closed woman, while you've got the chance.'

'Yes, ma'am!' Queenie said grinning in the darkness, the mood of uncertainty dispelled.

'We should get the children making paperchains for Christmas,' Billie reflected sounding wide awake. 'It'll give them something to do and to look forward to.'

Thinking of the joy of a possible reunion for herself Queenie asked, 'Will you go to your sister and her children?'

'Oh, no, I stay and help serve the patients' Christmas dinner midday, and we always sing carols around the wards on Christmas Eve.'

'So if Laura did manage leave perhaps we could all have a meal together here on Christmas evening.'

'Splendid! I'd love that. Are you a good cook?'

'I like cooking, when I'm left alone,' Queenie said remembering her early attempts at dinner parties, and Jock's meddlesome confidence-sapping interruptions.

'Have no fear, you shall remain quite unmolested.'

'Oh, I didn't mean you, of course. It's your kitchen.'

234

'I hereby convey it to you for Christmas Day in the year of our Lord one thousand nine hundred and forty. My father was a barrister,' she added, 'though brief he never was.'

Queenie giggled. 'Do you think we'll be able to get some kind of bird, possibly not a turkey, but perhaps a cockerel?'

'I'll arrange something. No use having relations lurking away the war in the countryside if they're not put to use. Now go to sleep, you always chatter more in the dark.'

'I think that's true,' Queenie pondered seriously.

There was a snort of laughter from the other bed.

The very next afternoon Queenie saw children, some lying flat on their backs, but with coloured strips of paper and paste pots cheerfully glueing the pieces into long chains. As the lengths grew she saw a nurse take the end of a streamer to a child in the next bed who had only been watching. She was soon, in spite of a bandaged hand and head, working on the opposite end of the streamer. The delight on their faces and the discussion as to what colour they should loop in next gave both more colour in their cheeks than they'd had since they arrived.

A week later their ward was strung and flounced with paperchains, and Queenie and Billie had arrived home after a late-night shopping trip hunting out crayons and white card, even some tiny gold and silver stick-on stars, for a Christmas card project. Perhaps it was anticipation of more pleasure for the children that made them sleep well that night. Queenie remembered rousing once to hear the passing clamour of fire engines, but had gone straight back to sleep.

The next morning as they walked to work they began to have some idea of what they had slept through. It looked as if a second Great Fire of London had only just been allayed; there was smoke everywhere, black smuts and flakes drifted on a breeze and the nearby streets were crossed and recrossed by hoses.

They hurried to the hospital, fearing they might find a charred wreck, but it was untouched. Inside much was changed, for there a new and terrible range of injuries prevailed – the awful trauma of severe burns – and still they were being brought in. They passed a trolley where a young man, fifteen or sixteen, lay waiting for attention. His hands and face were dreadfully blistered beyond recognition. He had on the remains of a telegram boy's uniform, and as Billie stopped to reassure him, he told her, 'My name's Gordon. I could do with a drink of Tizer. Please,' he added pitifully.

During the following nights thousands of incendiary devices were dropped. Fires raged all over the city and in the mornings still they blazed; radio reporters talked of walking between walls of fire during the nights. This new terror left a terrible frustration and heart-sickness. 'So near Christmas,' was the phrase repeated so often. It also brought many volunteers to the appeal made by Herbert Morrison, Home Secretary, for volunteer firefighters to help fire brigades and the Auxiliary Fire Service, so that small fires could be fought with stirrup pumps and sand as soon as they started, leaving the trained and the specialists to deal with larger blazes.

Queenie urged Billie to take some precautions for her own property and filled buckets with sand from some adjacent burst sandbags. 'While this goes on I think we should take turns to fire watch,' she urged.

'What, on the roof!'

'To do the job properly, yes,' Queenie affirmed and when her friend hesitated added, 'I'll do anything, everything, to keep our home. We should do it *now*, tonight.'

'Shamed into it,' Billie grinned. 'Pity we haven't got tin hats,' she added as she led the way up through the attics to a tiny door out on to the leaded roof space. They both shivered as the wind caught them, bringing with it the smell of wood burning, good wood, sound and dry. 'We'd be better behind the gables.'

But neither of them moved, the sight was already too awesome, too splendid, too horrific. The first waves of incendiaries were already burning. 'That must be all around St Paul's. Yes,' Billie breathed, pointing to the great dome, a black silhouette, the orb and cross surmounting it detailed and vivid against a rainbow of flame colours. As they watched the wind whipped up the flames and sent great showers of sparks high into the air, as if the city was to be one great bonfire, then they became aware of the noise of the fires: the ravenous crackling; the cracking of great wooden beams well alight; the bursting out of windows.

'The injuries . . .' Billie murmured.

The spectacle and the noise had a biblical quality, held them quite still, full of awe and incredulity. Billie pointed in the direction of St Paul's again, but then above the dome to another black silhouette, a plane. They watched as it swept in below a cross of searchlights redundant in the afterglow of the fires, and heard the deep intermittent drone and thrust of German engines.

They drew back instinctively holding their breaths as they saw a cluster of small bombs falling from the plane, like matches tipped from a box, at first in a dark group then separating into individual sticks of incendiaries; tiny things they looked, tossed around the sky by the wind. The plane passed almost immediately over their heads, and they realised that some of the 'matchsticks' were becoming alarmingly bigger very quickly and were going to fall nearby.

They saw some land and begin to turn on the houses with the damaged roofs, in the green square, then there was a crash and a rattle on their roof. They slid and slipped around the gable.

'Oooh!' Queenie gave a shuddering scream like one encountering a deadly snake, then without pause hurled herself along a narrow leaden ledge to where one of the incendiaries was lodged in the guttering. The bomb was about eighteen inches long and smoking furiously.

Behind her she heard Billie shout a warning, but she had her toe under it and hooked it wide, out into the street. As it fell it began to burn and when it landed it exploded into furious life, fizzing round in a circle like a great firework. Queenie was back beside, then beyond Billie shouting, 'I'll go down and put sand on it. You guard the roof.'

Clinging to the banisters with her good arm she half ran, half fell down the three flights. In the hall she hauled up one of the buckets of sand, enormously heavy, lugging it down the front steps towards the bomb, which was now in the middle of a great pool of fire, shooting flame like a grounded rocket.

She tried to hold the sand bucket up and hurl the contents, but it was way beyond her strength. Resting the bucket on its rim she was about to tip some of the sand out when she heard someone shouting. Turning she saw a bulky overcoated figure outlined by the fires further down the street. He came running, threw down a bag as he reached her. In rapid succession he took the bucket, pushed her behind him and threw the sand, kicked it up over the most persistent flames.

'Thank God I've found you,' he said.

She thought it was a strange way to announce his timely arrival, but she was certainly grateful.

'Let's get under cover.'

'Come into our house,' she invited leading the way. In the pitch black hall she could smell the scorch on their clothing, felt the brush of his uniform greatcoat as he passed her and she turned to close the door and pull the blackout curtain tight. Then she switched on the light.

'Surprise!' the naval lieutenant said taking off his cap.

Her hand flew to her mouth; she was quite unable to take in what her eyes were telling her. 'Jamie?' she queried. 'Jamie! Oh, my boy!' She rushed to him, trying to hold him and look at him at the same time. She saw changes, his chin and cheekbones had the sharper more exaggerated planes of a much older man; and many sleepless nights, or long watches, had darkly ringed his eyes.

There was a sound on the stairs and Billie came running,

238

asking if she was all right, then stopping as she came into the hall, nodding to the naval officer, 'You came just in time.'

'This is my . . .' Queenie stopped for she had been going to say her son, 'This is Jamie de Falla, my son-in-law to be. Jamie, this is Billie Chandler.'

'I'm very pleased to meet you,' he held out a hand, 'my mother-in-law-to-be,' he ran it all together making it sound cheerful, comic, 'has told Laura and myself how much she's indebted to you.'

'After this evening I think I owe her this house,' Billie replied shaking vigorously. 'That incendiary you dealt with down there, she kicked it out of the guttering.'

He looked at Queenie in amazement. 'You were up on the roof?'

'We'd begun fire watching,' she told him. 'The whole city looks alight from up there. How did you get here?'

'By tube, then walked.'

'What's it like?' Billie asked.

'It's the wind, it catches the flames, whips up great pieces of embers and throws them all over everything and everybody,' he paused and frowned. 'I helped wrap some children in coats and carry them across from a burning building to a shelter. At least there are no children at sea. It all made me desperately anxious to find you.' He looked from Queenie to Billie. 'I never realised it was as bad as this.'

'From watery wastes to fiery furnace,' Billie said, adding, 'I'll go back up on the roof, I'll let you know soon enough if there's anything to worry us. You make Jamie welcome. Are you going to sleep in the cellar with us?'

'I'll take turns on these watches. Roofs over heads are pretty important to us Gibraltarian evacuees,' he said, 'but I wouldn't mind a cup of tea first.'

Queenie drew him to the kitchen, putting on the kettle, getting out bread, the entire week's cheese ration and some tomatoes, lettuce and apples, sorry there was no meat to offer him. 'I think we've got an egg, I could scramble that.'

'I could just drink gallons of tea.' He took off his overcoat and began to unbutton his uniform jacket. He has the same long-fingered brown hands and nicely shaped nails as his father, she thought, smiling at him as he asked, 'Have you heard from Laura?'

'She rang, said there might be leave for Christmas.'

'There was a letter saying the same waiting for me when we docked. She should be travelling down the day after tomorrow, Christmas Eve, so I thought it was best to come straight here, you don't mind?'

'Mind!' She stood and shook her head. 'I am so happy. It's just so unbelievable, I wouldn't be surprised if you said you had The Rock outside.'

'With Father on it.'

'That would be heaven,' she said, 'but I'll be satisfied with heaven for you and Laura, that will be enough for one Christmas for me.'

He didn't answer, feeling at once humbled by such unselfishness, angry at the bloody war, and slightly embarrassed by the thought of what he hoped for this Christmas.

'And what's this then?' She picked up the sleeve of his jacket as it hung on the back of the chair. 'I don't know much about the navy, but an extra stripe?'

'Promotion,' he said, 'I'm what they call a Number One now, second in command on board our destroyer.'

'Congratulations!'

'Promotion comes quickly in wartime, I'm afraid,' he said then added, 'I mean new boats are coming into service all the time.'

'Yes,' she said quietly understanding the other reason without him spelling it out.

'And I'm here until after the New Year so you don't have to be embarrassed about asking that,' he said with a grin.

'Let's hope Laura gets the same then,' Queenie said, pouring tea into the largest mug she could find.

Jamie brought the house alive with his unexpected, self-appointed tasks (including plucking the turkey which arrived from Wiltshire), his sudden laughter, his reassuring male presence, even just his overcoat and cap hanging in the hall; life seemed safer, fuller with him around.

There was no message from Laura, but with only one day to go it could take all Christmas Eve to travel from Liverpool. The phone rang more times than she had ever known before, always for Billie – her family with festive catching-up as well as the hospital. Each time she saw Jamie stand quite still, anticipating, ready to lunge for the receiver.

'She'll be like you and just turn up,' she reassured him.

They made preparations for the Christmas Day meal for four of them. He brought a Christmas tree and to the scandal of Billie draped thin lines of cottonwool along all the branches. 'From my hospital box!' she exclaimed.

'Shouldn't your "hospital box" be at the hospital?' he inquired with mock severity, a glimpse of how he might be in command.

'True,' she admitted, 'but with a reckless type like your ma-in-law-to-be about, I felt I needed first aid at home.'

'I'm helping with the meals and packing stockings for the children tomorrow,' Queenie told him as Billie produced a box of childhood baubles, for which all three jostled and traded for prime places on the tree.

'I'll do some early last-minute shopping,' Jamie said, 'then I'll stick around, get some supper ready for when Laura arrives.'

'Then I'll stay and join the nurses singing carols on the wards, they have asked me.'

'Do that. It would be a nice thing to do,' he agreed.

By the time the nurses gathered to carol around the wards at midnight on Christmas Eve, Queenie regretted the decision. She was so exhausted, but once the candlelit procession began, all weariness was forgotten as she saw the pleasure on the patients' faces, and the tears. Standing to the rear of the red-cloaked nurses with just the candles and lanterns they carried lighting the wards, nothing could have looked more festive.

They sang 'Silent Night', as they approached each ward, then asked for a request, and so the repertoire of Christmas was gone through. When they reached the men's ward, Queenie looked towards Mr Moses as the first carol ended. She felt a sudden moment of alarm as she saw his head raised from the pillow and a long-fingered hand beckoning. She glanced at the nurses but all were still intent on the request for 'God Rest Ye Merry Gentlemen', so she went discreetly to his side.

'Hello, m'dear, is there something you want? Shall I fetch a nurse?'

He shook his head vigorously. 'No, no. I remember,' he said as she bent low to hear, 'I used to play the church organ. My favourite was "Christians Awake",' he said.

'I'll ask them to sing it,' she patted his arm. 'Rest back.'

She drew Sister's attention to the man who had not spoken since he was admitted, and she went quickly to him. Sister stayed with him holding his hand as the choir turned his way and sang the rousing rising words of the carol: 'Christians awake, salute the happy morn, Whereon the Saviour of the world was born.'

When they had finished he raised his hand in thanks. 'That's the best choir I have ever heard,' he told Sister.

It was with this moment in her mind above all others that Queenie made her way back alone through the silent streets. No raids tonight, a short respite. Billie had been invited to a party by an old acquaintance and would stay there overnight, returning to the hospital the next morning to help with the Christmas dinner. Queenie was not going back until after Boxing Day.

As she let herself into the hall the sight she most anxiously hoped and prayed for was there. 'Thank God!' she breathed taking off her own coat and hat and hanging them beside the navy cap and the Wren's hat. 'Thank God!' she repeated and reached up to touch Laura's hat. She had showed Jamie the flat earlier, and had later put clean sheets on the bed and been unable to resist turning both sides down for its two occupants.

She thought of them so close in the three-quarter bed as she made her way down to the cellar and her camp bed. Just the right size for a young couple, she thought – or me and Freddie come to that. 'Happy Christmas, my love,' she said aloud to the arched roof and using the string jerked off the light, 'thanks for your son.'

Chapter Nineteen

Laura woke slowly, realising first that she was very happy, then remembered it was Christmas morning, and that Jamie was fast asleep by her side. From Honeysuckle Cottage to Georgian mansion, she thought, and gave a wriggle of naked enjoyment – but she had not yet seen her mother.

She thrilled to the excitement to come, of the presents she had for her mother – a lambs' wool jumper, a bottle of lavender water and a pair of Fair Isle gloves knitted by one of the Wrens in her division. Wide awake she could wait no longer. She would make it the reverse of all other Christmases when the gifts had been brought to her bed and the two had shared the excitement of presents, before the balancing act of keeping her father and the spirit of Christmas in harmony.

She slipped out of bed, fumbled for her pyjamas, tucked the covers carefully in around Jamie, put her navy overcoat on, scooped up the bag with the Christmas presents – and went from bedroom to bedroom looking for Queenie.

She had seen little of the house either when her mother moved in or the night before. The kitchen and the bedroom had been all they needed – food, love and sleep, love and sleep, 'love and sleep' she whispered it like a mantra as she Santa Claused her parcels from room to room, and found every one empty and unslept in.

The realisation that her mother had spent the night alone

244

in the cellar came with an appalling jolt. She remembered Jamie pointing out the cellar door. Unable to find a light switch she located a candle on a kitchen shelf and, shielding the flame began the descent, still unconvinced her mother *could* be in this place.

After the bottom step a blank wall faced her, she turned and holding the candle a little higher saw what looked like a cavern – with beds and on one . . .

'Oh! Mum.' She wondered if it was her feeling of guilt after her own night of 'love and sleep' that brought her mother's startled look as she woke, for a moment studying her as if fearing she were a stranger. Then they were in each other's arms laughing, crying, asking questions of each other so fast neither had time to answer.

'Why did you sleep down here, all by yourself?'

'I never thought to do anything else,' she said. 'I knew you'd arrived, that was all that mattered.'

'Mum, Christmas Day, this is awful.' She looked around trying to find evidence of the dankness that should be in city cellars and found none. 'This underground . . . place.'

'Shelter,' her mother corrected, making her laugh as she used Billie's technique to pull on the light, revealing all, then as Laura agreed that as cellars went it *was* a superior kind, her mother added almost shyly, 'Like you then. Your photo is lovely, you look so smart and . . .'

'And?'

'Self assured . . .' Queenie paused not willing to say the word, distant, that had been around in her mind every time she had looked at the photograph, 'and different.'

'I'm certainly *not* different.' Laura was sure about that. 'Today's different though,' she said holding on to her mother's hand, 'we've only got Hitler to worry about this year.'

They both drew in a breath at the comparison, then burst out laughing. Hitler's threat was, at that moment, so much less personally vindictive than the domestic tyranny they had endured. Then she regretted the witticism as her

245

mother's gaze fell to her hands, so still, the pose she had so often found her in after one of her father's outbursts. Quickly she bundled the little pile of presents along the bed, nearer her mother's hands. 'Open your presents then.'

'Billie thinks the proper time to have presents is midday,' Queenie said doubtfully.

Laura wondered about Billie, she had met her only briefly before joining the WRENS. She was a hospital almoner, a figure of authority. She hoped her mother was not allowing herself to come under a new domination, a new bullying and insisted, 'Then this is our private bit of Christmas.'

'My presents for you are under the tree.'

'The two of them crept carefully up to Billie's sitting room and like children sorted and unwrapped their parcels for each other.

'Not very original are we?' Queenie had said when Laura unwrapped the navy blue cable-knit sweater she had painstakingly persevered with in her canteen, often a few stitches at a time, and would never have finished had Sister of women's surgical not enlisted the help of one of her favourite Cockney ladies.

'It's great, Mum, just what I needed.' Laura hugged it to herself. 'Great minds think alike. This'll keep the draughts off my back in the plotting room.'

Queenie soaked up the information, the plotting room, and hoped it was in a deep, deep bunker.

'Mum,' Laura queried, 'are you really all right here, working and your arm and everything – and with Billie?'

'Everything,' she confirmed, 'as well as it can be for anyone in this war.'

They embraced, held each other, managed to stave off tears.

'It's lovely to . . .' Laura began.

'I know,' Queenie said.

While her mother had gone to dress she crept back to Jamie, waking him as she slipped in beside him. He turned

246

and took her into his arms. 'You're dressed,' he accused, voice husky with sleep.

'Happy Christmas,' she breathed in his ear, clinging to his warmth, excited, twining her satin pyjama-ed legs between his and pushing a small gift-wrapped parcel into his groping hand. 'Happy Christmas,' she repeated.

'Happy Christmas.' He held her close, any present little compensation for having to let her go to undo it. In the distance he heard the front door close and Queenie investigating, then Billie and Queenie talking, animated Christmas greetings. He leaned over, recovered the small parcel he had pushed under his side of the bed and sat up.

They pulled up the pillows and leaned back side by side to undo their presents. They compared parcels, they were almost identical in size. Jamie pulled a comical face. 'You say you and your mother have exchanged jumpers?'

'You think we've bought each other the same thing?' she asked.

'I hope not.' He tore open his parcel and revealed a small jeweller's box, inside a handsome St Christopher medallion. The patron saint of travellers carrying the infant Christ safely over a stream was in silver relief, edged by a faceted circular gold frame.

'They say a lot of chaps are wearing them round their necks like army dog tags,' she said in case he thought it inappropriate.

'Thanks,' he said leaning over to kiss her cheek. 'Open yours.'

She wondered if he really liked the gift, or whether they had bought each other the same thing as she too revealed a small dark blue box engraved in gold with a jeweller's name, but inside her box was a gold cross and chain.

Then she realised the reason for his sudden solemnity. The same message was behind each gift and his card inside the box said, 'Stay safe for me, Yours always, Jamie.'

They sat propped up beside each other in bed, suddenly as much comrades in arms as lovers. Like the posters, she thought. Men and women striding off to war together, but the reality was different, behind the eager, glowing faces were many mixed emotions, many fears.

'Thanks, Jamie, it's beautiful.' She lifted the necklace by its brilliant chain, admiring the craftsmanship, the quality of the solid little cross. 'I shall wear it all the time under my uniform.'

'Me too,' he said raising his gift box in affirmation.

Too much affected by the mutuality of their gifts and their feelings to say more she pushed her feet under his thigh for warmth and to stop herself slipping down the bed.

'Just think,' he said rapturously, 'a lifetime of cold feet.'

It broke the spell and they slid right down under the covers.

Later Laura put the cross on and her new jumper. Billie declared the dinner party formal, but clothes informal. Jamie had immediately put the candelabra from the dining room sideboard on to the table and had gone down to dinner in balaclava, gloves and scarf – all courtesy of an unwoven navy guernsey which had belonged to Billie's brother-in-law (and the lady in woman's surgical.)

He had discarded the woollies before the meal and now leaned back spreading his hands over his expanded stomach. 'Now I know what they mean by a "blow out".'

'Room for a brandy though,' Billie said going to the sideboard. 'All round?'

'Why not,' Jamie answered for everyone.

'A toast?' Billie asked passing brandy balloons, and instinctively they all looked to Queenie, who was surprised but looked from one to the other as if wondering who to make the object of her toast. Billie first, unexpected benefactor, now friend. Jamie, as precious as any son she and Freddie might have had. Laura, whom she loved better than herself, than life itself. She wished she had the power to keep them all safe.

'Mum?' Laura prompted.

248

She smiled at her daughter, then raised her glass. 'Peace,' she said.

'To peace,' the other three echoed solemnly.

'Soon, and may all your men come home,' Billie breathed, then as if recollecting herself, added, 'my brother-in-law is with the British Expeditionary Force, got out at Dunkirk. He says they'll go back in, invade eventually.'

Jamie shook his head. 'Not yet awhile,' he said with certainty. 'There's too much to replace. We're just struggling to keep everything coming in, convoys down the east coast to keep London going, convoys across the Atlantic and back, that's my sector when I go back.'

'Yes,' Laura repeated the message that had been drilled into her section, 'it's the convoys that are vital.' She could see in her mind's eye the black outlines of ships she moved across the charts, like a huge but deadly board game with so many different pieces: destroyers, warships, submarines, U-boats, merchantmen – some 'yours' some 'the enemy's'. The merchantmen came off the board in increasing numbers and with every one she remembered the *Dromore Castle*, wondered if she was back coaling again, if Albert was still reading the Bible. She looked at Jamie, not leaning back now, but elbows on table looking at Billie, intent on the conversation. Now Jamie would be on one of those token destroyers. If she knew his convoy number she would know precisely where he was, exactly what was happening to him. Dear God.

'Yes,' Billie was saying, 'regrouping, and building up all the equipment left behind in France, that was the talk at the party last night. Planning, getting the strategy right. Perhaps staying in the corner for a bit licking our wounds.' She leaned back, hands clasped behind her head, 'and to really mix the metaphors, giving Hitler enough rope to hang himself. They say he's a man impatient for results, if one thing doesn't work quickly, he'll try another.'

Queenie thought of the changing pattern of the Blitz. The

Luftwaffe had received a stunning blow a few weeks before, since then no more daylight raids, now there was the fire bombing. She looked at her children and wondered what ordeal was next. Laura reckoned she was working in a safe environment and she shouldn't worry, 'safer than you here, Mum'. Jamie? Atlantic convoys. She remembered their crossing to Nantucket Light and back, the weather, just the one alert they had was frightening enough.

'I,' Billie said, standing and stretching, 'am going to wash up then go to bed, in my own bedroom, with another brandy and a book. What heaven!'

'We'll all wash up,' Jamie said and immediately began to clear the table. 'We can always leave the worst in soak.'

'Let's have some "Music While We Work".' Laura went to the gramophone in the corner.

'It's pretty scratchy, we had it as children,' Billie warned, 'put a new needle in, play waltzes to keep us going.'

Laura found the tin of tiny needles, released the old needle and screwed the new one into place, then winding the gramophone she selected Strauss waltzes already humming 'The Blue Danube', 'Daa, dah, da dah,' when as the needle fell into the groove she was snatched into Jamie's arms and waltzed, 'One, two, three. One, two, three,' he cried around the dining room, through the hall, into the kitchen and back to the sitting room, where he kissed her with great gusto.

'You're a ...' she failed to find the word as he gazed serenely down at her. She had thought she had outgrown such tongue-tied moments.

'I know,' he said and waltzed her back into the kitchen.

'Now your turn,' he told Queenie who from the kitchen could soon be heard pleading, 'Slower, slower. I'll be giddy.'

'About time!' he cried back and whizzed her ever faster back to the kitchen. 'Lastly the hostess with the mostest.'

'I've got wet hands.'

'Twice round the course to dry them then.'

Billie was heard to ask if he could do the Charleston. 'Always wanted to learn,' he told her. The music stopped, the needle scratching across the record and after a short rummaging the jerky catchy rhythm of the Charleston blared out as Billie turned the volume up to its fullest extent. 'Come on,' she said, 'I'll show you how. It's all in the knees.'

Soon Jamie and Billie were jerking around the room, Billie expertly. She grabbed a ribbon from a heap of wrapping paper and tied it around her forehead, then hitched up her skirt a little more and kicked up her heels, twirling her hands to what she obviously found an irresistible beat.

'Come on, you two,' she shouted at Laura and Queenie standing in the doorway, teatowels in hand. They were quickly drawn in, Laura came to suspect her mother had done this all before, she adeptly did she pick up the movements and so readily did she hurry to rewind the gramophone when the music slurred deeper and deeper to a halt. Then off they went again. Jamie careered around the room to the danger of everyone until he fell exhausted into an armchair and catching her hand pulled Laura down on to his knee.

'Let the flappers have the floor,' he gasped. 'I'm beat.'

'No stamina, that's what I say!' Billie cried then the next moment stood holding her knees. 'They are telling me they've had enough.'

Later with Billie and Queenie both settled in main bedrooms in the house, Laura and Jamie went out into the neglected city garden. It was incredibly quiet.

'No traffic,' Laura breathed looking up into a night where clouds drove across a starlight sky, 'but a bomber's moon.'

'But tonight we're let off.' He drew in a deep noisy breath. 'Good to be in the fresh air for a bit.'

'Oh! I've just seen a shooting star.'

'Is that lucky?' he asked.

Once more the words did not come because there were so many answers she could give. Yes, it was lucky at the moment. While they were together it was lucky. The last time she had stargazed with him in mind was when she had been sailing away from Gibraltar.

'What is it?' he asked gently and when she did not answer he said, 'I can guess.'

'How can you?'

'Because although I have told you when I have to go back, you have never mentioned to me, or to your mother, when *you* have to go.'

'Yes,' she admitted moving to sit on a stone seat, icily cold. 'I have to be back by midnight on the 27th.'

'Damn,' he said quietly. 'OK, so I'll come back with you, find lodgings in Liverpool until the 31st, give us four more days together.'

Before you go on Atlantic convoys and I plot them on a screen, she thought. But if I don't ask, don't know the number of your convoy, I won't be able to agonise so particularly.

Told on Boxing Day morning that Laura had to go back the next day, Queenie had stood silent for a moment then said quietly, 'I'd like to come and see you both off at the station.'

That night she had gone back to sleep in the cellar; it suited her mood better than Billie's elegant second bedroom.

What she did not voice was that she could not bear being left in the house alone after two days of such life and laughter. She would go straight from Euston Station back to the hospital, then perhaps returning would be more endurable after a work stint, when she would be tired, bone-weary, ready for the quiet desolate house.

252

Chapter Twenty

'You heard about Mr Moses?'

Queenie had not yet removed her coat and hat when the nurse rushed in to the canteen. She still felt numb with cold and loss after the separation from Laura and Jamie at Euston Station, going off in their naval uniforms with their bags and their youth, their love – but together – crowding the window to watch and wave to the last.

'Are you all right?'

The young Irish nurse looked at her with concern.

She focused on the youngster, always in trouble because her red hair escaped her cap, she could not have been nursing for more than twelve months and was, Queenie remembered, on men's surgical.

'Mr Moses,' the girl repeated.

Queenie recalled the frail skeletal hand lifting as they sang, and was not sure she wanted to hear, but she could see from the eager face of the nurse that she was going to be told anyway.

'Well, Mr Moses turns out to be the Very Reverend Thomas Taylor from Durham, so he is. He'd come to London to see his grandson while he was on leave but got caught up in the bombing and finished up in night clothes without any baggage and not remembering who he was, until the *carols*.'

'I thought you were going to say he'd died.'

'No! He's gone home!'

From first bed inside any ward to home was quite a leap for anyone, but especially for anyone as old and frail as Mr Moses.

'His wife's going to meet him at Durham station,' the nurse said grinning, waiting for the reaction.

'His wife! But she must be . . .'

'As old as Moses.' The nurse burst into laughter. 'I must go, I'll have Sister on my track, but I wanted to tell you after the carols.'

'So you mean he's left hospital and gone *on the train to Durham*?'

'The good Lord moves in mysterious ways.'

So had the frail old man been one of a crowd such as she had moved amongst at Euston Station? The bustling mass of uniforms, the travellers burdened with kitbags, cases, parcels and the emotions of those seeing them off. She had wondered if *she* had been right to go, but Laura's leave had been so short, every moment had to be garnered. She had looked along the platform as the back of the last carriage swayed out of sight, saw handkerchiefs being used more openly, then there was the doleful turning and walking away, as if all the spirit of Christmas had steamed out with the train.

The remarkable recovery of the Reverend 'Moses' Taylor was told and retold around the girders of the canteen, but Queenie found it impossible to throw off the sadness of her new separation. The trouble was, she thought dourly, that none of them knew when, or even if, they would meet again. If only, she thought as she pulled her chairs into sociable groups, we could say 'see you next week', or 'next month' – even next year if it was a certainty. She knew she was being peevish, illogical; life *never* was like that.

On her way home late that night the air-raid sirens wailed and she could hear the heavy droning pulse of enemy planes almost at once. She felt so dispirited she hardly quickened

254

her step. Her immediate instinct was to return to the hospital; so strong was the impulse she stopped and half turned. Ridiculous, she told herself, wasn't she totally worn out, exhausted with the ups and downs of the holiday? Perhaps the urge to go back was no more than not wanting to face Billie's house, the cellar, just the two of them.

As she neared the house the masked headlights of a passing car revealed a large black object at the foot of the basement steps. She approached cautiously, looking up above her head, examining the outline of the building against the sky, checking to make sure what lay below was not part of some dislodged masonry, and that more was not likely to fall at any moment.

She ventured a step or two down and saw that the object was rectangular, like a crate. Something for Billie, she supposed, and Billie was probably waiting for help to get it inside, the huge great thing.

'Hello!' Billie carolled from the kitchen. 'I've made us turkey broth, with the remains of the pudding for afters.'

'Big Christmas present,' Queenie said, then, seeing her friend's bemused expression, 'at the bottom of the basement steps.'

'What are you talking about?'

'There's a huge parcel, packing case I should think, at the bottom of the basement stairs.'

'What? I know nothing about a Christmas present, and I certainly didn't notice anything.'

They looked at each other, then both headed for the basement door, but the blackness was so total they could only feel.

'I'll get the flashlight,' Queenie said, 'if we shade it we should be all right.'

The flashlight was used only in emergencies, batteries were not easy to come by. She went out again, closing the door.

'There are two,' Billie told her as she fumbled for the switch on the torch. 'Two boxes of some kind. Heaven only

255

knows what they are. I can't feel any labels on them.'

Queenie shaded the top of the flashlight and switched it on. Immediately she gasped, her finger slipped off the switch and the light went out. 'It can't be.'

'What can't?' Even Billie sounded apprehensive.

Queenie shone the light a second time, forgetting to shade it this time and put her hand out to the brass-bound chests – Freddie's chests. 'But, but, we left them in . . .'

'Put that light out!' a stentorian warden's shout had them both scuttling back inside.

'What are they?' Billie asked, 'I'll have palpitations if you don't tell me soon.'

'I think,' she said, fingers covering her lips as if to utter the thought was ridiculous, 'they're the chests we had to leave behind in French Morocco when we were thrown out.'

'I wouldn't have thought . . .' Billie did not need to finish the doubts she felt about this supposition.

'No, and we left them in the rooms we had, in the charge of an Arab and his gimlet-eyed daughter.'

'We'd better try and get them inside so you can have a proper look.'

'There are handles,' Queenie said, then realised she was assuming what they had agreed was nigh impossible. She tutted at herself, tried to be practical. 'If we leave the torch on lying just inside the kitchen door, it'll help us see what we're doing.'

It didn't much, but they located the handles. 'To the count of three then,' Billie said. 'One, two three!' They heaved at the top chest. It reached the ground more or less by its own momentum once they had it off balance. It was only by half lifting and half sliding in a series of closely combined efforts that they managed to get it inside.

'So is it yours?' Billie asked as they recovered, then revised to, 'it is yours,' as she watched the other woman running her hands over the top, the brass hinges, the lock, looking more as if she was assessing the injuries of a living creature than a chest.

'There surely can't be many chests like this, so it must be, but ...'

'"But me no buts"'. Let's get the other one while our strength lasts.'

When both chests were in the kitchen side by side, Queenie stood looking as if lost in wonder, and while Billie appreciated they were very fine antique chests under the dirt, it was her friend's expression that fascinated. 'You look,' she told her 'as if you've just been introduced to the *real* Santa Claus.'

Queenie gave a short obliging laugh but still stood shaking her head.

'But how to open them. Where would the keys be?'

'In my case upstairs,' Queenie said still not moving.

'Oh!' and when there was still no move. 'Can I get them for you?'

'My suitcase is in the closet,' Queenie answered, 'the keys are in the inside pocket.'

'OK.'

Apart from her daughter's photograph there was nothing to see of Queenie's occupation of the rooms. She could do with a few more possessions, she thought, finding the keys. They were quite large, ornate, wrapped in tissue paper. How odd we are about what we treasure, she mused. These chests obviously either had something very special inside or were of some deep significance – they were certainly a lot more than just posh containers.

Returning, Billie watched as the first key was turned, someone, she thought, had kept those locks well oiled. She was full of curiosity as the lid was raised. Materials packed around a Singer sewing machine, and in the other yet more materials and a tailor's dummy. She was so disappointed, though quite what she had expected she was not sure. She had gathered her lodger liked knitting and sewing, but this looked either like an obsession or a profession.

Queenie was remembering how she, Freddie, Laura and Jamie had collected and packed all these things. She

257

remembered Jamie coming down the stairs swathed in one of the brightest dress lengths, how he and his father had gone off pushing the chests on the handcart.

'So they are yours, no doubt about that. Though how they got here?' She stood back and scrutinised the chests from all angles. 'The only thing it says on the back here is 'Not Wanted on Voyage'. It's on both of them.'

Queenie went to look. 'That certainly wasn't on when we left them, and . . .' she shook her head, 'I couldn't imagine our Arab landlord or his daughter writing that well in English. Come to that I couldn't imagine them not just keeping them, the daughter certainly admired them, coveted them, I thought.' She was ashamed of her conviction that as soon they had left, the chests would have been hauled down to the Arab's quarters. She remembered they had been roped up when they left them. 'But nothing's been touched,' she added aloud. 'I certainly owe the daughter an apology.'

'Judging by appearances, we all do it, I suppose,' Billie said.

'But the way the authorities threw us out of French Morocco at gunpoint, it hardly seemed likely they would send on our belongings.'

'Ridiculous things do happen.' She retold a story she'd heard at the Christmas Eve party. A box of malt whisky, twenty-four bottles, had been ordered at Fortnum's to go to the British Expeditionary Force before they got routed, then evacuated from Dunkirk, and this whisky had followed the man all the way from England to Belgium, France and back to his home in Kensington! 'He brought half a dozen bottles with him to the party. He swore it was true,' she added to Queenie's doubtful look.

'I just wonder if Jamie had anything to do with these arriving? He'd be the only one in this country who would know where I was – but he would have told me – surely.'

'Perhaps he didn't want you unpacking all this lot when they were home for the hols?' Billie said.

'Perhaps ...' She knelt handling some of the pieces of material, remembering what she had had in mind when she bought each piece in the Indian shops in Gibraltar, dresses, blouses for Laura, and herself. 'If these trunks had come with us to England I should never have taken the job in the hospital, I would have made and turned clothes for people,' she paused and smiled at Billie. 'I would have been sorry about that.'

'So would everyone at the hospital, particularly me. Now I'm starving, let's sit and eat our broth, and talk over this mystery.' She noted that Queenie closed the chests lovingly and it seemed to her that the mystery might well be why the chests meant more than the contents did.

'So they originally belonged to Jamie's father?' She was curious, interested in this Freddie they all talked about so animatedly, their faces all seeming to light up at his name. Construction engineer, tunnel and air-raid shelter maker. She also fell to wondering about Mr Maclaren, the husband who was never mentioned. An army officer who as far as Billie knew was never written to and certainly never mentioned, even over Christmas.

Queenie spooned her broth in silence, noticing neither her friend's scrutiny nor her attempt to learn more.

Billie asked twice if she would like more broth, then got up, cleared the dishes and produced the pudding.

'Your old cook must have been a wonder,' Queenie said making an effort to engage with the here and now, 'laying down puddings two years in advance'.

'She won't be making any more, she died last summer in the kitchen,' then at Queenie's startled glance added, 'no, no, not here, in Wiltshire.'

'Let me,' Queenie was just reaching over to serve the warmed-up pudding when the front doorbell rang. Billie tutted but beckoned to Queenie to carry on as she would go.

Queenie spooned out the remaining pudding, listening to Billie talking to someone, a man, she thought. The front door closed, but she could hear Billie questioning, laughing. It seemed she had a visitor, someone she knew. Queenie poured the custard, looking at the miracle of the chests. She had thought returning to this house would be a dreary experience after the gladness of Christmas, but so far there had not been time for it to be.

Billie came into the kitchen grinning like a Cheshire cat, gesturing for someone to stay behind her. 'I've solved the mystery of the chests,' she said, then standing back she let the man behind her walk through into the kitchen. A man in an overcoat, carrying a trilby, a man with the tanned skin of one who lived in the sun – all this she absorbed, as if her mind could only deal with this latest arrival one detail at a time. Then she dropped the custard jug with a thud on to the table, stood staring, riveted, this shock too much. 'Freddie?' A lot of half words began but none were finished.

'My dearest Queenie.'

He dropped his hat on to the table and went quickly to her, seizing her hands as shock made her knees fail and she looked likely to fall. He lowered her gently back into her chair. 'You'll be surprised to see me,' he said with a laugh at the understatement.

The phrase the 'onlooker seeing most of the game' came into Billie's mind as she watched the two of them. Here was the connection between Queenie's introspection over the chests and the man who had owned them. These two loved each other. They were totally lost in each other. She watched without embarrassment, but with many other emotions, as he knelt before Queenie and she leaned forward and put her head on his shoulder. So the love had been there the generation before Laura and Jamie. She wondered what had happened, and whether she was not seeing the beginning of a new life for the parents.

They clung to each other, asking quiet questions, the mundane general things that must come before the details. 'Are you well?' 'The youngsters?' 'You found the chests then?' 'Marvellous.'

Freddie looked round and smiled. 'I didn't mean you two

260

ladies to struggle with them.'

'So you did bring them?' Billie asked.

'Yes, in a taxi from Paddington, then there was no one here and I got the taxi man to help me unload, then take me to your hospital. It took me some time to find out that you had left, and I've just walked back.'

Queenie remembered her impulse to return to the hospital. She had not imagined it, her instinct had been right. Briefly the memory of her moment of terror in the hospital subterranean corridor impinged, but cavalierly she amended the thought to *sometimes* her instinct could be trusted.

'Would you like some turkey broth?' Billie asked. 'Sit down, let me take your coat and hat. I'll put them here for now.' She hung them on the peg behind the kitchen door, unwilling to miss any of this story.

Freddie clasped Queenie's hand tight on the table as Billie set a place for him, warmed up the remainder of the broth and cut slices of bread. He leaned back, beaming happiness and good humour as he told them how the chests had only recently arrived from one of the Gibraltan warehouses.

'They'd been there more or less ever since you were all brought back from Casablanca, but it wasn't until Fatima saw them in a warehouse that anyone knew who they belonged to, because the ropes and labels had gone. Fatima,' he glanced at Billie, 'is my secretary. It was seeing the chests again that spurred me to ask if they would let me come to England to work for the Ministry of Defence here. The contract in Gibraltar is pretty well complete, my men can supervise the finishing off and the maintenance without me. They told me they were sure I'd be welcome provided I could get here.'

'So, how did you?' Queenie was beginning to look better now, lively even, recovered from the initial shock.

'I hitched a life on a destroyer,' he told them.

'Is that allowed?'

'The MoD declared me as a desirable to the captain, then there was no problem. The chests started off as deck cargo, but in the end I had them below and slept on them.'

'So you're here to stay?' Queenie asked. 'Really here.'

'In England, yes, I've come to work here for the duration of the war. Where shall I stay in London?'

'Well, here of course,' Billie interrupted. 'Here, in Queenie's flat.' She suddenly felt her throat thicken with emotion and she rose and cleared the crockery from the table. 'Look,' she said, 'you two have got a lot of catching up to do. I'll go up if you don't mind – and if the raids get bad I'll see you both down the cellar – that you will have to share with the two of us,' she told Freddie.

He stood up as she made for the door. 'Thank you,' he said, 'for everything, for looking after Queenie for me, you know ...' he made a kind of gesture between Queenie and himself and repeated, 'you know ...'

'I think I know all I need to know,' she smiled at him. 'See you both in the morning.'

She closed the kitchen door after herself and the tears began to fall in earnest. She stumbled and nearly fell flat over Freddie's case in the hall, but as Queenie called to ask if she was all right, she ran upstairs afraid one of them might come after her. Fat chance, she thought, they would be totally engrossed in each other for the rest of the night, for the rest of their lives most likely.

She went into her bedroom and leaned back on the door. 'Oh, Harry!' she mourned. 'We loved like that, our eyes shone when we looked at each other. It was just like that from the first moment we met, as if invisible threads ran between us.' She stood and ached for the young man who had been killed in 1916 leading his men on the Somme; she had been twenty and he twenty-four. Truly a perfect match, people had said; not only had their families approved, but their circles of friends had rejoiced; everything was right for them and they loved each other.

'To distraction', she whispered to her empty room. 'I have tried to make my life count, Harry, make it useful, but it's been a dry old shell in every other department.'

Chapter Twenty-One

The telegram came the day Laura had recommenced her duties; it was brought to the main plotting room. She saw a fellow Wren go to the group of Royal Air Force and Navy officers concerned with these joint operations rooms, single out her commanding officer and whisper to him. He looked annoyed, frowned over in her direction then nodded curtly.

The telegram was put into her hands. She looked for permission to read it and received a swift jerk of the head. She left the central arena with its walls of maps, route lines, ship and plane markers and the tall movable sets of ladders she had to climb to help pinpoint the convoys. She stood contemplating the telegram. Telegrams were synonymous with bad news. Thank God she knew where Jamie was – but her mother? The BBC had reported bombing on London again last night.

Her hands trembled as she tore open the undersized buff envelope, she had to read it twice to take in the fact that it was good news. 'Jamie's father in England for duration. Love, Mum.'

Jamie would be outside waiting for her when she went off duty, she consulted her wristwatch, in two hours' time. She pushed the message into her pocket and went back to her duties. She looked over to her commanding officer. 'Good news, sir.'

'Well done.' He nodded adding, 'Now let's get on with the war.'

Jamie stood shoulders hunched as she ran to him and pushed her arm through his. 'Colder here than on the bridge,' he said before she could speak, then hanging back when she tried to rush him on, tell him the news. 'Who's that guy over there, d'you know? He's been hanging about as if he's waiting for someone.'

'Probably is,' she answered, then in a moment of unguarded concern asked, 'He's not an airman with a red moustache, is he?'

'Y . . . e . . . s?' he answered the question with an implied greater question.

'I think I've managed to give a chap the wrong impression,' she said shivering, being careful not to glance around. 'I'll tell you, but let's walk on, and *I've* got news that'll warm the very cockles of your heart,' she told him.

'Good,' he said, 'I need it after watching that type ogle every Wren who's come out *and* never made a move until you appeared. There's a pub around the corner, let's get in there out of this wind.'

She decided to wait until they were inside to produce the telegram.

'I've found something else, too,' he said nearly good-humoured again and teasing, 'but I'll tell you about that later.'

The pub was alive with merchant seamen already well into drinking the pub dry and creating a cigarette fug that well obscured the vision. Jamie fought his way to the counter to cries of 'Look out boys the navy's 'ere!' and 'So what kept 'em?'

'Rounding up you bloody stragglers,' Jamie retorted to a general roar of laugher.

He came back with two small tankards of beer. 'Short rations for non-regulars,' he told her as they sat in the corner as far away from the uproar of talking, laughing, arguing, as possible. Nearby the printed silk handkerchief

264

and spinner of the illegal Crown and Anchor game appeared from a pocket and was restarted now the newcomers had been assessed.

'So who is that chap?' he wanted to know.

'Important things first.' She was going to pull the telegram from her pocket but he captured her hand.

'No,' he said suddenly tense again, 'nothing's more important that this. That man was watching for you, I could tell the moment you walked out.'

'Well, he's wasting his time, I've made it as clear as I can.'

'But he's not got the message yet, and,' he growled, 'he's followed us in here.'

Laura glanced quickly then dropped her gaze as the pilot pushed into the bar and looked around, then made for the bar, ordered a drink and stood so he had her in his view.

'I'll go and thump him now and be done with it,' Jamie muttered. 'Look at him! No, don't! I'll do the watching. What have you done to make him think he's in with a chance?'

She could see there was going to be no settling this until she told him exactly what had happened.

'Can't you see what it is?' she whispered at him, urgent and frustrated. She wanted to tell her good news, not have it spoilt by this unwanted man's presence. 'Can't you see who he's like, that's what made me stare at him, it was almost uncanny. It was at a dance, I went with a lot of the girls, you don't mind that, do you?'

He looked at her swiftly. 'No, of course not,' he said, then returned to glaring towards the man at the counter.

'Look at his colouring, red moustache, black hair, such a vivid contrast, and just his general expression, sort of arrogant, leering.'

'Oh!' the exclamation was quiet. 'I do see,' Jamie said slowly, 'I do see. He's like your father,' he looked back sharply to her, 'but *he* doesn't know that.'

'No, I can't very well explain that I was appalled to see

someone who reminded me of my father. *That's* why I stared at him and he took it as a come-on and asked me to dance.'

'And did you?'

'Just once.'

'But now he's found out which section you work in,' he grumbled over his tankard, unable to tear his gaze away from the airman.

'It looks like it, but Jamie, please ...' She foraged in her pocket.

'I'm going to have to deal with him.'

'I can handle it, there's nothing to worry about.' She pulled the telegram from her pocket, smoothed it out on the table before him. 'Read that, it came about two hours ago.'

It was with difficulty he looked away, at first glancing, then seeing the telegram form with attention, flattening it between both hands to read. His mouth gaped and she thought he was going to whoop in delight, as he would have done in sunlit Gib she thought, instead he said very quietly, 'The old devil. I wonder how he's managed that.'

'I thought we could phone in a little while. They'll be down in that cellar if there's a raid going on but Billie has a phone down there.'

'Good idea, come on drink up, we'll leave *him* behind.'

They ran hand in hand through the cold drizzle and crowded into the urine-redolent phone box. The phone rang for some time before a male voice answered, Jamie heard it and grabbed. 'Pa?'

'Jamie!'

'How d'manage it? How are you? Just missed us, didn't leave until yesterday.'

'I'm fine and it's a long story. Hitched a lift with the navy.'

'What did you do, tell them your great-great-grandfather sailed with Nelson?'

'Something like that.'

'So is Billie letting you stay?' holding the phone higher

266

away from Laura who wanted to speak. 'Thought she would. Salt of the earth, been wonderful . . .'

'Marvellous,' Laura corrected.

'. . . to Queenie. Have a word with this woman here before she scratches my eyes out.'

'Freddie? It's good to hear your voice.' She was aware of Jamie stooping to peer through the dingy rectangles of glass out into the street. 'Has Mum got over the shock yet?' She remembered her mother floating in borrowed robe across the courtyard in the middle of the night.

'Just about. I've been to work with her today, in the canteen. I'm going to put her some extra shelves up, make it more workable.'

'Can you do anything about the chairs?' she laughed.

'Chairs?' Jamie repeated.

'They're the bane of her life,' she said to the men at both ends of the line. 'Jamie's coming back to you in a moment, but is Mum there?'

'She is,' he said.

She had a picture of them standing side by side, his arm around her. Then her mother's voice, warm, husky. 'Laura. What about this? What a surprise,' she went on to tell about the chests being on the doorstep.

The stories and the chatting went on, until they had nearly exhausted every last coin in their pockets. 'We could try to ring you back,' Queenie suggested.

'We'd thought of that but we can't read the number, it's all scratched out.'

'One piece of unwelcome news,' her mother's voice fell. 'Your father's in a psychiatric hospital.'

She was neither surprised, nor did she consider it bad news.

'In this country,' her mother added.

'Oh, they've brought him back.' It was not a question. 'Are you all right?' She meant worried, are you worried.

'I was upset when Freddie first told me, but now I'm OK. Just felt you ought to know. Don't worry about me, *we're* fine.' The voice faded a little as if her mother had turned to Freddie. 'No more worries.'

Freddie's voice came in from aside. 'Just the divorce, then we'll marry.'

'Divorce?'

'Yes,' he said soberly, 'there's grounds.'

'Oh, yes,' she said quietly as the last coin dropped out of use and the line went dead.

'Your father's talking of divorce and,' she paused to make her voice stay level, 'and my father's in this country . . .'

'I heard,' Jamie said as she put the receiver back on to its rest. 'But he's obviously under restraint.'

She was surprised Freddie was talking of a divorce, it was unusual, expensive, involved barristers, lengthy evidence, often private investigators, almost unheard of in Gibraltar with its high percentage of Catholics.

Jamie put his arm around her waist – difficult in a telephone box in overcoats carrying gas masks. 'My father will want to do the right thing,' he said as if he was thinking on the same lines, 'no matter how difficult, he'll get there in the end. He'll want to make sure your father can never interfere with their lives again, should he ever . . .'

He left the sentence unfinished leaving her in a quagmire of questions. Should he ever . . . what? Be let out? Escape? Was this why Freddie thought they must both be told? She became quite overwhelmed by thoughts of such an occurrence, scenarios ran through her mind – accostings, awful dramas – jeeps careering down streets. Would he find out where her mother was? Could he possibly? Would the officials running the Gibraltan evacuee scheme tell him? She remembered the paper she'd watched being filled in before they left Anerley, with Billie's address and the words 'left the scheme' added in bold black pen. Would they perhaps delight in telling a husband that his ungrateful wife and daughter had gone away – and where they had gone?

'Would it be like a lunatic asylum?' she asked.

'More a hospital I would have thought, but the patients would be watched, restrained.' He really knew little of such things, tried to think of reassuring but honest things to say. Then both of them started as someone knocked impatiently on the door of the telephone booth, shouting, 'You two about finished? It's for telephoning, not smooching.'

They came out quickly, Jamie apologising as an elderly grey-haired woman with a greyer shawl over her head and shoulders bundled past them grumbling.

Jamie held her close into his side as they walked heads down against a spiteful sleet which drove into their faces. She resented her father's ability still to take the edge from her happiness, and his doppelgänger's persistence. It was weeks since the dance.

'Look!' he said suddenly drawing her into a shop doorway, a newspaper shop with wet and wind-torn newspaper placards behind wire frames lined up under the windows, inside faded displays of things no longer available: dummy tins of Gold Cut and Navy Flake tobaccos; a tattered stack of phoney chocolate bars, the wood showing through the silver paper.

'I've found somewhere nearby we could go for an hour or two before you have to go back to quarters...' He sounded doubtful.

'But?'

'It's 'orrible.'

'Is it dry?'

'Yes, and there's a gas fire.'

'Come on, what are we waiting for, it can't be worse than a shop doorway, or that pub.'

'We'd be in the dry on our own for an hour or two.'

He led the way back past the pub and to a doorway set above a tier of steps strewn with crumpled fish-and-chip newspapers. As they climbed the steps, a sailor opened the door and came out, bumping into them. 'Sorry, mate.' He must have glimpsed the epaulettes, for he hastily corrected himself, 'Sir!'

They went in, closed the door then fumbled their way through the inner blackout curtain. Inside was a middle-aged woman, hair bleached a brassy blonde. 'What d'you want?' she asked without preamble and without any show of interest or enthusiasm for their arrival.

'The room I looked at earlier.'

'Which room was that, dearie, I have a lot of "tenants."' They heard the door reopening behind the blackout.

'The one to the left at the top of the stairs,' Jamie said hastily.

'Short stay, out by ten, a pound.'

Jamie seemed to have the note ready in his pocket. He paid, received a key, took Laura by the hand and led her up stairs lit by a dim bulb 'blacked-out' by a piece of ragged towelling. Below they heard the next tenants, a man's curse was muffled as he fought his way through the blackout curtain but the girl's laugh was a high-pitched screech flailing the eardrums.

Jamie turned left and unlocked the door, stood back for Laura to enter, then stopped in the open doorway. She felt around and switched on the central light, no shade here though the bulb was perhaps dimmer.

'Oh God!' Jamie exclaimed, 'it looks even worse now than it did before. What was I thinking of? Come on let's get out of here.'

She moved behind him and closed the door, after her dour thoughts this was refuge against the night, against the rest of the world. 'It's all you said it was, dry and it has a fire. Can you light it?'

He fished out a lighter and stooped to turned on the tap. The fire lit reluctantly with a blue woosh of flame and a strong smell of gas and damp. But even as they watched the radiants began to warm to a pleasant orange. There was, he noticed, a meter in the corner.

She turned and skimmed her hat over on to the bed, then unbuttoned her overcoat. 'Put the light out,' she said, 'by the glow of the fire it'll look . . .'

'Less awful,' he hoped.

'Cosier.' She confirmed. 'Better than the phone box, or a shop doorway on a night like this.' She didn't really mean the weather, she meant the briefness of their time, as the woman so bluntly put it 'Out by ten'.

He had been about to say better than the pub, but he didn't want to remind her, or himself, of the airman, of the predator as he began to think of him.

He watched as she spread her overcoat over one side of the bed and with the gesture invited him to do the same with his.

'I've got a small clothes brush in my handbag,' she told him. 'I don't fancy madame's bedlinen.'

The remark reminded him of the way she had swept and dusted before they left Honeysuckle Cottage. She was wonderful, caring; he must never lose her to anyone, then he remembered their walk through the wood above the cottage, how she had run in front of him and he'd felt such a sense of loss, such panic. He'd found her at that strange eerie centre of the wood, the pines dense, the low ferns in the bluey-green gloom as if all were under deep water.

It made him fearful, not for himself, but of the stakes – the gamble. He had found her in Gibraltar and at Anerley. What were the odds on their staying together? Did they go up, or down, as the war continued? The last time he had seen his mother, he had not known he would never see her again. There was always a last time, but no one knew just when that would be.

'Jamie?'

He glanced quickly to where she sat on the edge of the bed, he was doing it again, lagging behind. He unbuttoned his overcoat. She stood up and took it from him. 'We'll be careful not to crease it too much.'

'Who cares,' he breathed, catching her into his arms so the coat was between them, then pulling it out and throwing it towards the bed. It landed on the floor. They left it there.

Later she thought that though the bed squeaked and the

271

fire smelt fumey she could willingly stay there for ever and, as she moved her thigh away from a metal button, she sighed; this was true love.

'We mustn't go to sleep,' he whispered.

She hummed contented agreement, listening to the hiss of the fire and to fierce sleet sounding like elastic bands being pinged hard at the window panes, and watching through lowering lids the orange glow on the walls and ceiling.

'I am a fool,' he said suddenly, 'the town may be full but I could surely find a vacancy either in a hotel or a boarding house in the suburbs.' He warmed to the idea. 'I could book us in as a married couple for two nights. We could have our evenings in comfort and I could order a taxi, whisk you back to your quarters in good time.'

He raised himself on one elbow when she did not answer and saw she was asleep. Looking down he thought what an idiot he'd been not to have thought this out earlier that day, instead of bringing her to this knocking shop. He looked at the luminous hands on his watch. He would let her sleep another fifteen minutes. He lay so he could watch her face as she slept, lips just parted, the fire lighting her body from feet up so it looked as if she was like some beautiful Phoenix rising from the flames, or Aphrodite from the waves. He buried his face into her neck, kissing her lightly, waking her gently, he did not want to think of waves or of returning to the sea just yet.

He spent all the next day tramping around Liverpool in ever widening circles. He began to feel like a hawker with unwanted goods for sale. It was not until he was some distance to the south of the town, that he realised he would soon have to give up to be back in time to meet Laura. He was in a district with much larger residential houses. Garston the front of a bus said. He came to a road called Cressington Park and decided he would just try along one side, then he would catch a bus back into the centre.

He met with polite refusals at the first two houses, no one at home at the next house, but the front door of the fourth house was opened by an old man whose eyes lit up when he saw a naval uniform. 'Hello Jimmie,' he greeted him with the naval slang for a second in command, 'what can I do for you?'

Jamie, in the end, told the ex-commander the truth. 'But I guess your young lady would prefer me to pretend I think you're married,' the old man concluded.

'I guess,' Jamie said before he ran to catch a bus.

When he returned with Laura, the ex-commander opened the door to them and gave Laura an approving nod – more of a bow really.

'Commander Leonard Briggs, Laura Maclaren,' Jamie made the introduction.

'My dear, I'm just sorry your stay is going to be so brief. Left at the top of the stairs,' he told them briefly, 'my quarters are downstairs.'

Left at the top of the stairs, same instructions Laura thought – but all else was different. The ex-navy man had lit a fire in an enormous bed-sittingroom. There were sandwiches and biscuits as well as a flask of tea on the table.

'He knows, doesn't he?' Laura stated.

'He's such a nice old guy I couldn't deceive him. Do you mind?'

'No, I guess not.' She thought that wartime separations and brief meetings had robbed of her of such niceties as false modesty and strict moral rectitude some time ago.

The following night not only was the room as well provendered as before but when the time came for Laura to leave, the commander 'call me Len' backed an ancient Riley out of his garage and drove them back, waited while they said goodnight and drove Jamie back to his house.

'This is very good of you, sir,' Jamie said, 'beyond the call of duty, as they say. It's made all the difference to our last two days.'

'I can imagine,' he said drily, 'I'm not too old to do that.'

'Tomorrow's my last day but if I can do anything for you in return . . .'

'You can, as it happens,' he said as he swung back into his drive. 'First you can have a drink with me to celebrate. Then you can help me put the house in cold storage before I sail.'

'Sail?'

'Yes, I'm into this bloody war at last, been trying for long enough.'

'Not a desk job then?'

'No!' He aimed a short triumphant jab at Jamie's shoulder before climbing out of the car. 'Come on, I'll tell you.' Over very large whiskies and sodas he said the Admiralty and the merchant navy had at last seen the benefit of using men such as himself, 'old men but with the experience' to be convoy commodores. 'I'll be in charge of the merchantmen but *advising* escorts.'

Jamie looked at him as he lit his pipe and stared with joyful determination into an action-packed future. He was a rather undersized man who had lost most of his hair, but it would be a brave captain or senior officer who went against this man's *suggestions*.

'We'll likely be serving in the same sector.'

'Here's to it then!' The newly appointed convoy commodore refilled their glasses. 'The sooner we get it finished the sooner you can get back to that girl of yours.'

'I'll drink to that,' he said giving up the idea of keeping a clear head for his last day as he downed the drink and the commodore reached for the bottle.

'There's not much to choose between them for such as us,' the commodore ruminated after several more drinks, 'the sea and a woman, they both want to be wives.' He laughed with his whisky glass resting on his stomach making the amber liquid dance.

'My last day tomorrow.'

The older man chuckled. 'You have mentioned it.'

'Your family, sir,' he decided he could never dream of calling this man Len, 'you've known some separations.'

The whisky glass tossed towards the grand piano and the

photographs standing on it. 'My wife died giving birth to our third son, Ritchie, while I was involved in the battle of the Dogger Bank, 1915. Didn't much care after that whether I lived or died. Never got a scratch. Been on my own ever since, series of nannies and housekeepers.'

'God, I'm sorry. And your sons?'

'All in the navy, conceived 'em in one war ready for the next.'

They drank until the whisky had gone, the commodore becoming first belligerent, then lachrymose, then falling fast asleep. Jamie pulled the glass from his hand, put the guard before the fire and a coat over the old boy's knees. 'Must be seventy,' he said.

In bed he tried to remember what Laura had said about the sea, something about not trying to compete with it. He moved his head on the pillow and the room spun; he'd think about it tomorrow. Tomorrow never comes, some bloody idiot said; he fell asleep on the anguish that he knew it would.

Neither of them began to feel much better until around teatime. Jamie made tea and knocking at the door took it into the commodore's sitting room. 'I'll go in on the bus tonight, sir.'

'No such thing, I'm ready when you are.' He picked up his duffel coat. 'I've things to say on the way in. Things I should have said last night, instead of getting blotto.'

He said no more until they were driving along the promenade through Otterspool. A papery white, wintry moon lit the sea which looked almost oily it was so still, the opposite of the other nights he had spent in Liverpool when wild winds full of sleet had lashed from sea to shore.

The commodore cleared his throat. 'You asked me last night about separations. I just want to say that I learned the hard way that you must leave your beloveds with only good memories. They'll remember you best the way they saw you last, they will remember best the last things you say. That's what they'll take with them when you separate.

275

Make sure it's all the best you can be, every word the best you can say.'

Jamie swallowed noisily. 'Thank you, sir, I'll try to remember.'

'You remember!'

Jamie grinned. 'Yes, sir!'

When they arrived outside Laura was already waiting. 'You're early,' he said, 'or are we late?'

'Both a bit,' she answered climbing into the rear seat with him, 'and I've permission to stay the night, all night, as long as I'm early tomorrow. Some of the other girls are filling in.'

'That's a bit of good cheer.' The commodore puffed his pipe more vigorously, clouding the car, making himself and them cough and laugh.

When they neared the house he added, 'I'm off to see an old colleague so I'll drop you off and see you in the morning, take you to the station, Jimmie, and then the good lady to her headquarters.'

'But I've brought things to cook for the three of us tonight,' Laura said. 'I've ...'

'Bless you, m'dear. If it's a lump of steak, leave mine and I'll cook it tomorrow.'

'Well, it's sausages and eggs.'

'Right, I'll have mine tomorrow. See you both in the morning.' He passed the house key out of the window. 'Goodnight both, sweet dreams, well ... I mean if you get as far as sleep.' He took his pipe out of his mouth to waggle it roguishly at them, then reversed the car out of the drive.

'Do you think he's made that up to leave us alone?' she asked.

'Yes, of course. And we have all night?'

She nodded. 'The evil moment put off.'

'Let's just eat and relax then, forget tomorrow.'

'Yep! Sufficient until the day ...' The Americanism gave her away and when they were inside he drew her into his arms and told her all that the commodore had said.

276

'He's very wise,' she said, 'like your father, keep busy he says, do what has to be done. So!' She laid a parcel on the kitchen table and like a conjuror drew out a length of sausages. 'Don't ask where they came from,' she told him, 'they're strictly illegal black market goodies.'

They ate, drank coffee, lay on the rug before the coal fire ready lit for them in the sitting room, talked of Gibraltar, made love, went to bed, talked of the whale and its rainbow spout, of the wonderful huge moons that were part of the warm nights on The Rock, of the brilliant green phosphorescence in the waters at night. 'It is both place and myth,' he said.

'Do you see us all back there?' she asked. 'You and me, your father, my mother, after the war?'

'My father and your mother certainly, but us? Would you want to go back there to live?'

'Hmm,' she considered, 'I guess wherever you are . . .'

Chapter Twenty-Two

'Gone?' Nadine asked in a whisper as she arrived on the plotting floor. Laura nodded sadly.

'Not the best way to begin 1941,' Nadine sympathised, then in an effort to dispel the rueful countenance, 'but at least you *know* him.'

She glanced quickly at this tall, elegant young woman who had left Cambridge University to join the war, and who said she despaired of ever meeting the 'right' man.

'I mean in the biblical sense, of course,' she added.

Behind them her commanding officer cleared his throat. They turned to each other and Nadine surreptitiously mouthed, 'Let's get on with the war shall we.' Then they hurried to either end of the room to prevent a burst of giggling, definitely not expected of Wrens on special duties. Thank goodness for Nadine, confident, observant, she had that rare gift of knowing when to speak, chivvy along and when to give space to her friends.

Even while she was busy Laura's mind ran short replays of the early morning departure. In a last-minute flurry of anxiety Jamie had made a point of telling her not to worry about her father, to watch out for that airman, not to wander the streets on her own and to keep with a group of friends at dances 'at all times'. She had tried to reassure him in those last seconds caught in a hubbub of passengers and deafening streams of steam expressed from the train.

'Don't worry,' she had told him and forced a smile, emotionally very costly, for him to remember her by. Then the handclasp from train to platform was broken. 'Stand clear!' A whistle, a green flag.

'Write!' he shouted.

'Tonight!' she had shouted back, waving until he was well beyond sight, then not really remembering making the journey back to these underground chambers.

They were kept busy; convoys in ballast were moving outwards from the north-west coast, while from the other side convoys left Canadian ports laden with troops, armaments and food, zig-zagging towards their destinations. Too often the white discs representing U-boats had to be put into position, always 'popping up' as Nadine put it – not, Laura considered, a very happy phrase. Her only consolation that day was she knew Jamie was not yet at sea. His destroyer would be waiting for its complement of men to return from leave. Then tomorrow, probably in the morning, there would be the conference of all the masters of the merchant ships, the commanding officers of the naval escorts, the convoy commodore and shore controllers. After the conference the convoy usually sailed the same day.

'Going straight back to quarters tonight?' Nadine asked as she passed her pushing one of the huge giraffe-like ladders they had to climb to reach the further parts of the wall chart around Iceland, Greenland, Nova Scotia.

'Yes, got some catching up to do, and I'm going to write to Jamie, I promised. He may just get it before he sails.'

'I ought to write home,' Nadine said, 'the trouble is we can't tell details, so to the outsider the job's routine office work. I believe my mother thinks we're sitting around in a sewing circle, or something, like the women's groups she entertains at home – sewing shirts for soldiers, or whatever they do.'

As they made their way out through the labyrinth passages towards the street, somewhere on the Mersey a tug hooted and her heart gave a downward lurch. He'd be aboard by now, conference in the morning, then away. She envisaged the journey as she would see it, across their wall, grey-green, the colour of a sunless sea, across the Atlantic, the North Atlantic most likely. She remembered his fear of cold water. She also finally admitted that she would always either know, or be able to judge, the departure dates either side of the Atlantic. She would know when he was on the high seas, when he was in range of German bombers, or in U-boat alley. Those markers on the chart had always been important; everyone silently grieved when a ship was lost with the faces of the 'ancient mariners', the senior officers who had served in the last lot, set rigid, eyes shuttered as they pushed everyone harder to their duties. Now the symbols would have a poignant significance for her – almost beyond bearing.

Outside the wind had dropped and low over the Mersey were the remains of a brilliant sunset, long red streaks of orange, down to storm-red on the horizon, criss-crossed by broken lines of steel-grey cloud. She was grateful that Nadine Boston didn't chatter, leaving her free to begin to compose her letter to Jamie. 'If I hurry I can write my letter and nip back to catch the last post,' she said aloud.

'My mother, I'm afraid, will not get hers that quickly.'

'But I might get mine.' A man's snide voice interrupted. 'It must be my turn, now the navy's gone back to sea.'

Laura steeled herself not to turn but Nadine spun round; she had been at the same dance, knew the man and Laura's detestation of him, though not why.

'Laura,' he called and laughed causing her to vent an exasperated groan; even his laughter held that same hint of malicious pleasure as her father's did when he tormented. Nadine glanced at her friend then stopped suddenly and swept round on him. 'Bugger off, don't you know when you're not wanted?'

'Wasn't talking to you, madam,' he retorted.

'No, but I'm bloody talking to you, clear off.'

'Not quite the lady you pretend,' he said still laughing.

'There's a dance same place we met,' he addressed himself to Laura. 'I've bought the tickets.'

'No, thanks.' This detestable creep had come near to ruining her last few precious days with Jamie.

'Come on, don't let your hoity-toity friend put you off, you know you want to.'

Enraged, Laura turned to face him, though he was too near for any satisfaction in the confrontation; she could smell his slightly peppery breath and rank perspiration. 'There's only one thing I want, and that's for you to stop hanging around. The only reason I stared at you at that wretched dance is because you remind me of someone I hate. Do you understand that? Have I made myself clear?'

Behind them they could hear more men coming. 'It's the CO,' Nadine said and made as if to go back.

'I'll be waiting,' he said in a low voice, no hint or pretence of any kind of humour now, just raw threat, then he turned and strode quickly away.

The men coming the other way were merchant seamen, strangers, who bade them a goodnight, one turning to ask, 'You both all right?'

'Fine. Thanks for asking,' Nadine called back as they too began to walk on again.

'Did you hear what he said?'

'I did and I reckon your chap's right, you have got to be careful. He's an evil bit of work. There's something wrong about him too, something not kosher. For one thing,' she reasoned, 'he's been around a long time. Has he been on leave all this time, ever since that dance? That's weeks and weeks ago. Where's he based?'

'Thank goodness there's usually people around when we leave headquarters,' Laura said addressing the present situation.

'We'll make sure there are from now on,' Nadine mused, 'but I'd very much like to ask him a few searching questions. We should be able to out-manoeuvre him, arrange for backup of some kind.'

Laura glanced at her questioningly.

'What we need to do is organise a personal convoy system, get ourselves a few naval escorts.'

'We'll have even more problems if you're not careful.' Laura's attempt at a joke was spoiled by the tremor in her voice.

'Not if we choose the right type.' Nadine was as always totally confident.

Laura wrote her letter to Jamie; she would just make the last post if she hurried. She pulled on a topcoat over her skirt and blouse and ran for the nearby post office which operated a late collection. She dropped the letter into the box with a feeling of satisfaction. 'Made it.'

She turned back, walking now. The next moment her heart thumped in alarm as a man stepped out from a back way to a row of houses as she passed and caught her arm. 'I said I'd see you later,' he hissed as he pulled her tight against himself, one hand half under the revers of her coat brushing her breast.

Completely taken off guard she was half dragged from her feet towards the denser black of the narrow way. He wrenched at the front of her coat again. Was he was going to try to rape her? Revolted, she kicked furiously back at his shins, anger taking over after the first fright. There was no way, she told herself, no way was she submitting to this beast, she'd rather die. But he was strong, intent. He pulled her some way further into the alley and was kind of chuckling in his throat as if he were enjoying this struggle with her. Panic surged over her as she wondered if she might even be fighting for her life. She must have help. Almost as if sensing what she intended his hand left her breast and groped for her mouth as she shouted at the top of her voice. 'Let me go! Let me go! Help!'

There was the trick of getting your knee up sharp between the legs if she could manage that, but she was hampered by her own coat and skirt. Then she half slipped on the wet grass. His fingers went over and into her mouth.

She bit hard. He swore as she shouted again. He pushed his leg hard behind her knees and was forcing her down, but then they both heard the sound of men running, boots noisy and sliding as they came nearer.

His hand clamped with a clawlike grip on her mouth, but she kicked out towards the wall, anything to make a noise. Her shoes hit wood, a gate. A man's voice reached them, out of breath, but near, 'It's from up 'ere.'

A light was flashed into the alley. By the torch one held she could see they were two elderly men encumbered by their special gas masks in haversacks and wearing tin hats with the white letters 'ARP' on the front. Air raid wardens.

''Ere, what's going on?'

She was released so suddenly she fell.

'None of your business, just delivering this.' The man reached down to ostensibly lift her up. She pushed him away and scrambled to her feet. 'She slipped,' he added.

'He attacked me. I thought . . .'

'Do you know him?' one of the wardens asked.

''Course she does, been to a dance together.'

'That right, miss?' the other warden asked sternly, making her feel she was the trouble-maker.

'He was at a dance,' she began and felt sympathy drain away from her, men aligning with their own kind. 'Look,' she tried to explain, furious with herself as her voice thickened with distress, 'he's just attacked me. I thought he was going to rape me . . . or murder me.'

By the dim torchlight she saw the man spread his arms. 'You can't please 'em. She panicked, that's all.' Then he turned and began to walk away, not to the road, but further along the alleyway – escaping. 'See you Saturday then, Laura,' he called back.

'So he can just walk away!' Laura was stunned, she gestured after him, towards the men, who shuffled uneasily.

'He knows your name,' one of them said.

'He heard someone use it . . .' The impossibility of trying

to explain was so obvious she began again. 'Well, I don't know *his*, and . . .'

'Walk you back to your quarters, miss?' one interrupted.

'No, thank you!' she exclaimed. 'I just hope you're better at fire watching than you are at . . . other things.'

All the day's emotional experiences overcame her as she rushed back into quarters and encountered Nadine. 'Have you been to the post already?' Nadine began, 'I was going to walk with you . . .'

Laura burst into tears.

'What's happened, your coat's filthy . . .' Nadine paused to take stock of her friend. 'It wasn't him?'

She nodded, beginning to sob uncontrollably. 'He was waiting near the post office.'

'Are you hurt?' Nadine put her arms around her and held her, patting her back, comforting and questioning. 'He's not hurt you, he didn't . . . ?'

'No, some air raid wardens came.'

'Let me have your coat.'

As she unbuttoned the coat and pulled out her arms a white piece of card fell to the floor. 'Huh!' she kicked violently at it.

'What is it?' Nadine asked stooping. 'A dance ticket. You don't mean . . .'

'He fooled the air raid wardens into thinking he knew me well and was just inviting me to another dance. He called me by my name.'

'He knows far too much about you,' Nadine decided, 'but I think I know something about him. He's just arrogant enough to go to this dance,' she tapped the card thoughtfully on her fingernails. 'Time to have *our* convoy conference, I think, and get our escorts detailed.'

In the days that followed Nadine took over the situation, quite sure the man would turn up on the night. 'Surely not,' was Laura's private reaction, while wondering whether she and her mother were just people who attracted the same bullying, sadistic type of man, that he should also have the same colouring was just a tormenting coincidence.

'He'll try,' Nadine was convinced, 'Somewhere along the line he'll try to waylay you.'

'Well, he certainly won't expect me to go to this wretched dance.'

'Oh I don't know, these people are sly and devious, but there's often something compulsive in their fixations.'

'Very reassuring.' She did not say that the reason she was letting herself drift along with the plans was that she was finding it increasingly difficult to write fluently to Jamie. She felt her letters must sound stilted as she kept so much back. She couldn't write about her work, or about the airman, while the news from London was soon told – Queenie and Freddie were enjoying a beautiful reunion (a honeymoon her mother had written) in spite of the raids. Happiness, she thought cynically, did not make for much wordage in letters or in newspapers. She filled her letters with anxieties about *him*, his convoy, and felt acutely dissatisfied with her efforts. She wondered whether she would tell him if there was any kind of outcome to all the plotting. It was as if Nadine tapped into her thoughts as she said, 'You want peace of mind, you want to be able to give Jamie peace of mind. We've got to deal with this creature before he does do you some real harm.'

She knew Nadine had contacted someone who had been a close family friend of her father's before the war, but she would not reveal who. 'Better you don't know.' On the night all Laura had to do was walk back to her quarters at the usual time, then leave with a crowd to go to the dance – and from then on 'everything's taken care of'.

She did refuse to use or touch the ticket that had been stuffed into the front of her coat. Nadine presented her with an unsullied ticket, no doubt using the other for herself.

On the evening of the dance Laura sat motionless on the edge of her bed, thinking that what she'd really like as underwear was not silk French knickers but a metal chastity belt – she could always send Jamie the key.

'Look!' her friend came and took both her hands. 'Tonight

285

may settle this once and for all, make him too scared ever to show his face again, or better still he may be locked up for ... something or other.' She waved an airy hand.

'Something or other?'

'Intimidation, I should think, we'll leave that to the experts.'

'What experts?'

'Oh, the goodies, the good men.' She indicated Laura's midnight-blue satin dance dress. 'On with the motley!'

Unconvinced, uncertain, unhappy, she changed and they waited for their escorts to arrive. When they did Nadine said as an aside to her, 'These are just the corvettes, the battleships and cruisers will be already in position.'

The young men had been well schooled. They walked alongside the girls smartly, but not too fast, seeming to look straight ahead, but Laura had the feeling that nothing was escaping these sub-lieutenants who were used to sighting the merest whisper of a plume in the sea that might mean a U-boat periscope.

'Jeremy Taylor,' her escort introduced himself, then he'd cleared his throat. 'We've been well briefed, you don't need to worry. We have either to dance with or take you to the bar for a drink. We won't let you out of our sight.'

'I'm sorry to spoil your free time, I understand you're due back on board by midnight.'

He grinned down at her. 'Don't mind this kind of spoiling any time.'

The gala dance was going to be well supported, as most social occasions were, service people and civilians, mostly girls, crowding in. The big band sound met them as they reached the hall. The strains of 'In the Mood' had most feet tapping before coats were left at the cloakroom. Nadine and Laura handed over their coats, brushed their hair, reapplied a little lipstick. 'All right,' Nadine asked. 'Nothing sighted so far.'

It was on the tip of her tongue to ask how she knew, but Nadine gave her an authoritative nod and led the way out and along a short corridor into the crowded interior, where at that moment the only lights were those reflecting in many coloured prisms from a rotating ball of mirrors, and on the stage the lights on the music stands.

Jeremy was at the door waiting with his fellow sub-lieutenant; he held out his arm. 'My dance, I think.' When she hesitated he added, 'You mustn't waste my free time. I love dancing.' He led her first into the trio of quicksteps, and he *could* dance. She was a passable performer but he made her feel brilliant, and she forgot her role of decoy as they went from quickstep to a series of foxtrots. Then the dance band leader announced, 'It's jitterbug time!'

'Will you?' Jeremy asked eagerly as the lights switched from mirrored moody ball to spotlights circling the floor into which the couples began the individual dancing techniques of the jitterbug as seen in American movies. The athletic included acrobatics, as the fellows swung and bounced their partners from hip to hip without the girl's feet touching the ground, or slid them almost on the floor through their legs and back.

'I couldn't do the throwing-about bit,' she said.

He took her hand and led her back on to the floor. 'I do that,' he said and before she could protest she was jitter-bugging with the best, and doing all the acrobatics to his yelled instructions. 'You're good,' he exclaimed, 'when you let yourself go you're wonderful.'

Marvellous, she mentally corrected him and missed his hand finishing in a half sprawl on the floor.

'All right?' He was all concern. 'Sorry, sorry, so sorry. I get carried away.'

She tried to reassure him she was fine but he insisted on taking her to the bar and fetching her a drink. He came back with a port and lemonade. 'It's what all the girls seem to be drinking.'

'Thanks, quench my thirst and give me energy for some more of your wonderful dancing.' It was not flattery, and she really was grateful that these officers should fall in so readily with Nadine's strategy. She wondered if her friend had finally given up on the attendance of the airman. She looked around more carefully as the lights went up for a spot prize waltz. She saw several of their own staff and Nadine just going out towards the cloakroom, leaving her chap on guard at the door.

'I won't be a moment,' she said then added as he looked concerned, 'Nadine's just gone to the ladies, and your friend's at the door, so I'll be all right.' She felt comforted by his concern and by the presence of the other sub-lieutenant who nodded to her as she left the hall. 'Just joining Nadine,' she told him.

In the hallway was a complete contrast. After the heat of the dance floor it felt as if someone had left the outside door open, it was freezing cold and deserted for a few seconds until a man came out from the gentlemen's cloakroom as she walked past. She was thinking of how she could rag Nadine about all the elaborate plans, all the theories which were obviously all wrong, when she was grabbed from behind, a hand over her mouth. 'Keep walking,' the voice said. 'Told you I'd be here, now you're coming with me.' When she tried to twist round in his grasp he hissed in her ear, 'I've got a knife, don't struggle.'

She believed him, through her flimsy clothing she could feel something pointed just over her right kidney; she tried to arch her back away.

'Walk to the exit,' he told her.

She had little choice, for when she tried to stop, the point of the knife pressed harder. Her only hope was that someone, Nadine, anyone, would come out of one of the cloakrooms, or from the hall ... but they were already nearing the first set of swing doors. Where was the attendant who *always* sat on the door?

'Push through,' he breathed in her ear. Even in the terror and panic she knew to leave the hall could be her last mistake. The only thing that occurred was to pretend a faint, to slump down. She tried to assess the angle of the knife, which way was best to fall, but in those few seconds it was too late, the point pressed harder, his right foot kicked out to open the door and she was propelled violently forward.

The opening of the door seemed to act like a signal. She felt rather than saw movement behind them, then his hands were ripped from her and she heard the sound of the knife as it fell, ducked and draked across the floor hitting the far wall. The foyer was suddenly full of people, men, Nadine.

The pilot was protesting, shouting his outrage, his innocence. 'She's always leading me on.' A man in plain clothes picked up the knife with a handkerchief and held it up before him, 'At knife point,' he said before wrapping it.

She began to appreciate the full extent of this 'operation' as two senior officers, one Royal Air Force, one a civilian policeman, walked out of an office at the back of reception. The air force red cap went quickly forward to the man being held by Jeremy and his companion. He studied him a moment then pulled open the man's tunic. He had on a striped shirt with a piece of air force blue material caught up under a blue collar.

'I think,' he said, to the civilian chief superintendent, 'this is one for you. Probably a draft dodger – among other things.'

She suddenly felt something warm on her back and putting her hand to it, withdrew it smeared with blood; before she could react Nadine and the plain clothes policeman were at her side. 'She's hurt,' he exclaimed.

'It can't be much, surely,' she hoped, 'it didn't . . . hurt,' she struggled with the last word as she felt herself falling.

Dearest Jamie,
I have good news to tell you. I know you were worried about the pilot who so dogged our tracks in the days before you sailed. Well, he is out of harm's way – in prison awaiting trial.

His real name is Brian Begg and he is not only *not* a pilot he is a conscript dodger.

It's such a relief to be able to write to you and tell you

all that has been happening here . . .

Well, not quite all, she thought, she saw no reason to tell him that she had spent a night in hospital and had two stitches in a back wound. Time enough to tell him about the attacks and the knife when he was home and could see she had come to no harm.

> . . . I saw no point in worrying you when you could do nothing about it, and Nadine and her uncle *Chief Superintendent Boston* were wonderful (marvellous). It *had* become a worry. The man had turned up on two other occasions, presented me with a ticket for another dance – rather forced it on me – so as Nadine said something had to be done – and done it was. His final apprehension was a fine example of combined forces operations – the RAF, the navy and the police. I don't think you need have any worries about me with Nadine and her relations on my side!
>
> I think about you every moment, Jamie. I want this war to stop wasting our lives, every moment we are not together is a desert. God bless you and keep you safe. I send honeysuckle memories to you, think of them and you can smell the flowers, inhale deeply and be back in that beautiful bedroom, or on the hill looking down on that shepherd with his sheep. The high and lovely places will always be ours. I love you, until Europa Point lighthouse and all the stars stop shining.
>
> Yours for ever
>
> Laura

She wondered where he was at that moment, and where he would be when he finally received his next batch of letters and this news.

'But my letters will be better from now on,' she promised as she kissed below her signature.

Chapter Twenty-Three

'Signaller make to our straggler, "Long may your lum reek."'

'Sir!' The message was flashed from the bridge of the destroyer to the floundering merchant ship.

'Reply from the *Clansman*, sir,' the signaller reported. 'He says he'll tell his chief engineer.'

'Huh!' the captain received the message half laugh, half grunt.

Jamie often thought Laura would appreciate these laconic witticisms that passed between ships even in times of the most foreboding circumstances, like this one.

'Take over, Jimmie, I'll go below for half an hour. Call me any sign of *more* trouble.'

'Sir.' Jamie answered to the nickname for first officer more often than to his own name. He saw his captain take a final regretful look back at the merchantman astern of the main convoy. The decision to abandon the *Clansman* to whatever German U-boat, Focke-Wulf, or the weather would throw at her had just had to be made. Every ship that could not keep up with the main convoy was at the same risk. Once the escorts began to put the many at risk by rushing back to circle and harass the straggler, like sheep-dogs with a recalcitrant sheep, then the odd arse-end Charlie had to trust to her luck – and there wasn't enough of that to go round on these Russian convoys.

This was Jamie's third, interspersed with duties in the North Atlantic, all convoy work, shepherding merchantmen; many like the *Clansman*, ships that should never still be at sea, would have been in the breaker's yard years ago were it not for the war. The *Clansman*'s decks were stacked with planes in sections, its holds with armaments and food for the Russians, and the engineer couldn't even keep the engines turning. Jamie could imagine the language that was passing between bridge and engine room.

He turned his binoculars back to the merchantman they were fast leaving astern. You just never knew; worry about a straggler and it could turn up in port unscathed while the convoy itself lost as many as thirteen ships out of thirty-six. He'd seen that happen on an HX convoy heading back to Britain from Halifax, Nova Scotia, with Canadian troops, ammunition, and food to keep Britain from starving.

But the war had moved on, rapidly. Hitler was not apparently going to let Great Britain, that pesky little island that 'did not know that it was beaten' stop him from pressing on with his greater ambitions. Russia, in spite of the Russo–German Pact of 1939, was invaded in June 1941, and Japan had bombed the American base at Pearl Harbor on 7 December 1941. America, having declared war against the Axis powers earlier that year, had declared war on Japan the next day.

The balloon had certainly then gone up on a world scale. Two years on his war had been ... what ... seeing merchant shipping blown out of the water ... leaving survivors screaming as they died in waters covered by burning oil ... watching a young Canadian soldier leap from a converted liner when he thought they were going to be torpedoed, only to meet his end among the churning propellers. There had been just two leaves in England, a weekend in Portsmouth, when his destroyer had been diverted around the southern end of neutral Ireland to chase U-boats thought to be hunting a special convoy with VIPs aboard – Prime Minster Winston Churchill had been the rumour. Jamie had been grateful to whoever it was, for Laura had come south and they had had two nights and one day together. The second leave they had spent in Liverpool. He had been properly introduced to, and had properly thanked, Nadine. The longer leave had made it harder to separate, made them both long and ache for the next time.

He stifled a sigh, tried to concentrate on the present trouble, which was just too few destroyers and too many merchant ships to try to look after. He just wished the whole damn war over. Two years on and he was still hoping for southern duties, that his destroyer might, with a lot of luck, be sent to *his* home waters of the Mediterranean, where the water was blue most of the time, not like liquid black treacle stirred with ice for good measure.

He gave the orders for the turn aligning the destroyer with the direction of the convoy, then for 'Half speed ahead', acknowledging that his wish for that kind of luck had more to do with his dread of these glittering black Arctic waters than commonsense. He frowned, checking the ship was precisely back into its normal escort position.

The convoy was due to make one of the sharp-angled turns which took them zig-zagging onwards to Murmansk. It was a time when everyone worried, when the best men checked and rechecked their calculations, and prayed that *all* the other skippers of *all* those merchant ships had got it right too, otherwise there could be mayhem. They had enough enemies without running into one another, and in these latitudes, at this time of year, the twenty-four hours consisted of dark twilight and night, another reason for constant vigilance whatever watch it was.

He hesitated whether to report they were back in position, not really wanting to disturb the old man, who spent more time on his bridge than was strictly necessary. Jamie could have resented this, taken it as a sign that his captain had not complete confidence in his first officer. He knew better. Just before he had joined this command Captain

293

Harold Smithson had been on compassionate leave. His wife had died, cancer, he believed, but the big C was not openly talked bout. The captain had opened his heart to his second in command, who had found him gripping a family photograph until his knuckles stood out white, when he had first come aboard. For everyone except a captain the one compensation about any ship was that there was constant close companionship, men cleaved together. 'All in the same boat' took on its true meaning, shared hardships and danger drove every other worry out of a man's mind – for a time. The captain's position set him apart; served by his own steward in his cabin, working usually as he ate, he only messed with the other officers on special invitation. Perhaps the only time he really mixed was on the bridge.

Jamie knew he was a lucky man in that respect, all the letters he'd received in various ports told of cheerful things. Laura, his father, Queenie, even Fatima in Gibraltar, were all full of great plans for the future. 'When the war is over' was the stock phrase. Fatima told him of an RAF ground crewman, 'very handsome, a blond Englishman, who wants to marry me and have lots of children'. Jamie thought he'd jolly well better have good intentions, or this RAF type would have Fatima's brothers to deal with. He wrote back to her full of good wishes and saying she'd better wait until they all got back so they could be at her wedding.

He added to his letters to Laura every day, even if it was only a few lines, and often reread the log she had kept during her time on the *Dromore Castle* and all her letters. She was eloquent on paper. The only other times when her words followed as smoothly as her thoughts were after they had made love. It was something that endeared her to him, for while she was often shy at speaking out, it was as if love-making released all her inhibitions. He had usually listened without speaking, sometimes even falling asleep, at others roused to make love to her again by the rush of feelings, the great passionate endearment he felt for all she said, all she was.

His father's last letter had hinted at hush-hush war work which, to Queenie's disappointment, was taking him to the south coast for several days at a time. 'But she refuses to leave her hospital canteen and come with me,' he wrote. She says no one else knows how to deal with her chairs.' The chairs had become their family joke. 'I do not like leaving her and Billie alone in London, though while I'm away she is occupying what spare time she has sewing for the nurses. The blouses and dresses she has run up from the materials in the chests it just nobody's business. I tell you she's the most popular woman in that hospital!'

Laura had told him how her mother used to sew when Jock Maclaren had been at his most tormenting. It had been a way of staying sane, doing, all the time, something useful, something usually for someone else. Now she filled the hours when his father was away by sewing. Two women, he thought, mother and daughter, who both deserved a really good life once this bloody war was over.

He imagined the four of them back in Gibraltar – at Fatima's wedding. He felt a smile try to move lips stiff with a film of ice. Everything on board was iced up in these waters, he thought cynically, only the thickness varied.

'Ere y'are, sir,' a mug of steaming hot cocoa was thrust into his hands by Smiler Harris, the captain's steward. 'Captain thought you might like one.'

'Give him my thanks, Smiler.' Smiler had experimented with all kinds of drinks, laced with all kinds of spirits, to keep warm, but in the end this chocolate drink came top. It both fed and warmed.

He had taken one sip when there was a flash as bright as a sunburst on the far side of the convoy and an almighty boom rolled across the water to them. 'Christ!' Smiler muttered.

'Don't expect it was,' Jamie muttered grimly, flipping the lid of the speaking tube. 'Sir!' There was no need to say more: the captain had heard the noise like the beginning of an imminent and violent thunderstorm.

*

The war didn't have any regard for Christmas, and Laura found herself on duty the whole of the festive season. Like everyone else they made the best of it. Sprigs of mistletoe appeared over doorways, even a small artificial Christmas tree had found its way down on to one of the tables.

It all seemed by the way; Laura's mind was focused on Jamie's convoy, to the exclusion of most else. German codes had been intercepted and broken and it was known that the *Scharnhorst*, a German pocket battleship (a slicker, faster model of the more powerful but cumbersome battleship proper), was on its way to attack this particular convoy. The *Scharnhorst* and its big sister, the giant battleship *Tirpitz*, lurked in the Norwegian fjords and were a permanent threat to the Russia-bound convoys. Laura had seen in graphic detail how, when the *Tirpitz* stirred, everyone got edgy. In July 1942, when Convoy PQ17 had scattered and been largely annihilated, the ship symbols had lain in a small pile on the table and all those on duty had left looking grey and feeling they had been part of the battle, of nerves at least.

Now, as she always thought might happen, she knew that Jamie, his destroyer, his convoy, was in the most imminent danger, and she could do nothing but pray. She reminded herself that it *was good* that the *Scharnhorst*'s orders had been decoded. A powerful Royal Navy force was being deployed to try to encounter the pocket battleship off Norway's North Cape.

When the Russian convoys had begun she and Nadine had laughed about the long climb to the top of the near vertical ladders to move ships around the top of Norway. 'Should keep us trim,' Laura had said. 'Reckon the commander-in-chief likes to see us flitting up and down,' Nadine had cast the merest nod towards the office window which overlooked the great wall chart.

Climbing the ladder to move this particular attacking force Laura's legs felt leaden. Under her fingers was the convoy, the *Scharnhorst* and the approaching navy attacking force. She tried to reassure herself, it was a powerful force: cruisers; destroyers, and the battleship *Duke of York*. It looked as if the navy really intended to get the *Scharnhorst* this time. It also looked as if there was quite a battle developing. She had to hang on tight to the ladder as this thought sent her head swimming. She didn't want to be sent off duty – not at this point.

She was extra careful as she began the climb down to the floor. She wondered what kind of place the North Cape was, the last landfall of Europe several hundred miles further north than the Arctic Circle. The land of the midnight sun in summer, then three months without a sunrise, but with the phenomenon of the Northern Lights.

She had just reached the last step when she was immediately sent back to alter the position of the pocket battleship and to add four white discs near to the convoy. These felt like a personal affront, U-boats as well as the *Scharnhorst* – what kind of Christmas was this!

She thought of the last Christmas they had spent together, two years ago now, with her mother and Billie, a happy, happy time, though sometimes she thought you only really appreciated *how* happy in retrospect.

The first casualty was a tanker; they knew before the reports from neighbouring ships. There was a way a tanker went up and burnt on – and on – as few other merchantmen did. Ammunitions ships exploded and often went on exploding until the sea swallowed them up, sometimes even after then, spewing up flames and wreckage, and men.

'Action stations!' Jamie had made the call as second nature when the distant ship had been hit.

He thanked God they had no troopships in this convoy, liners hired as troop carriers were prime targets for the U-boat attacks and prime cares for the escorts. If escorts or merchantmen were hit, sailors, unlike soldiers, at least had an idea what to expect, knew what to do. He knew convoy commodores found army officers a pain in the neck, particularly if they tried to give advice while under a sea attack.

All the time these random thoughts raced through his mind, his eyes scanned the waters and he called for reports.

'No asdic?' the captain asked at his side.

'Nothing yet, sir.'

'Sir! Bearing red 135. U-boats, sir, at least two.' The report came from their asdic officer who with one man tended his sonar equipment at the rear of the bridge.

Almost at the same moment the sub-lieutenant on the starboard wing of the bridge reported a visual sighting. 'Could be a pocket battleship, sir.'

'The *Scharnhorst* d'you think, Jimmie?' Captain Smithson asked, binoculars trained on the horizon.

'Time she came out of those fjords so we can get at her, sir.'

'Torpedo trail on port bow, red ninety.'

Smithson had seen it a second before and was already ordering the destroyer to swing round to be bow on to the oncoming torpedo, lessening the target area. 'Make to the freighters,' he yelled.

The destroyer responded quickly, swinging round. Their eyes went from the approaching torpedo which in the rising swell jumped out of the water on its way towards them, then over to where the merchant shipping would be a bit more cumbersome in their manoeuvres.

'It's going to be close,' the captain hissed as the torpedo came towards their bow, then they lost sight of it, held their breaths, then someone from the stern rejoiced, 'Missed us, sir!'

'The trouble is there's a lot of bottoms the other side of us,' the captain muttered, 'and it may not be the only one.'

'And,' Jamie added, 'it may not be from the U-boats asdic picked up.'

About fifteen seconds later a small freighter caught it. 'She's hanging on, sir,' the port sub-lieutenant reported, 'just clipped her, I would say, she may ...'

'All right sub, we don't need a running commentary, nothing we can do for her at the moment.'

The asdic now came to urgent life. 'Contact, sir,' the asdic officer reported. 'U-boat bearing red 40 and closing.'

'Come about. Prepare depths charges.' The asdic officer made his guess at the depth of the U-boat and the men ran aft to set the charges to detonate accordingly. They circled. The ping and the echo of the asdic quickened, as did every man's pulse.

The tension in the ship could be felt like an electric charge holding them all together, gathering them up for action.

The ping of the asdic and the responding echo merged. Jamie knew the submarine was directly under them. He looked at his captain who nodded, saying as if to himself, 'He's going for the supplies, not the escorts.'

The signal was given and the depth charges were launched from the back and sides of the destroyer, a V-shaped formation of explosives, which with an asdic contact as strong as that should give some result. Many necks craned as the barrel-like weapons plunged down, breaths were held as the seconds passed. They waited, Jamie and the captain watching out for signs of attack from other as yet undetected U-boats, also keeping a weather-eye on the approaching pocket battleship.

Signal lamps were flashing from the convoy commodore's merchant ship. 'What's that?' the captain demanded, still keeping his eyes on the surrounding sea.

'Naval force closing on the *Scharnhorst*,' the signaller reported.

'Yes!' Captain Smithson rejoiced, though whether it was for the navy coming to their assistance or for the depth charges as they boomed and erupted under the sea, was never to be known. Jamie was just pointing to what he thought might be oil from a stricken U-boat when there was a tremendous explosion, the deck under their feet heaved, flames and noise overwhelmed all senses. Jamie was blown upwards and sideways against the port bridge wing. His shoulder hit some piece of superstructure violently, stopping him being cannoned overboard.

What seemed like hours later, but was probably only seconds or minutes, he came round to find the remains of the bridge in flames. Captain Smithson lay near the asdic housing. Jamie struggled over to him; trying to turn him, he realised how much his shoulder hurt and blood was running down between his fingers. Smithson was dead. Instinctively he drew his fingers over the eyes and lowered the lids while at the same time he yelled for 'damage reports', noting the asdic officer and his man had both been killed outright.

'No use, sir, she going to go.'

He hardly needed to be told, the destroyer was already settling.

'Abandon ship, make the order.'

'Right, off you go,' he ordered the sub-lieutenant, then caught sight of someone below the mangled superstructure, with fire lapping the man's legs. He grabbed one of the ship's hoses and played it before him until he got to the unconscious signaller. He pulled him clear and taking him to the side, tied a rope around his waist and lowered him down to one of the subs standing in the boat.

'Come on, sir,' the sub shouted, 'nothing else you can do.'

Then he saw another man lying in the scuppers. He repeated the same procedure lowering him by rope. He glanced around, the ship was settling. He was endangering the lifeboat by staying aboard longer. 'Pull away,' he said already half over the rail and ready to jump.

Then he heard a scream. In the ship's alleyway he saw the captain's steward, his arm raised in appeal for help. Smiler's clothes were well ablaze. He went back, seized the hose again and played it on the man, who fell and lay still.

Beneath his feet the whole boat shuddered, a death rattle, Smithson had told him about that. 'Once you've heard it you'll never forget.'

He grabbed the terribly burnt sailor and dragged. This man was heavier but desperation gives strength. He roped the man, lowered him as carefully as he could, the sub-lieutenant in the lifeboat trying to catch the man's legs and haul him in.

'Come on, sir,' he shouted, 'don't want to land in that bloody water.'

'No,' he said and jumped.

It was as the attacking force was moving in on the *Scharnhorst* that Laura was suddenly struck by a premonition so strong that she neither heard nor saw what was going on around her until Nadine came to her and drew her to one side.

'What is it?' she asked. 'Laura!' She looked over to their superior officer, a Wren whom she had thought it prudent to tell of the situation her friend found herself in. 'She won't thank me for telling you, but if anything happens, I thought . . .'

'You did right, if the need arises take her off the floor, and I'll step in.'

'Can you hear me?' Nadine asked as she led Laura through to the rest room. 'What's happened?'

These were the words that brought her back to reality. 'Something,' she said, 'something has just happened to Jamie, I felt it.' She put her hand over her mouth as with complete conviction she knew what had happened. 'He's gone into the water.' She covered her face with her hands.

Nadine held her tight as she rocked. 'He dreaded the cold waters, he had nightmares about it, it was the one thing, more than the enemy, anything.'

'Don't give up on him too easily,' she said after some time.

'No,' Laura's head shot up and she stood straight, determined. 'I won't. Let's go and see what's happened on that board.'

'Sure?'

'Very.' But when they returned her officer turned her away again. 'I think not Maclaren, can't afford any mistakes. I'll send all the news through by Boston as soon as it's over.'

'I'll be in the canteen, ma'am,' Laura said reluctantly.

'One of the escorting destroyers has gone,' the Wren officer told Nadine, 'think she's better waiting outside until we're certain which one, and there's a lot to do. We can't have distractions.'

Nadine knew she was right, but her heart ached for Laura, waiting no doubt alone in the canteen.

The *Scharnhorst* was surrounded near the North Cape and was repeatedly hit by gunfire and torpedoes. She finally succumbed to a torpedo from the cruiser *Jamaica*. There were 36 survivors and 1,864 lives lost.

When Nadine was finally released from duty she found the canteen empty. She hurried back to their quarters, Laura was sitting on her bed with a letter in her hands. She looked up when her friend entered.

'A letter from my mother,' she said. 'More trouble.'

'What is it?'

Laura realised that this she could not tell, certainly not at that time anyway. 'Jamie's ship?' she asked.

Chapter Twenty-Four

Queenie stood looking at the dead flowers in her vase. For the first time since the Blitz had ended and she and Freddie had shared the flat, she had forgotten to buy fresh flowers. Every week she went specially to the station flower seller and bought flowers for the flat, and flowers for Billie, their discreet landlady.

It wasn't the first time Jock Maclaren had ruined her efforts with flowers, her heart beginning to pound at the recollections, uprooted flowers, ruined gardens, torn oleanders. He could destroy everything. It was just another sign that she was already certain who this man was. Three times now she had seen the same tall, but gaunt and ravaged figure, lift itself spectre-like from where he lingered in doorways. In the shuttered headlights of passing cars she had glimpsed a haggard face, thin, no red moustache and he wore a wide-brimmed old trilby pulled right down over his hair. He *could* have been any man of similar tallness, it was her instincts which convinced her it was Jock who had been following her home from the hospital these dark December nights.

Tonight, the third time, when he lurched towards her she had run, panic-stricken, straight into a group of American soldiers. They had caught her, steadied her, then cheering urged her to turn round and go with them. Then as they turned away one of them seemed to glimpse the figure she was afraid of.

'Say, you in trouble, ma'am?' he asked.

'I . . .' at the full extent of her night vision she was sure she saw the same tall figure outlined against a stationary vehicle. 'I've had a fright,' she gasped, 'I only live around the corner.'

'Say no more.' He called back to his friends, and in the end they all walked her home.

'Thank you all so much, I'll never forget how kind you've been.'

'Have no fear, the Allies are here.'

She smiled, not making the usual response linked to what England, Churchill anyway, saw as their late entry into the war, 'What kept you?'

Alone in the flat she had been unable to calm down, and with Freddie away she had needed to tell someone. She had written to Laura asking her advice. Should she contact the authorities to find out if Jock had escaped, or worse, whether they had discharged him? If they had thrown him out of hospital *and* the army, that indeed would finally have turned his brain.

She had never confided her marital affairs to Billie, and Billie was so desperately busy at the hospital with war casualties now being nursed in former clinics, outpatient departments, even corridors, and her mainstay, Wendy, gone. Wendy had fallen in love, got herself engaged, married, pregnant and gone off to live with a Welsh mother-in-law she had never met, all in four months.

Laura would give her the best comfort and advice. She could always rely on her daughter. She expected a telephone call as soon as Laura received her letter, which could be today – or perhaps tomorrow.

There was a noise at the flat door, it opened and there was Freddie.

'Freddie?' she questioned his unexpected homecoming, then her heart leapt for joy. 'Freddie!' She took a few hurried steps towards him as he just stood holding his attaché case, not moving to kiss her, hold her, speak to her.

'What is it?' she asked, suddenly so fearful. Had he come to tell her Jock was free?

'You haven't heard the news?'

'The news?'

'Jamie's ship's been lost.' He dropped his case to a chair and looked around the flat. 'There's been no word, no telegram?'

'Jamie,' she repeated in a whisper, trying to adjust from the expected trouble to this terrible news.

He reached for her then, their grip on each other tight, as if both felt all the world might well be crumbling away around them.

'Laura,' she said, 'she would know?'

'You've not heard from her,' he shook his head knowing she had not, adding 'sure to I would have thought, working where she does.'

'Can we do anything?' She regretted with all her heart the letter she had written, worrying the girl, appealing for help. It was Laura who would need *her* help now.

'Hope,' he said grimly.

At that moment the telephone rang downstairs in the hall. Freddie turned and ran down. 'Hello!' his voice was hard, firm, prepared, then he exclaimed, 'Laura! My dear ... yes, it was on the news. You've not ... no. You don't know any more than just the sinking?'

'Not really.' Queenie who was by his side gripping his arm heard her daughter's flat despairing words.

'They say no news is good news,' Freddie said having to work hard to make the bland platitude sound new. 'We must just hope and pray. You'll ring us if ...'

'Yes, and I'll give you a number if you need to contact me urgently.'

Queenie listened to Laura's voice, a bad line making it sound like a crackly old gramophone record and so remote.

Queenie took the receiver as he wrote down the number. 'Laura, are you all right? Is someone with you?'

305

'Nadine, she's been wonderful,' there was a pause, 'I can't believe it, Mum.'

'No, nor us.' In her daughter's utter despair Queenie found a new immediate mission and she said firmly, 'No, and we won't while there's hope.'

Laura did not answer, then she said, 'Your letter, Mum, that came on the same day, I . . .'

'I was wrong about what I thought,' she told her daughter firmly. 'There's nothing to worry about after all.'

'You're sure?'

'Sure,' she said firmly. 'Freddie wants to come back to you.'

'Would it help if I came up to Liverpool, or both of us? I've been given time off.'

'I'd rather you two stayed together. They've put me on less important duties, but I'm being kept busy, and I'm still on the spot if news comes. I'd sooner do that. Perhaps later I might come to you.'

'I understand my dear.'

Queenie went back on to the line and they made their goodbyes, the flat forced words poor messengers for all the love and hopes they carried.

Freddie had taken off his coat and stood waiting for her in the hall. Without speaking they linked arms and walked back upstairs to their flat, and she saw utter grief come over her darling Freddie.

'I thought at least Jamie and Laura were going to spend their lives together,' he said.

'Come on, we mustn't give up,' she swallowed hard. 'We must do things, that's what you always say. We'll . . .' she wasn't sure what they could do, so she changed tack. 'You must tell me why you're home early, is it because of Jamie's ship?' She didn't wait for an answer. 'We'll have a brandy before we do anything else.'

He looked at her suddenly as if the mention of brandy had reminded him of something. 'How are *you*?' he asked. His eyes seemed to stray to the vase of dead flowers. 'I

306

thought you looked startled when I came in.'

'Well, I was!' Automatically she moved to the vase, swept it up and took it into the kitchen, where she disposed of the dead blooms, rinsed the vase and put it upside down on the draining board. Turning she saw him watching this show from the doorway.

'What was it you told Laura not to worry about?' he asked.

She turned back to the sink, pushed the vase along the draining board, stood it upright, then turned it upside down again. 'Just hospital gossip,' she turned to him, nodding as to force his acceptance of her explanation. 'The brandy's in the sideboard.' She led the way back to the sitting room.

'What do you really think?' she asked as they sipped their drinks.

'I think there must be survivors, or the navy *think* there are survivors. They won't report people officially missing – or dead – until they're sure who has been rescued. In convoys men can be picked up by several different ships. It could take weeks.'

With Freddie at home and the anxiety about Jamie, she managed to put her worries about Jock aside, also several days she and Billie were able to leave for home together.

It was just a week later, when she was once more leaving alone, that he appeared again. This time he was much nearer the hospital, where there were more vehicles, so she saw him not once, but time after time in jerky repeats like a very old cinematograph film. Then her name was called.

Startled she stopped, swung round, confused by the sound and direction of the voice. Looking behind her she saw in the next headlights that the man had stopped too. She had an impression of clothes hanging on a skeletal frame, his stance, one of intentions thwarted. The dim lights passed but she felt unable to move. Was he still coming after her? Then someone caught her forearm. She shuddered, screamed.

'Queenie!' Freddie's voice was urgent, raised in alarm.

'What is it? You looked quite the wrong way when I called.'

'I don't know,' she almost shouted, then striving for control, 'it was traffic, I was disorientated. I didn't expect you.' All she wanted was to be home, she pushed her arm through his. 'Sorry.'

'Well, expect me from now on. I shall be meeting you every night,' he told her.

She almost stopped walking, so great was this surprise, so just what she needed. 'Every night? But how can you? Not if they send you back to the south coast.'

'I've heard today, I'm to be part of planning in London, instead of supervising in the field. It should be kind of office hours, for quite a time anyway. So I shall come straight from the office to meet you from the hospital.'

'You mean beginning soon?'

'I mean as from now,' he reassured her.

'Oh, marvellous.' She laughed briefly, shakily. 'Now let's hurry, get back into our flat.' When they were inside, had climbed the stairs and closed the door she continued on the same theme. 'We've been happy here, haven't we Freddie? I know not now, not waiting to hear ... but before that we've had nearly two years. We wouldn't have expected that.'

'It's been the only thing that has kept me going.'

She knew he meant *now* while she, momentarily unhinged by Jock's near presence, was reviewing their whole lives. She did not attempt to explain; she appreciated he could not see beyond this waiting time, this time when every knock on the door or ring of the telephone sent sheer cold fear running down the spine.

'This is no news,' she told him, 'but Laura rang last night.'

'Yes,' he said, alert for any snippet of information from Liverpool.

'She said the feeling is the news of survivors can't be much longer coming, even from Murmansk. She also said that even though the convoys deliver things there, it seems very much a closed port to the men. There have been reports of damaged ships having to wait for spares to be taken by following convoys, before repairs could be done, and of the stranded crews having to eke out and beg food from other British ships. There's nothing available from the shore. Do you believe that?'

'I think I do, it's a damn bleak place.'

'But if men were injured surely they'd care for them in hospital?'

'I wonder where the nearest hospital would be,' he mused, sighed deeply. 'Convoys are usually turned round in a week,' he said, 'so we must soon hear.'

Later as they lay in bed together she asked about his posting to London. 'Did you ask for it?'

'Begged,' he admitted. 'I couldn't concentrate, I had to be with you, Queenie, you're the only other person I really care about in the world.'

She turned into his side, she felt his arm raise and she lifted her head so he could put it around her shoulders, pulled the pillow down so she was comfortable enough to sleep when the time came.

'Queenie,' his voice in the darkness sounded full of anxiety, 'you would tell me if there was anything else worrying you? Anything to do with Jock.'

She did not answer, the unexpectedness of this direct question and the way they were, lying so close, made her bite her bottom lip hard so she did not blurt out all her worries. But if he met her each day from the hospital . . .

'Have you heard something about him?

She felt him raise himself up from the bed as if he could see her, assess her answer.

'No,' she said truthfully, 'I've not heard anything, and we've more important things than Jock Maclaren to worry about.'

She felt him slowly lie back down. 'It's you I care about, you I've always loved,' she told him and for the first time since he had come back to London this time he made love to her.

His love-making was like the man, gentle and caring, and because of the consideration so much more arousing for her. There was such a mutuality of honest regard, respect which served to build a passion of tender giving, so when they lay still afterwards she felt tears running down her cheeks. She did not move to dry them, kept them silent and secret. 'I love you so much, Freddie, if only we could hear Jamie was safe I'd want nothing more ever in life.'

'Or me,' he whispered. 'You and me. Jamie and Laura. Ah, me.'

She held him around his waist until he slept.

The next day at the hospital Freddie, Laura and Jamie were never far from her mind. She had such a premonition that something was about to happen. She was finished earlier than usual and thought she would surprise Freddie by being in the foyer first. Only the previous night he had decided they should wait for each other there, rather than risk missing each other outside. She had made no complaint about that.

The corridor was for once quiet, no porters rushing about with trolley loads of supplies from the subterranean storerooms, or nurses and doctors rushing down for quick refreshment. Her quick footsteps echoed on the concrete floor as she anticipated seeing Freddie. What he said was so true, in times of such terrible troubles being with the one you loved was a mainstay, a life saver. Her thoughts were interrupted as someone came from one of the doorways just ahead of her, and stood barring her way. She stopped, gasped, hand flying to her mouth. 'Jock.' The whisper was fearful but for a second she felt pity for this travesty of a former military man.

She might have tried to help him, or appeal to him, but she recognised the thin humourless sneer curling his lips.

'Oh, no,' she breathed.

'Oh, yes,' he hissed with relish. 'Oh, *yes*!'

310

She turned and tried to run but he was upon her, grabbing and gripping her fiercely in hands that were thinner, sharper, crueller, than they had been before. She struggled desperately, looked up and down the corridor, someone must come.

'I've caught up with you at last.' The throaty sneer was still the same. The pleasure of having caught his prey and having it to torment was the same. 'It's taken time, but I'm a patient man as you know.'

She opened her mouth to scream, but he saw the intention coming and clamped a hand over her lips, his nails piercing her skin.

'This,' he told her, 'is it Queenie, my love. This is my *wife's* swan song. Say goodbye to life Queenie. If I can't have you ...' His free hand was on her throat, and in a curious movement she found herself brought backwards over his knee as he suddenly knelt. She was forced backwards, painfully bowed over his knee, rocking, no contact with the ground. Then both his hands moved to her neck and his fingers drove deep, restricting blood and air. She seized his wrists, tried to pull his hands apart. Hanging on. Her last thought before she felt herself somersaulting into blackness was, 'Where is everyone?'

In the foyer Billie saw Freddie coming in, she stopped to speak to him. 'No news?' she asked.

'Nothing.' They talked for a moment or two then Billie said 'I'd go and root her out, she's probably rearranging those chairs. It's become a hospital joke, Queenie's chairs. If we could have those upright girders taken out she'd be a happy woman.'

They parted on a smile.

As Freddie pushed through the first set of swing doors he frowned; in the distance someone was shouting, a young woman with an Irish accent, he thought. It sounded urgent and he quickened his step through the next doors so he could see the length of the passage. Several people were on the ground. One a nurse, a big man in a dirty army great-coat and a woman flat out on the floor. Queenie?

311

'Hey!' He shouted as he sprinted to help the red-haired nurse who was hurling herself time and time again at the man who shouldered her aside. Before he reached them he saw the slightly built girl grab at his hair, then try to deter him by digging her fingers into his eyes, as he bent to his murderous attack.

With the speed and strength of the utterly desperate, Freddie seized the collar of the man's greatcoat and hauled him aside. In that second he glimpsed spume-flecked lips and recognised two things: Jock Maclaren and madness. 'Get help,' he told the young nurse as he wrestled Jock away from Queenie, who lay so still. 'Go on!'

Jock got to his feet and seemed to recognise Freddie, for he launched himself viciously at him, his hands going straight for his neck, and he was strong. He had all the strength of a maniacal beast.

Near their feet Queenie groaned. Freddie registered, 'Thank God she's alive,' as he tried to prevent Maclaren getting back to her. The man was quite beside himself, uncaring for anything that was done to him, he came on like a great, scrabbling, unstoppable monster.

He hoped the nurse would soon be back with help, for as he punched him with all his strength, he felt no one man could stop him. Jock Maclaren was laughing, with blood pouring from his nose and mouth. 'It's the end!' he shouted. 'The end is nigh!' He screamed with hysterical laughter, but as his voice dropped and he muttered, 'for both of you!' it was more sinister. He must know that the young nurse had run for help, obviously did not care. Freddie realised this *was* his own life he was fighting for, but all he wanted to do was tend to Queenie.

He felt the man's nails down the side of his face as again Jock reached for his neck. Freddie punched hard into his stomach, heard the gasp, echoed by his own as Jock's feet kicked into his crotch. He doubled up, vaguely aware of hearing other people – shouting, running – and suddenly it was over. Jock Maclaren was being held by several men, porters and soon policemen. Freddie, down on his knees, crawled over to Queenie, bent close to her face.

'Don't move her, Mr de Falla!' It was Billie's voice, formal, urgent and looking up he saw the red-haired nurse by her side. 'It may be her back is injured, we must be careful.'

Immediately there was a doctor, several men, perhaps all doctors for all Freddie knew, kneeling by Queenie. He was marginalised, a concerned onlooker, as the professionals took over. He heard the nurse explaining what she had seen, Queenie racked over the man's knee, bent backwards.

Broken, was the word that intruded into Freddie's mind as he listened, saw the care with which she was moved on to a back board, then a trolley. Still she was unconscious. Then he saw the marks on her neck and semi-circular incisions on her cheeks where Jock's fingernails had been, and he wanted to hurt someone back, at that moment anyone would have done, any Aunt Sally, any wall to punch.

Billie came to him. 'Stay where you are for a bit longer,' she said, 'we'll have a look at you in a moment.'

'Queenie?'

'Everyone in this hospital loves Queenie, nothing will be left undone, I can assure you.'

'I must be with her.'

'In good time,' she hesitated, 'the police need to know about . . .'

'Her husband,' he told her, 'the last we heard he was in a psychiatric hospital.'

'This time I should think he'll be sectioned, kept in permanent protective custody.' Billie leaned down to him and with the help of a porter got him to his feet. 'We'll get a wheelchair,' she said, 'take you to a cubicle.'

'I'm all right,' he said.

'The sooner you're cleaned up, the sooner you can go to Queenie.'

Billie came back to Emergency Admissions as soon as

she had obtained the news from the side ward Queenie had been taken to.

'Freddie,' she came to sit by him in the cubicle.

'Oh, God!,' he breathed as he saw her face, 'she's not . . .'

'No,' Billie said quickly, 'but it is serious.'

'Can I see her?'

'I'll take you now,' she rose seeing that this man would not take in anything she or anyone else had to say until he had his beloved Queenie under his gaze once more.

She led him to the small room just outside the main ward, which had a door from the corridor and another from close to Ward Sister's desk. A white coated consultant of senior years greeted him, held out his hand. The two men shook, each assessing the other. 'My name's Albertsunn, senior consultant in the spinal injuries department.'

Freddie glanced at him, all the questions in his eyes.

'Sit down man,' he said and once Freddie did so he did not delay. 'First her heart is not as strong as I would like, then there are two major problems,' he said and seeing Freddie's eyes on the bandaged neck and the brace beneath it he diverted to mention, 'the neck bandages are on wounds that are in no way life threatening. The main problems are a head injury, and the longer she remains unconscious the more worrying this can be. The other . . .' he paused here and drew in a breath as if to clue in his listener that this was the major worry. 'The other is the spine. I fear there may be damage to the spinal cord. I've had X-rays taken, but I don't want to risk moving her about at this stage. I shall wait to make a more in depth assessment when she recovers consciousness,' he paused. 'I understand there is a daughter . . .'

'Yes, she is in the WRENS,' Freddie's eyes never left the man's face.

'I think,' he said, 'if it's possible, she should be sent for.'

314

Chapter Twenty-Five

Never had Queenie listened so intently, for no other senses registered, only sounds.

Never had she felt so much on the brink of such portentous decision making. She was like a set of scales in perfect balance.

She was aware of different people at her beside, mostly there was a man who stayed nearly all the time. They came and tried to influence the equipoise, but she sensed that only she could do this.

Now there was someone else trying to make the decision. There had been the other voices, kind, persuasive, but this one was curiously like her own voice, almost like another part of her brain giving her a good talking to. She became more attentive.

'Mum,' Laura begged, 'don't let him win, not now. Not after so long. You've everything to live for now, Freddie, being with him, marrying him.'

Marry Freddie. The idea was nice, made her feel quite able to drift away on such a pleasant thought. Freddie of course had been the man who had been here all the time.

She listened on but there was silence now. Perhaps after all the decision not to stay was the best one. Another voice, a far more powerful voice from a different source told her she could go now if she wanted to. It was an option she could exercise, to move into acceptance of the state from which the voice came. A journey.

'Mum! Mum! Don't go!'

This voice was strident, urgent, made her balanced mind flinch and tremble. This other person, this daughter, was claiming a part in the decision making. Children should be seen and not heard. This is not your death we're talking about, it's mine ...

'I need you!' Laura insisted. 'I stood by you when you needed me, now I need *you*.'

This was an accusation, a recrimination.

'This is too much ...'

She could hear that her daughter was sobbing now and another woman was interrupting.

'My dear, this is only upsetting yourself. Perhaps you should leave your mother now for a few moments.'

'I can't bear it, Mum, first Jamie, now you. Mum!'

There was more urgent whispering, the sound of movement. Laura being taken away, sobbing, out of control.

Queenie sighed. Always trouble. First Jamie ... Freddie's Jamie ... and she remembered the loss of his ship. What had they heard? She should be with them all. Times of trouble. Loved ones together.

She had the strange feeling she shrugged off a hand. She felt suspension slipping away, earthly things returning. The scales were moving.

She opened her eyes cautiously. It was not like Laura to make such an outcry about anything, but the excitement seemed to be over, for turning her head just a little she saw Freddie. He sat with his head bowed over her hand, which she realised he was holding. She squeezed his fingers. She felt him grow still with attention, then very slowly he raised his eyes, very slowly as if he were looking at every tiny fraction of her arm on the way to her face. So before he reached it she'd time to prepare muscles stiff with disuse, and she smiled at him.

She saw his lips part.

'Queenie?' he asked.

She thought she nodded but was unsure her head responded to the command.

'I'll get someone,' he said coming close to her face, then lifting her hand to kiss it. She tried to hold his hand tighter, wanting to say, no wait, no fuss, not yet, but he was unsure of her, afraid she might slip away again without help, she saw it in his face.

'Nurse,' he called and immediately the curtain around her bed was opened.

The rest seemed to be done in dumb show, Freddie looked from the nurse's face to Queenie's. Nurse looked. 'I'll get Sister,' she said.

Sister came and officially declared the miracle so. 'It's late but I'll see if Mr Albertsunn is still in the hospital, and I'll tell your daughter, she's just taking a little walk outside.'

The consultant came hurrying to the ward shortly afterwards. 'Just caught me,' he said coming to the bedside. 'Now, Queenie, how are you feeling? Been having to make my own tea in the canteen.'

Queenie's focused on the senior consultant. 'I'm sorry,' she croaked.

'Mum.'

She heard Laura coming, running, choking with tears as after five days her mother's first words were of apology.

Queenie's eyes then focused on her daughter and she smiled and lifted her hand, the gesture meant I came back for you. Laura took it in both hers.

'Here's a drink for your mother,' Sister said as a nurse arrived with a long spouted cup.

Queenie was given just a little fluid, her eyes never leaving her daughter's face as she drank, then she asked. 'Jamie?'

Laura shook her head trying not to let the awful sinking despair show in her face. 'No news yet,' she said. It was going on too long, even Freddie had said so. They had stopped, everyone had stopped, repeating hackneyed phrases about it being only bad news that travelled fast.

317

'I have an operation to do in another hospital,' Mr Albertsunn said, 'but before I leave I would like to make a preliminary examination now your mother's obviously fully with us.'

Queenie wondered if that was quite true. She could feel no sensation, no sense of sheets on feet or legs, no movement when she ordered her toes to flex.

'Of course,' Laura said stooping to kiss her mother's hand before she released it. 'We can come back later?'

'Being as she's such a special patient,' Sister agreed.

'She has spoilt us all,' Mr Albetsunn said, 'now it is our turn.'

'Let's go down and tell Billie,' Freddie said as they left the ward, both of them quite unaware that they were holding hands until they reached the staircase. Here they paused, looked at each other, aware that they had crossed one bridge together, but that there were more to come.

They were allowed back into the quiet ward for a few more precious moments, for reassurance that in mind at least Queenie was restored to them. The consultant's report, relayed by Sister, was that there was extensive and deep bruising and swelling, and that Queenie would be kept flat on her back for some time yet. 'It's early days yet,' Sister said, 'and there's a long way to go.'

Queenie had just sighed a little when she said that, the tiny noise had sounded so tired, so weary. Laura had heard, she recognised the sound she'd heard so often after one of her father's onslaughts. It was the sigh of a woman about to make one more effort, one more fresh start, of a woman who knew there were more mountains to climb.

Then she and Freddie walked home, both too exhausted for talk, the stress, the long days and nights of waiting and watching finally allowed to sweep over them. Only once did Freddie break the silence.

'I shall look after her no matter what,' he said 'and eventually I shall take her home with me to Gibraltar, where she belongs.'

Laura did not answer, perhaps because she knew she would make the same commitment to his son – given the chance.

When they let themselves into Billie's house the telephone was ringing.

Freddie was there first but handed the receiver to Laura, not moving away, the wire taut across his chest to reach her ear.

'Laura?' Nadine queried.

'Yes,' her voice was full of caution, daring to hope for nothing.

'There are survivors,' Nadine said, 'and his name's among them.' She waited for the reaction. There was none. Nadine went on. 'Jamie's name is on a list of survivors who were picked up by a freighter with damaged steering. They only reached Murmansk yesterday.'

She sank down to the hall chair.

'Laura?' It was Freddie now who questioned.

'Jamie's on a list of survivors.'

A distant voice rose anxiously. 'Laura, Mr de Falla? Are you there?'

He took the receiver, gripping her shoulder tight with his other hand.

'Thank God,' she heard herself say, 'thank God.' She vaguely heard Freddie recovering speech, then questioning. 'Just twenty-six,' he repeated the number, 'twenty-six survivors.' She looked up at him then and he nodded to her. 'I'll hand you back to Laura now. Thank you for this news, I ...' he paused to regain control, 'you'll know what it means.'

'The commander-in-chief is trying to obtain more details. He's doing all he can. There are some injured,' she added cautiously, 'the boss is being great, he knows what you're going through, your mother and all. He asked after ...' Nadine broke off. 'How is your mother?'

'Conscious, today, just a little while ago,' Laura said with a choking laugh, 'we've just got back from the hospital. I was going to let you know. Sensible, thank God. No brain injuries, but we don't know about her spine.'

With the phone call completed Laura turned to find Freddie putting his hat back on. 'There is a chapel near the hospital. I am going to give my thanks,' he said.

'I shall come with you.'

Chapter Twenty-Six

During the following week Laura had to return to her duties in Liverpool, while her mother's condition remained the same. She spoke to Freddie every evening, and he seemed to consult Mr Albertsunn almost as frequently.

'He says he's never seen such deep and extensive bruising from a physical attack. He thought if he'd been told your mother had been in an air raid and buried under her home he would have believed it more readily.'

'Nadine's uncle, the policeman, believes my father will end his days in a prison for the criminally insane.'

Freddie thought that it was no more than he deserved, having condemned his wife to the possibility of a different kind of confinement.

The following night she had good news for him. The survivors were being brought in stages from Murmansk to Scapa Flow, from there they would be transferred and brought to the north of Scotland, assessed, then flown to different centres according to their needs.

'So it shouldn't be long before we see him,' he said, 'or you'll be able to. I've been detailed back to the south coast. I heard today. I can't tell you more, except that I *have* to go.'

Laura thought of the rumours that were circulating of a recrossing of the Channel, of liberating Europe. Freddie was an imaginative engineer, he would be invaluable.

'The tides are beginning to turn,' she said. It was a phrase she'd heard several times recently at headquarters. Certainly the pattern of naval warfare had changed. March 1943 had seen Britain's heaviest shipping losses of the war, but the old year had gone out with the sinking of the dreaded *Scharnhorst*, and, in the following May, Convoy ONS 5 had sunk forty-one U-boats. The excitement in the underground headquarters had been intense, astonished disbelief might have summed up their feelings at the time, but later the same month Admiral Dönitz had withdrawn his U-boats from the Atlantic.

Freddie was wondering if he should try to prepare Laura for what she might face when she remet his son. The dangers of fire on a torpedoed ship – and in deadly icy waters – it would be a miracle if he had escaped unharmed. 'You may have to be the strong one for a time,' he told her.

It was a remark she remembered as she began her journey by train and bus to the outskirts of a Northamptonshire village, where a local mansion had been requisitioned and made into a hospital for convalescent servicemen.

All the way there she had gone over in her mind the few extra facts that they had been able to glean about the condition of the survivors. The captain's steward had horrific burns and had been taken to a special burns unit, six more of the survivors had died on the way home, but the rest, nineteen, Jamie included, were in this place.

She could not believe that she would shortly be able to see him, to touch him, to talk to him, that he was here within walking distance. She was suddenly overwhelmed. For goodness sake, she told herself, I can't cry walking up the drive. She diverted behind one of the enormous and majestic elm trees that dotted the vast expanse of lawns. She had a good nose blow, told herself she was only delaying the glorious moment of meeting by such behaviour. The tears refused to be stemmed. Then, getting desperate, she used a ploy Nadine said her brother used at public school

322

when tears threatened. You had to say 'Rats, rats, rats' crossly to yourself, then you couldn't cry. It seemed to help, particularly when she saw another woman walking up the drive.

The entrance hall was huge, went up several storeys and had sabres and pikestaffs arranged in huge fans, interspersed with ancient shields. Otherwise it reminded her of the school buildings at Anerley, an official place where one should report one's presence. She was looking around unsure in which direction to move when she heard footsteps, brisk, hard-soled shoes on tiles, coming rapidly nearer. A tall dark woman in elegant tweed suit, knitted stockings, came smiling towards her.

'Hullo there, can I help you?'

'I've come to see Lieutenant James de Falla,' she paused as there was a heightened attention from this very self-possessed young woman. The smile left her face and she tipped up her chin, looked down her nose you might say, as she studied Laura. 'May I ask what your relationship is?'

'I'm his fiancée,' she added feeling defensive. She had the distinct feeling that this young woman had formed a relationship with Jamie, but her next words seemed to contradict this idea.

'You're Laura then.'

'Yes,' she said. 'He's not dangerously ill or ... or anything?'

'Not physically,' she said, 'in no way in my opinion, but see for yourself, then perhaps we could have a chat. It's not my place to make medical judgements, but ... Well, damn it! I do own the house, I'm entitled to some say about what happens here.' She gave a tiny determined stamp. 'He's in the orangery, but before you leave,' she pointed to a baize-covered door in one corner of the huge entrance hall, 'that's my private quarters, just come straight in, I'll be waiting.'

'I don't understand at all,' Laura began.

'I think you will, when you've seen him and when we've

323

talked.' She led the way into a huge conservatory which ran the whole length of the back of the house, like a miniature Crystal Palace.

'By the way, my name's Monica Shardlow.'

She stopped just inside the conservatory and pointed to where a man lay in a long chair some way from the others. 'Right, bright smile and off you go. He may be asleep,' she added, 'he has terrible nights.'

She looked sharply at this woman who nodded meaningfully as if this was a piece of important information. She was aware other men greeted her as she passed, but her gaze was on the reclining figure. It seemed a long way through the easy chairs, the wheelchairs, the men with crutches instead of limbs.

She reached his chair, and looked down at a man she would not have recognised, not immediately. She would have walked past this gaunt-faced man, whose tan had faded to an unhealthy yellow, whose hands twitched as he slept. But she thought, he has two legs, two arms, all his fingers, as far as she could see. Carefully she pulled up a chair and sat by him, then put her hand over his, realising as she did so how cold her hand was compared with his.

He started, half cried out, snatched his hand away. Nearby she heard men tutting to themselves, as if this was something he did regularly to their annoyance.

'Jamie,' she said quietly but urgently, 'it's me, Laura.'

He half turned in the chair. 'Laura?' he said. 'Laura!' he said her name with urgency as if calling her from a distance. 'You've come through then, out of the wood.'

Had he been dreaming? She did not allow her alarm to show. 'Of course, we always come out of the wood together,' she said, then as if inspired she went on, 'don't you remember the wood on the Downs, the wood above the cottage?'

She saw she had his attention.

'That was strange, do you remember, like being underwater, green, greeny-blue.'

324

'Oh, God!' he moaned.

'I waited for you, we came out into the sunshine together, then walked back hand in hand to Honeysuckle Cottage.'

'Yes,' his hand gripped hers, she noticed how discoloured all his fingers were, blue, purple, like bad chilblains. She noticed the nightmare in his eyes and wondered what it was he had seen, what experience could have so swept away his exuberant joy for living. She wanted to throw herself into his arms, but she remembered Freddie's remark. She was the one who had to play the comforter. She sensed just making contact, reminding him of all he meant to her, was what was important now.

She took his hand again and for a moment he shivered. 'Yours hands are very cold,' he said, but when she would have withdrawn it he caught it by the fingertips and held it. 'It made me jump before.'

She saw that his eyes were clearing of sleep and the fright she had given him.

'Laura,' he said. 'I've been waiting for you for a long time.'

'And me you,' she said then smiled at him, 'all my life, and several lifetimes before that I think. Do you remember our first meeting on Gib? In the street with your father and my mother.'

'Pa?' he queried.

'Well, and he's on the south coast again.'

'And Queenie?'

She hesitated. 'The whole hospital loves my mother and her chair problem,' she said.

He laughed and she could not resist putting his hand to her cheek and whispering, 'I do love you, Jamie, more than anyone else in the world.'

'I can't believe you are here, no one told me . . .'

'I didn't know until late last night that I could come, and I've a week, so I could stay somewhere nearby, come every day.'

'There is some talk of moving me,' he said.

325

'Where to?'

He shrugged. 'They don't tell me. I think it has something to do with the nightmares I have.'

She was not sure what to say, just regarded him attentively.

'Every time I sleep. I dread going to sleep. I shout out, and,' he glanced towards the other patients, 'upset the others.'

'You wouldn't upset me,' she said. 'Could you come home with me to Billie's? Is there any reason why not?'

She learned that he had gone into the sea, that he'd had bad frost bite, hands, feet, face, followed by severe kidney trouble, all due to the intensely cold water. 'Lucky to survive, they told me. Perhaps I was lucky, but not Smiler.'

'Smiler?' she queried.

'Steward to the captain.'

'Isn't he in a burns unit?'

'Yes,' he said harshly, 'he's still alive – they tell me.' He looked down at his hands, turned them over, and over again. 'How can he be?' He shook his head looking down at his hands, which he wrung and drew through each other repeatedly. Then he looked up at her. 'It wasn't my nightmare about going into the sea that came true, it was his.'

So many platitudinous words came to her mind, but she did not utter them, she had heard too many at her mother's bedside.

'I met Monica Shardlow as I came in,' she told him. 'She invited me to look in on her before I leave.'

'Lady Monica,' he said, 'she's A1 to all of us. The lads reckon she beats most of the doctors here put together.'

When the nurses began to fetch the patients in for their evening meal, Laura made her goodbyes. 'I'll try to find a room at a local pub, or something.'

'That would be good,' he suddenly grinned and she saw a glimpse of the old Jamie. 'Wish I could come with you.'

She wanted to say, 'Why not?' but felt perhaps Lady Monica would be telling her that very shortly. She leaned

326

forward and kissed him gently on the lips; his hand came up and pressed her more closely to him.

She found the green baize door, knocked and entered. 'Well, my dear, what's your verdict?' Lady Monica asked without preamble.

'He's obviously had a terrible time.' She told briefly of his dread of falling into cold water.

'That explains a little more,' she said, then suddenly she got up, paced to the window and back. 'Look, I'm going to be perfectly frank with you. There's talk of sending your fiancé to a psychiatric unit.'

'No! No!' Laura was on her feet. 'Never. Never.'

'That's my feeling. His nightmares come from actual bloody awful experiences, they're not fantasies, or imaginings. He needs time and he needs you.'

Laura paced the room unseeing. There was no way Jamie was going to be taken to a ... like her father. 'For God's sake!' she exclaimed.

'Quite,' Lady Monica agreed. 'Come and sit down, we must talk. I have taken a great interest in your fiancé. We have a very pompous doctor here who feels if he writes a long report about the odd patient, he justifies his position. He's made mistakes. I don't intend him to make any more. What your man should have is a medal for bravery. I've been and interviewed other survivors from his ship, his sub-lieutenant in particular. Your James saved several men's lives before he left his sinking ship, including the captain's steward.'

'He mentioned him.'

'His nickname was Smiler,' she shook her head, sighed heavily. 'He was terribly burned when the ship was hit but James got him over the side. Unfortunately, both Smiler and James landed in the sea, but they were hauled out pretty pronto, or as you know they would have had no chance – but they were in wet clothes which froze. Smiler thrashed about quite a lot and, as James tried to help him, his blistered skin ...'

'Came off,' Laura said remembering Jamie's examination of his own hands. 'Is he still alive? Jamie said he was.'

'Yes, he's in a special burns unit in London, I have the details. There's no doubt the man has suffered beyond anyone's imagining, faces endless operations.'

'But Jamie just needs time,' Laura said, looking fixedly at this lady of the house. 'What can I do? Will you help me get him away? There is no way he is going into a psychiatric hospital. I'll kidnap him.'

'That the spirit,' she said 'and I'll help you. I've a few strings I can jerk.'

'And I'm going to write to Smiler and to Jamie's father.'

Three days later a reply came from Smiler dictated to a nurse. Jamie was waving it to her when she arrived. 'Read it,' he urged, 'read it aloud.'

Dear Jimmie,

I've only just learned where you are, so I am writing to say thank you for saving my life. I know, from what little I remember and from what I've been told, that I owe everything to you. You got me off then looked after me in the lifeboat and on the freighter. Greater love has no man and I thank you from the bottom of my heart.

Looks like I'm going to be here a long time, so guess my war is over. Look after yourself, sir. I'll never forget you.

Your obedient servant,
Gordon 'Smiler' Harris

She looked up to find tears in his eyes. 'So do you think he doesn't remember the worst in the lifeboat?'

'They say nature blocks the extremes out,' she said.

'There is another letter,' she told him. 'Billie has written a wonderful letter, on hospital notepaper, detailing how if they will allow you to come back to London to live with her and your father, whatever care you might need would be immediately available at her hospital. She's listed various experts they have on call.'

328

Two days later the meetings, the jerking of strings and the telephoning of anyone they thought could help, was over. A senior naval doctor had attended and ruled that he saw no reason why Lieutenant de Falla should not be allowed to go home for a few further weeks, to finish his recuperation. 'We need officers such as this, men with courage and initiative, back on active service.'

Laura added the final impulse by saying that if this could come into effect immediately, she could travel back to London with Lieutenant de Falla, see him safely settled before she had to return to duty.

Lady Monica walked to the end of the drive with them the day they left. 'Well, I got rid of my *bête noire* doctor and you two got each other.' At the bus stop she stepped back to look at them both in their navy uniforms. 'You know you remind me of that saying when you're together – 'the sum of the whole is greater than the parts'. Be good to each other. Goodbye.' She stood and waved the bus out of sight.

They travelled first class and when they boarded the train they found a compartment to themselves. 'Our luck is in,' he said.

'It won't last long, by the next station we'll be packed solid like the rest of the train.'

'I need to talk to you,' he said.

'And me to you,' she said soberly, 'before we get to London there is something you have to know.'

'Me first.' He sat close taking her hand in his. 'You wrote to Smiler didn't you?' I must have been fairly thick, or too wrapped up in myself, not to realise straight away. That letter has made a tremendous difference, you know. Suddenly I saw that I'd only witnessed the man's suffering. He'd gone through it, come out the other side and was saying *thank you* for the life he says I saved.'

'I don't think there's any doubt about that.'

'I just felt I'd been wrong to save him, that oblivion would have been a better option seeing what ...' He stopped then. 'I shall go and see him, the hospital's in London.'

'Good! I wish I could come with you. But ...'

'But? This sounds a serious "but".'

'It is,' she cut in before he could say more. 'It's about my mother.'

When the full story of the attack and its consequences were told he said, 'My father never mentioned this in his letter.'

'No, we agreed it would be better not to.'

'We must go and see her as soon as we get to London.'

'I'd like to do that, and she'll be overjoyed to see *you*.'

They were both shocked when they reached Queenie's bedside. She looked so much frailer, so much paler, but when she saw who was with Laura, her daughter thought for a moment she was going to levitate with sheer excitement. She raised both her arms and shook them about in greeting and celebration.

'Jamie! My dear, dear, boy. How I wish Freddie was here as well.' She laughed then. 'We're never satisfied, are we? Don't sit down yet, let me look at you properly.' She caught his hands and steered him to lean over her so she could soak in his looks.

'Hmm! Pale but interesting,' she said, 'like me probably. There's something I want you to do for me.'

'Of course,' Jamie said.

'What is it, Mum?' She looked on the locker to see if there was a drink available.

'I want you to get married right away,' Queenie told them.

330

Chapter Twenty-Seven

The wedding was arranged for the first Saturday in March by special licence. Queenie was not only determined to see them wed, she was also determined to be on her feet by then.

'Please don't put yourself through this,' Freddie begged as she laboured in the flat with crutches, walking sticks, chair backs. 'You're home, that's all any of us care about. We've got the wheelchair and I can carry you up and down the stairs, you're no weight.'

'I can do it on my bottom now.'

'There's no need,' he implored.

'I'm standing,' she had insisted, 'my daughter will remember me on my feet at her wedding.'

He appealed to Billie. 'She's not strong, she should be resting – and now she's sewing!'

'It's only her determination that's got her this far, the consultant's amazed. You're not going to stop her trying, and perhaps,' she put her hand on his arm, 'you're wrong to try. As for the sewing, that's my fault I'm afraid.'

He watched her that evening poring over her sewing machine, using both feet, one on top of the other, to press down the electric pedal which powered it. She worked with a kind of urgency, but on the completion of each seam, she lifted the lacy pieces and smiled at them. It was as if she was sewing in dreams.

'What is that?' he asked at last.

'Don't you know?' she laughed. 'Can't you see?'

'Well it's white and has bits of this and that.'

'Billie has given Laura the wedding dress she would have worn if her young man had survived the First World War.'

'But you've cut it up.'

'Not exactly, remade it would be a better word. It would not have been long enough for Laura, but I've taken off some of the lace flounces and put in a deep V section from under the bust to the waist at the front and a deep plain band at the back.'

'Getting a bit technical for me. How will you know it fits?'

'I'll show you. You can help.'

Together they fitted the pieces of the dress on to the tailor's dummy.

'I wouldn't have believed it. It looks fantastic.'

'I think Billie's home, go and fetch her to look at it.'

The dress astonished Laura. 'It must have cost a fortune.' She was tearful and inclined to be over humble about it until Billie said, 'You will wear that dress with pride for your man, as I would have worn it for mine.'

The wedding day, Saturday 4 March 1944, was cold but fine, and they arrived at the Register Office to find a small crowd of nurses and doctors from the hospital in attendance all rallying to throw confetti and cheer bride and groom, then accompany them to a wedding cake and champagne party back at Billie's house. Here the newly promoted Captain Jamie de Falla, resplendent in uniform with his extra stripe, referred to his 'beautiful bride, radiant in a wonderful dress courtesy of the marvellous Billie Chandler, without whom none of them would manage.' Loud cheers. 'And the skill of my mother-in-law Queenie, whom I understand has dressed most of the ladies here today from her stash of prewar materials.' More cheering. 'Thank you for coming everyone, God speed to you all.'

332

'And you both! The bride and groom!' The toasts drunk, they were seen off in a taxi to honeymoon overnight at the Savoy Hotel. This was what Billie called her 'proper wedding present' to them.

On Sunday morning they arrived back aglow with love and enjoyment. 'There was more champagne in the room, we're still awash,' Jamie reported.

'And flowers, masses of flowers,' Laura added. 'It was all wonderful. Thanks so much, Billie.'

'Yes, thanks all of you, Pa, Queenie, Billie, and now we have to go.' Jamie had to be aboard his new destroyer in Portsmouth the next morning, and was then bound for the Mediterranean, he hoped.

'A captain, marvellous!' Freddie clapped his hand on his son's back. 'Marvellous.'

'I know a song about a captain,' Laura said and catching her mother's eye they both laughed. 'As our final performance,' Queenie said. 'Both together,' Laura prompted.

'On my feet though.'

Laura put her arm around her mother and they stood together. 'You have to imagine us doing a kind of tap dance,' Queenie told them, 'after two. One, two ...'

> A captain? A captain?
> Yes, of course, I am.
> I'm Captain Sam
> Of the *Frying Pan*.

'Oh! very flattering,' Jamie said, 'I could clap you in the rattle for such behaviour.'

They made their final goodbyes, their excitement was such that tears were very nearly kept at bay. They were all looking for better times. The wedding had made them all feel they had claimed a stake in the future.

Queenie had certainly pushed the matter, but she had been right was the thought that came to Laura as her train sped north and she thought of Jamie speeding south. Their stars were moving apart again, and the trouble was he was dearer to her than ever. She wondered if that was how their life would be, the more time they spent together, the more precious each would become to the other. 'Just get this war over,' she said to herself.

The country's expectations reached a high pitch when on 6 June 1944 the expected invasion took place. The British Second Army and the American First Army landed on Normandy beaches code-named Sword, Juno, Gold, Omaha and Utah. Once the landings on the five beaches were linked, the Allies were kept supplied by Mulberrys, artificial harbours which so transformed and speeded the supply situation they badly upset German defence calculations.

Freddie was full of the success of the Mulberrys, but the one supplying Omaha beach was virtually destroyed after a three-day storm culminating on 19 June. He was late back from the Ministry of Defence that day, and was surprised as he opened the flat door. There were no lights on, and there was a small of burning, of something badly scorching. He snapped on the lights and rushed through to the sitting room.

On the ironing board a piece of material was smoking, on the floor lay Queenie.

'Queenie!' his exclamation was soft, full of fear. 'Queenie,' he lamented, fearful as he saw her open eyes, but she was watching him, her lips attempting a smile. 'I'll get help,' he said.

'No,' she gasped, 'come here,' and when he knelt by her she added, 'it's too late. Hold me.'

He swallowed hard, opened his mouth to protest.

'I know,' she said with certainty for, after the first devastating pain, hadn't she heard the voice again, and hadn't she agreed that this time she knew she must go. 'It's time,' she whispered to him, 'just be here for me, just the two of us.'

He slipped down to the floor and drew her head and shoulders on to his lap. 'Comfy?' he asked, his voice breaking on the memory of the times he had asked her that after they had made love. 'Comfy.'

'Hmm.' She made the same noise of satisfaction. 'Hmm. Talk to me, Freddie.'

He looked down at her dear face and he would have died instantly for her if it would have helped, instead words flooded into these final moments between them. 'I always thought you had the right name, Queenie. You've always been queen of my heart, queen of my world. You've been a queen to your daughter and to my son, a noble lovable figure.' He saw a sudden realisation in her eyes, as if she saw not only him but beyond, yet she expected something of him too. 'Marvellous,' he said stooping to kiss her lips.

Her lips curved to a smile as he drew away. Her eyes held all knowledge, and she was gone.

It was some time later that Billie came up the stairs and through the open door of the flat. 'I can smell something burning,' she began then rushed to stand the iron erect. Stooping to switch it off she saw Freddie sitting in his hat and coat cradling Queenie.

Laura arrived in London the following evening. Freddie met her at the station. They held each other tight. 'I can't believe it.'

'Nor me,' Freddie agreed tucking his hand under her arm. 'Do you want to talk here?' he nodded towards the buffet.

'I think I do a bit.'

'It was her heart,' he said as they sat fiddling with full cups and saucers. 'They have decided against a post mortem in the circumstances, because of her recent history.'

'History?' Laura queried. 'You mean the attack.'

Freddie nodded.

'So he did kill her in the end,' she said. 'My father began killing her spirit and mangling her heart before I was born and probably ...'

335

'No, no,' Freddie shook his head gently at her. 'Such talk with not help, and she had plenty of spirit left to the end,' he told her, then paused as a young family went by obviously seeing their soldier father off. 'Strange, isn't it, these war years your mother and I have had together have been some of the happiest in my life.'

'I wish she could have known my news,' Laura said and when he looked at her questioningly she added, 'you're going to be a grandfather. I'm expecting. You're the first to know.'

He looked at her for some time in silence. 'One goes and one comes,' he said, then he added, 'I'd like it if you would agree for your mother's body to be cremated so that I may take her back to Gibraltar with me, when the time comes.'

The reality of her mother's death suddenly hit her for the first time. 'Come on, m'dear, let's see if we can get a taxi.'

Before she had to return to what would be the final weeks of her service in the WRENS, for she would be discharged once it was known she was pregnant, she wrote to Jamie:

My dearest Jamie,
There is no easy way to tell his news. My mother died suddenly two days ago. Two doctors agreed that it was heart trouble, so mercifully where was no need for a post mortem. Your father was with her when she died, and I know he is writing to you about this and about how he intends to take my mother's ashes back to Gibraltar.

I can't really believe it has happened. I thought my mother would be around until she was old. She deserved a good long life, didn't she? I know people say things about no one ever promising that life would be fair, but this is so awful. I suppose what I'm feeling is the anger they say comes with loss, I'm like a child crying for the moon, or for the sun that's gone out of my life. For so many years, until I met you, she was the one bright thing in my life. She was a light who was there for me, no matter what. We were mother and daughter, sisters, comrades-in-arms – you know what I mean by this last, and I don't want to contaminate this letter with his name (he is, by the way, permanently locked up, too mad to be brought to court).

I could feel very bitter if it were not for you and your dear, dear, devastated father – and one other thing.

The other thing is that you and I are going to have a child. You are to be a father, which somehow seems less surprising to me than the fact that *I'm* going to be a mother! The sadness about it is *my* mother was not to know.

It has all made me wonder if she did not have some kind of premonition about her health, I mean being so keen we should marry so quickly. I'm so pleased we did – for many, many reasons. I love you and ache for you to be home – but perhaps by the time our child is born you will be, God willing.'

More when I get back to Liverpool.

Your loving, loving, wife, Laura

Leaving the WRENS and parting with Nadine, who declared she would be offended if she was not asked to be a godmother in due course, was more difficult than she imagined. Waking alone in Billie's house after the other two had gone to work was torment, the anguish of her mother's loss came every day afresh.

She tried to busy herself for Freddie's sake. He looked dreadful, an old man. 'I'll be all right,' he said. 'I just feel I had heaven in my hand, and now it's been dashed away. That takes a little getting over.'

Then as July 1944 came and the Allied foothold on Europe was strong, Freddie came home with astonishing news, or it seemed astonishing to Laura.

'There a lot of agitation for some of us Gibraltarians to be repatriated, and I think the first to be taken back will be those in London. Gibraltar's position is no longer considered open to invasion or attack, and of course most of the evacuees have had a far more perilous time here in England than they would have if they remained on The Rock – but that's hindsight, of course.'

'You mean we could go home?' Laura was surprised to hear herself call The Rock home, but at the same time recognised that it was true. Her home like Jamie's would be Gibraltar. Though where precisely 'home' would be was unsure, as many houses had been requisitioned by the military forces, and now Freddie understood the housing situation was under great stress. 'Frankly, the Gibraltan authorities don't want their evacuees all back too soon, they wouldn't know what to do with them. I think I can persuade them they need *me* over there, and of course I should want to take my daughter-in-law as she is expecting a baby, and we would want it to be born on Gib.'

'You think there's a chance?' Laura asked, heart bumping at the idea. If Jamie was still in the Med then she knew sooner or later all navy ships called at Gib.

Fourteen days later they packed their cases, and said goodbye to Billie. 'But we'll meet again,' Freddie assured her.

'Have no fear about that,' she told them. 'I shall pack those beautiful old chests and bring them to you when the war's over.'

'We'll keep you to that,' Laura told her. 'I don't know what we would have done without you.'

'Look after yourself, m'dear. They say friendships made in hard times last the longest. Keep me posted about this baby.'

They travelled to Cardiff, where they were to await passage on the *Stirling Castle*, a Union Castle liner delayed for windlass repairs.

Once aboard though the voyage seemed swift. They were well escorted this time with no diversions, and it took just a matter of days rather than weeks. Most fantastic of all, aboard were Doris and her children, but in four years how they'd grown. They were young ladies now, and the baby a schoolgirl, experimenting, not very successfully at first, at climbing in and out of the hammocks they were supplied with. But they were a pleasurable few days compared with the way they had been evacuated from The Rock – twice.

Their arrival back was very different, too; no one waited to cheer their arrival, for neither Fatima nor her brothers knew they were on the way. Laura saw the Hewitt children being photographed by the *Gibraltar Chronicle* holding huge slices of watermelon, not a commodity they had seen in the four years they were away. Marjorie and Beryl she guessed would soon be working girls, while Lorna and Paddy would have to go back to school – and all home to their father at the lighthouse on Europa Point. He'd be pleased to have Doris back.

Freddie procured a taxi. 'Where to first?' he asked.

'Fatima's house, do you think?'

On the way up to Cumberland Hill they began to appreciate just how crowded the town was with servicemen, but when they knocked on her door they did not expect it to be opened by an airforceman in shirt sleeves carrying a teatowel.

'Who is it?' Fatima's voice came from the kitchen.

'That's what we want to know!' Freddie shouted back.

'That can only be—' Fatima's exclamation was cut off as she flung herself past her guest into Freddie and Laura's arms. She retreated at once from Laura and pointing at her stomach cried, 'Hey!'

Laura flourished her rings. 'All legal,' she laughed.

'But you didn't let me know.'

'There's not been much time. There's a lot of catching up to be done.'

'This is Mike Parker, by the way, we're ...' she rushed back into the kitchen then came back slipping a ring on to her engagement finger 'engaged. We were washing up!'

Laura watched Mike's face as Fatima, exuberant and flamboyant as ever in black skirt and brilliantly flowered

339

blouse, displayed her ring. He obviously adored her and was as blond as she was dark.

The congratulations, the proper introductions, then the news, good and bad was exchanged. 'You'll stay here,' Fatima said. 'Josh and Carlos can double up.'

'I was hoping to go home,' Freddie said.

Fatima shook her head. 'The military have your house. We had to pack up all the furniture we could, plus anything else we could manage into one room, and it was sealed, but the rest of the house is still being used.' She looked at Laura. 'Your mother's house is still shuttered and barred. There were so many rumours about the army and your father,' she shrugged, 'no one took the initiative, so we just kept quiet. With Freddie's locks and bolts, it should be as it was left.'

It was, dustier, full of memories but untouched.

'How do you feel about us both living here?' Freddie said. 'For the time being anyway. We could soon clean it.'

'Wipe away the bad memories,' Laura mused looking round at the dull hallway. 'I could make it how my mother always wanted it to be. We used to talk about it. If there had been just the two of us we said we ...' she stopped, turned back to Freddie. 'Yes,' she said, 'let's do it.'

The work of cleaning and sweeping was begun; everyone joined in. Carlos and Josh came to whitewash and paint. The house began to glow with new colour, polish. Laura even regretted not having her mother's machine to make covers. 'Never mind,' Fatima said, 'do what the Spanish do, throw shawls and coloured rugs over settees and things.'

'Oh, good, I've not had a good shop since I've been back.' They went together. Fatima's mother was still marooned in Spain and the two young women found great comfort and pleasure in each other's company. Particularly as now the hard work was done, Freddie had begun to spend more time back at his business picking up the threads.

As Laura's pregnancy became more cumbersome she enjoyed being in the garden. She re-established the oleanders, set a pomegranate tree and masses of geraniums. One day as she worked, thinking of her mother, she heard herself singing quietly under her breath. Had she stopped mourning her mother so soon? She knew it was not so, rather it was that out here in the garden her mother felt very close. 'Be here when the baby comes, won't you?' she asked.

'Are you all right?' a gentle voice said behind her.

'Fatima! You really startled me.'

'I've just come back with Freddie. He left some blueprints here. We knocked and called, but you were much too busy.' She held out her hand and pulled Laura up off her knees and they sat together on the stone seat where she and her mother had so often sat.

'You know Freddie's worried about the baby's birth. Gibraltar's hardly geared up for English mums and babies. He asked me to sound you out about going into the military hospital.'

'I really don't want to do that. I'd rather it was here, at home.'

'There's a midwife who comes over from La Linea, all the locals book her. How would I get in touch with her?' Fatima asked, then answered herself, 'Oh! there's a woman who had the baby in the flats.'

'I'd like to meet her,' Laura decided. 'See if we could come to some arrangement.'

Freddie would only be satisfied if Laura also saw the doctor at the hospital, and Señora Isabella, the midwife, agreed to come and live in from the end of October until some weeks after the birth.

The birth of Peter James de Falla on 30 October 1944 was not only some weeks earlier than expected, but was as straightforward as any first birth could be. Tended and inspired by the wonderful Señora Isabella, Laura progressed from a very long hot bath to a consoling walk around with the Señora rubbing the bottom of her back in just the right place. She reached the second productive stage of labour being told she was a model patient, and could now work hard and shout loud if she wanted to.

Freddie did not reach home that evening until the pushing and panting was all safely over. He rushed into the house and Señora Isabella forestalled all his anxieties, all his questions by beckoning him up the stairs.

'Come and see your grandson,' she said, 'and his clever mother. We had him perfectly.'

After reassuring himself that Laura was all right, he sat in the easy chair by her bed and the midwife placed the lightly swaddled baby into his arms. 'While we tidy up,' she said. He beamed down at his grandson as mother rested and the midwife prepared to bathe and dress the child. Then they realised Freddie was asleep. 'There's a camera over there,' Laura whispered. 'Take their picture, I can send it to my husband.' For the only person missing from the celebrations was Peter James's father, now in the South Pacific working with the American Fleet against Japan.

But on 11 January 1945 the Royal Naval destroyer, escort to a convoy of walking wounded returning to Britain, steamed into Gibraltar harbour. Fatima heard the news first from Mike Parker – the RAF had been keeping air cover. She sped to Laura's home almost unable to speak with excitement.

Feeling it was something wives of seagoing men must have been doing from ancient times, Laura gathered up Peter in his shawl and ran to the quayside. Here she was joined by Freddie and Fatima and her brothers.

Jamie's destroyer came into harbour, her crew standing along the deck of the ship in smart order, with her captain on his bridge.

How they cheered.

She knew he saw her and she and Freddie lifted the baby high above their heads. The destroyer siren rang out triumphantly, and the crew raised their hats in three rousing cheers across the waters of the great harbour. Other ships took up the siren call.

'People will think the war's over,' Fatima said. 'Never mind, it soon will be.'

Laura peered up into her son's face, wondering if the noise might upset him. But the four month old was gazing wide-eyed and entranced up and out towards the sparkling blue horizon. 'You recognise the sea, don't you,' she whispered to him, 'and soon you'll know your father.' She gave him a little triumphant upward flourish.

'I thought for a minute you were going to throw him up in the air,' Freddie said.

'He wouldn't have minded,' she said. 'He's Jamie's boy.'

Epilogue

Laura regarded the ape on their tree. It had a large baby by its side and a smaller one on its back. 'There should be three,' she told it, for Peter James had been followed by David Frederick, both navy career men, and then by Grace. Laura gave a half laugh, half sigh. Grace was the reason she was at this place once more, this appointed place. The place most laden with memories.

Grace. She had only known Jamie lose his exuberance twice in his life. The first time after he had believed he had saved a man only for him to suffer a fate worse than death, though that had not been so. Smiler Harris had gone on to own a Portsmouth restaurant and be a grandfather.

The second time had been when Grace, named for Jamie's mother, had, after being the joy of his life, rebelled in late teenage years and told her father that she would run away. 'I'm going to live in London, and I'll never come back, not to you anyway.' Jamie had been in despair. 'What did I do wrong?'

'Nothing,' she had told him, 'you and Grace are just too much alike.'

Freddie had been the calming one – his rooms in Queenie's old house had become the Mecca for anyone with a problem, where certainly all the family sought and found a listening ear, and a reasoned judgement. He had urged his son not just to let her go, but to take her to London to

344

arrange a place at the art college he knew she yearned to attend. 'Trust her,' he had urged.

Five years later Grace had come back to them without rancour, or even seeming to remember the anxiety she had caused her family. What they were to realise was that Grace had inherited her namesake's talents. She came back to them a brilliant and inventive embroideress, designing and executing magnificent modern altar pieces for churches and cathedrals, beginning to make a name, be in demand, and with the added talent of being able to pass on her enthusiasm and skills.

Freddie had just funded her in her own shop and studios on Main Street, Gibraltar. The opening ceremony was to be that night. The upstairs studios had been given their final touch when Freddie had presented his granddaughter with the unicorn tapestry her grandmother had worked so many years ago. Jamie had hung it in place of honour and Grace had festooned it with broad red and yellow ribbons for the opening. At street level the shop was a blaze of colour. Every silk, wool and ribbon, every bead and sequin, all the breathtaking examples of Grace's work, every item, large and small from pomander cushions to shawls, throw-overs, bedspreads invited the touch of acquisitive fingers. Prices ranged from £2 to £2,000. Something for everyone, Grace declared, whether it be embroidery kit, pin cushion or enrolment for a course of classes. It was dazzling, full of vitality, like Grace, like her father. Every Gibraltarian VIP had been invited months ago, a surprising number of guests from London were expected on the evening plane.

She turned to see if Jamie was coming. She had suggested this break, this breath of air. It was almost inevitable he and his daughter would clash on such an occasion, both wanted so much to succeed for the sake of the other, both wanted perfection.

Below a cruise liner hooted its arrival. She stepped forward: a liner docking would mean many extra customers in Grace's shop. They would have to put up notices welcoming the liner by name and offering discounts for passengers, as other shops did. It suddenly occurred to her how much her mother would have loved all of this.

She recalled how Freddie had asked if she would mind if he scattered Queenie's ashes, rather than have them interred. She had thought he would like a set place to visit, a fixed shrine. He had said she would always be everywhere for him.

They had brought her mother's ashes to this place and he had performed a very simple, but memorable, act. He had made a special box, one that opened flat like a conjuror's box. He had stood beneath this old eucalyptus tree and offered them to the elements. The wind had seemed to sigh in its task as it slowly bequeathed the ash to the blue sky and blue sea. They had stood quite still for a long time after all, all, had gone.

The tree had witnessed so much that was meaningful in her life. On the edge of this ancient gateway to the Mediterranean, on one of the Pillars of Hercules, its roots thrusting down between the limestone, withstanding the tearing winds of winter and the lashing storms. Like Freddie, she thought, a lively nonagenarian still enjoying life.

Looking up she was surprised to find that there were already stars out, including the bright mariner's star, as if entangled with the branches.

Lost in a lifetime of memories, she heard someone calling. She turned to see Jamie hurrying up the cliff towards her. He was beckoning her urgently back to this grand opening, this new beginning on this old Rock, and as her heart lifted at the sight of him she thought he was as beautiful as ever.